THE RISE OF SYN

THE CHILDREN OF CHAOS
AND
THE RISE OF SYN

K.D. THOMAS

Nightmarish
Tales

Copyright © 2024 by K.D. Thomas
First Edition: 2024
ISBN: 979-8-9910014-1-0 (trade)
ISBN: 979-8-9910014-0-3 (eBook)

All rights reserved.

No part of this publication may be reproduced, distributed, or transmitted in any form or by any means, including photocopying, recording, or other electronic or mechanical methods, without the prior written permission of the publisher, except as permitted by U.S. copyright law.

The story, all names, characters, and incidents portrayed in this production are fictitious. No identification with actual persons (living or deceased), places, buildings, and products is intended or should be inferred.

Book cover by Nightmarish Tales | Cover illustrations by Seven and Euforiadesign | Maps by K.D. Thomas | Interior illustrations by K.D. Thomas and Seven | Copyediting and proofreading by Oren Eades.

Published by Nightmarish Tales
Tallahassee, Florida
https://www.nightmarishtales.com

I would like to thank my family for always believing in me and aiding me throughout my journey.

To all the non-human animals of Earth, I would like to thank you for your tenacity in such a cruel world.

I dedicate this tale to the misfits and the forgotten. The Shadow King sees you and will not drag you to his kingdom, for he shares your pain. It is why he cries.

Keep your chin up and show the world that you are not weak—you are strong.

And you matter.

U.S.A
SOUTHEAST
Kentucky
West Virginia
Virginia
Appalachian Mountains
Tennessee
North Carolina
MOONLIGHT HILLS
Satan's Web
PERK
South Carolina
Atlantic Ocean
Alabama
Georgia
TALLAHASSEE
Florida
Gulf of Mexico
South Florida Sea Break
THE BAHAMAS
CUBA
Caribbean Sea
Caribbean Islands
JAMAICA
HAIT

2224 CE
Era of Science & Magic

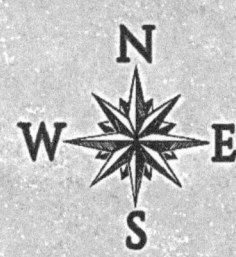

BERMUDA

Bermuda Triangle

BIRDSONG

BIRDSONG ISLAND

AND CAICOS ISLANDS

DOMINICAN REPUBLIC

PUERTO RICO

LEGEND

COASTAL REGIONS HAVE BECOME SUBMERGED

– – – – –	Bermuda Barrier
– – – – –	Trade Routes
	Fae Trails
🏠	Cities
	Drowned Wetlands
⛰	Mountains
🌴	Trees & Plants
⛺	Fae Camp
☠	H.C. Branch
◉	H.C. Headquarters
◆	Miami Ruins
▢	The Council
■	Mage's Guild

"When one opposes rules written by the stars, energies from all over shall clash, and the end of all will draw near."

—Ezra, *the Fall of Kanaria*

CONTENTS

THE RISE OF SYN

† PROLOGUE: *The Shade* 1

† I: *A New World* 4

† II: *Deathly News* 19

† III: *The Mage's Guild* 30

† IV: *A Bode To My Eternal Love* 38

† V: *Hate Crime* 42

† VI: *A Strange Appetite* 46

† VII: *The Atomic Years* 56

† VIII: *Year 2208* 61

† IX: *Fire Dancer* 71

† X: *Lemon Leaves* 76

† XI: *Dark Reunion* 79

† XII: *Mutt* 87

† XIII: *Memories Of Cross* 91

† XIV: *Laughing Iron* 105

† XV: *Sparrow Manor* 107

† XVI: *The Kanarians* 117

† XVII: *Old Friends* 125

† XVIII: *Alien Gods* 135

† XIX: *Identity Crisis* 149

† XX: *Under A Violent Moon* 168

† XXI: *Ghostly Ghouls* 178

† XXII: *Thorns & Wine* 189

† XXIII: *Ashes* 200

† XXIV: *House Of Freaks* 213

† XXV: *Space & Time* 229

† XXVI: *The Crown* 243

† XXVII: *A Festive Morning* 256

† XXVIII: *Chicks 'N More* 270

† XXIX: *One Sly Ally* 287

† XXX: *Syn* 299

† EPILOGUE: *A Broken Wing* 313

MEMOIRS OF THE 3 REALMS

∞ *Shadowlands* 327

∞ *Yellow Sky* 337

∞ *Nightmare* 351

FAE COURTS & COUNCIL

✪ *Sapphire Court* 363

✪ *Willow Court* 364

✪ *Dragon Court* 365

✪ *Onyx Court* 366

✪ *Ruby Court* 367

LOST GLOSSARY

☠ *Glossary* 371

PROLOGUE

THE SHADE

BOVE THE BLUE SEA, birds flew in flock. An abnormally tall man with a black hooded trench coat walked out of a fog of shadows, staring up at the cloudy sky. Looking around at what used to be a city called Miami in South Florida, he surveyed the marshes that conquered the area. The drowned city of ghosts had only a few thousand residents who were too stubborn to move. He turned and saw an elderly man fishing off the coast.

The frail fisherman noticed the man staring at him in shallow water. "Aren't you a tall fella?" the man asked, prying his eyes from his fishing pole, looking over at the seven-foot-tall man who had emerged from a hidden path of shadows.

"What year is it here?" the visitor asked the fisherman.

"2224... You don't know the year? Don't tell me you're one of them aliens the news be talking about." The old man studied the being, who did not look entirely human. "Wait, are you one of them fae folk? I saw you teleport."

The two locked eyes for a moment.

"Oh!" the old man exclaimed, realizing his words could have been harsh. "I don't mind if you're fae. I'm just asking. Not my business if you are."

The man in black held back a laugh and watched the fisherman reel in his line.

"But you really should keep up with the date. It'll do you some good," the old man said, raising his eyebrows, giving what he felt was sound advice.

"Thank you for that guidance." He nodded at the old man, who looked back at the brackish sea, tossing his fishing line in an area that had no fish. "No... I am not of the fae, nor did I teleport. The Shade is not a portal. It is a path that moves very fast between the three realms, with many doors."

"Sounds like a portal to me." The fisherman shrugged.

"Portals and The Shade are not—"

A group of teenagers a quarter-mile away distracted the two from their private conversation with loud screams.

"Damn kids," the old man said. "They're always fighting. Crime's getting worse, despite the country trying to enforce peace. People blame y'all and that Isis lady. But for an old man... you lot bring me peace."

Rather than correcting the man in his old age, the man from The Shade allowed him to believe that he was fae.

"At least you can die," he told the fisherman as he tried to find the door to lead him back into the shadowed path. Before opening the door, he turned to the old man and said, "I have no end. Therefore, my soul can never know rest."

The man stepped through a translucent door.

Not realizing he had dropped his fishing pole in the water, the old man muttered, "Teleportation." Then, he laughed like an innocent child. He looked around the scarce beach and exclaimed, "I just met a fae fella!"

No one heard his excited words.

"I am not fae," the other man said from within the shadows.

"Then, what are you?" the old man hollered, trying to find him. "Well, at least tell me your name before you go to God knows where!"

"I have many," the man said and vanished.

As the man with many names walked away from the hazy door that led to the beach where the fisherman searched the waters, the entryway shrank to a window the size of a basketball. And voices echoed within The Shade.

He pinched a particle in the air and twisted it, flinging himself down the dark path. After he reached his destination, he approached a new window that hovered in a pit of shadows.

He grinned darkly and watched a woman walk down a sidewalk on the other side. "Maybe the orb was wrong..." he whispered.

The man walked to another window nearby. He gripped the edge of the new window, which led to the woman's house, and turned it into a door. Then, he raised his hood and stepped through the gateway.

I

A NEW WORLD

N A SATURDAY MORNING, many people slept comfortably in warm homes, while others shivered from the cold front that tormented the state. The normal array of signs supporting the rights of fae was put on hold, for the people who waved them were mourning the death of a man named Simon Coy. As Novus Episcopal Church held a packed funeral for Simon, most of the city wept for what they feared was to come. Tragedy often sparked unrest, and those who opposed mixing with the fae had a twisted way of blaming them for everything.

Newsstands with a recording of a woman talking to the public were on the corners of practically every street in the capital city of Tallahassee, Florida. Her image hovered in the air in a holographic form. She stood tall, with rich brown skin and short black hair formed in a pixie cut.

"All Earthlings are one. The anti-fae rebellion must end. We all come from Eden." The woman repeated the phrase throughout the city.

"Fuck that woman!" a rebel yelled, glaring at a newsstand. He reeked of meth and hatred. "You call her *The Mother*?!" he scoffed. "You call her a god?! There's only one God! Isis is one of the fae! Why can't y'all see that?!"

The angry rebel spotted a pale woman with blue eyes and light blond hair rushing his way. Her long braid swung behind her, and smoke was escaping her nostrils. Frantic, the rebel turned, only to be intercepted by a police officer of the Old Precinct. The officer was tan, like sunbathing was his hobby. He had graying brown hair and dark blue eyes. And he irritably yanked the rebel into his arms.

Close to twenty-five years ago, during the summer of 2200, humans had been met with a twist in their perception of what was real. As the human world continued to create inventions that made one's life easier and came up with methods to pacify climate change, bizarre discoveries made headlines after a humanoid group of fae came out of hiding. Nymphs, elves, fairies, trolls, and goblins were the five species of fae, and most human societies froze when they left their hideouts in the Southeast of the United States.

But when the fae drifted solely to Tallahassee, the city quickly formed an alliance with them. Among those who grew notorious for their support of fae rights were the Sparrows and Acostas, the Adams, Novus Episcopal Church, and most of the local police department—specifically, the Old Precinct.

However, not everyone was welcoming in Tallahassee. As if the nation had not already been thrown into a web of confusion, the nation's government was not surprised by the fae's existence. Soon, millions of American citizens became paranoid.

And paranoid people had a habit of creating a mess of things...

"Let me go! I did nothing wrong!! It's called freedom of speech, you pig." The rebel struggled to free himself from the handcuffs being placed on his wrists. He locked eyes with the cop, who pulled up a holographic warrant from his watch. "That's not me. I don't participate in vandalism."

"I'm pretty sure this is you," the officer said, staring at a large scar on the rebel's cheek that matched the photo of the man who looked like him.

"That's probably some fae that did magic to impersonate me," the rebel said confidently. "You should be going after them, not me. You probably won't, cos the cops here just *love* the fae. Don't y'all?"

"I somehow doubt that." The officer dragged the rebel to his police car. He looked back at the woman, whose nostrils were no longer emitting smoke, and said, "Wait there, Wren."

Wren nodded and fixed her hair. Black ribbons were woven into her fair locks, forming a long braid reaching her mid-back. She looked down at her black gothic dress to see if any debris was attached.

After the officer placed the man in the backseat of his car, he returned to the woman who had helped intercept the crazed rebel. "I told you not to interfere," the officer said, scolding her.

She defended herself. "I'm the one that told you he was out here."

Wren had spotted the rebel who the police were looking for on her way to buy coffee before her friend's funeral. She was surprised that the anti-fae radical was proudly standing near the Old Precinct right after a warrant was announced for his arrest.

"You're not a cop," the officer said. "Eudora would have the entire department's head if she knew you were out here tackling rebels."

"But I can do weird things, Jackson," Wren said and hunched over, spreading her fingers wide, acting spooky. "Didn't you know that?"

"Speaking of weird things—we need you to come down to the station sometime this week to retrieve information from the rebels," Jackson said. "We need to know what the Human Coalition is planning. That okay?"

"So, I can't tackle rebels, but I can read their minds to help the police?" Wren asked the cop.

"Correct." Jackson nodded.

"Just making sure that you're aware that you're all a bunch of hypocrites," Wren said.

"If you want to tackle criminals, become a police officer," Jackson told her, his eyes becoming stern.

"No. I'm perfectly happy being a dollmaker." Wren folded her arms. "I can make a doll in a cop uniform, but as a cop, I can't wear dresses. Just let me tackle the rebels."

The officer turned away and walked back to his car, shaking his head. "You're a nut!"

"Takes one to know one, Jackson!" Wren yelled out to the officer.

Inside the patrol car, the rebel was staring at Wren, who was walking toward a coffee shop. When Jackson slid into the driver's seat, the rebel leaned forward and asked, "Ain't that the Sparrow girl?"

Jackson turned around and looked at the fanatical man through the glass. "Mind your business."

"It is, ain't it?" the man in the backseat hollered. "Well, I'll be damned. I met *the* Wren Sparrow."

"Leave her alone," Jackson said seriously. "You guys come after her, and we'll make sure you never see the light of day again."

The rebel scoffed. "Why would we go after *Ms. Darling*? Everyone knows she can do magic."

"Cut the crap. We know the Human Coalition wants her dead." Jackson cursed and started the engine.

The rebel was shocked. "How'd you know that? I mean—no, we don't."

"Fucking hell," Jackson muttered. "You guys are morons."

The rebel started shouting, cheering on another extremist who was holding up a sign. Jackson looked at the poster: **I Didn't Evolve. I'm A God-Fearing Man!** He grumbled as he drove slowly by the crazed man who was proudly holding his sign.

The arrested rebel became louder. "Settle down, or I'll make you," Jackson shouted toward the back. "I should have used the tranquilizer cuffs on you. Do you want to be re-cuffed?"

"Fuck yeah, man! That shit makes you feel like you're flying." The rebel in the back looked excited.

"For fuck's sake," Jackson cursed. "You're getting high off handcuffs?"

The rebel shrugged. "You're the ones who added drugs to the things."

Jackson eyed the other rebel with the sign. "Well, you guys are right about one thing."

"We're right about a lot of things," the detained rebel told Jackson arrogantly.

"Not all of us evolved. Some of you are still stuck in the stone age." Jackson looked back at the rebel with a smirk.

The dimwitted rebel grumbled and noticed something dangling from the officer's rearview mirror. It was a braided charm promoting primate studies—a gift from Jackson's daughter, who was going to college for anthropology. While it brought the officer luck, it troubled the rebel, and the hateful man frowned as he read what was woven into the braid: **Zyula**.

"Zyula this, zyula that. Y'all arguing about where you come from. But y'all just a bunch of heathens. We come from the one true God." The rebel nodded with his eyes closed. "Y'all going to Hell."

"Do you really believe in the crap you're spewing?" Jackson laughed and stopped at a red light. He glanced at the jail on the other side of the light, then looked up at the mirror to gaze back at the rebel. "They have evidence that the zyula were real."

"You sound like a science man, pig. Don't tell me you agree with the fae?" the rebel asked with wide eyes. "You're a fucking traitor to this country and not worthy of that badge. Let me out!"

"Science denier? Consider me shocked," Jackson said dryly. Under the swinging charm was an interactive hologram of the car's center console, and he quickly pushed a preset on his satellite radio to turn on Science Now, a fae network. As if it was perfect timing, a human scientist and fae scholar were talking about the zyula and katani...

"Let me get this straight—you're still saying the katani came to life from clay idols?" the scientist asked the scholar. "All these years, and I still don't understand why you all believe in this nonsense. The katani are part of the animal kingdom, just like the zyula. Why does this offend you?"

"Because it's simply not true," the elven scholar retorted politely. According to the fae's evolutionary theory, two ancient humanoids had roamed the planet over two hundred million years ago. The fae called them the zyula and katani, but human scientists named them *Vetus lupo primatus* and *Edax ossium*, after the fae had shared their fossils with them.

During the Triassic Period, the zyula had emerged alongside small shrew-like animals. While the shrews had descended into various groups of mammals, populations of the zyula lines had evolved into primates during the Late Cretaceous Period. Since the zyula and small shrews had shared a common ancestor, descendants of both became tied by blood.

Around the same time the zyula had evolved into primates, most of the katani had descended into what would be known as fae. A few species of both fae and primates varied, such as goblins and monkeys, while others remained closer to their ancestors, like nymphs and humans.

"You agree that Earth is a part of Eden, correct?" the elf asked.

"Well, yes..." the human mumbled about Eden—the giant planet Earth was only a fragment of.

"Then, why is it so hard to understand that some Edenians could have survived and created the katani?" The elven scholar was getting upset.

"Because the Edenians are all extinct," the human scientist answered. "You guys claim Eden exploded and created the solar system. Well, that's all fine and good—we're in agreement with that. There's proof of *that*. But how could lifeforms survive on different planets with different gasses? Don't tell me they're all running around in spacesuits—"

The radio host chimed in to prevent the two from arguing.

"Let's see if we can find something else," Jackson muttered, shifting through the presets on his radio. He eyed his audio file. "Oh, I know."

"God, no. Turn that horseshit off!" the rebel yelled.

Pressing the **Play** button, Jackson grinned as Isis' voice filled the car...

"Abiding by the natural law of the lands, the zyula were once viewed as the perfect apex predator," Isis said, describing the two species of Pangaea.

"Due to a genetic anomaly, the zyula could transform from human-like to wolf-like and had intelligence beyond any other animal. They had a stronger bite than a *Tyrannosaurus rex* and reached almost fifteen-feet tall. Being cruel monstrosities, they had often hunted out of boredom."

It was a recorded lecture Isis had given at a convention held by Science Now. "But the katani proved to be a worthy contender. Coming to life from clay idols, the katani were made from magic to offset the zyula, who were conquering the planet like a pestilence. Standing much shorter than the zyula at around six feet, the katani made up for their missing height by wielding powerful magic. Their bloodlust was reflected in their eyes, and their dull teeth were strong enough to shatter bone—"

"Turn it off!!" the rebel shouted behind Jackson. "Turn it off!! Turn it off!!"

Jackson paused the audio. "Are you going to be quiet?"

The rebel released a hot breath of air, grumbling.

When the fae first shared their theories with the humans, much of the human world laughed. The allegations sounded like the ramblings from a conspiracy theorist who was stuck in a cave. Though they were one to talk, since human science was often criticized within fae society. But the communities of both groups eventually came together.

"You better be careful, officer," the detained rebel warned Jackson, leaning forward in his seat. "The Devil will snatch you and drag you to Hell. I've seen him. He's got these chains and smells like death." The rebel looked through his window and saw a woman in the car next to them singing to herself. "A war is coming, and you need to make right with the lord."

Jackson rolled his eyes.

"No, sir." The rebel banged his head on the window when he noticed the most *disturbing* of signs. On the woman's car door, there was a decal of an infinity symbol and the words: **Support The Mage's Guild. We All Come From Eden!** "No, sir! Eden and the mages are the workings of the Devil. That woman there is fae. You should be arresting her! Let me out!"

The woman driving the car heard banging and turned her head to look at the patrol car next to her, noticing the rebel throwing his head her way. Even though Jackson waved an apology to her, she quickly rolled up her window.

After the light turned green, Jackson turned into the parking lot of the Old Precinct and walked to the back to re-cuff the man, who immediately entered a trancelike state.

"You damn idiot," Jackson hissed. "What? You didn't like her sticker?"

"Fuck... you..." the arrested man said with slurred speech.

"Do you ever think before you speak, or do you just vomit bullshit?" Jackson asked.

The rebel mumbled and leaned back into the seat, closing his eyes to enjoy the high.

Across from the downtown jail that Jackson had pulled into, stood a group of elven mages on break. They were staring at the detention center, which was becoming full of lunatics. A mage saw Jackson struggling to haul the rebel out of his car, so he snapped his fingers, and the arrested man floated unwillingly.

Jackson looked over at the mages and noticed that one had summoned a luminous rune, which he was holding, for levitation. He waved at them, only for the mages to turn their backs on him.

"What's up, guys?" Wren walked up to the group of mages, her black-gloved hands holding a coffee she had just bought. She had already drunk half, and the caffeine had her rushing around the area in a manic frenzy. "You know where Rose is? I want to check on her before the funeral."

She saw Jackson enter the station across the street. "Did you see the guy Jackson arrested? I helped catch him," she bragged.

The mages turned to Wren. While they normally detested humans, they did not mind most of the ones in the city—especially the daughter of the Sparrows, who was known for her odd ability of telepathy. Thankfully, the mages were trained to harden their minds.

"She's patrolling the art district," one mage told Wren. "It has the least rebel activity, so she was assigned there for her first day. She's with Marie; don't worry."

"Marie?" Wren asked.

"Her mentor," another mage chimed in. "Marie's a scrawny thing, but very powerful. She's in good hands."

Wren nodded and said, "I'll just call her." She walked backwards from the group, waving. "Thanks, guys."

She spun around and headed toward Novus, but she stopped when she noticed a new hologram appearing next to where Isis hovered at a nearby newsstand. It was a poster of both Isis and her top assistant, Tabitha, waving from Mars.

Wren walked up to the poster and stared at the image. She lowered her gaze to a message scrolling across the poster that read: **The Dynamic Duo Is At It Again. Edenian Fossils Found On Mars!**

"Isis found new fossils," Wren whispered.

Isis and Tabitha had become a worldwide sensation over two decades ago, after being interviewed by the White House press. During the interview, humans were startled by their claims: a soul, magic, three parallel realms, godlike aliens—the findings were numerous.

"Damn fae." A man in a suit glared at the poster, walking swiftly by the newsstand. "They should all just move to Mars."

Before Wren could yell at the man who sided with the rebels, he merged with the crowds who roamed the sidewalk. While Isis and Tabitha had won over the hearts of many humans, they also received a lot of hate. It was a difficult period of change, for some skeptics kept a harsh tongue.

Wren brushed off the man's words and turned back to the poster.

"Fossils," Wren said excitedly to a woman who was reading a virtual magazine at the newsstand.

The woman reading about a pop singer did not care about the fossils and ignored Wren, thinking loudly, *Can't she see me reading? How rude.*

Wren scowled at the woman, who cared more about the entertainment world than scientific discoveries.

"They found fossils on Mars!" Wren exclaimed to the woman and walked away from the newsstand. Looking back, she shouted, "And you're the rude one!"

The woman looked up at Wren, startled, and watched the odd dollmaker walk around the corner and toward the church.

Wait, isn't she the one that makes the protection dolls? the woman thought and looked away from Wren to search through the rows of news and entertainment. Her eyes landed on the cover of Tallahassee's local business magazine, where Wren was smiling, holding a porcelain doll. The woman picked up the magazine, staring at the cover. Then, a hologram of the new protection doll emerged from the cover, singing a lullaby. "I've been waiting for these to come out!"

The woman looked back to see Wren, the heir to a global wine company who preferred to be a dollmaker, but she was gone.

The woman then turned to the poster to read about the fossils.

As identical fossils kept appearing on Mars and Earth, connecting the two planets together, Isis had gradually revealed her phylogenetic tree of life for Eden: the Ossa Antiquorum. While this chart helped everyone understand the lifeforms of Eden, there was one thing both human and fae scientists struggled with...

What happened to one's energetic self after death? Surely, not everyone could rise from their grave like Isis.

After Isis had allowed an international group of human scientists to examine her body in 2202, it had been hypothesized that her atoms went through a drastic change that had left her in a frozen state. Initially, they did not believe a soul was driving her corpse, but when the scientists scanned her head during the exam, there was no brain to be found—only a cluster of gas forming a cloud of stars. And when the puzzled scientists of the chilly lab tried to theorize what Isis could actually be—most of them spouting alien theories—she took it upon herself to show them her true form. She raised her hand to her own throat and ripped it open, pouring her essence from her body and onto the floor. The gas and energy that formed her soul weaved back together, creating an energetic copy of her physical form. She then entered her corpse, and when she opened her eyes, the wound in her throat sealed. Looking around the room, she had told them, "If you want further proof, you can also leave your shells."

In the end, they had agreed Isis was whatever she claimed to be, for no one from that day wanted to leave their "shells." Respectfully, they called her The Mother—after she had told them it was her title—but they did not quite understand the meaning behind the name.

The sixty-seven physicists, biologists, and neuroscientists who had tested Isis released the examination results. And it was enough for most humans to believe in the soul theory.

While Isis' anatomy may have proven that there was a soul, no one knew where the souls of the dead went. Isis was technically a demigoddess, but she was limited in her knowledge, as the blessing given to her had its restrictions. She could not take portals outside of the solar system or instantly know the truths of the universe, like a god, so she had to resort to earthly ways of study.

Science.

Despite not knowing where one went after life, the discovery of a spirit made humans not fear death. This resulted in a chaotic transformation among human societies. Some people became happier, but many became darker, and a few came up with conspiracies that the fae were sent by the Devil to test one's faith in *God*. And while the passing of loved ones was not met with the same intense emotions, the deceased were still being mourned. No one knew where anyone went or if they would ever see each other again, and this brought unease.

The worst part of the discovery of a soul was that murder and suicide rates increased drastically among humans. It was as if no one cared that the details of what happened after death remained a mystery. Where the soul went could be worse than not existing. What if the soul remained in the body, stuck between the bones and ash for all eternity? What if death was an eternal punishment, and rebirth was just a fairytale?

※※※※※

When Tabitha requested to have a meeting with the president of the United States during the spring of 2201, they ended up doing a national interview. Tabitha was enraged that their theory on how the katani came to be was being mocked by human scientists—especially since they had gifted some of their ancient fossils to the humans months ago. As the fae scientist complained and tried to explain the validity of their claims, people only saw a short woman who spoke in fast riddles while flailing her arms. And humans quickly grew to adore Tabitha, a very short nymph with light skin covered in freckles and bright-red hair.

After the president reassured Tabitha that they were not mocking the fae's claims and were just adjusting to the discoveries, she felt comfortable enough to share more of their scientific findings. She explained how the fae were capable of magic, but it was not magic in the sense of fantasy. And when she mentioned their proof of life after death, the president laughed from a place of endearment.

After realizing she was not being taken seriously, Tabitha began to stutter. She explained their research on multiple pantheons of godlike aliens, only for the host to break out into a loud laugh. Humans did not see Tabitha as a scientist at the beginning, and her words were perceived as comedy. The host kept interviewing her because of her witty charm, often asking her if she was performing a skit that the fae arranged.

"Whatever's going on, I love it." The president laughed. "I could use you in the White House. First clay idols and now alien-gods?"

Tabitha jumped out of her seat; her tolerance was fading.

Proving the existence of magic was an easy feat, considering the fae themselves were capable of magic. And Tabitha conjured water on the stage. But the understanding that magic was just manipulating energy seemed to escape the human populace. As Tabitha grew annoyed, trying to explain how energy could be controlled by one's hypnotic cells, which were common in the fae, an icy breeze filled the room. A slight twist of air formed in the middle of the stage, and the president and host stopped talking.

The short scientist raised her arms as if she were forming a cheer, and she announced to the audience that her boss was arriving. The proof that the gods were not a fabrication, and that consciousness survived bodily decay, came from the life of a person who had survived the clutches of death.

Her name was Isis.

The viewers flipped out when Isis walked on stage from her portal. Isis sat next to Tabitha, scanning the room, and everyone dropped into an eerie silence.

Then, Isis said a few words in a voice that seemed to echo softly off the floor. Staring the president in the eyes, she stated, "I was born human, and I died human, but I came back as *this*."

While Isis kept the details of how she came back from human ears, she spoke about other things. She explained their theory of three parallel realms and how one's energetic self did not end upon the decay of flesh, but the humans did not know what to think. A resurrected human with godlike powers? Portals? Three realms? Scientific evidence of a soul? What in the world was happening? The fae's discoveries were getting stranger.

"W-what are you?!" a woman yelled from the audience.

"Bet she's a nymph," a man whispered to the woman.

Isis snapped her head toward the person who had accused her of being a nymph, and the man slouched in his seat from her ancient glare. She stood up from her chair, nodding at Tabitha, and left the stage through her portal. She had no time for fools. If she was not to be believed, then she would let the fools stay blind.

Even though the audience viewed Isis as a long-lived fae, despite none of the fae living past two hundred years, the fae knew otherwise.

Isis was blessed by the Shadow King.

And the Shadow King was the first child of Chaos...

Isis was born on the outskirts of Egypt in the year 2500 BCE of the Old Kingdom. Being raised by her blind grandmother, she was taught the art of magic and divination. When Isis was mortal, humans and fae lived together. But as new kings came to power, prejudice toward the fae blossomed, and hate had spread like a poison throughout Egypt.

When Isis was thirteen, she made a vow to a creature hiding in the shadows. Mistaking the being for a frightened nymph, she had dedicated her life to saving the fae who were being persecuted for being different.

At twenty-five, Isis turned her grandmother's house into a temple. While all the fae would seek her out for aid, it was mostly the nymphs she had become familiar with, for they remained living within human society after most of the fae fled. The nymphs did not want to flee their homes, for they were a species who took pride in their dwellings, most never moving from their birthplace. Nymphs could have easily blended into human civilization, as they looked a lot like humans, but they were honest about who they were. They were a wonderful blend of honor and humility. And the humans took advantage of this, often forcing them into servitude.

When Isis turned forty, she had become so proficient in magic that her mind attracted a god, and attention from the gods was never good. While Isis sat upon her stone throne, healing the common fae and human, a god named Nao walked into the priestess' temple in the guise of a pauper. He tossed a coin at Isis, and thousands of coins started spilling out of her mouth. An ominous laugh escaped his greedy lips, and he watched as her followers rushed toward the gold. People dug into Isis to grab more coins.

Shoved under the crowd, she died a painful death. Nao returned to his shattered kingdom in Kanaria before the shadows could claim him.

However, Isis was stolen from death by the creature who hid in the shadows. But life was not what she returned to. When she came back, she stopped aging and did not need to breathe oxygen. Her magic became stronger—strong enough to lead the fae into hiding while human empires fought and enslaved each other. She had created remote communities across Earth for the fae to live.

Isis became the fae's messiah, though a messiah, she never wanted to be.

Tortures that would give nightmares a fright were inflicted upon other humans in the fae's absence. As time went by, Isis could hear the pain and suffering of others. One day, she unknowingly walked through a portal and stood before a huddle of nymph children, who were crying over the murder of their animal companion. Humans were always cruel to the fae, and the year 2459 BCE was not any different.

Watching Isis bring the kids' cat back to life, the very being who had stolen Isis from death gifted her a crown of shadow, giving her the powers of half a god.

At that moment, Isis understood who the creature from the shadows was: the Shadow King, the tortured and isolated god from the shadow realm.

The god had watched Isis from within his shade, and as she had healed the downtrodden, she had reflected the purest of hearts. Because of that virtue, the Shadow King granted Isis a title, and she became known as The Mother of Lost and Abandoned Children, and her pain never ceased. Temples to honor Isis were built, and many deities representing her were created.

But the truth of who Isis was had been lost in the tragedies of history.

DEATHLY NEWS

S THE WINTERY CHILL flew through Tallahassee, Novus started ringing a hollow-sounding bell. Rushing through the side entrance of the church, Wren found her way to the front pew and sat next to a tan man of Korean descent, Ha-Ru "Ray" Kim. While staring at the closed casket in front of them, Wren took hold of Ray's hand to calm her nerves, and he gave her a light squeeze.

"I was worried you'd be late," Ray whispered.

"Never," Wren said. "Where's Esme?"

Ray shrugged. "I bet she's hiding somewhere—"

"No," Wren said, cutting him off. "She was swinging by the bookstore..." She paused. "She probably got caught up with something. I mean, she left home before me, and I had time to tackle a rebel."

Ray stared at Wren's foolish grin. She was proud of helping Jackson.

"Wait—what?" Ray asked. "Oh, never mind. It's about to start." He tried to take his hand out of her hold. "Wren, let go."

Wren released Ray's hand reluctantly, not wanting him to leave her alone during their best friend's funeral. She stared into his dark brown eyes as he stood up. Then, she batted her eyes away from him and peered down at her hands covered in black lace.

"I feel so bad for them," an old woman whispered to another woman a few rows back, causing Wren to turn around. "Those four were inseparable."

The other woman said, "I saw Esme not too long ago. She's picketing with the kids that live in the bookstore. One of the orphans was attacked earlier this morning."

The old woman widened her eyes. "Are you serious?"

Wren stared briefly at the two older women, who continued their gossip. "*That's* why Esme isn't here," she whispered to herself.

Wren smiled at a small huddle of kids standing in the back, scared of mixing with the humans. One of the goblin girls waved at her, but then quickly hid behind a tall troll after Wren waved back. The tiny goblin peered around the protective-looking troll while giggling. They were the orphaned fae children the priest housed, mostly goblins and a few trolls.

Like goblins' golden skin, trolls also had unusual flesh. Trolls often varied from light blue to dark blue, and even had purple hues. While goblins stood between three and four feet tall, trolls stood between five and six feet. And while goblins had pointed ears, trolls' ears were floppy.

"Why are you hiding, Samara?" another goblin asked the shy girl, who was full of giggles. "It's just Wren."

"The Spirit could start fire," Samara said with hopeful eyes. "Wren blew up her yard last week... She *really* is the Spirit."

An older goblin boy who did not believe that Wren was the reincarnation of the Spirit said, "No, she isn't. Wren is just odd. The Spirit is in India. Even the Council thinks so."

"Isis thinks it's Wren," Samara said quickly, glaring up at the older boy. "Are you disagreeing with Isis?"

Samara peeped around the tall troll and continued to smile at Wren. As if a cloud of invisible bees manifested before her, Samara ran away from the nave and toward the orphanage to hide. Wren held back a laugh as a few other orphans followed Samara away from the service.

Wren did not want to be laughing at Simon's funeral.

"Are you okay?" Ray asked Wren, staring down at her.

Brushing his hands over his black suit to smooth out any wrinkles, he began to worry. He was preparing to meet the priest at the podium to give the eulogy for their deceased friend, but he noticed Wren's distraction and grew hesitant. Observing her glossy eyes, he asked, "You're not having a panic attack, are you?"

Wren shook her head, pursing her lips. Ray saw her suppression of a smile and grew annoyed. He looked back at the kids, who were making faces. He sighed and narrowed his eyes at Wren, disappointed in her demeanor.

"Really?" Ray muttered under his breath. "This is not the time to be joking around. Esme isn't here, and you're not acting properly. This is a fucked way to honor Simon."

Wren heard him and composed herself, but as soon as he walked up to meet Father Bernie at the podium, she looked back at the kids. She needed joy amidst such sorrow.

"Is your sister really from Moonlight Hills?" a short, plump man loudly asked a few benches back, trying to get Wren's attention. He was holding a small notepad and pen. "Hey!"

Wren eyed the man she did not know, then looked around at the people who were seated in the pews. She recognized half of them as members of the church and friends of Simon's, but the other half were reporters and strangers. The funeral was crammed, and half were only there for the popularity of how Simon had died. Growing irritated, Wren glowered at the short reporter and flicked him off.

The troll who stood in front of the goblins released a roaring laugh. As if that was what those who cared about the deceased needed, a few attendees started barking for the reporters to leave.

Ray panicked at what was happening and looked nervously over at the Holo-disc, which was a narrow pedestal with a holographic version of a nineteenth-century television with communication capabilities. Simon's grandparents were hovering above the pedestal, sitting on their couch near the front pew. Their fair skin looked pale pink, as the old Holo-disc needed maintenance. They had decided not to attend the funeral in person, for they feared the city's civil strife.

Father Bernie observed the loud crowd and said, "To all the reporters, I must ask you to leave."

"We have a right to be here," a woman with a recorder in her lap protested. "This is a church and a public funeral."

The woman held up her flyer, inviting all of Tallahassee to attend the service.

Father Bernie nodded and said, "I was hoping the people of the city would attend, but not in the form of the press. Please, I must ask that you excuse yourselves."

Most reporters left politely, but the short reporter who had asked about Wren's sister, Esme, would not budge. A few attendees grabbed the man's arm and dragged him to the door to leave. "You can't do this! I'm filing a complaint at city hall!"

"File it," a detective hissed down at the extremely short man. "And make sure to add the name Connell B. Hayes of the Old Precinct as one of the people who kicked you out. Don't forget to mention how you were being disrespectful."

The short reporter looked up at the detective looming over him. Connell's dark brown cheeks were flushed from anger, and the reporter's own strawberry cheeks were fluffing in brewing frustration.

Everyone knew the officers of the Old Precinct were not to be taken lightly. It was the closest precinct to the state's downtown capitol, and it had been built to honor a police chief named Fredrick S. Old, who had died protecting protestors at a peace rally. And while the entire Tallahassee Police Department took the rights of fae seriously, the Old Precinct took it a step further, trying to live up to Old's ways.

"And me," a petite woman with bronze skin and Arabic roots said, waving at the short reporter from her seat near the front. "Your mayor." The mayor glared at the reporters with chestnut eyes and stood up. "My apologies, Wren, but I think it's best I leave with them." The mayor looked down at Wren, fixing her raven-black hair. "Give your aunt my regards."

"I will, Mayor Adams." Wren nodded.

"Stop calling me that," Mayor Adams told her. "Our families have been friends for generations. Call me Zara."

"In public, I will never." Wren smiled up at Mayor Adams.

Mayor Adams walked away after patting Wren on the shoulder and helped escort the reporters outside. The short reporter looked embarrassed when he was shoved through the door. "We should *not* vote in another Adams," he mumbled about the mayor.

When he was in the doorway and holding onto the doorway's edge, the reporter's eyes lit up. "Ah, I see Esme across the street!" he shouted and looked back at Wren. "I can ask your sister myself!"

"I dare you." Wren stood up, her eyes turning an icy blue as tiny flames of smoke exited her pores.

The reporter stopped taunting her, and his cheery face disappeared. "Freaks!" he shouted. "You don't even look like an Acosta! I bet you're adopted like Esme, *Wren Sparrow*! Bet you're fae! They should overturn your rights!"

"I'm my parents' daughter," Wren said, seething angrily. "*And* an Acosta."

"Come on," Connell said, pushing the short man through the door. "Let's go for a ride."

"I think the rebels have the right idea about y'all!" the boorish reporter shouted outside. He glared across the street at the church's bookstore, where he spotted Esme, who was writing something on a picket sign. Two goblins were standing near Esme, laughing as they read what she wrote.

Connell shoved the reporter into the back seat of his car. "Maybe I should join their rebellion!" the reporter shouted from inside the cruiser.

As he pounded his chubby fists on the window, Esme held up her sign with the new words **Be Quiet! Your Voice Is So Horrible Sounding! Please?** scribbled on it, which only angered the reporter more.

The two goblins who laughed on both sides of Esme pointed at the man, who was screaming from inside the detective's car. Esme's minty eyes watched the car drive away. She shivered from the cold and wrapped her arms around her long coat, which framed her white dress. She had planned to wear her new outfit to Simon's funeral, as it was customary to wear white to funerals among the nymphs, but her plans changed when she saw one of the goblins being harassed earlier that morning.

Esme yawned and rubbed her arms from the breeze. Her skin was almost the color of onyx, and goosebumps covered every inch. Her long black hair flew in the wind, and the sun highlighted her natural streaks of blue and green.

"Will they take away our rights?" one goblin asked, looking up at his older brother.

The three at the bookstore had heard the mad reporter shouting from within the church before being hauled away.

"What rights?" the older goblin muttered and leaned back on the wall of the bookstore.

"No," Esme said, as she snapped her eyes back to the two goblins she was protecting.

Not long after the fae emerged, the United States had held a nationwide vote about granting the fae fundamental rights. It was revealed that the governments of the world had already known about the fae's existence and kept it classified because they wanted both groups to live peacefully. Peace had become a priority after so many wars across the globe. Plus, humans and fae did not have a harmonious past.

After the vote proved inconsistent, the country made a radical decision: The federal government had officially proclaimed that they were creating new laws within the United States, and any form of assault inflicted on the fae would be seen as a hate crime. Learning from their past, the country knew how horrible humans could be.

As the laws were being created, Tallahassee entered an alliance with the fae who had traveled from a city called Moonlight Hills. And in 2203, three years after the fae left their hideouts, the first bill was officially declared. It read: **The Fae Are Given All Rights As Human Citizens, And All Are Equal In The United States**. It was a simple and purely ethical rule that most people agreed with for a variety of reasons.

The day the president had endorsed the new law was a day of celebration.

On the day the bill was passed, Tallahassee's reigning mayor, Zara's uncle, held a masquerade gala at Sparrow Manor. They were formalizing a peace treaty with Moonlight Hills. While the mayor and the Sparrows played host to the diplomats from Moonlight Hills and the governor of Florida, the two humanoid groups mingled. Reporters were at the party, recording the event live, and the nation watched the news on Holo-discs or looked up at the footage in the sky via U.S. Sky News—a global industry that brought national news to everyone by sending muted holographic footage down from satellites.

The party at the Sparrows' was a sight that the country, and the world, had never seen. People from all over stared up at the sky in awe at the majestic jewels and gowns the fae wore. Since Sky News was restricted to a country by satellite borders, the rest of the world watched the news coverage above them using their own nation's Sky News, or on Holo-discs.

The union of humans and fae had begun, and the future seemed bright.

While more than half of the United States was supportive of the alliance that took place in the South, people across the Southeast were enraged that Florida's governor was a supporter of federal fae integration. Florida had a history of being separatist regarding civil rights ordeals, but within the past century, the state had strayed from its quasi-militant governorship.

And those who stood against the alliance completely lost their minds.

The vile fanatics called themselves the anti-fae, as if originality escaped them. They had drifted toward Tallahassee and set up camp right outside of city limits. Eventually, they came together and formed an organization called the Human Coalition. However, as ethics became the trend, hate became the minority, so most people had little tolerance for the anti-fae. The number of political candidates who continued to choose goodness as their platform only grew, and Florida was not exempt from this. The mindset the nation had adopted was simple: "All humans are one."

And the fae were being included in that philosophy.

Back inside the church, Ray pressed a button on the clicker he was holding, holographic pictures of Simon flickered on, and the lights dimmed. The service was beginning.

"Ignore them. Come sit down, Wren. It's starting," a woman with light brown skin and iron-curled brown hair named Ms. Beckman whispered next to where Wren was standing, prying her from her concentration on the closed door. Wren turned around and sat down next to Ms. Beckman, who was once Wren's second-grade teacher.

Ms. Beckman's grandson leaned around his grandmother and told Wren, "I don't think you're a freak."

With the blend of his words and seeing the pictures of Simon, tears formed in Wren's eyes. She could not reply to the boy and only nodded between muffled weeps.

Simon had once helped Wren conquer her sadness with his laughter, and he had eased her suffering with his very existence. Without the antidote of Simon, Wren did not know what to do—fear paralyzed her.

During the gala the Sparrows had hosted, Wren was only three years old. She had been playing with Esme, who was the same age as her, outside while the adults discussed the alliance.

But the party was interrupted by a horrendous slaughter. Masquerading as allies, a group of anti-fae had made their way into the party. Before anyone could see, twenty fanatics pulled out explosives and machine guns hidden under their coats and dresses. With over fifty fae and humans dead, the city of Moonlight Hills retracted their agreement.

There were only two people who survived the massacre: Esme, the daughter of the McKnights, who were noble aristocrats from Moonlight Hills, and Wren, the daughter of the Sparrows, who were part of the Acosta dynasty—a family of old money whose ancestors from Spain had created the most successful winery in the world.

The attendees inside the church grew quiet as pictures of Simon continued to rotate in the air for everyone to see. Ray stood at the podium and was reading a page from *The Hymnal 2224*, the church's modern book of hymns that had been altered to include fae songs.

While Ray was preparing his speech, Wren noticed a new notification on her phone about Isis. The tiny holographic headline read: **The Mother Has Found Giant Fossils! We Repeat, The Mother Has Found Giant Fossils!**

As most people perceived Isis as an undead deity who loved exploring the solar system and were amazed by what she could do, Wren viewed her as family. Wren's mind wandered, and she then remembered being comforted by Isis as she laughed in her mother's terrified arms—a memory from an age no one should be able to remember.

※※※※※

In the summer of 2200, Isis led the first group of fae to Tallahassee three months after Wren was born. The demigoddess had witnessed a prophecy that the spectral wanderer she had met in Egypt of the Old Kingdom had been reborn, and Isis swore that the child of the Sparrows was her reincarnation.

However, the highest of the fae courts would not hear it, despite the Spirit having been their ancestors' guardian. The Council, formed from the five fae courts, insisted that no fae were to emerge from their hidden communities across the globe and ordered them not to follow Isis on her migration to Tallahassee. Humans were not tolerant of fae in the past, so they had to remain cautious.

Most of the fae followed the Council's order, but not all listened. The closest fae city, Moonlight Hills, from the mysterious woods of North Georgia, was deaf to their own government's order. And their diplomats followed Isis toward Tallahassee like it was summer vacation. The visitors from the woods wore bright clothes, and a few had unusually long ears. Some strangers were not even three inches tall and flew with glittery wings.

Nymphs, elves, and fairies were the ones who first congregated in the front yard of Sparrow Manor, a house that was more than a house—a masterpiece of stone that had been designed by the Sparrows when they were newlyweds. With tall trees, expansive yards, gardens, and an iron fence, the estate was a mix of modern architecture and Gothic structures.

Mia Acosta, a woman with olive-toned skin, and Calvin Sparrow, who was almost as pale as a dove, were excited about the family they were planning. But when the fae rushed out of Isis' portal, everything changed...

The Sparrows were standing on their front porch as Mia held their baby in her arms. "She's not her!" Mia repeatedly yelled at the strangers invading their yard, wanting to believe her own lies.

However, Mia knew her words were untrue, for when she was pregnant with Wren, she had dreamed of bizarre things. She had turned her dreams into a series of children's books that followed the space adventures of two beings named Lynn and Lock. Staring at the strangers, Mia realized the visions she had dreamed and the books she had written were not fiction, but her daughter's fate.

And Wren was calling a hidden civilization out of hiding.

A tall woman wearing the jewels of the pharaohs walked up the porch steps to where the Sparrows stood. As if knowing who the strange woman was, the baby giggled. "If she is not *her*, then why does she recognize me?" the woman asked Mia in an archaic Egyptian accent.

The Egyptian woman then said to the child, "Hello, Wren. My name is Isis. We met long ago." As Isis and Wren both laughed at the other in a shared joy, Mia moved her eyes over the people. Recognizing the picture book she had written, *The Adventures of Lyn and Lock*, being held in the arms of a tall man with pointed ears, she released a disturbed laugh. She placed her hands over her face and clawed at her cheeks.

Isis brought Mia and Wren into her arms, humming an ancient tune. As she hummed, Mia calmed down. And with her hums, rain poured from the sky.

It would have been easy to brush off the appearance of the elves and nymphs as cosplay, but how could one explain the chattering fairies sitting on the flowers?

The Sparrows then led the fae inside after they listened to Isis explain who they were. Afraid of what could befall the people who looked odd, the Sparrows quickly invited Tallahassee's mayor over to speak to the ambassadors from Moonlight Hills.

Days later, Tallahassee was introduced to the three species of fae and Isis, and the reception was mostly positive.

The goblins and trolls wanted to see the child of the Sparrows, as they, too, believed in the legend of the Spirit, but the nymphs, elves, and fairies had beaten them to it. And since the fae had a caste system, goblins and trolls were forced to stay in their hideouts.

Well, at first...

III

THE MAGE'S GUILD

AS IF IT HAD become a religious practice, prejudiced people attacked Tallahassee routinely after the tragedy befell Sparrow Manor. The Council noticed this from their home in the city of Birdsong, which was located on Birdsong Island, an island shielded by a barrier dome in the middle of the Bermuda Triangle. To conquer the raids on the human city they had grown to like, the Council gifted Tallahassee a guildhall for the Mage's Guild—a society of healers, who threaded breaks in the energetic sequences of living things, and fighters, who specialized in offensive magic.

With the addition of the Mage's Guild, Florida increased its support of integration, and a summer festival was created from that allegiance. With the Mage's Guild, Florida's governor and Tallahassee's mayor presented a fae parade throughout the capital city each year. Vendors lined the streets, and booths would educate humans on fae culture. Over time, a few of the local humans were even recruited to intern with the guild if their energy was strong enough to learn the disciplines of magic. Since humans lacked hypnotic cells, magic was hard for most of them to learn.

The mages were called demons by the anti-fae radicals. And the anti-fae would constantly try to destroy Tallahassee as if it were tradition.

While Simon's funeral was taking place and Esme was protecting the two stubborn goblins who would not go inside the church, mages of the guild and police officers patrolled the area. They were looking for anyone who posed a threat to the fae, which mostly were the rebels.

"It's the end times!" a madman in his older twenties shouted with a strong southern accent into a bullhorn. "The world is ending!" He wore a brown coat, and his hands were wrapped in cloth. "The fae were sent to us to test our faith in God! Science is destroying us! I'm not a primate! I'm a man of faith!" He was preaching from the corner of a busy street in the Art District. "Come, join the rebellion!"

A fair-skinned woman was standing quietly on the corner of the street, eyeing the rebel with her doe-like brown eyes. She widened her gaze at the man shouting about the nearing apocalypse. Her navy suit was decorated with emblems of the Mage's Guild. **Rose** was sewed into her blazer.

"Hey! Hey!" The dangerous rebel approached an elderly man walking out of a shop. "Can you hear me? Can anyone hear me?" The older man froze when the rebel leaned into him, grabbing his arm, and shouted loudly into his bullhorn, *"We are all doomed!"*

"Okay," Rose whispered, trying to hype herself up as she looked down at the new ribbons on her brand-new suit. She had officially joined the guild, and her nerves were going haywire.

She turned to the hateful fanatic and the poor man. "You are disturbing the peace. Release your grip on this gentleman and lower your voice."

The crazed rebel was slouching and turned to look at the mage. The older man rushed from the rebel and ran down the sidewalk once his arm was released.

"What did you just say? Did you threaten me?" The maniacal man who was part of the rebellion walked toward Rose.

"O-oh, I would never." Rose held up her hands and crossed them timidly. "I just want the city to be at peace. That's all." The shy mage laughed nervously at the rebel glaring at her. "Can't we all just get along?"

"I think you threatened me." The rebel looked over at a police officer climbing out of a parked car nearby. It was Jackson. He was on his way to check on Rose. "This mage threatened me, officer!"

Jackson glanced at Rose, who looked rattled. He walked up to her and the angry out-of-towner.

"Thank god!" the rebel scoffed, thinking Jackson was there to aid him. "Now, we're getting somewhere. Officer, this damn mage just—"

"Hands behind your back." Jackson quickly approached the rebel and grabbed the man's shoulder.

"What?!" the rebel shouted at the officer. He was used to the police who shared the same hate as him in the town he was from. "I did nothing wrong. I'm just doing my American duty and warning the *true* citizens about the fae!"

Jackson placed handcuffs around the man's wrists and shoved him to another officer, who was jogging up, spilling her coffee. The rebel rattled his fists against the energy-infused handcuffs. He gritted his teeth from the soft buzz that was sent to his brain, sedating him.

The newly arrived officer looked down at the coffee dripping from her hand in a trance and asked, "What should I do?"

"Take him to the car," Jackson told the officer. "I'll be there in a sec."

The officer nodded and took the detainee to their patrol car.

"Man, the station is getting full of these lunatics." Jackson scratched his head and bowed a little at the mage. "I'm sorry about this, Rose. They just keep piling in from out of town. Talk about a great first day for you, huh?"

"It's okay, Jackson." Rose calmed down at the sight of a familiar face. She looked past him. "I don't remember you having a partner."

Jackson gave Rose a blank stare. "I don't. I was dropping off some idiot, and she was sitting at my desk. I told her to move—made her cry," he said, rubbing his neck. "I didn't know she's in the process of being reassigned. She was Terrance's partner."

"Is she okay?" Rose looked worried. "I know your voice can carry."

"She's fine. She's just timid, like you." Jackson grinned. Then, his grin flatlined. "I just want to let you know that Wren is bounty-hunting rebels on the wanted list again."

"My lord..." Rose's cheeks flushed in anger. "Don't let Eudora know. I'll handle this."

"By the way... I heard Wren set her yard on fire." Jackson widened his eyes and leaned in closer to Rose. "Mind reading and now fire-starting. Are you sure she isn't a fae? Maybe a nymph, like Esme?"

Everyone was aware of the strange human who harbored even stranger abilities. Wren's abnormalities had become well-known throughout the city after she went through a phase of repeating everything people thought out loud back to them. It brought her comfort to know that the voices she heard were not imaginary as she saw people's reactions—though the people whose secrets were being revealed did not find it comforting in the slightest.

"You know very well that Wren is Eudora's biological niece. She's not a fae. She's just gifted." Rose did not want to talk about Wren's strange abilities. The pain of losing Simon had affected everyone immensely, and Wren had reacted explosively.

Rose looked down at her hands clasped together. "So... how's Terrance doing?"

"He's all messed-up," Jackson said. "He's on leave and in therapy. That's why I have his partner."

He rubbed his eyes from lack of sleep. The police officers and mages hardly slept because of the frequent attacks in the city. "Shit. He may never return to work. Did you know Simon's mom was laughing at the scene? Terrance said she even sang—"

Jackson noticed Rose's teary eyes and bit his lip, frustrated about not thinking before he spoke. "I'm so sorry, Rose. That was tactless of me—damn it." He looked up at the sky.

Rose extended her arm and patted him on his elbow. "It's okay, Jackson.

You mean well." She looked around him and noticed that his temporary partner was being screamed at by the drugged lunatic caged in the backseat of the police car. "You better go help her."

Jackson looked back at what was going on in his car. "Later, Rose," he said, waving.

Rose waved at Jackson, who hopped into the driver's seat and drove toward the Old Precinct. Novus and the Old Precinct were about two miles away, but everyone in the Art District could hear the bells that came from the church.

Rose sighed as she was left alone on the sidewalk, listening to the bells. Her two-hour lunch break was at twelve, and she planned to swing by the funeral for the after-service lunch. She was depressed that her first day was the same day as Simon's funeral. But death was viewed differently in the fae world, and it was not severe enough to miss work.

Rose feared she had impulsively joined the guild when Simon died, trying to find answers of where souls went when the body perished, but what was impulsive about joining an agency after interning with them for twenty years?

❋❋❋❋❋

"No need to live in fear," the priest told everyone inside of the church, staring at the orphans, who were no longer goofing around.

"What if the Mage's Guild don't help us?" one of the goblin boys asked the tall troll who stood in front of everyone.

"They will. The mages here like us," the troll who stood between the funeral and the other orphans told the boy. "Wren and Esme's aunt is a mage."

"She's not their aunt," the boy said, correcting the troll. "Rose is their mom's cousin."

"*Actually,* you're both wrong," a goblin girl told them, feeling superior in her understanding of Wren and Esme's family dynamic. "Wren's real aunt,

Eudora, adopted her and Esme after their parents were killed. Rose is Eudora's friend and acts like Wren and Esme's aunt."

"Whatever... Still, what if they don't care about us?" the boy asked the troll. "What if we get hurt, and the mages don't help because they hate us? We belong to the Lower Courts."

"Well, then..." The troll looked back at the short goblin asking all the questions. "If the guild doesn't help us because of our class, then we don't need them."

The formation of the Council had begun with the merging of the five fae courts with equality in mind, but the nymphs, elves, and fairies had become classist over the centuries. The Council consisted of the kings and queens of each of the courts, and when the new generation of leaders came to power, they voted to split the courts into two ranks. Since three out of five were in favor of separation, the majority vote had won. The Council then divided the five courts into Lower and Upper to appease their people. The three leaders of the nymphs, elves, and fairies who sat on the Council did not agree with the classism their people had grown toward the trolls and goblins, but they each had their own court to run.

The six trolls who were orphaned with the twenty-two goblins released sparks of flame at their feet. And the goblins felt safe once more.

"We'll create our own guild," a younger troll who stood behind the protective troll softly bellowed. "We'll call it the Trolls' and Goblins' Guild."

"Yeah," the goblin girl exclaimed. "We aren't afraid. We're brave!"

An older woman with dark brown skin and gray hair walked out of the kitchen and hushed the orphans, who were getting rowdy, with a gentle smile. "Go play in the North Wing."

"What are you cooking, Bettie?" a troll asked the human who volunteered to cook for the funeral service's lunch.

"It's a surprise. Now, go play." Bettie waved for them to run along.

"I bet it's meat," one of the goblin boys said, scrunching his nose at the goblin girl, who had shouted too loudly.

"Gross," the girl replied, and they all ran away down the hall toward the North Wing, where the orphanage was.

Not allowing the shooting at Sparrow Manor to intimidate them, the goblins and trolls who lived in the South took advantage of the fact that Moonlight Hills had abandoned the fae-allied city. So, they migrated to the Floridian city over the years, wanting a better life. If the Upper Courts were too good for Tallahassee, then the trolls and goblins would seek to claim the city as their new home.

At first, the presence of the Mage's Guild caused the trolls and goblins to think about fleeing from the city, as elves primarily ran the guild, and elves were notorious for loathing the Lower Courts. However, the Mage's Guild in Tallahassee was run by a few elves who had strayed from their species' prejudice, and they did not mind the fae from the Lower Courts.

Catching wind that the mages were nice to the Lower Courts, more trolls and goblins continued to travel toward the city. Anything was better than what they were experiencing. Looked down upon by the people of the Upper Courts, mostly because of their barbaric looks, goblins and trolls were often vagabonds. Traveling in communities, the Lower Courts never had permanent homes.

When the rejected fae first appeared around Tallahassee, they were not the fae the city was used to. They lacked the Upper Courts' grace, but most people welcomed them. Since the reception of their presence was mostly positive, the fae of the Lower Courts felt confident that a new era was beginning and that their lives would change for the better by living in Florida. So, more trolls and goblins drifted away from their temporary hovels.

They had once traveled boldly with gold banners and smiled at the humans as they walked in the streets of southern cities. Most humans waved curiously at the trolls and goblins, but a few lunatics tried to kill them during their voyage.

As a result, the Lower Courts chose to migrate discreetly.

Traveling in groups, trolls and goblins would hide their children in sacks under their caravans. It was not unusual for many of them to have witnessed their families murdered in their youth. It was all too common.

The Lower Courts did not have Isis' aid of teleportation, like Moonlight Hills had. Isis was setting up her new lab on Mars when the goblins and trolls were first attacked in the streets of North Alabama. Feeling the pull back to Earth, the demigoddess had notified Birdsong of what was happening. The Council wanted to give the Lower Courts aid, but they also wanted to avoid angering the Upper Courts, so they tried to tell the goblins and trolls to travel the wooded paths with members from the Tallahassee Mage's Guild standing guard. But they did not listen to the very council who had placed them in the Lower Courts. They would rather risk their lives than kneel before the Council, including their own court leaders who had betrayed the original council's creed of equality.

Since the fae had evolved from the katani with cells that hypnotized the world's elements, they could manipulate the forces of the world. Goblins were known for their defensive magic, but their power took a large amount of energy. During migration, the parents summoned everything they could to protect the children. Even though the goblins often traveled with the trolls, the trolls' power of fire did not protect them from unseen bullets and traps. The fae were restricted to their species' hypnotic element unless they were mages. But becoming a mage was a long and tedious venture, and one had to be specifically recruited into the Mage's Guild.

In the end, the orphaned children continued the journey, and it became routine for hordes of kids to arrive in Tallahassee. In no time, fostering the fae became as normal in the city as fostering humans.

However, the process had turned strict in recent years, as the newly elected mayor, Zara Adams, grew protective of the fae orphans. Knowing all too well how human fostering customs were flawed, the mayor granted the responsibility of overseeing fostering and adoptions to Father Bernie.

IV

A Bode to My Eternal Love

Father Bernie walked up to Ray at the podium to see if he was ready to begin the eulogy. He pried his eyes from the book and nodded at the priest.

"I am going to recite Simon's favorite song, 'A Bode to My Eternal Love.' Don't worry—I'm not going to sing it." Ray began the service with a lighthearted joke. "Wherever Simon is now, I hope he is listening."

Wren tried to smile at Ray. She knew the song he was referring to. Everyone did—it was the most cherished song within the fae community.

"'Onto my back, I lay. Onto my stomach, I pray. Though no one hears my plea.'" The ballad was written by a man named Danny Vice. "'My darling, my darling. I was blind in my youth. There is no wrath like a man who was blind to sin. Though time will come again—'"

Wren picked up the hymnal from the stool before her. She opened it, flipping to the page Ray was reciting. While the life of Danny Vice was taught in schools for his act of freeing enslaved humans, the human world was once blind to his influence within fae society...

Danny was a man who had lived in the South during the 1700s, and he had fallen in love with a woman who was plagued with many scars.

Not only did Danny's parents participate in the sinful act of enslaving people, but they also enjoyed it. As a young child, Danny was ignorant of the atrocities of slavery that occurred in his father's land. His mother always took him inside the house whenever his father was angry at someone. But as Danny grew, and when he could run from his mother's grasp, he started to see horrible things.

Eventually, he became close to a few people who were there against their will, for he was not like his parents in the slightest—in particular, a girl named Janette, and he played with her in the fields. Listening to her stories from her village in West Africa, he fell in love with her, and he even learned Janette was not her true name.

Her name was Zuhrah.

Danny rebelled against his parents as he spoke with more people in the fields. It was common for children to wish their parents to be heroes, but his parents were not the heroes he thought them to be. He became reckless, and he would play marbles with the people who were stolen from their homes. And he would always make sure his father saw.

That proved to be a fatal mistake.

When Danny was seventeen, he returned home to find the man and woman who had behaved like Zuhrah's parents lying dead in the field. Danny ran over to where the other workers stood, but his mother yanked him back. Feeling the fury rush in, he released a scream while he shoved his mother to the ground. He rushed for his father's shotgun, and he aimed the gun at his father, who was laughing at the crowd who mourned the dead. Without hesitation, he pulled the trigger. After, he killed his mother in the same manner, and he set the house on fire.

Through the small crowd of men and women shouting at the burning house, Danny finally noticed Zuhrah. Every detail of her face haunted him until his dying day.

There was a third corpse lying in the field: Zuhrah.

After Danny parted ways with the free people from his father's fields, he walked into the woods. From the horror, he blinded himself with twigs that he had broken from a tree. He hiked further into the woods, not knowing where he was going. He wanted to die—for a bear to maul him. He regretted not jumping into the fire, and he stumbled as he felt the trees.

And then he felt a person.

Stopping his staggering through the woods, a group of tall elves looked down at the man who had gouged out his own eyes. The elves were the tallest of the fae, and they were also the ones who had the best musicians among the courts, for air was their magical element by birth.

As Danny shouted at them to kill him, they almost fulfilled his wish. But an elder came out of her hut and ordered them to stop.

After being taken in, Danny found a new home with the small elf camp hidden in the Virginia woods. And eventually, he became a renowned bard and poet. Every song he wrote was dedicated to Zuhrah, and every tale was about his father's evil lands.

Human history claimed Danny died in the fire, but that was not what had befallen Danny Vice.

"'—and I will free you from him,'" Ray spoke slowly, eyes clouded. "You will not recognize me. For I lashed lashes upon my back. It is okay, my dear. I could not feel the pain. I feel the scars, so I know I have been struck. My heart is numb; my skin is cold. And I scream your name. As I lie on my deathbed, I cannot see. For the eyes I used to gaze upon your face, I plucked the moment you left. My dear, my sweet. Zuhrah, we shall meet under the tree where we used to sleep...'"

"'Onto my back, I lay. Onto my stomach, I pray. Though—'" The two older women who had been gossiping at the beginning of the funeral were now standing, and they sang the song right after Ray finished reading it.

As more people stood to sing the song, Wren remained seated. Ray tried to urge her to join the others in harmony, but she acted like she could not see him. She then smiled at a young girl singing the song loudly.

After they all sang the song that a gravely heartbroken man had written, they sat back down. Ray reminisced about how Simon would always sing the song to interrupt Father Bernie. People smiled through their tears, remembering how much Simon had loved interrupting the priest's lectures.

Ray paused, finally realizing why Simon was obsessed with the story of Danny and Zuhrah. Then, he almost broke down at the podium. But he was able to hold in his cries.

Like Danny's parents, Simon's parents were monsters. Also, like Danny, Simon was in love with someone his parents loathed. Thinking Wren was fae because of her odd abilities, Simon's parents had never liked her, and they would always try to separate them whenever they played as children. Going against his parents, Simon had often sneaked out to hang out with Wren, Ray, and Esme.

Nothing could keep the four best friends apart.

Death could only try.

V

HATE CRIME

AS THE CHURCH'S BELLS stopped, signaling the funeral had begun, Esme stared across the street. She was upset that she was going to miss Ray giving the eulogy for Simon. But she felt it was wrong to leave the two goblins alone. Standing close to four feet tall, one of the goblins was leaning back on the church-owned bookstore with folded arms, looking up at the sky.

It was hard enough that a third of the city still opposed the fae. **Kind Human Slaughtered By Rabid Fae** had been written as an opener in the city's newspaper, and each local fae lived in fear.

"Stop worrying, Rolf," said a shorter goblin, who stood close to three feet tall with a light gold complexion. He twirled his picket sign, which read **Leave Us Alone**, while looking over at his brother. "They can't blame any of us for Simon's death. Simon's parents killed him in public."

"Stop telling me to stop worrying, Kyle." Rolf, the taller goblin with darker gold skin, slid down the wall and sat on the sidewalk, scratching his head out of irritation. "They will accuse us. Watch. We are the *new arrivals*."

Rolf and Kyle were new in town, having arrived the prior month. They had been part of a small caravan that traveled through the woods from West Alabama to Tallahassee. For years, the hidden road they had traveled proved safe, but during the last migration, the kids had watched their families be murdered. Anti-fae fanatics were mapping the location of the scattered fae, and the fae's routes were constantly being ambushed.

After becoming separated from the other survivors, the brothers had continued their voyage to Tallahassee, where their first shelter was behind Novus Episcopal Church. When Rolf had stolen a bag of chips and bread to feed him and his brother from a nearby convenience store, the priest of Novus saw him run off toward a tiny gathering of woods.

Approaching the two, who hid inside some bushes, the priest sat down and stole a chip from their pile of stolen food. The goblins just stared at the priest, who slowly chewed. "Welcome to Novus," Father Bernie had told the two goblins hiding in the shrubs.

At first, Father Bernie tried to encourage Rolf and Kyle to live inside the church with the other orphans, but goblins were not a trusting bunch, especially of other goblins. After they refused to live inside the church or sign the city's roster to list them as residents, the brothers feared that staying isolated was their destiny. However, the priest was known for his charity, and through that generosity, Father Bernie gave them a copy of the keys to Novus' bookstore. Some people called the priest a fool for his blind trust in the orphaned fae, but he was a man who only knew compassion.

"They won't accuse you. You two never leave the bookstore. Plus, the Mage's Guild is standing guard," Esme said. At five feet and nine inches, she was much taller than both, and she was seated next to Kyle, clutching a picket sign. "It's obvious that Simon's parents killed him." She squinted her eyes to stop the tears that were trying to fall. "A cop witnessed everything. You'll be fine."

"Easy for you to say. You can pass as human," Rolf muttered. In the past, he and Kyle did not have a good experience with nymphs. But he liked Esme. She was the only nymph who was ever nice to him and his brother.

"And you guys also have those human ears... You look like humans, especially when you're not swimming," Rolf said. "Those scales you guys get when you're in the water are *uuugly*." He laughed and then looked worried about hurting Esme's feelings. "No offense."

Esme released a soft smirk at Rolf's snide remark. She understood his disdain for the Upper Courts. She was a nymph, but she did not like her own people much of the time. Her people were no longer the peaceful species that swam alongside the orcas and whales in the sea.

Thousands of years ago, when the nymphs used to live in the ocean, they were peacekeepers, and they made sure the ocean was in harmony with the creatures below the waves. They only wanted to govern sea life and live quietly. But sailors would discover them when ships were first invented, and humans kept invading the sea. Being spotted always created trouble for the nymphs, as sailors would become obsessed if they saw one. The humans eventually created myths about them, calling them mermaids, and they would hunt them for their golden tails. But the nymphs could swim far and hide in the deep.

This was not the case on land. On land, the nymphs were slower and weaker. A world where their essence was depleted frightened the nymphs.

So why did they live in a habitat that scared them?

Loyalty.

The empress of the nymphs had formed an alliance with the other fae courts to oppose the humans' dominance, forming the Council. And the monarch then led her people to land...

"Can't you go inside and ask Wren to read those mean women's minds?" Kyle asked Esme. "She'll know if they're planning anything."

That morning, Kyle had returned from the nearby general store with bags full of markers and posters. He and Rolf had planned on protesting while the funeral took place. But a gang of ex-Novus members had harassed him, causing him to drop his shopping bags.

When Esme went to check on the brothers before Novus, she had found Kyle sprawled out on the sidewalk, crying as the women who surrounded him bullied him. In a fit of rage, she had blasted the small group of women with water, which nymphs could conjure. Fearing Rolf and Kyle would suffer more bullying, she had stayed at the bookstore, picketing with them. She was the manager of the bookstore, and she had grown protective of the two.

Rolf corrected his younger brother. "Old hags, Kyle. They're wretched old hags."

"Not right now. Simon's funeral has started." Esme looked over at Kyle.

Rolf and Kyle stared at each other, feeling bad for not attending the funeral. Having met Simon before he was murdered, they had grown fond of the overly cheerful human. The two thought that if Esme, who was far from human, was friends with someone like Simon, then he could not have been that bad. They had used the same logic for Esme's human sister Wren and their friend Ray.

"Ms. Norris and her lackeys won't do anything else, guys. You saw how scared they were this morning. They are the least of our concerns. Verbal insults are the peak of what those cowards can do. I'm worried about the actual supporters of the rebellion." Esme looked up at the dreary morning. "I'll ask Wren to scan the city after the funeral."

"If those women aren't part of the rebels, then why were they yelling at my brother?!" Rolf asked.

Esme lowered her eyes from the sky and turned to stare at Rolf's enraged ones. "Prejudice," she whispered to the two goblins, who grew quiet.

VI

A Strange Appetite

INSIDE NOVUS EPISCOPAL CHURCH, Ray switched from a formal tribute to a more relaxed one when he realized that the energy was too dense for him to concentrate. He abandoned his written script and began talking about the pictures of Simon they had chosen to honor his life. He was describing a picture of him and Simon holding up horribly sewn dresses in a photo that he froze in place with the projector remote. Wren and Esme's outdoor raccoon had been run over by a car in the fourth grade, and Simon viewed it as a tragedy. And since the girls had always worn dresses as kids, he had wanted to make them one to cheer them up.

In their youth, Wren had been obsessed with porcelain dolls and wanted to look like one, and Esme wanted to befriend every animal. The girls always mimicked each other, so both ended up wearing dollish dresses while holding raccoons, rats, birds, snakes, and many other creatures. Eudora never got used to the critters flocking to her house, but she allowed them to stay because the girls viewed them as their friends.

Older women used to horde around Wren and Esme, as their elaborate dresses had always attracted a particular crowd. Whenever the women gathered, Esme would run off to hide, vanishing into the wind. Wren did not like the attention they received because it always made Esme freak out, and whenever Esme was frightened, Wren became upset.

So, Wren began to destroy things and kept wild rats in her dress pockets. The women would be shocked and, quite frankly, disturbed to see an innocent-faced child ripping the heads off dolls, laughing while doing so, often with a rat poking their head out to watch. She would twirl in her dress, talking to her beheaded dolls and curious rats, and Esme would feel safe enough not to hide from the humans when forced into public. To say Wren was successful in keeping the women away would be an understatement.

"So, we made two dresses," Ray said, then vented about how badly a sewing needle hurt, making much of the crowd chuckle. "But I assure you, both Wren and Esme will confirm how bad the dresses were. They were like potato sacks!" He twisted his mouth up to one side, expressing a somber grin.

"Simon was angry that the dresses turned out badly, so he looked around town for a new racoon. Nothing can ever remedy the loss of a life, but when Simon came to school the next day covered in scratches from wrestling a wild racoon, Esme and Wren laughed the entire day. He always did things like that whenever one of us was sad..."

Wren locked eyes with Ray, and tears finally fell down his cheeks. He clicked the remote to try to find a new photo to talk about. Feeling himself on the verge of breaking, he cleared his throat and shifted his feet. He set the photos to auto-cycle and turned his attention to his parents, who sat on the bench behind Wren. They were encouraging him to continue his speech and were sitting next to Markus Rowans and his parents. The Rowanses were the only goblin family at the service.

Then, a memory that was not connected to any of the pictures came to Ray. "I remember when the first family to survive the fae trails arrived. I was ten. How many of you remember that?" He moved his hands as he spoke. Most of the crowd looked at each other, raising their hands.

"It was a huge deal because the fae trails are *very* unsafe, so every news station was covering it." Ray looked at the back pews, where the few orphans who had stayed for the service were seated. "The Rowans family signed the city roster, and fourteen years later, they're still here." A few people who sat near the Rowanses patted them warmly on the shoulders. "They moved into a house next to Eudora since it was vacant. Anywhere near Eudora is the safest place in town. She has *Vaan*." Ray warped his hand into a claw and bared his teeth, making a few people grumble. The city had mixed feelings about Vaan, a ruthless man with the Mage's Guild who followed Eudora around everywhere. "Simon was beyond thrilled that the Rowanses were Wren and Esme's neighbors. Fun fact, did you know goblins love pranks? Of course, you do! How many of you are tired of coming to church to find frogs hopping on the pews?"

Numerous people nodded, a few chuckling. All eyes drifted to the back to smile at the orphans, who were happily swinging their legs while sitting on the benches. The kids enjoyed playing with frogs and loved the fact Ray mentioned them. It meant their frogs were appreciated.

"Simon had convinced Wren to read the Rowanses' minds when we were over one night. We were planning to work on our volcano project after dinner, but that never happened. Don't get Esme started on how we got an F. She always wanted to go to school with us and hated being homeschooled. She volunteered to help us build our volcano and even bought all the supplies." Ray paused, grinning at Esme's neuroticism about education. "A volcano was never built, but we did have dinner and a show. Wren stormed outside, and not even five minutes later, she ran back into the house and told us that the Rowanses were eating a human head and drinking cow's blood."

This was news to most of the attendees, and everyone burst out laughing, many eyeing Wren, who became embarrassed. The Rowanses, who sat behind Wren, were nodding their heads proudly.

"We all now know the fae are herbivorous, but back then, we didn't know that." Ray allowed himself to join the laughter. "So, we were all a little scared, to be honest. Even Esme. I mean, we should have known that the Rowanses were pranking Wren, because whenever Isis was in town, Esme would hound her with a million questions. One was why animal products made her sick. You don't know how many times Isis told Esme that none of the fae eat meat. The world wouldn't think Isis is this mystical being if they saw how she blew up at Esme for asking the same questions! But we were kids—we didn't listen."

People started talking to each other. Everyone was forgetting they were at a funeral when Isis was mentioned. The demigoddess visited the Acosta family throughout the year, and the city loved when she came to town.

The priest, sitting in a chair near the stand, helped Ray regain control over the service, clearing his throat loudly and quieting everyone down.

"That night, Wren kept trying to read the Rowanses' minds," Ray said as he resumed talking. "She even passed up ice cream to play detective. Wren never passes up dessert! But she got tired of not knowing the truth, so she knocked on their door and spoke to Ms. Rowans. We all heard her shouting at Ms. Rowans from inside the house. She flat-out asked Ms. Rowans if they were eating human heads and drinking cow's blood!" Ray laughed. "I don't know exactly what Ms. Rowans told Wren, but she came running into the house shouting at everyone that she was a nymph."

When Wren had run into the house after spying on the Rowanses, shouting that she was a nymph, Esme abandoned her vegan ice cream and argued with her. Simon and Ray were eating their own ice cream cones while eyeing the bickering sisters like they were watching a sitcom.

Wren was confident that she was controlling the air after speaking to Ms. Rowans. To Wren's defeat, Esme explained that air manipulation was far different from the vibrations Wren manifested. Plus, nymphs could only control water. The best Esme could come up with was that Wren was an enigma.

After Esme informed Wren that she had powers that all the fae courts were foreign to, Wren cried.

And Vaan had become irritated.

Eudora had been attending an opera with Rose, which meant Vaan was subjected to the horrors of babysitting. The man who was far from human marched over to the Rowanses and pounded on their door. After Ms. Rowans answered, expecting it to be Wren, she dashed down the hall. Wren had followed Vaan, pointing at Ms. Rowans, asking him to punish her.

After Vaan ordered the goblin to explain what happened, he dragged Wren back to the house and sent her to time-out. "Stop reading people's minds!" he had barked at Wren, slamming her door shut.

It was a fond memory for Ray, but he did not experience Vaan's wrath.

Wren rolled her eyes and looked away from Ray. She peeked back at Ms. Rowans, who was smirking. She anxiously snapped her head back to the front to stare at Simon's flowers.

"Simon always made us laugh, whether by fighting raccoons or having Wren play detective. Back then, we didn't know he was goofing around because of his parents..."

Ray's voice wavered—he should not have mentioned them.

He tried to resume the eulogy. "If Simon never forced us to hang out as kids, the four of us wouldn't have become friends to begin with. Simon was a good man—a rare man."

Before Ray could continue speaking, his mask completely crumbled. Everyone stared at him, pounding his fists on the podium, his sadness turning to rage. He normally had control over his emotions, which was why he had volunteered to give the eulogy, but the mention of Simon's home environment destroyed him.

Father Bernie walked up to Ray and whispered into his ear. The priest took over speaking to allow him a moment to breathe.

After Ray walked down from the stage and to the flowers in front of the podium, where the pictures of Simon hovered above, Wren walked up to him and gave him a tight hug.

"This city has suffered too many sorrows," Father Bernie said, rubbing his eyes. "I'm sure most of you are aware that Simon was in the middle of moving back. This weekend was supposed to be his welcome-home party," he said into the microphone. "We will now open the stand to whoever wishes to speak."

Ray leaned back from Wren, wiping the tears from his eyes. "Sorry."

Wren smiled gently.

"I need air," Ray whispered, then walked toward the door that led to the inner courtyard.

As Wren followed him, Ms. Rowans walked up to the podium. "Well, Simon succeeded," she said quietly. "He and Markus became good friends after that night, and we all were pleased to hear that Simon was moving home. But let me tell you what I told Wren that night..."

Before Wren could shout "No!" to Ms. Rowans, Ray pulled her outside.

"It can't be that bad," Ray said as they walked to a wooden bench under a tree.

After they sat down, Wren slouched and leaned her head back on the bench, staring up to watch the leaves of winter. "Yes, it is," she said, embarrassed that she had ever believed Ms. Rowans. "She said I had nymph's eyes."

"How's that bad?" Ray asked.

"Because she said Isis had cut the eyes from a nymph and gave them to me when I was born, turning me into a nymph. And that was why Isis came to my house back then," she muttered. "I should've known better. She obviously wanted to mess with me. I mean, why would Isis come all the way to my house to turn *me* into a nymph?"

"To be fair, you were obsessed with the fae when we were kids... and you did read her mind. Can't wait until Isis finds out about this one," Ray said humorously. "She takes a lot of pride in thinking you are the Spirit's reincarnation."

"She knows. I called her the next day," Wren muttered, remembering that week vividly.

"Well, what did she say?" Ray asked.

"She told me to stop being gullible and go to bed." Wren sighed. "When I told her that Eudora took away my Holo-disc for a month, she said, 'Good,' and hung up on me. I needed her, but she was too into whatever was going on in Antarctica."

"Think that was when they found that zyula village," Ray said.

Extracting an eighty-million-year-old frozen city to place in the museum in Birdsong was not as important as Ms. Rowans' prank, according to Wren's ten-year-old mind.

"Who lets someone like Vaan babysit kids?" Wren complained. She had a vendetta against him for convincing Eudora to take away her Holo-disc whenever she read people's minds as a child.

"Eudora," Ray said, answering her rhetorical question. "You should have seen everyone's faces when I mentioned him. He is *not* liked."

"I heard them cursing. They like him when he cleans up the city. Freaking hypocrites." Wren rolled her eyes.

"You were just complaining about him." Ray turned his head sideways, looking at her.

"He helped raise me and Esme. He's practically family, so I'm allowed to," Wren spat. "They're not grateful at all for what Vaan does for the city. Without him, the rebels would have taken over Tallahassee years ago. And we would have thousands of David Henrys running around."

Wren folded her arms, arching her eyebrows down in irritation. She fell into a grim silence, thinking about what Vaan did to David Henry, the perpetrator of the city's second mass shooting after the fae became residents of Tallahassee. She had been in the third grade when their school became infested with bullets.

After the incident with David Henry, the rebellion became bigger, drawing in more hateful people from the outskirts of Tallahassee, and the rebels started protesting daily on every corner of every street, near the newsstands.

✹✹✹✹✹

David Henry was the son of the man who had orchestrated the attack on Wren's house when she was three. He was the most terrible man around, inheriting his late father's hate. Always wearing his father's torn biker jacket everywhere he went, he mocked the Sparrows' tragic death. He would yell and threaten Wren at her school, telling her that she should have died with her parents.

Threatening children would not go unnoticed.

The mayor tried to keep the vile man away from the city, especially from the children. But David Henry was persistent in his quest to torment the last Sparrow. He wanted to finish his father's mission.

One day, he almost completed it.

At Wren's school, David Henry ended up shooting and wounding forty-five people, and thirty were kids. While the teachers tried to protect the children, Wren managed to escape. She ran onto the playground as David Henry ran after her. She screamed at the surrounding energy, and the air began to vibrate. Darkness seeped into her heart, and coldness spread through her veins.

Before she could test her expanding abilities on the shooter, she saw Vaan with his hand clasped to David Henry's throat.

In front of everyone, Vaan ripped out a part of David Henry's spine. He was delicate, trying not to kill the shooter. The teachers tried to block the windows and told the kids inside the rooms not to look.

Vaan's stomach grumbled, and his eyes turned a dark red. He leaned down and started crunching on the bones protruding from David Henry's back. The nineteen-year-old cried in agony as Ray and Simon ran to the playground, bypassing the teachers. Ray turned around at the sight, close to vomiting, but Simon grinned enthusiastically at the man in pain, then shook his head, scared that such a thing fascinated him.

"Attacking my niece's class is not something one should do." Eudora walked up to Vaan's side. Her eyes were wild with anger. "Did you think we would allow you to harm the kids?"

Eudora tilted her head to gaze into David Henry's eyes. "I thought it was well-known that Tallahassee has a Mage's Guild. Only a fool would come here alone knowing that." She smiled at the shooter, who was screaming at the top of his lungs. "Vaan, be a dear. Can you deal with his tongue? He's too loud."

Eudora looked away while Vaan ripped out his tongue with his teeth.

"As I was saying, we have mages throughout the premises. So, I fear you have wasted your ammo," Eudora said.

The Mage's Guild members, all wearing dark blue suits, rushed down the sidewalk and entered the classrooms. They were frantically drawing out energy from the air to fuel their magic. There were so many casualties that the mages only healed the injured to the point that they were no longer dying, with plans to rush everyone to the hospital. They had to reserve their energy, or they would be consumed by friction and combust. The mages could only do so much when it came to binding one's flesh, which was why the guild had a rule that their healing capabilities were to be used for the benefit of children and animals. However, the circumstances were dire, and the mages temporarily ignored that rule and also healed the adults who were on the verge of death.

Eudora gasped over at the mages healing the wounded. "Look at that—no one's dying."

She tightened her lips at the man whose face was butchered, skin flapping down his cheek while Vaan licked his cheekbone.

"As for you, not so much." Eudora beamed at the young man's pain. "Your father killed my older sister, and my friend killed his son."

Eudora widened her eyes at her mistake.

She then leaned into David Henry, fearing his earless ear would not hear her. "Oh, my apologies. My friend *will soon* kill his son."

In front of the three kids, Vaan chewed on David Henry's flesh and bones until the shooter was no longer breathing. Ray kept his eyes closed most of the time, while Wren and Simon watched, and the two would often glance at each other with menacing grins.

VII

The Atomic Years

RAY PRIED WREN FROM the memory of Vaan ripping a man apart and said, "At times like these, I wish I could go invisible, like Esme. Must be nice..."

Wren shook her head, trying to rid her mind of David Henry's guts on the sand.

"Are you okay?" he asked her.

"Yeah, just distracted," Wren replied.

"Understandable." Ray nodded.

"Esme was hiding all week." Wren stared at a dead leaf on the ground.

"You know how she is. She doesn't like others to see her cry," Ray said.

Wren leaned her head on Ray's shoulder, closing her eyes. They knew all too well how much honor Esme had. Being born from nobility, Esme carried herself with an aristocratic demeanor. But the last McKnight had often cried alone in her youth...

A few weeks after Eudora adopted the girls, Esme had developed an ability to turn invisible. She would always fret over why she could vanish—that was until a goblin, who came with the first wave of orphans, overheard Eudora talking about Esme to Father Bernie one day.

It turned out that it was just something nymphs could do on land when they were scared or did not want to be seen. It surprised the goblin that Esme's first disappearance was at three, and that she did not know what atomic camouflage was.

But no one told Esme that it was a general trait of hers until they were almost four, meaning she had spent nearly a year thinking she was broken. Turning invisible was something she felt she should have known, and then she developed a whole new concern about not being a real nymph.

As Esme combated atomic camouflage, Wren stopped talking. And around the same time that Esme found out that her invisibility skill was genetic, Wren realized that the whispers she was born hearing were not imaginary and the images she dreamed were not just her thoughts. But she did not know how to communicate with others about what was happening inside her head—she had forgotten how to speak. This led to her behaving strangely around other people, and she would stare everyone down, trying to understand why she could hear them speaking without their lips moving. As she tried to understand others, people would see a silent girl sending death glares.

So, Esme took it upon herself to communicate for Wren. Well, when she was not disappearing. A fantastic duo, Esme and Wren were.

Seeing how the two girls were inseparable, Eudora was insistent that Esme should attend Wren's preschool, after Esme adjusted to living with a human family. It was a short-lived attempt. The once peaceful preschool was shifting into an anti-fae mindset, and Esme lasted not even one day before turning invisible in front of everyone. She had spent the morning crying in the corner of the classroom, while Wren tackled everyone who bullied her to the ground, biting their arms.

Furious, Eudora showed up with a wrath like no other. She threatened she would ruin them—and ruin them she did. She bought the private preschool, bulldozed it, and turned it into a park. No one ever saw the teachers who had mocked Esme again. Everyone suspected Vaan was the reason for the disappearances. It was the most logical guess, since people who crossed Eudora often went missing, and Vaan had a strange appetite.

Fearing the non-human man who protected Eudora like she was his liberator, the city both loved and cowered at the sight of him. Vaan was a significant part of the city's security against the anti-fae, so no one interfered with his activities. Knowing Eudora and Vaan ran the metropolis more than the city officials, no one even asked questions.

At around the age of five, Wren and Esme were separated when they reached kindergarten because Eudora wanted to keep Esme safe. So, Esme spent her days being taught by private tutors within the walls of Eudora's mansion, and she would surpass her tutors, skipping a few grades. Meanwhile, Wren was forced into a public school to socialize with other humans. She lacked human interaction because she was always around Esme.

The separation from Esme led to Wren spending many of her days isolated from the others on the school's playground. Wren would always bring one of her headless porcelain dolls to class, but no one liked them, and for some reason, no one wanted to play with her—until a boy from her kindergarten class felt obligated to annoy her.

Wren panicked when Simon first approached her, and she stared down at her doll to save herself. Having been separated from Esme, she was forced to learn how to speak again. But at first, all she did was grunt for Simon to leave her alone.

However, Simon would not stop talking to her, and he made it a habit to run around Wren during recess. He would often chant, "Sad girl, don't cry. Sad girl, don't cry." He felt it was his purpose to make Wren smile, and one day, he succeeded.

Immediately, Simon dragged his best friend of two weeks up to Wren during lunch in the cafeteria and introduced them. She stared at the boy from one of the other kindergarten classes. She recognized him, but she did not like the boy named Ray at first. He would always rip rose petals off flowers during recess, and Wren liked the flowers being intact.

Ray tried to leave, but Simon forced him to sit beside Wren. He told them, "Sad people shouldn't be alone. We should stick together."

The three formed a club after Wren became friends with Simon and, eventually, Ray. It was a club for sad guys, as Simon called it. But he was always happy, so Wren wondered what made him sad.

In the middle of her kindergarten year, Wren introduced her two school friends to Esme and her aunt. It intrigued Simon that Esme was a nymph. This affection made Esme vanish until Simon clung to her and cried for her not to disappear. Startled by Simon's sincerity, Esme fell when she tried to run from him. Ray helped her up, inspecting her scratches.

From that moment on, Esme lowered her guard around the boys, and the Sad Guy's Club gained a fourth member.

Even though Esme wanted to go to public school with them, she was not allowed—Eudora was not risking her being mistreated again.

While Wren, Ray, and Simon went to the same school, Esme was homeschooled throughout their elementary and middle school years. After middle school, Wren and Ray attended the same high school, and Esme was accepted early into the local university for physics. Fae rights were better there, and the university even had goblin scholars, causing Eudora to allow her to pursue higher education with humans. As the three stayed in Tallahassee, Simon moved away to live with his kind grandparents after his parents had lost custody.

At eighteen, Wren moved out of her aunt's three-story Victorian mansion and back into her parents' two-story manor. She wanted to live in her parents' house despite the haunting memories of the shooting. Not wanting Wren to live alone, Esme followed her to Sparrow Manor.

2224 was supposed to end well for the Sad Guy's Club. Simon had moved back, Ray had just bought the motorcycle he had been saving up for, Esme loved being Novus' bookstore's manager even though she had a Ph.D., and Wren was used to her weird abilities.

But now, without the one who had formed the club, the three left behind were shrouded in nothing but despair.

The Sad Guy's Club was not a place of rainbows and unicorns, no matter how peppy Esme was.

VIII

YEAR 2208

THE KIDS RAN AROUND the playground as Wren watched in all her gloom from a shaded bench. It was the year 2208. As the world was changing, some things remained the same, and she was a target for bullying.

"Why aren't you playing with the others, Wren?" their second-grade teacher asked, walking up to her.

"I don't want to," Wren replied, glancing down at her mother's illustrated storybook in her lap.

"Is it because Simon's sick today?" the teacher asked, worried about her.

Wren stayed quiet. Simon had become her confidant, and facing school without him was misery.

The teacher smiled and sat down next to her. She looked over at Ray playing dodgeball with friends from his class. "Aren't you friends with Ray? Why not go play with him and his friends?" The teacher tried to comfort the saddened child. "Who knows? Maybe you'll make some new friends?"

Wren looked up at Ms. Beckman and said very seriously, "Ray's friends are all fucktwats, Ms. Beckman."

"Where did you learn that word?" Ms. Beckman asked, trying hard not to laugh at a child saying an offensive word at school.

"My aunt," Wren said and swung her legs. "Well, I guess... she's my mom now."

"Ms. Beckman," another teacher called out, interrupting their chat, "may I speak to you?"

"Of course," Ms. Beckman replied. "Excuse me, Wren. Go and try to make some new friends, okay? And don't call people... f-twats. It's hurtful to call people names."

Wren nodded and looked up at the afternoon sky. She had no intention of making new friends.

Prying her from her melancholy, a girl from Wren's class quickly approached her. "Why do you wear those dresses?" the girl asked Wren. She had been playing dodgeball with the class, but she was now judging Wren's attire of a puffy doll dress. The girl was tiny, with black-rimmed glasses. Her brown hair was held in pigtails. Her name was Amanda, and her brother was Wren's biggest bully.

"Because..." Wren muttered.

"Because why?" Amanda asked.

"Because I do," Wren answered. "Why do you wear those glasses?"

"I need to," she said pretentiously. "You don't need to wear those dresses."

"You don't know," Wren replied. "I could have a need."

Amanda stared at Wren and then looked down at the storybook in her lap. "I get why you annoy Max... Is that your mom's book?"

Wren did not reply and gripped her mother's book.

"Let me see that." Amanda snatched the book from her hands and flipped through the pages of *The Adventures of Lynn and Lock*. "There's no such thing as many worlds and the Shadow King. Max said your mom is in Hell for being a Satan worshiper. Lynn and Lock are dumb—"

Wren left the safety of the bench, stormed over to the girl, and pushed her to the sand. "Shut up!" she screamed down at Amanda, whose glasses fell off.

Amanda cried and reached for her glasses, but Wren stomped on them. As the glass cracked, she felt a darkness rise inside of her. "Yes, *cry*," Wren, stuck in a trance, hissed quietly down at Amanda, who was sobbing. "Bullies are not honorable."

"Max," Amanda yelled out to her older brother, picking up her broken glasses.

Max and a few second and third graders ran over to where Wren and Amanda had fought.

"Did you push my sister?" Max asked Wren, helping his sister up from the ground. "Did you break her glasses?"

"Yes," Wren replied, not scared of him.

"What happened?" Ray asked and ran up to them. "Seriously guys. Y'all need to stop picking on Wren—"

"Shut up, Ray," Max yelled and shoved Ray, stopping him from getting closer to Amanda. "She broke her glasses." Max's eyes looked frightened. "Our dad's going to be pissed..."

Max eyed the book Wren was picking up from the ground. She brushed off the dirt from the cover and analyzed her mother's storybook.

"Give me that crap," Max yelled and snatched the book from her. "You broke her glasses because of this?"

"No. She said my mother is in Hell. That is why her glasses broke," Wren hissed. "Now, give me my mother's book back."

"I'm tired of how you talk," Max told Wren. "Like you're better than us."

As Wren watched Max tear out the pages of her mother's very first copy of *The Adventures of Lynn and Lock*, she felt her heart break. By the time Ray pried the book from Max, it was too late. The torn pages flew in the wind.

Wren let out a high shriek, charging at Max, pinning him on the dirty sand. "I hate you! The gods hate you! Everyone hates you!" she screamed down at his scared face.

Max pushed Wren off him and ran away with the other kids, scared by the darkness he saw inside Wren's eyes.

She stayed on the ground, heaving, while Ray picked up the pages. She closed her eyes and focused on the breathing techniques she and Esme had been taught by their therapist.

"Wren?" someone asked, ripping her from her concentration.

Wren opened her eyes and saw Simon's face hovering above her.

"Oh, no," Simon said, staring around at the pages surrounding her. "Who did this?"

Simon squatted on the ground and helped Ray pick up the pages.

"I thought you were sick?" Wren asked him.

"I feel better," Simon said, tugging at his long sleeve, trying to hide his bruises.

Wren forced a smile.

"Don't cry." Simon shook his head and hugged her.

Wren cried like a normal eight-year-old. She acted like the child she was, muttering in broken sentences. She lost her high-class demeanor to childish tantrums.

"Max did this, right?" Simon yelled and ran toward the group of kids playing dodgeball. "Y'all are dead!"

After Simon fought it out with Max, both were sent to the principal's office, where they were given after-school detention. Then, both ran back to their classrooms, clutching their detention slips.

Hours later, intercoms chimed with the end-of-day bell, and kids rushed outside—they were eager to leave. But school was not over for those who broke the rules.

Ray walked up to Wren, who was sitting at their usual hangout spot, and said, "You should say you're sorry."

Wren looked baffled. "For what?"

Ray sat down next to her at the outdoor picnic table and waited with her for Simon to leave detention. "I know Amanda started it, but their dad is mean."

"Many people are mean." Wren shrugged. "Simon's parents are mean."

"Not like Max's dad," Ray said, unaware of the truth about Simon's life. "I saw his dad hit him last week."

Wren flashed her eyes to Ray. "Like hit-hit, or a slap?" She lightly slapped Ray. "Like this?"

"Like this," Ray said and punched the air. "He punched his bookbag."

"So... he didn't get hit?" Wren asked. "His dad hit his bag?"

"It was on his back. It still must have hurt," Ray argued.

Ray lived in the same neighborhood as Max and Amanda, a few houses down. He was very aware of the dynamics of their household. While their father was not physically abusive, his words cut deep, and he would often hit their bags if they acted up. While most logical people saw Max and Amanda's father as a single dad trying his best, the kids viewed him as a villain.

"I don't care. I don't want to." Wren fluttered her eyes from Ray and smiled when she saw Simon approaching them.

"You don't want to what?" Simon asked Wren.

"Say she's sorry to Max and Amanda," Ray told him. "They have to go home to their dad... Saying sorry may help."

"Or make it worse," Wren chimed in.

Ray argued with Wren. "If you say you're sorry, it'll make them feel better. Just do it."

As Wren and Ray argued in front of Simon, he looked down at his feet, tugging on his sleeves. "You should, Wren. You should say you're sorry." He looked up at his two best friends as they bickered. "Ray's right. It will make them happy." He flashed a smile.

"Fiiiiine." Wren exhaled the word and collapsed on the table, placing her arms over her head to tune out both Ray and Simon.

Ray noticed Max rushing out of the classroom, jogging toward the front of the school. "Go, say you're sorry," Ray ordered and shoved Wren off the bench. "He's leaving."

Wren jumped up and ran after Max. She was not happy about it, but it was two out of three, and the majority always won in ethical situations like these. She then thought if it had been a tie, they would have had to battle it out another way, and her apology would therefore be delayed. It was one of their codes in the Sad Guy's Club.

Right when Wren was about to turn around and protest, planning to argue her case about how they should ask Esme if she should apologize to her school bullies, she saw Max grab hold of his sister's hand. "Come on," he told Amanda. "I'll protect you."

Wren abandoned her idea of protest, finally understanding the severity of their home dynamic. She ended up following Max and Amanda to where a police car was waiting for them. Their father climbed out of his car and smiled at the principal, who was approaching him. Whether it was the status of being a police officer or the fact humans were merely selfish and immoral, no one cared if the officer occasionally hit his kids' backpacks.

The horror.

At that moment, Wren screened their father's mind. But all she could hear were muffled echoes from his shrink. Wren assumed their dad needed a therapist because he was a bad man, but she and Esme both had shrinks of their own—a child's failed logic.

Before Max and Amanda climbed into the backseat of the car, Amanda locked eyes with Wren. Wren mouthed the words "I'm sorry," and Amanda suddenly cried.

Instinctively, Wren ran up to Amanda before she could enter the car. "You better not hit them!" she shouted when she approached the open car door, glaring at the officer. "I know about you! I heard your doctor in your head! You leave them alone! I broke her glasses, you hear me?! I'm a mean bully! That's why Max bullies me! My aunt will kill you if I ask her!! She will!" She started beating on the car door after Amanda closed it. "Her name is Eudora Acosta, and she drinks tea with the mayor!! Vaan will eat you, Jackson Barlow!!!"

The officer looked shocked at Wren screaming at his car, her face plastered to the window. He knew who the crazy child was. She was one of the adopted daughters of the chicken chain's eccentric entrepreneur, who was known to be associated with not only the fae, but the man from Birdsong Island. Like the rest of the city, Jackson knew about Vaan, the grotesque man who had arrived a couple of years prior with the Mage's Guild to help the local police department fight off the increasing crime. But Vaan committed crimes of his own.

Jackson drove quickly from the school. "You never said the Sparrow girl is in your class," he said.

Max and Amanda were silent.

"Is she your friend?" their father looked in the rearview mirror at the two.

Before Max could answer honestly, Amanda interrupted, saying, "Yes."

"Great." Their father rolled down the window to get fresh air. "Eudora is her goddamn mom. She's always at the station barking orders. We don't get along too well. Fuck!" He rubbed his eyes roughly, his head aching.

Max and Amanda jumped slightly at their father's voice, catching his attention.

"It's my fault," Max exclaimed, misreading his father's anger. "Wren broke Amanda's glasses, and I tore up her book. That's why I fought."

Jackson looked back at his son's scared face. "Stop apologizing, kid. You're not in trouble." His heart felt pinched when he realized Max was scared of him. "Sorry, I'm under a lot of stress." After a moment to calm down, he looked up at a picture of him and his deceased wife hanging below his rearview mirror. "Didn't we used to eat Mexican food on Wednesdays with Mom?"

The kids were silent.

"What day is it?" Jackson asked.

The two looked confused. They had not eaten out since their mother was alive.

"Want Mexican for dinner?" Jackson asked.

"Yes?" Max replied and looked over at Amanda, worried that it might be a trick.

When their father reached back in the backseat to grab pain reliever from his briefcase for an approaching headache, both of his kids flinched. The fact that Amanda and Max feared him finally sank in for Jackson, and his eyes grew so cloudy he had to pull over on the side of the road.

"I knew this was a trick," Max whispered to Amanda. "I'll protect you from his swings."

Their father heard and broke out crying like a child.

"Mexican and ice cream, it is." Jackson wiped his tears from his face. "And then... let's go visit Mom. I have a lot to apologize to her for."

Amanda's and Max's eyes lit up when their father smiled back at them with red eyes in the rearview mirror.

"I miss Mom." Their father turned around. "I love you both. You know that?"

The two children did not move or speak.

"I'm sorry. There's no excuse for how I've been acting," Jackson told them. "I don't expect you to forgive me... but let me try to make things right. I have not been a great dad to y'all."

Thinking back to when he lost his wife in a car accident before that moment of clarity, their father held back a choke. Registering that he should have walked a path that would make his deceased wife proud, rather than succumb to his anger, the officer pledged to do better. He was not just a husband—he was a father.

"I want to bring mom queso and chips!" Amanda blurted out after realizing their old dad was back. "Mom always ate it."

"Good idea," their father said as he drove them to the restaurant that was once their mother's favorite.

"And Rocky Road ice cream," Max said slowly, unsure if their dad had returned from a phase of rage.

"Queso and Rocky Road." Jackson nodded. "The ants will love that."

"Oooo, let's have a picnic!" Amanda clasped her hands together.

As the two continued suggesting things they could do when they visited their mother's grave, their growing nightmare of a father was turning back into the caring man they had once known. Grief could shred all good from one's bones—it needed to be monitored when a man had two children to raise.

"Just so you know, you weren't all that bad. I mean, Amanda hits harder than you. And it never hurt anyway," Max told Jackson after they climbed out of the car at the restaurant, patting his dad on the back. "Your screams were kind of funny, too." He rushed ahead toward the front door with Amanda, laughing at the outing.

Frozen, their father turned around and tried to calm down before walking into the restaurant. He did not want to be sobbing while ordering food.

Back at the school, Wren was sitting with her two friends at the picnic table.

"What are you smiling about?" Simon asked Wren.

"Oooh, nothing," Wren said, swinging her legs happily. "Just Max and Amanda and their dad are nice to each other again."

She smiled wider at Ray and Simon and said proudly, "Because of me."

"Wait, can you read people's brains on purpose now?" Simon exclaimed.

Wren nodded cheerfully.

"See?" Ray narrowed his eyes at Wren being smug. "Apologizing helps."

"Nuh-uh." Wren shook her head at Ray. "I threatened their dad. It's scaring people that works."

While Wren and Ray argued like cats and dogs, Simon watched. He shifted in his spot on the bench. He was slightly disappointed. It seemed like everyone's family life was improving but his. He shook his head and tried to think positively. "It doesn't matter why. They're better!"

Both Wren and Ray nodded at him.

Ray turned to Wren. "What do my thoughts sound like?"

"Probably static because you're an egghead," Wren told him and crossed her arms. "How would I know?"

Wren panicked, realizing she had just revealed a defect in her ability. "You can't read Ray?" Simon asked her. "What about me?"

Wren stared at the two boys, eyes watering. Flaws in her abilities often embarrassed her. "I can't—leave me alone!" She ran from the table and toward where Eudora and Vaan normally picked her up from. She halted and turned to them. "Don't tell anyone I can't read some people! Or I'll make Vaan eat you!"

❋❋❋❋❋

Amanda waltzed into class the next day with fancy glasses. She showed off her new designer dress her father spent some of their savings on. She and Max had been told to pick three things from an upscale store when their father was trying to find durable glasses for Amanda. While Amanda chose a doll set, a dress, and sparkly eyeglasses, Max got a hydro-skateboard, a jacket, and sunglasses.

Sidetracking her from talking about her dress to her friends, Amanda noticed a girl was making fun of Wren's beheaded doll. Before Simon could come to Wren's defense, Amanda walked up to Wren's desk and picked up the headless figurine. Wren looked up at Amanda, alarmed.

"I don't know. I think it's pretty cool." Amanda smiled and laid the doll back down on Wren's desk. "Sorry I said your mom is in Hell... We're not even religious. I'm just always mad because I miss her..."

"Sorry I broke your glasses." Wren's tension subsided. "I miss my mom, too. And my dad."

"Sorry Max tore up your mom's book," Amanda said.

The two girls smiled at each other. Simon watched the scene, and then he placed his head back down on his desk. Finally, Wren had another friend in their class. He could rest.

IX

FIRE DANCER

WHEN A COLD BREEZE rushed through the courtyard, hundreds of dead leaves fell, and the chilled grass swayed. The wind released a haunting moan, echoing off the stone walls that framed the inner courtyard.

"We should go back inside," Ray said, flinching when a gust of frigid air reached them. He looked down at Wren and shoved her off him, as she had fallen asleep. "Wake up."

Wren yawned, saying, "I had the weirdest dream. I think I was screaming at Jackson."

"That's not a surprise. You scream at everyone," Ray joked.

"No, I don't." Wren eyed him.

She grumbled, standing up with Ray, and they walked away from the courtyard.

After walking inside, Wren sat back down next to Ms. Beckman and Ray returned to the podium. Ms. Rowans had been talking the entire time they had been outside, but she hopped down, happy to have helped Ray with the tribute.

"Are you going to speak, Wren?" Ms. Beckman asked her.

"It's best if I don't," Wren replied.

The teacher nodded slowly.

"This is too much," Ms. Beckman whispered, tears staining her makeup. "Too much death..."

Ms. Beckman's grandson hugged her, trying to comfort her. Like many people of the modern age, Ms. Beckman had lost her daughter and son-in-law to suicide a few years ago, and she had gained guardianship of her young grandson. As humans kept ending their lives to discover what was next, those left behind suffered.

Like murder, suicide had turned into a morbid trend.

Wren closed her eyes, trying to enter a peaceful state of mind. She had developed a new ability, and she was worried she would blow up the church. Sitting stiffly, she suppressed the flames she had recently learned to manifest as she tried to tune out Ms. Beckman's muffled crying. She cracked her eyes open, feeling smoke trying to escape the slits.

When Simon was killed the prior week, only days before Christmas, Wren's entire distorted reality blew up as fire seeped from her pores and eyes. She was used to her ever-evolving powers, but she had panicked when flames engulfed her body. She had sent out force fields, destroying her gardens, and she had clawed her arms, barking out into the night. Giving Esme a fright, she had manifested the opposite of the nymph's water in a fiery rage.

That night, Ray had visited Sparrow Manor and was forced to climb the tall iron fence, as the gates were locked. Esme had been hosing down the yard, but she ended up blasting Ray as he quickly approached the gardens.

Then, exhausted, Esme had fallen on the baked grass, and when Wren regained her sense of self, she had panicked when she saw her sister lying motionless. After Ray placed Esme carefully in their indoor pool to heal in the medicinal water, he went to help Wren.

Before Wren could even finish suggesting she was part troll, Ray pushed her not-so-delicately into the herb-infused water.

It was a night that lit up the neighborhood...

Ray was going through the donations before ending the memorial. The only thing Simon had wanted was for Novus to be given more support, so more orphans could have a home after surviving the fae trails. The Acostas and the city helped Novus fund the program for the orphans, and they had enough resources to foster an entire town, but Simon believed there was no such thing as too much support. He had made many posts promoting Novus' mission—helping the fae survive and thrive—on his public social media accounts throughout the years.

And when Simon was killed, and the nation chatted about the murder in the South, strangers from all over had sent thousands of donations to Father Bernie via U.S. Sky Mail—the nation's satellite mailing system.

"Thank you, Rodney Clarkins, for your donation," Ray said while reading the stack of papers made from coconut pulp. He was not going to read thousands of names, so he settled on addressing the largest contributors. "Thank you, Helen—"

Wren straightened her back. She recognized that name.

Couldn't you have read his mind? Rodney Clarkins had sent an audio email to Wren two days after Simon was killed. *What's the point of having superpowers if you can't save his fucking life!?* He did not know Simon. He was an avid supporter of fae rights and conspiracy theories, and he followed Tallahassee news like it was a football team from his small apartment in North Dakota. After hearing about the murder, he had researched who Simon Coy was and stumbled upon his social media. When he had found out that Simon's best friend was the Acosta heir in Tallahassee who could read minds and do magic, he felt Wren should have been able to prevent the murder.

Rodney's words had made Wren's blood boil.

Just because Wren could read minds, it did not mean she could read everyone. And like Ray, Simon was one mind she could not explore. But that did not mean she did not try to unravel the mysteries of Simon's home dynamic as a kid. She had often ventured into his parents' hectic minds because she wanted to see what Simon was up to, as he would repeatedly stay home from school due to "sickness." To her unfortunate luck, Simon's parents were too insane to comprehend, and she could only hear muddled voices. Back then, she was only a child, so she did not think the chaotic voices were cause for concern.

"Vaan better kill them slowly," Ms. Beckman hissed as she stared down at her phone, a holographic article of Simon's parents smiling in handcuffs was displayed on her screen.

Wren stared at Ms. Beckman, shocked. The teacher never spoke harshly, no matter the situation. The decades of abuse Simon had silently suffered and then his sudden murder had unnerved all of Novus. But Ms. Beckman was not just a member of Novus, nor just a teacher from their youth—she had been Simon's maternal figure.

Before Simon's abuse was uncovered, someone on the police force who was friends with the Coys had always covered up the neglect whenever they received welfare calls. With documents they did not know were falsified, the cops would reassure the concerned citizens—Ms. Beckman included—that Simon was just rambunctious and often got sick. There was even a medical doctor in on the cover-up, and the facade had worked for years until Connell joined the local police department when Simon was in middle school. Teaming up with one of the few officers, Jackson, who suspected the Coys were abusing Simon, the two had found the confidence needed to pursue the truth in an environment built on gang mentality. And after they had started working off the radar, they had revealed Simon's abuse.

Connell had been the missing link for Simon's parents to lose custody.

Simon's parents were part of the Human Coalition, also called the H.C., an organization of anti-fae radicals throughout the Bible Belt. After the Coys lost custody, they escaped to South Alabama, where one of the club's main branches was located. They were able to avoid charges by using one of their most prominent connections—a Florida Supreme Court Justice who kept his connection to the Human Coalition a secret. Vaan had tried to claim the Coys as supper, but the radicals were a slippery bunch, and they had managed to place a few of their own in government positions.

Everyone thought Simon would have a better life after he was taken from the Coys—and for a long time, he did. He had been rescued from his deranged parents and lived with his doting grandparents for years. His grandparents had even paid for him to attend a private university near the South Florida Sea Break, a southern region slowly breaking due to violent hurricanes. It was the best university for the sciences in the nation, and their climate research was often published worldwide. Every young scientist wanted to go there, despite the erratic weather—and he had the grades and passion to get in. Things were going well for him, but he made one mistake: He thought it would be safe to move back to Tallahassee because it had been years since his parents moved from the city. He had missed his three childhood friends.

But moving back had not proven so safe in the end.

When the Coys were informed that their son was in Tallahassee, the monsters had traveled back to the city. As the rumor that Simon was eloping with Wren spread throughout the Human Coalition, the Coys had snapped from embarrassment. They swore Wren was a nymph. They did not know what they would do when they found Simon, but murder proved not to be off their agenda. Simon had been murdered by the very beings who brought him into the misery of life.

Plastering his face on picket signs to oppose integration, claiming Simon's parents were the victims of fae magic, the Human Coalition was using Simon as a martyr for their cause.

And it was making Wren spiral out of control.

X

LEMON LEAVES

INSIDE THE CHURCH, EVERYONE was silently watching Ray. He had just finished naming the top donors, and he was gripping the edges of the podium. His mannerisms were much like those of his stern mother, who had migrated with her husband from North Korea twenty years after North Korea's revolution. A lot of emotion hid behind a structured solid shell.

He announced that lunch was going to be served in the inner courtyard and then walked to the front pew to sit on the other side of Wren. His parents were seated behind them, and they leaned forward, whispering to him, trying to ease his mind.

After the funeral ended, everyone spoke to each other. Wren roamed aimlessly around the pews as Ray walked his parents outside to their car. She was utterly detached from reality, and she did not even see him when he returned. He pinched her arm to snap her out of her trance. After she glared at him for disturbing her disconnect from what was taking place, the two friends stared at the priest, who was rushing around the church.

"That man worries me," Ray said, wrapping an arm around Wren's shoulders. He did not want her to leave his sight. "Simon would've made him some tea and ordered him to take a nap. Let's go make him some."

Wren stepped out from under his grasp and turned away. "It's okay. I want to check on Esme and the kids," she said. "But you should go make Bernie some tea."

After a moment's hesitation, Ray turned away to walk toward the kitchen. Despite their habit of arguing, he was not in the mood to disagree with her.

He stopped walking and turned around to look at Wren. "Oh, do you guys want to go to lunch with us? My parents would love it if you and Esme came. Rolf and Kyle can come, too. Unless you're eating here..." Ray scratched his cheek. "I'm meeting them in about an hour."

"I'm not hungry, but you should ask Esme. She and the boys may want to. Want to come over after?" Wren asked.

Ray nodded and vanished into the kitchen.

"Hey, hon," Bettie said to Ray after he walked through the door. She was stirring a wooden spoon in a pot of gumbo. "Did you see the swan napkins outside? The kids helped make them. Find a spot at the tables. We got the heaters going, too. We're serving fried chicken, greens, chicken gumbo— you name it. You know Simon *loved* his chicken."

After meeting Father Bernie, Bettie had volunteered to cook for the church. She had cooked for Novus for over fifteen years, while helping with the orphans. She was a retired mathematician from New Orleans, and she had moved to Tallahassee after the fae movement surfaced.

"Sorry, I can't. I'm meeting my parents for lunch," Ray told her. He walked straight to the kettle next to Bettie. He could not help but worry that Wren would do something foolish—something that would reunite her with Simon. He clenched his fist and grabbed the canister of tea leaves. "I'm just making Bernie some tea first."

Prying Ray from his worry, a few of the orphans rushed in to talk to one of the few humans they trusted. The others were Wren, Father Bernie, Bettie, and the friendly detective named Connell. Breaking into a laugh at a young boy's golden face twisting to cheer him up, Ray decided he had time to help Bettie serve the kids their lunch. He reached for the other pot on the wide stove—a mix of seasoned greens, beans, tomatoes, and potatoes.

"I wanted to make this at Simon's welcome-home party, not for lunch after his funeral..." Bettie stared down into the pot of gumbo as a young troll scrunched his nose at the chicken. "It was his favorite as a kid. He always pestered me to make it for lunch after Sunday school."

Bettie quickly looked away from everyone. She released a million tears, which she tried to hide with her hands. The kids, who had been playfully making gagging sounds at the meat, stopped and looked at Bettie with concern.

"Wait... wasn't Simon the guy Father Bernie introduced us to?" one of the young goblins asked the others. "Is he dead? Is he in the casket?"

Another child tugged on Ray's sleeve. "Who was Simon?"

Ray looked down at the girl. "My brother."

XI

Dark Reunion

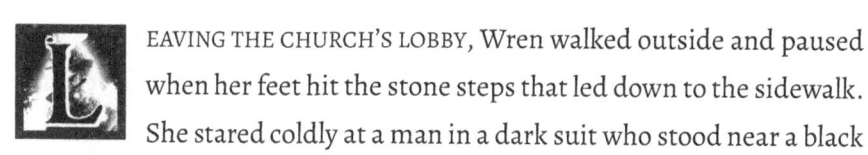

LEAVING THE CHURCH'S LOBBY, Wren walked outside and paused when her feet hit the stone steps that led down to the sidewalk. She stared coldly at a man in a dark suit who stood near a black car. He was extremely tall, with hair of a lighter blond than her own. She looked both ways and tried to sneak away before he could see her.

But she could not become invisible like Esme.

"Wren," the man in the black suit called out to her. "Wren Sparrow?"

Wren tried to ignore him.

"Can I speak to you for a moment?" the man asked, displaying an FBI badge.

"About what?" Wren asked sharply, sending cold daggers into his gray eyes.

She knew all too well who the man was. She wanted to laugh and claw at the invisible demons surrounding her.

"My name's Leonard Frost," he said, ignoring her scolding glare. "I have reason to believe you are being targeted by a man named Kieran Cross. He escaped Perk City Jail this morning, about four hours ago. We estimate his arrival early this evening or tomorrow morning, depending on how he's traveling."

"I don't know anyone named Kieran Cross." Wren batted her eyes, her tongue full of lies.

Blood was everywhere in her mouth. She was biting her tongue, pretending not to know who the agent or Kieran was. As it settled on the tip of her tongue, she tasted the sweet metallic taste of the liquid she craved.

Wren only knew one other human who desired the taste of blood. While she mostly craved the blood of non-human animals, the monster craved his own kind.

And that monster's name was Kieran Cross.

Kieran was a cold and sarcastic man who seemed not fully human. He resembled marble statues—expressionless and dreadfully pale. He was born in North Georgia in a small eighteenth-century vibe of a town. And he was one of the first minds Wren had fully explored at the young age of four. As she continued to watch him throughout the years, his life began to unfold like a dramatic series.

Viewing Kieran's saga usually gave Wren ease during her troubled times, but he had become unhinged. And through that derangement, he became aware of Wren telepathically spying on him. So, her troubled times were just that... *troubled*. Her constant prying into Kieran's mind was what attracted the monster's attention in the first place.

Too much of something often led to ill consequences.

"Why is he after me?" Wren asked the agent, walking up closer to him, smiling the southern smile she learned from growing up in Tallahassee.

Frost cleared his throat and said, "I don't know. He kept repeating your name on the cameras. Do you mind if I smoke?"

They walked away from the area near the church's entrance. Wren was five feet and six inches tall, and she appeared extremely short compared to his lengthy frame of six feet and five inches. She did not respond to his question and only stared at him silently.

Ignoring her silent glares, the agent removed a cigarette and lit it when they got under the shade of a tree. "This isn't a game, Sparrow. Cross is very dangerous. He's currently going through a trial for a murder back in October. He's also a suspect in a federal case, and he escaped Perk City Jail around seven this morning."

"Seven?" Wren asked him, looking down at her watch. "How fast did you drive? It's only a little after eleven."

Frost did not speak for a moment as he puffed on his cigarette, and then he said, "I was already near Tallahassee when my partner called."

"How did you find me if all he said was my name? There could be another person named Wren Sparrow," Wren said. "What were you doing *near* Tallahassee?"

"Not that hard to figure out who he was talking about. Cross kept shouting that you were reading his mind." Frost blew the smoke away from her. "And I was near here because I have a graduation reunion tonight."

He was lying. It was painfully obvious. He did not even bother to try to hide his facade.

A few times in the last couple of months, Wren had tried to read the agent's mind from Kieran's memory of him, but it never worked. She was now in a closer proximity to Frost, and she tried to extract Frost's memories once again, only to be rejected. She huffed from agitation. She had seen part of Kieran's own memory that morning, so she knew part of why Frost was in town. But that still did not answer how he got to Tallahassee as quickly as he did.

In Wren's vision of Kieran's life, Frost's spunky partner Aria Daniels was in Perk earlier that morning, trying to investigate who a federal hacker named Ezekiel was. Daniels was also not convinced Kieran had murdered his long-term boyfriend, and the agent had gone rogue to investigate privately into the matter.

As she was snooping around the jail, she heard Kieran screaming about Wren from his blood-stained cell. Daniels had left Kieran's cell briefly to get the guards, but when she returned, Kieran had broken through his window, leaving the iron bars of the very old jail window on the floor.

"Okay." Wren grew annoyed. "Where did you graduate?"

"The local college in the next city over," Frost replied.

"What city? What college?" Wren asked, raising a single brow.

Frost hesitated. "Are you seriously interrogating *me* right now?"

He studied her with his analytical eyes. Something tugged at her mind as Frost took his last puff on the stick of death, then smashed it into the tree.

"Don't hurt the tree," Wren hissed before she could even decide not to scold an FBI agent.

"Excuse me?" Frost scrunched his forehead.

"You burned the tree," Wren said. Something inside of her was getting angry. The agent annoyed her. "Apologize to her and please leave me alone."

He raised his eyebrows. "I can't leave you alone. You're a target—"

"I refuse any sort of protection from someone low enough to vandalize Mother Nature," Wren said bitterly.

"I think you are underestimating Cross. He left Perk in a very bad state—"

Ignoring Frost's warning, Wren pushed him away from the tree and wiped the ash from the bark. "Enjoy your *reunion*, Frost."

She glared at him and walked across the street to the other side of the road, where the bookstore was. She walked up to Esme and the two goblins, who were yelling at the agent under the tree, preaching about how trees deserved more respect. "Always fighting injustice, aren't you guys?"

Esme turned her attention to Wren, but she kept eyeing the FBI agent. "Who's that?"

"You know how Kieran went to jail?" Wren reminded her. "Days after Halloween?"

"Of course." Esme widened her eyes, fascinated by the human from the same state as her.

"That guy's with the FBI. He's looking for him." Wren nodded back at Frost.

"You mean..." Esme looked around Wren and eyed Frost, who was still staring at them. "Did Kieran escape?" She saw the look on Wren's face. "He did, didn't he?" Her jaw dropped.

Wren nodded nervously. "He broke out this morning. And he's on his way here."

"Why didn't you tell me sooner?" Esme asked. "I know you can read his mind like a freaking large-lettered magazine."

"With Simon's funeral and all..."

"Forget Kieran's life for a second. How was the funeral?" Esme asked. "Did Ray give a good speech? What am I saying? Of course he did."

"It was... a funeral. Pictures, memories—you know the drill." Wren shrugged, not wanting to talk about it. She moved her eyes from Esme and took in Rolf's and Kyle's nervous faces. "You two would be safer inside the church. Novus supports fae rights. You know that, right?"

Rolf and Kyle looked hesitant. Wren glanced at Kyle when Rolf looked at his younger brother defensively. Rolf grew mad, and his golden skin darkened. "Tell that to the old hags that cornered Kyle this morning."

"It was Ms. Norris and her friends," Esme added. "When I came to check up on the store, they were screaming at Kyle. He was sitting on the ground crying! That's why I couldn't attend the funeral. I told Father Bernie. Did he tell you?"

"No. He was probably too busy getting the service ready and forgot. Two women were talking about it before the funeral. I was going to come check on you, but everyone else was absent today, so it felt wrong to leave," Wren said.

Eudora and Rose were busy working and Esme had become sidetracked, so Wren had felt obligated to stay—even though she hated funerals.

"Sorry. I really wanted to attend." Esme's eyes watered.

"You had a good reason not to," Wren told her. "Protecting the kids is the best way to honor Simon." She peered down at the goblins. "Ms. Norris isn't even part of our church anymore. Why were they here?"

But she knew why...

After Father Bernie announced he was opening his doors to the fae, half of the old congregation left. The priest had preached how the serial murders of the fae were genocide. He urged everyone to come together and not repeat humanity's dark history toward a peaceful nation of people.

When he had announced that he would not turn any of the fae away, Ms. Norris was one of the members who had left to join a non-Episcopal church in the Northside that catered to humans who were against coexistence. And while the northern church was not part of the rebellion, they often provoked the fae in the streets.

Novus may have lost half its congregation, but Bernie had started a shift within the Episcopal Church, and the sect merged fae beliefs in with their faith. The Episcopal Church had become a mesh of Christianity, fae magic, and modern science, with Isis being their collaborator. And both the non-religious and religious flocked to the church, supporting what they stood for.

"Where did the assault happen?" Wren asked Kyle.

"There." Kyle pointed across the street near the tree Frost was standing under. "I was being yelled at for ten minutes before Esme found me."

"Did no one hear you from inside the church?" Wren asked.

"They didn't know." Esme defended Father Bernie and the members. "The choir was singing during the early service. It's not their fault."

"Yeah, Esme actually went all Hulk on the hags." Rolf laughed. "The women ran away drenched in water. It was awesome."

"I told Bernie right after the morning group ended," Esme told Wren. "I didn't see you walk into the church, so I tried to tell you using my thoughts, but I don't know how to do a reverse communication."

"I entered through the side entrance. And I don't think reverse telepathy is a thing." Wren raised her eyebrows at Esme and pointed at her temple. "Or Kieran would be screaming at me nonstop."

"Is he here?" Esme looked around the area, but only saw police officers, mages, a few passersby, and Frost, who was still staring at them from across the street. "Is he mad? How'd he find out about you anyway?" She then pointed at her own head. "Can you read his mind to find out?"

Rolf and Kyle just stared at the two women, who were pointing at their own heads. They knew very well about Wren's eternal confusion about what she was and her mind tricks. That was one reason they had magical wards in place to protect their minds from being spied on. They liked the weird human—they just did not trust her. She was not fae or a mage, and they viewed her abilities as odd.

"No, his mind is pretty garbled at the moment—"

"Hey!" Rolf interrupted the sisters' bantering. "Can you do your mind crap on the city?" he asked Wren. "Like, just do one massive woo-ha!"

"Woo-ha?" Wren asked the older goblin, who had his arms spread out wide.

"They want to see if you can read everyone's minds so we can know if any rebels are up to anything," Esme said.

Wren widened her eyes. "That is a fuck no. Are you trying to kill me?" She glanced down at the goblins. "My brain would explode."

Kyle looked up at his brother, who looked disappointed in Wren. Then, Rolf turned to Kyle and started making exploding noises. Esme stared down at the brothers and nervously played with her ankh necklace.

"Can you just scan the Human Coalition, then?" Esme asked. "I fear they are going to do something."

"I don't need to read minds to know things are about to get worse. Those creeps will be in the city soon, especially since Simon's parents are members. They will most likely try to break them out of jail. Lock up early and come home," Wren told Esme, then turned to Rolf and Kyle. "No picketing for a while, guys. You two can stay with us if you feel unsafe here."

"No way," Kyle said. "Your house has ghosts."

He believed that the spirits of everyone murdered during the shooting at Sparrow Manor were trapped inside.

"And it's too big. It's like a fort!" Rolf exclaimed, shaking his head.

The brothers were loyalists of the small bookstore. Something about living in bunk beds in the back of a small building full of books appealed to them. They sought comfort in smaller abodes. Most goblins loved small dwellings, and the other orphaned goblins inside Novus often slept under their beds or in closets.

Wren did not think her house was that big, nor was it haunted.

It was smaller than Eudora's house.

XII

MUTT

ESME EYED FROST AND then told Wren, "Don't worry about Kieran. I'm sure everything will be fine." Her tone seemed optimistic, but her smile was grimmer than the funeral. "Go home and get some rest."

Wren stared at her sister. "I can't just ignore him, Esme. Did you just forget that he's on his way here?"

"Yeah, but..." Esme trailed off.

"Kieran may kill me." Wren stared at Esme, trying to get a reaction from her. "He may *kill* me."

"Still... he *might* not," Esme replied with hope in her eyes. "He might just want to meet you."

Wren nodded slowly. "*Or* he may kill me for spying on him for most of his life, then eat me because he has cannibalistic tendencies. Just a thought."

"Are you sure you can't read his mind?" Esme asked.

"Yes." Wren sighed. "His mind is too crazed at the moment for me to understand any of his thoughts. I can only recall the memories I've already read." Kieran's thoughts were muddled, but she could tell he was coming for her. "It's fine, Esme. Remember, we are more powerful than some mutt."

It was Esme's turn to nod slowly. "I don't like that word. Calling someone a mutt is insulting. How would you feel if someone called you a mutt? Wouldn't that hurt your feelings?"

Wren shrugged. "Not really. I mean, I am mixed..."

"Forget that I asked." Esme looked defeated.

"Well, what do you want to call him then?" Wren asked.

"You said he's a human mixed with something unknown..." Esme paused for a moment and then suggested, "HMSU!" She clasped her hands together, proud of her idea.

"Mutt is shorter... and easier." Wren raised an eyebrow. "I like mutt."

"You can be so offensive sometimes," Esme told her. "Like Mom."

Wren patted Esme on the shoulder. "I know."

She turned to leave the bookstore, but she stopped and looked back at Esme, who had resumed waving her sign at a car driving by. Esme glanced over at Wren and noticed her concern.

"What?" Esme asked.

"Don't forget we're having a small dinner with Bernie tonight," Wren said.

Esme nodded.

"Oh... and Eudora wants to take us to the Diamond Club after the arraignment next Friday." Wren looked horrified. "She texted us this morning, but I know you don't like your cellphone. She wants us to browse the new season catalogs."

"I saw." Esme sounded excited. "I'm getting better with technology."

Esme looked proud of herself. Nymphs were not tech-savvy, and they feared the contraptions humans and other fae adored. Considering the nymphs came from the sea and were masters of manifesting water, they feared the possibility of electrical shocks.

"About time..." Wren mused at her sister.

"I saw that Mom's coming back early Monday afternoon." Esme's eyes lit up.

Though Wren preferred to call Eudora by name, for she had childhood memories of calling her Aunt Eudora, Esme found it more comfortable to call her Mom. While Wren often squabbled with Eudora because the two were a lot alike, Esme took on the role of the good daughter. After Eudora proved she would never abandon the orphaned nymph, Esme had attached herself to the Acosta woman.

"See you at home." Wren rolled her eyes at Esme, who was naming things she wanted to buy from the catalogs of high fashion the Diamond Club was known for.

Esme did not hear Wren's farewell as she started scribbling down a list of items she planned to purchase on Friday on the back of her picket sign. Rolf and Kyle began adding things they wanted to her list.

"Damn it," Wren muttered as she walked from the bookstore, noticing that Frost was still standing across the street, smoking another cigarette.

The agent eyed Wren. Unable to help herself, she winked at the FBI agent and whistled at him playfully, causing him to look somewhat stunned by her behavior. She then headed toward her house, which shared the same street as the church and bookstore.

"Wren," Father Bernie yelled, walking out of the back entrance of the main building directly across from the bookstore, smelling like lemons.

Wren grumbled under her breath. She was not in the mood for more talking. But she met the priest on the sidewalk along the side of the church, her back toward Frost. "What's up?" she asked.

"Bring a memory of Simon for the chest tonight," Bernie reminded her. "Wear pastel, none of that gloomy attire you love."

"I will," Wren told him and then looked offended. "'Gloomy?' My clothes are not gloomy."

The priest stared at her in disbelief. "You and Ray are two of the gloomiest kids I have ever known."

Wren scoffed and walked away. Father Bernie eyed her gothic dress, scoffing himself, and then he looked at the FBI agent, who was crushing his cigarette in his hand. He was about to call out to the agent to ask if he needed anything, but the priest stepped back when he saw shadows dance around Frost. So, the church was the priest's destination.

As Wren walked down the road, she moved her eyes back and forth, scanning the memories of Kieran's past. She was trying to prepare herself for the monster's arrival. She could not read everyone's thoughts, as a few were unscathed by her telepathy, but Kieran was not one of the few. He was strange and wild, and she had instantly become glued to his life when she first ventured into his mind.

When Wren first entered Kieran's thoughts accidentally, through his love of her mother's storybooks, she could not understand what was going on. Not knowing what to make of her vision of a boy two years older than herself, she had tried to draw portraits of him. At four years old, they were primarily scribbles, resulting in poorly drawn sketches of what looked like a fangless vampire.

After Wren had finally started speaking again when she was five, she told Eudora and Esme about Kieran, only to confuse them. After Esme had complained because she could not see Kieran, Wren had tried to explain that she could only see Kieran inside her head. Eudora knew what was happening, and she found Wren's ability very troubling. The cold, stern woman dreaded the very thought that her niece may have been what the fae claimed.

While Eudora remained on the fence, Wren did not believe in the fae's accusations of her being the reincarnation of some ghost.

But she did believe in Kieran. *He* was real. And he was coming for her.

Kieran's life used to bring her relief in the past, but his saga became terrifying one year ago—on the day of Christmas.

Immediately, Wren tapped out of her reality and entered the horrors of Kieran's mind...

XIII

MEMORIES OF CROSS

KIERAN WAS THE PRODUCT of a humble married woman and a charming devil of a man passing through the small town of Perk, Georgia. The traveler had bewitched her to cheat on her husband, and when she gave birth to Kieran, the entire town fell under the devil's son's spell.

However, as time went on, Perk began to wince at the boy's presence.

During the last month of 2223, Kieran was making Christmas dinner for his parents—and his father found out about his mother's affair with the traveler. Kieran had forgotten one thing at his parents' house when he had moved out: a journal. He had recorded everything, even about the day his mother told him who his biological father really was. His mother cried so much when she told him the news, but he somehow already knew.

He did not resemble the man that raised him at all.

Kieran's dad was looking for the gold ring he had bought to surprise his wife. He wanted to replace her wedding band, but he had forgotten where he had hidden it. During his search, a journal fell out of the closet in Kieran's old bedroom. Grinning and wondering what kind of adventures his son might have gone through in his younger years, he picked up the journal.

He had smiled no more than a second, for when he opened the journal, he landed on the most shocking of pages. It was as if someone had thrown him the journal and said, "Hey, read me and kill your wife."

Kieran was placing baked fish on a platter while his mother was setting the table. She was admiring tulips in a crystal vase that was propped up on top of their piano. They were flowers that her husband had recently given her. She began humming just when her husband started shouting from upstairs.

The metal spoon fell from Kieran's fingers as he turned to see his father strangling his mother. In a flash, he was on top of the man he had spent his entire life calling Dad. He threw him off with strength he did not know he had and started yelling, saying it was Christmas—a time to forgive and forget. He kept repeating himself as he compressed his father's face into the hardwood floor.

Kieran watched his father's blood splatter on the floor. He stopped what he was doing, but his father was already dead. He stared at his bloody hands as he heard his mother's bloodcurdling screams.

Then, Kieran had feelings of hunger. Unable to control himself, he crouched over the corpse and began tearing at his father's flesh with his bare hands. And he drank the blood that dripped from the meat. Shoving the meat into his mouth, he slowly chewed. His mother tried to pry him away from her husband's corpse, frightened by what was happening.

Out of instinct, Kieran slung his mother back. The crystal vase fell when she collided with the piano, and the tulips spread over the bloody floor. She snatched a piece of glass and pleaded for Kieran to stop his horrific behavior, tears rushing down her face.

Panicked by the sight of her son eating her husband's flesh, she gripped the shard tightly as her tears slowed to a stop. Hypnotized by her husband's corpse, she brought the piece of glass to her throat and shoved it into her skin.

Kieran stopped eating his father's flesh when he saw his mother faint from the blood loss. He stood up and caught her from collapsing entirely to the floor. She stared up at him and said a few words he would never forget.

"Ezekiel." Her eyes fluttered as death came for her. "Find him..."

✻✻✻✻✻

Kieran had a knack for attracting ruin. And on the night of Halloween in 2224, his boyfriend was murdered. He had once believed his mother when she told him that funerals were created to help those left behind to deal with and understand death. He wanted to believe her, but she was dead—dead, like everyone he seemed to have ever cared for...

Oh, so quiet were the people who mourned in a stone-statue manner. Their eyes were all glued to the casket that held the deceased. A daunting question was in each of their eyes, but no one dared ask. Kieran was among them.

When Kieran listened to the bells' soft song of sorrow, it was as if it was calling him to death. His pale features were cold and structured, with dark blue eyes that harbored a tragic misery. His short, shaggy, dark brown hair waved lightly in the breeze. He stood while everyone else sat on the steel chairs outside in the widespread cemetery.

"Did you?" was the question everyone wanted to ask Kieran.

Kieran's dim eyes moved among the people, who all stayed motionless out of fear toward him. He was not to be feared—he had a sincere smile and handsome features. But that was before he had killed his father the year before. It was written off as self-defense, but one still wondered. The recent mystery of Johnny's death allowed the town to speculate whether Kieran was the one who ended his boyfriend's life.

Two dark suits who reeked of the FBI stood a few yards from where the town's local sheriff sat. They both wore dark sunglasses and had stern looks. Kieran just ignored them altogether.

"Kieran..." a frail woman said quietly from the chair in front of the small service. "He couldn't have killed..."

Kieran stared at the chairback of Sarah, Johnny's twin sister, who was crying into her trembling hands. Sarah's parents were crying next to her as they mourned over the loss of Johnny. The Williams family had once adored Kieran, but now, they would not even look at him.

The sun was covered by many clouds, which wanted to pour the sky's tears. People stood up from their chairs when the funeral ended. But no one dared look the monster's way. Sarah hurried along with her parents, as her mother clutched her hand tightly, not letting her peer back at Kieran.

"They fear him," Daniels said to her partner, Frost.

"Well, if he's the one hacking into government files, he should be feared." Frost folded his arms and peered at Kieran.

The two FBI agents stared through their thick sunglasses at the man leaning against a slender tree. Kieran looked at the grave being filled with earth, then turned his gaze to the two suits.

"What exactly are these files?" Daniels asked Frost. "Did you ever find out?"

"I don't know. They're classified," Frost lied.

Daniels nodded. "Are they sure he's Ezekiel?"

"That's why we're here." Frost turned to face his partner.

Daniels folded her arms. "The director reported Ezekiel's activity as coming from this area, and Cross does fit many of Ezekiel's marks. He said Ezekiel commented about cannibalism and his father's downfall in one of the hacked files. Cross not only killed his father, but he ate him. His father was butchered. There's a good chance that Kieran Cross is Ezekiel."

"I guess so," Frost replied.

"Gah—I don't know. All fingers point to this town, but Cross doesn't give off the hacker vibe. Murderer? Yes. Federal hacker? No. This doesn't make any sense." Daniels was frustrated with their assignment. "Only if I could read those files..."

"This town doesn't make any sense," Frost grumbled as he glared at a kid's **Fae Are Going to Hell** shirt.

Kieran turned away from the two agents and left Johnny's freshly dug grave. He wandered over the cemetery grounds, staring at the tombstones.

"Kieran," a middle-aged man in priest's garb said. He was once a Catholic priest who had been defrocked, and he was following Kieran away from the burial. *Preacher*, they all called him—a preacher in name, but a monster in heart. "Kieran?"

"Yeah?" Kieran asked sharply, raising an eyebrow.

"You should speak to the people from the FBI," the ex-priest who still preached told him. "They are investigating a cyber threat."

"Why?" Kieran's eyes pierced through Preacher's false serenity with such hatred that it shook the older man briefly. "I know nothing about that kind of thing. I barely use my computer."

Preacher went silent for a moment—and Kieran realized what the man was insinuating.

"First, you accuse me of killing my boyfriend, and then you accuse me of being a terrorist?" Kieran asked with calm anger.

"No one is accusing you, but for this town, will you speak to them? I want to ask you before they start forcing questions down your ears," Preacher asked.

"Oh, how considerate of you, old man," Kieran said nonchalantly with a twisted sneer. "I'll speak to them only because that's what Johnny would have wanted me to do. Not for you, and not for this town."

Kieran walked away, leaving Preacher to dwell in his fake aura of peace.

"I'm tired." Kieran stopped walking and turned back to the unholy man. "Tell them to come by tomorrow, and I'll talk."

Kieran walked away from the vile man and toward the white car that once belonged to his mother. He entered the familiar car and stared into his rearview mirror at the former priest speaking to the feds. He detested the man who still wore Catholic robes.

"What fucking timing." Kieran cursed and started driving away, turning the music up. He screamed over the deafening music. "Fuck!"

Kieran's entire body went cold during his drive home, exhausted from his living nightmare. He tried to focus on Johnny's smile to quiet his painful mind, only to remember a very somber day.

Kieran and Johnny had been lying on a hill when they were twelve. Under the clouds, he had listened to Johnny's confession. He had grown so angry that he felt the rage of a killer and he screamed like a creature from horror tales, shrieking until his voice had gone out. He had wanted to destroy Preacher, but Johnny pleaded for him to stay quiet, so he had kept what Preacher did to Johnny a secret.

But the promise Kieran and Johnny had made long ago was no longer valid—Johnny was dead.

Kieran was going to kill.

He was getting hungry.

And he hungered for the kill.

The next morning, Kieran was sitting at his wooden table staring at a hallucination of his boyfriend. It was almost as if a corpse was sitting across from him. Johnny was the same as when he was alive, but that was impossible. Kieran's mind was playing with him.

"You're dead," Kieran said coldly.

Johnny did not speak.

Kieran threw his wineglass at the hallucination of Johnny, causing him to disappear. It was morning, but Kieran could not face the day sober.

"Leave me alone," Kieran hissed.

He moved his arm ferociously, causing the wine bottle to fall. Releasing an inhuman growl, he stood and looked toward the foyer, hearing a car drive up his driveway. He marched from the dining room and slung open the front door.

"You got me," Kieran said to the two feds who walked up to his house.

He smiled forcefully and walked down the stairs to meet them in a wide-open blue robe and shiny red boxers. "I'm your hacker."

The agents hesitated. They had been told Ezekiel came across as eccentric, but something about Kieran created doubt in their minds. However, this was a confession, and they had their orders.

Kieran did not recoil when Daniels grabbed his arm. "We'll question you, Cross," she said, leading him to their car. "Just remember, a false confession is obstruction of justice."

"I'm not lying. I'm your criminal, and I killed my boyfriend because he wanted me to stop." Kieran glared at her. "What more do you want?"

The agents exchanged looks, tired from their yearlong hunt for Ezekiel. "Get in, Cross," Daniels said. "Just... get in."

Frost sat in the passenger seat, and Daniels started the engine. They drove for about five minutes in silence until Kieran broke it when they pulled into the parking lot of Perk's only jail.

"Living in a town like Perk makes you rebel... at least for some of us," Kieran said from the backseat as Daniels parked the car.

"Who's 'us?'" Frost asked.

"Johnny and I," Kieran said with a quick tongue. "The peak of Sarah's rebellion was metal music. She drew the line at digging up graves."

"Who's Sarah?" Frost asked, ignoring what he meant by grave-digging.

"'Digging up graves?'" Daniels asked, looking at Kieran in the rearview mirror.

"Sarah's Johnny's sister," Kieran replied to both. "I went through a phase of digging up graves when I was younger." He shrugged. "No biggie."

He fell silent.

He had nothing to hide.

"Come on," Daniels said, pulling Kieran out of the car.

Kieran stood up, squinting at the dim light from the sky. Frost walked on his other side, holding his arm.

"You smell like a bar," Kieran told Frost. "You should stop smoking."

Frost ignored the twenty-six-year-old fiend who was sniffing him. Then, the agent looked down at Kieran in alarm as an odd vibration emitted from Kieran's forehead. Frost quickly looked over at Daniels, taking in her lack of awareness, and then he walked in front of Kieran.

"What are you doing?" Daniels asked Frost when he bent down to look Kieran in the eyes.

"Checking," Frost mused.

"Checking for what?" Daniels asked him.

Frost studied Kieran's eyes, ignoring Kieran's complaints. "For drugs," Frost mumbled, a man addicted to lying.

People stopped talking as the three of them entered the city jail—a small and quiet building. Perk only needed one jail, as crime was often minimal, and their population was under ten thousand.

"I knew he killed the Williams kid. Lock 'im up," a deputy snapped at a few underlings, who were only too eager to obey. "We should just send him to Saint's Prison. Screw the flippin' trial. Everyone knows he done it."

Frost eyed the cross that was hanging above the receptionist's desk.

The town was highly religious, and since all of their money went to their beliefs, it had left them with practically nothing when they were founded in the 1800s. So, when Orchid Group, a company known for its private prisons, reached out to the town in the early 1900s, they offered to strike a deal. If Perk gave the company rights to a specific area of its land, the townspeople would not only have first choice of employment at their Perk location, but each person would also receive a monthly stipend. As for the City of Perk, they would receive even more.

It was an obvious win for the small town.

And when Orchid Group built one of their well-known secured prisons on a portion of their land in the mid-1900s, the people of Perk became prosperous. Surrounded by trees and hills, Perk was in one of the prettiest woods of the South—full of ancient trees with twisted and brilliant bark.

However, the woods held secrets of hauntings, which were well-known to the CEO of Orchid Group. The rumor that the woods were haunted was what attracted the company in the first place. It was a prime location for one of Orchid Group's prisons.

And the more money Perk received, the more fanatical the people became. Gaining a reputation for being cultish throughout the years, it was only natural for Perk to become isolated from the rest of North Georgia. Soon, no one wanted to visit Perk for its historic trees, let alone live there.

Aside from the town full of lunatics needing severe mental help, it became public knowledge that the extensive woods Perk was surrounded by had a habit of "eating people." The woods had become known as Satan's Web in the late 1930s, and almost three centuries later, the nickname lived on.

"We wish to question him first in one of your rooms, please," Daniels said sternly. She gripped Kieran's arm and pulled him away from the cops who tried to take him from her. "He's a suspect in a federal crime."

"Suit yourself," the rude deputy muttered, walking over to get coffee, shaking his head.

Coffee spilled on the cop's white shirt, making him swear. "Feds, fuckin' feds," the cop said to the secretary, who sat at her desk to his left. "Taking our offenders, ruining our cases."

The two FBI agents led Kieran into a small room, where he was seated in the center. It was just an empty room with a wobbly chair and no table. He looked up at the flickering light. The broken light bothered him—not the agents or the smell of smoke surrounding Frost. For being a city with funds they could start a million fires with, Perk looked nothing but poor.

"Kieran Cross." Daniels turned the tiny recorder on. "Age: Twenty-six—"

Kieran looked up at Daniels as she spoke. Her red hair had streaks of natural blond, and her almond-shaped eyes were bright green, flattering her lightly tanned skin. Short but strong in bite, Aria Daniels was not one to be messed with. She kept talking into the recorder, pacing back and forth, often peering curiously at Kieran. He turned to look at Frost, who was standing near the door with arms crossed. Frost looked down at him, and the tall agent clenched his jaw, his veins popping lightly under his fair skin. He stood calmly, despite the vibrations from Kieran bothering him.

Chills came from the darkest corner. He was not the tallest man. Standing at five-foot-eight with medium blond hair and honey-brown eyes, he could light up a room with his innocence. *Johnny.* Kieran tried to ignore the hallucination of his boyfriend, who kept judging him from his spot in the corner near the two agents.

After the interrogation and the police processed Kieran for the murder of Johnny Williams, the agents walked outside to talk privately.

"This doesn't add up," Frost said after they entered their car. "I don't believe Cross is Ezekiel. And I think Perk is wrong about him killing Johnny Williams—even if he confessed. It doesn't fall in line with how he killed before."

"People lie, you know that, but the murder is not ours to deal with. I don't believe he's Ezekiel either, even if he has some similarities." Daniels shook her head. "Something is going on with this town. Did you see the deputy's reaction when we asked for a room to question Cross? It feels like they're hiding something."

"Well, we know Ezekiel is in Perk. Should we continue investigating?" Frost asked his partner. "Next stop, city hall?"

Daniels did not hear him. She had become consumed by Kieran's father's death. "Even if it was self-defense, Cross' father was brutalized…"

Frost eyed Daniels. "Let's not discuss that case. Focus. We need to snag Ezekiel."

"It should be re-opened." Daniels looked distracted from their current job. "The coroner would know—"

"It's a closed case. The report says an animal attacked the corpse. Maybe Cross didn't eat his father's skin, and we're just seeing cannibalism in a case where it may not have happened. Let it go." Frost tried to calm Daniels down from her need for truth, but she had a certain influence over him, and he gave in. "Fine... we can go to the morgue to talk about the Williams kid and Cross' father because it can help us find out who Ezekiel is. Everyone knows everything in towns like these."

"Deal." Daniels nodded and drove the car from the jail's parking lot.

Inside Perk City Jail, Kieran was placed alone in a cell with a cot, sink, and toilet. A blanket and small pillow were lying folded on the cot. He had changed into the blue uniform reserved for inmates awaiting trial, and soon, he would be transferred to Saint's Prison—well, after the trial and all, but who were they kidding? Kieran would be convicted of murder and transferred to the prison a few miles away, and Saint's Prison would be his new home.

The guards walked down the cracked halls every hour. It was the first night in the jail for Kieran. There were only eleven inmates, and ten still wore street clothes. Most of them were drunks and vandals.

"Lights out," a guard yelled from down the hall, and the cells turned pitch-black.

Kieran sat against the cold stone wall. Dark bangs hung in his eyes, and his arms rested on his knees. He stared at the iron bars before him. He had impulsively confessed to end the madness, but the madness was only beginning. On the verge of freaking out, he banged his head back against the wall, ignoring the spreading pain.

Footsteps echoed throughout the jail as he kept banging his head. The dim night lights turned on. The footsteps hurried as the other inmates started screaming like drunken wild animals.

Kieran banged his head faster, causing a loud sound to pass through the cells of wildness. Blood gushed from his head, falling down his body and onto the ground.

"Stop." A guard named Roger Cope stood in front of Kieran's cell. "Cross, stop it—"

The sight of the boy who the town had once been fond of stunned Cope.

And the guard's old compassion for the young man returned briefly. Kieran had once held a smile that cheered up everyone. But Cope was now staring at a man glaring dead at him with poisonous eyes and covered in his own blood.

Kieran smeared his hands in the newly formed puddle as he grinned down at the blood. "Go away," he mumbled, hunching over.

Cope called for help, for the medics to come. Kieran laughed and held up his bloody hands, catching fresh blood falling from his chin.

"I don't need help." Kieran stared at the red liquid he was capturing in his cupped hands. "Don't come near me."

He felt the change rising in him—the change that had led to his father's death, the change that gave him a constant hunger. It was getting stronger.

Cope's eyes widened as Kieran drank his own blood. The expressions of the arriving guards were as expected. They practically shat themselves in place. They did not know what to make of the madman that looked like Kieran Cross.

"Screw prison. Maybe he needs to go to Saint's Asylum instead?" Cope asked the others, spooked. The mental institution was owned by Orchid Group as well, and it was located across from the prison. Often, they would send their criminally insane there for treatment before moving them to prison.

"Wherever they send Cross, I hope he gets help," another guard said as he restrained Kieran so a medic could sedate him.

"He can't be helped. He has the devil inside him," the medic blurted out as she ran forward with a needle. The woman injected fluid into Kieran's bloodstream, and he quickly became dizzy.

❋❋❋❋❋

After months of self-inflicting wounds and dissociation, the noise of blood rushing inside Kieran's head made him moan, and he woke up to the dullness of his cell. He was lying face down on the dark stone ground. He did not know how long he had been confined. He had checked out of reality when Johnny died and entered a hell of his own creation.

Johnny's voice entered Kieran's ears. "Why are you doing this?"

Kieran tried to ignore the illusion.

"Why?" Johnny asked.

"Leave me alone," Kieran muttered to the imaginary Johnny. "You're dead."

With those mumbled words, he burst out in a hard sob, and Johnny took his leave by disappearing slowly into the air.

Clink. Clink. Clink.

Kieran was puzzled at Johnny's departure and was pondering his remaining sanity when a piercing sound came closer to his cell. Turning toward the sound, he focused on the shadows drifting near the bars.

Clink. Clink. Clink.

A pain Kieran had to accept as pain, and not relief, came to him in a matter of an eighth of a split second. His deadly eyes could not open from the weight of the chains sinking into his flesh. The coldness of the metal burned deep into his skin. It was a brief horrendous suffering, and he had to bear it for a reason alien to him.

Kieran's surroundings changed, and he was instantly transported to a darker and more disturbing cell, bigger than the one he was in just seconds before. The new cell had a transparent glass wall in front of him, not iron bars like at Perk's jail. On the other side of the glass, shadowed figures walked in and out of his sight. Some vanished into the thick, smoky air that surrounded them.

The air smelled like death and rot.

"You..." A low and eerie voice came from all around him. "What... are you?"

"What are you doing? Send him back," another voice said from the shadows. "Stop invading people's dreams, Aaeon."

Kieran rattled his fists in the thick chains that bound him to the brick wall behind him. The sinister voice cried like a child as the chains loosened around Kieran's body.

"Kieran?" Wren shouted from the air above him. She was getting dressed for Simon's funeral in Tallahassee, but her mind had drifted inside his when she sensed that he was in danger. "Kieran!"

Kieran glanced up at the woman yelling down at him. It was almost as if he could see her, but that was impossible. She was not there. He stared up at the shadowy silhouette of a woman that danced across the ceiling while the chains fell from his body.

In an instant, he woke up in his tiny cell, covered in sweat from the nightmare. His ears rang from the woman's voice, and at that moment, he knew who she was. His wrists and neck still burned from the chains as he tried to move. Blood from all his self-inflicted wounds stained him and his cot.

XIV

LAUGHING IRON

WREN BROKE AWAY FROM Kieran's memories and realized she was standing in front of her tall, double pedestrian gates—two iron doors, one welded in place. Kieran had found out about her because she had been sloppy when she ventured into his mind that morning.

She turned to look at the vacant houses on the street. Most people had moved after the Sparrow Manor massacre, but a few remained, and an old man was mowing his lawn.

Wren placed her thumbprint on the left gate's lock to unlock it, but her finger slipped. She froze when she heard the recording of Simon's laugh escape the intercom. She did not know that he had recorded his voice in her security system after he arrived three weeks ago. When he was alive, he was an electrical engineer with expertise in holographs, and he had found it easy to infiltrate her house mechanics...

When Simon moved back, he had stopped by Sparrow Manor. He knew his three best friends were there—they were always there. He was buzzing the intercom to the left of the gates. His eyes were wild. Before Wren opened the door, he had hacked into the lock system and recorded his voice to sound whenever Wren or Esme failed to unlock the gates.

Simon had always liked a good prank.

On that day, while Wren had rushed to unlock the gates, Ray left the front porch to greet Simon. And Esme had turned invisible. After one of the gates swung open, Esme flapped a bat next to Simon's ear. He screamed when he saw the bat, while Esme laughed maniacally.

Simon calmed down when he had realized it was just Esme, and he tried to joke about the Halloween decorations still being up. Twisting his expression and acting afraid of the morbid décor, he did not want to admit that she had successfully scared him.

Wren had left the Halloween decorations up in memory of Kieran's boyfriend, but she never had the chance to inform Simon about the murder. The four friends were reunited, and Wren did not want to begin the reunion by revealing how Johnny was killed.

It would have broken Simon's heart.

Growing up, Wren had told her three best friends about Kieran, and each of them had a favorite person in Kieran's saga. Ray's favorite person was Johnny's twin sister, Esme's was Kieran, Simon's had been Johnny, and Wren favored Kieran to the point of being his telepathic stalker.

Wren placed her thumbprint over the lock again, but she smudged it on purpose so she could hear Simon's laugh. She then looked up at the sun above her and watched birds fly overhead.

Kieran had lost the one dearest to his heart months before Wren lost Simon. Both Wren and Kieran craved blood, and the two held many similarities.

Wren was starting to think that Kieran was a key that could unlock the mystery of who she really was.

As a strong vibration traveled down her spine, Wren's eyes glossed over.

XV

Sparrow Manor

BACK AT THE BOOKSTORE, Esme was placing protection runes Rolf and Kyle had made above the doorframe while they played card games. The two were tired from protesting. A knock came at the door, almost making Esme fall off the stool she was standing on. She cracked open the door and peeked out to see Ray holding up a large bag of leftover Chinese food from the church's fridge.

Looking spooked, Esme said, "Sorry I couldn't attend the funeral. I'll be at the dinner—promise."

Ray flashed an understanding smile. "Everyone's talking about it. You're the hero of the morning!"

She almost grinned, but her mood was still bleak.

Ray looked down at the bag of food. "You guys want some Chinese for lunch?" he asked, looking back up at Esme. "I took out everything that had animal product in it. Or are y'all eating the veggie soup Bettie made?" When he noticed her uncertain look, he added, "You can come to lunch with me and my parents. Rolf and Kyle, too. We're going to Pumpkin Vines."

"Going out today isn't safe for them. Thank you for the invite, but I'm going home soon. I may just wait for dinner," Esme said. She then looked back at the kids. "Do you want Chinese food or Bettie's soup?"

Rolf huffed and shouted from inside the bookstore, "I don't like onions! Bettie puts onions in everything!"

"I like Bettie's food," Kyle argued with him. "It's tasty."

"Then you can eat it." Rolf slammed his cards down. "Gimme the Chinese food."

Esme snatched the bag and slammed the door in Ray's face. Puzzled, he slowly turned away from the bookstore.

She cracked open the door again, making Ray look back at her. "Sorry about that. Thank you for the food. I'm setting up runes for Rolf and Kyle, so I can't open the door too wide. The magic is already in effect."

"Don't they have protection wards up?" Ray asked her. "What are the runes for?"

Esme widened the door slightly and poked her head out, whispering, "It's extra protection. Kyle is extremely scared, even if he doesn't act like it. Rolf's been trying to cheer him up all morning. They're playing poker."

Ray tried to look around her to see the brothers playing their game, but they were sitting on the floor hidden behind the door.

"Tell them I'll be over to play cards after things calm down," he told Esme.

"We're playing Texas Hold 'Em right now! Come join. Bring cash!" Rolf yelled and walked up behind Esme with a spring roll in his mouth. He then turned to face Kyle, who was rummaging through the mix of food. "Kyle, stop eating all the fried tofu."

"Then share the spring rolls," Kyle said right before Esme closed the door.

Ray walked to his motorcycle in the bookstore's parking lot, spotting Frost. The agent was leaning back on his black car, parked on the side of the road, with his arms crossed. Ray glanced at the car's plates and noticed the government seal.

Instead of rushing to meet his parents for lunch, he decided to meet with Wren first. Something told him that Wren knew who the guy was.

She was telepathic, after all.

Wren was unlocking her front door when she heard Ray's motorcycle drive up. She turned around and looked through the tall iron bars. He was parking his bike outside her gates. "I thought you were meeting your parents for lunch?" she asked.

Ray walked up to the left gate. "I am, but who's that guy parked outside the bookstore? The serious-looking blond guy with the government car?"

"He's with the FBI," Wren told Ray, walking back to meet him. "You remember how I told you Kieran went to jail?"

"Yes... but what does he have to do with the FBI?" Ray asked.

"He broke out of jail," Wren replied, and then she noticed Ray's face waiting for clarification about why Frost was lurking nearby. "The FBI guy is looking for him. Supposedly, Kieran is on his way here to meet me." She shrugged. "He's being watched by the feds. They think he may be some cybercriminal. Ha! Can you believe that?"

Ray kept staring at Wren for further explanation. "Why is Kieran headed here to *meet* you? Last time I checked, only one of you knows about the other."

"Kieran found out that I have been mind-stalking him all these years, and he is *not* happy." Wren laughed briefly. "He may actually kill me."

"Unlock your gate. I'm staying with you," Ray said.

"I'll be fine." Wren rolled her eyes. "Remember, I can set things on fire."

"How could I forget?" Ray asked with both eyebrows raised. "Fine. Come to lunch with us. My parents really want you to go, and I don't like this FBI-and-Kieran situation."

"I want to be alone for a bit. Don't worry about them. I doubt Kieran will kill me, and the agent is not a threat—just some guy doing his job. I was joking." Wren reached through the bars and tried to fix Ray's messy bangs. "You really should wear a helmet."

Ray swatted her hand. "Okay, *Mom*. I'll be over right after lunch."

He drove off, and Wren walked away from the gates and toward her roofed front porch. She walked through the front door and stopped as soon as she entered the spacious foyer. After closing the door, she stared aimlessly toward the split staircase that led up to the second floor, which was blocked off by a heavy red rope. Wren only had a few memories of the second floor, but she treasured each one.

She locked her eyes on an enormous picture of her parents and Esme's, framed in silver. It was hung high on the wall above the staircase landing. The picture of the Sparrows and McKnights had been taken on the day of the gala at Sparrow Manor.

Wren leaned back on the closed door and slid down, staring up at the photo. Eudora thought it was insane for the two girls to return to the house where the shooting occurred, but Wren wanted to honor her parents' creation by living in it.

Slowing her panic attack, Wren stood up and walked toward the living room. To each side of the staircase's landing was a silver-framed archway that connected the foyer to the living room, and on both the right and left walls of the foyer were two more archways leading to the wide rectangular hallway within the house separating the kitchen, study, bathroom, Esme's room, and Wren's room from the inner living room.

Wren walked under the archway to the right and into the living room. She headed toward the couch near the right wall, where she often made dolls, and placed her purse on the onyx stone side table. Feeling numb, she flopped face down on the black cushions of the silver-framed couch.

As time passed, she entered a staring contest with one of her dolls that was perched on the silver-framed coffee table with a glass surface. She could not help but feel judged, as the doll she had been procrastinating to finish was staring at her with one painted eye.

She slid to the floor and sat drearily upon a gold oriental pillow from Japan. She moved her eyes to stare at the Holo-disc, which rested on a narrow black pedestal behind the coffee table. She debated whether she should watch the local news. Exhausted, she leaned back on her couch. A loveseat sat to her right, and an oversized chair was to her left. Both were the same Victorian design as the couch and faced the coffee table, creating an enclosure. The living room set rested on a large black-and-silver area rug atop a white marble floor.

Facing in from the foyer, the other three walls that helped form the living room each held two archway entrances near the corners, as well as paintings, wall candelabras, and hand-crafted bookshelves, mimicking the wall that separated the living room from the foyer.

And under one archway that connected to the left hallway stood Esme. She stared at Wren for about twenty minutes before saying, "You should take a nap in your bed and get some actual rest."

"I'm fine, Esme," Wren told her. "Weren't you just at the bookstore? Don't tell me you can teleport now."

"No, I'm not Isis," Esme replied. "I left the bookstore not too long after you left. Went by the church first. Is your panic attack gone?"

"I haven't panicked in forever," Wren said proudly.

"Ah, that's why you didn't hear me walk in about thirty minutes ago," Esme whispered with a nod, knowing that her words were untrue. "You may have fooled our therapist, but you haven't fooled me or Mom."

A crackling noise came from the elevator to Esme's right.

She walked into the living room and looked toward the elevator, which was to the left of Wren. It traveled from the underground garage to the living room on the first floor and up to the hall on the second floor. The ruby-framed vessel hummed faintly, and the lights flickered.

Esme moved her eyes from the elevator, looked at Wren worriedly, and asked, "Do you feel okay?"

In an instant, Wren folded over, causing Esme to run to where she was lying on the rug. Esme screamed down at her sister to wake up, but her eyes would not open, and her body began to convulse.

A twisted spiral of images invaded Wren's vision, and she tried to calm herself by listening to the family of fairies chattering in her kitchen as the gargoyle named Red threatened no one in particular.

"Don't say you're fine when you're clearly not," Esme said, panicking at Wren's body shutting down. "You even made the lights flicker!"

Esme sat on the floor and leaned over Wren, worried. Sweat bordered Wren's brow as Esme felt her forehead. She stared down at Wren, whose body was becoming covered in light blue lines, then snatched her hand from Wren's face, not wanting to touch the weird-looking veins.

"I wonder if Ray's done eating." Esme glanced at the clock on the wall. She sighed and looked up at the second-floor balcony crowning the living room walls. "Should I call him? I don't want to interrupt their lunch... but he'll know how to bring you back." She looked back down at Wren, almost expecting her to answer. "He always knows what to say."

Waiting for Wren to finish downloading a new premonitory vision, Esme was trying to figure out how to help restore her mind. Normally, Ray was always around when she entered a mental lock, and his sarcastic words were enough to snap her out of it.

While Wren stayed in the dark, Esme tried to think of what she could do. She widened her eyes, having an idea. Whenever a new vision came, Wren would wake up craving meat—raw meat. Why? That remained a mystery.

Esme summoned water to help place her on the couch. She knew she had to prepare raw meat, or Wren would run out of the house hunting a poor animal.

Wren had done that before.

Esme walked briskly under an archway behind the couch and into the wide hall. She rushed past the talking gargoyle near the study, who was cracking jokes about Wren being weak. Having no time to deal with the statue, she jogged toward the kitchen at the front of the house. If one stood at the front door, looking into the foyer, the kitchen was the first room through the right archway.

Esme turned the corner and opened the door in the middle of the wall. She walked up to the refrigerator and threw open the freezer door. She stared solemnly at a large steak. As an herbivorous species, it went against the fae's principles to partake in the serving of an animal's corpse.

Esme brought out the frozen steak and placed it into the sink. She placed her hands over the steak and extracted the excess juice from the meat, which was Wren's favorite part. But Esme only cared about sanitizing the meat.

A ball of liquid hovered between her hands, stinking of blood and fat. She scrunched her nose and sent the liquid quickly down the drain.

"I don't know why you do that for her," someone said from the dining table.

Esme looked at the small ceramic statue of three fairies dancing on top of the half-wall separating the dining room from the kitchen. Each had wreaths on their heads, and their hair was long and curly as they danced around a tiny clear crystal ball. A fairy emerged from the crystal ball and flew to the kitchen counter to judge Esme, her sheer wings flapping like a hummingbird's.

"If you don't like Wren, then why do you come here?" Esme asked the fairy. "Wren adores you three."

"We are loyal to the Sparrows, and I never said I didn't like her." The fairy hovered over the sink and pointed down at the steak. "But a nymph should not handle meat. It's sinful."

"Leave her alone and come back," another fairy said from the statue. "The lullaby is incomplete without three."

"I am. I am." The fairy who had emerged through the portal hesitated to fly back and looked up at Esme. "Humans raised you, so you most likely don't understand, but your ancestors are crying."

"Oh, my goddess, Twila," the third fairy said. "Leave the poor nymph alone. We must finish this song before night falls, or the birds will not sing."

Twila flew back to the statue and stood on the crystal ball, looking down at the image of her two sisters in their home in Moonlight Hills. "One morning of the birds being quiet will not end the world."

"If the birds don't sing, we don't dance," the third fairy argued. "I don't know about you, Twila, but I love dancing in the snapdragons."

Esme chuckled at the three sisters bickering. As Twila returned to Moonlight Hills, Esme placed the meat on a large serving platter and put it inside the fridge.

"Did dey go back?" a snarky voice asked from the hall.

"Yes, Red," Esme replied loudly to the gargoyle.

"Good!" the gargoyle replied. "Damn fairies, always singin' and dancin.' Pisses me off."

Esme walked out of the kitchen after she had washed her hands and walked up to the gargoyle, whose eyes were glowing red. The gargoyle had used to keep their station in the foyer, but they had grown to prefer to keep their lookout in the middle of the right hall.

It was near Calvin Sparrow's study.

"Why are you always so annoyed by them?" Esme asked Red. "They stay in Moonlight Hills to write songs for the birds, and then they visit our gardens so they can dance to the birds' lullabies. They don't even bother you."

Similar to elves, fairies loved music. While the elves manipulated air and crafted instruments that twisted with the element, fairies communicated with the planet itself. The music the fairies composed was so connected to Earth that it made the birds sing.

"They be too happy," Red mumbled. "I don't like happy. Can't they stay in de hills all de time?"

"No, they love our gardens, as do the birds who live in the yards." Looking at the gargoyle with four faces, Esme patted the statue on the top of one of their heads. "It's okay to laugh, Red."

Red stopped talking, and their red eyes turned gray. The gargoyle was once happy, and they had even sung throughout the house with the fairies.

One year after Wren was born, Red was gifted by an elven couple who were visiting the Sparrows. The couple were stone crafters from Moonlight Hills, and they were in Tallahassee to meet Mia and Calvin, wanting to give their daughter gifts. Red respected their makers, and if their makers wanted to give them to the Sparrows, then they vowed to protect them.

However, Red felt they had failed the Sparrows as a house guardian, and ever since the shooting, the gargoyle had kept a serious composure near Calvin's study. They admired Calvin.

"Wren," Esme said, walking into the living room to check on her, "are you back?"

Noticing that Wren's eyes were open and staring up at the high ceiling, Esme was about to tell her about the steak. She stopped walking suddenly when she saw that Wren's dilated eyes were a light blue, and flames were exiting her pores.

Blue flames.

✸✸✸✸✸

Wren was playing outside with Esme when bullets flew through the windows and Molotov cocktails exploded in the trees. It was 2203, and while most people were supportive of the human-fae alliance, fear still ran rampant among many.

And that fear found its way into the gala at Sparrow Manor.

Esme's and Wren's parents had been watching the president on the Holo-disc in the living room, while the governor talked up a storm with the diplomats and families from Moonlight Hills, who had volunteered to test out integrating into Tallahassee's community.

But when the anti-fae revealed the guns hidden within their clothes, the gala came to a deadly halt.

After some of the rebels approached the two young girls, who were trying to hide behind a tree, a loud storm manifested, and rain fell. A pale man emerged from the shadows, and the anti-fae rebels collapsed to the ground one by one, throwing up their insides. White wings extended from the man's back, and his long white hair swayed in the wind.

The man turned to the two girls who were crying near the tree. "Remember this day." The man's eyes blazed with a coppery haze as he glared down at Wren. "This slaughter is no one's fault but your own."

Wren tried to hold Esme as they cowered away from the tall man with wings.

"You and Cain's selfish actions—"

In the middle of the winged man's speech, cold chains materialized, which quickly wrapped around him. A taller man of ghostly flesh stood in a fog of shadows, gripping his links of cold steel. He wore an executioner's hood, and black drool dripped down his chin as he smiled down at the two girls.

The eerie-looking man then dragged the winged man deep inside his realm of shadows.

XVI

The Kanarians

DING-DONG. THE BELL ECHOED throughout the house, ripping Esme away from her thoughts. She looked up, as if the sound was coming from the second floor.

After a moment, Esme went to check the nearest intercom on the living room wall to see who was buzzing at their gates, and she saw Ray standing there. He had changed into khaki pants and a white button-down shirt for dinner. She looked down at her crystal watch and noticed an hour had passed. It was already two.

"One moment," she said nervously into the speaker and rushed into the foyer.

The front door opened, and Ray stared through the bars of the left gate at Esme, whose face looked spooked through the small opening of the front door. "Are you going to let me in?" he asked her and shook the bars of the iron gate. "I'm too full to climb."

"O-of course," Esme said and pressed her thumb on the fingerprint scanner on the main intercom in the foyer, unlocking the gates.

"What happened?" Ray asked as he walked up the pathway, the gates locking back into place. "You have *that* look."

"No, I don't," Esme argued.

Ray walked into the house and closed the door. "Why is it freezing in here?"

"Wren is covered in these blue flames," Esme blurted, leading him into the living room.

They walked up to Wren on the couch. Every inch of her was covered in icy flames, and her skin had turned pale blue.

Esme rubbed her arms from the chill. "I thought she was entering her mental shutdown like normal, but her veins kept darkening until these blue flames appeared."

A twisted fog of darkness kept Wren paralyzed as Ray and Esme stared down at her. Seeing flashes of being stuck in shards of glass surrounded by fire, Wren witnessed a future that made no sense.

"Well, this is new... Wake up!" Ray yelled at Wren. "We have dinner in a few hours. Stop doing your mind crap."

Frozen in place, Wren listened to her friends argue about how to wake her. She did not know what was happening to her body, and her anxiety escalated. She tried to keep her mind calm by listening to Ray and Esme shout at each other, but new visions of the past overwhelmed her.

Never had she seen both past and future in one download before. But deeds Kieran had committed before leaving the town of Perk dominated her mind while she stayed motionless on the couch.

Then, Wren realized what Frost meant by "leaving Perk in a very bad state."

When Kieran had broken out of jail that morning, he did not leave the town as soon as he was free. No—he hunted. And his first target was the corrupted former priest.

Wren tasted the blood of Preacher's heart, which Kieran had torn his teeth into. She felt Kieran's vengeance when he had burned the church down with the early morning service inside. The screams of the people echoed over the crackling fire.

After Wren watched Kieran vandalize more of his hometown, she found out that he was already in Tallahassee. And he was staring at her house from across the street. Surprised by his fast arrival, she let her guard down.

And she shivered from the coldest frost.

Across the dreary street, Kieran stood on the grass between two empty houses as he stared at the two-story manor. He was wearing a black athletic suit he had stolen from a house on his way out of Perk, not wanting to wear the jail uniform any longer. He clutched a *Welcome to Tallahassee* pamphlet he had taken from a gas station that was already being robbed. Reacting to a loud mower, he eyed one of the few residents of the street who was doing yardwork a few houses down.

He then turned his gaze to another man who was staring at him: Frost.

The FBI agent flicked his cigarette Kieran's way and started walking toward him. Kieran was about to run, but something kept his feet frozen to where he stood.

"You arrived *much* earlier than scheduled," Frost told Kieran.

Kieran shrugged, not scared of the agent. "Are you taking me back?"

"No." Frost looked over at Wren's house. "Your arson burned most of Perk and half of the jail."

"Nice," Kieran whispered to himself.

Surprising Kieran, Frost patted him on the back. "Well done, kid."

"Wait, what?" Kieran looked up at the agent praising him.

"There are some things I can't do," Frost told Kieran. "That's why we have people like you."

Frost flipped open his cell phone and read a message from Daniels. The agent glanced up at Wren's house. "Are you going to go talk to her?" he asked. "Or are you just going to watch her house?"

"This is *so* weird," Kieran said.

Frost did not reply. He walked away from Kieran and back toward his car, which was parked at the corner of Wren's fence.

Kieran shifted his eyes away from the odd agent and continued to watch over Wren's house. He was trying to figure out how to introduce himself.

He had heard Wren yell at him when he was stuck in his nightmare back in jail. As if reading a biography of her, he had woken up knowing precisely who she was, and he hoped she could figure out what was happening to him.

Before Frost entered his car, he looked back at Kieran, whose eyes stayed fixated on Sparrow Manor.

Ring.

"Yeah?" Frost asked after he answered the incoming call from Daniels.

"How's it going?" Daniels asked. "Did you find Cross?"

"No." Frost turned the ignition on and drove away from the street.

"Don't lie to me." Daniels sounded annoyed.

"Why do you ask if you already know the answer?" Frost asked. "He's in Tallahassee."

"Grab him," Daniels said.

"The kid is not Ezekiel." Frost narrowed his eyes and slowed down as he approached a stop sign. "And his murder charge is not our case."

"You still need to bring him in. We have ATF, the DEA, and more field agents arriving to investigate the fire. Hacking isn't the only reason he's wanted now." Daniels was worried about her job security. "If he's not Ezekiel, he's connected somehow."

"Well, I think we should let him go," Frost said, turning the corner.

"What? We can't just let him go! Are you insane?!" Daniels shouted at her partner. "Who the hell are you anymore? The Leonard I knew would have already been handing Cross over. Why even drive to Tallahassee to intercept him if you weren't planning on dragging—"

Daniels paused.

"You weren't ever planning to bring him in, were you? And how the heck did you get down there so fast? You left Perk around eight! Start talking,

Leonard. You have been weird about this case, and now you can practically teleport!?"

Frost hung up on Daniels after she paused to breathe.

While Daniels had wanted to snoop around the burned-down Perk, and more agents were arriving to help her investigate the fire that had burned down several federal buildings, Frost had taken the car and left. Fearing that the human government would catch on to who Kieran and Ezekiel were, he had frozen the highway with a tundra of ice and sped to Florida on tires that practically smoked.

Avoiding teleportation was something Frost tried to maintain, for the Shadow King could detect all transport via portals in the light realm.

And the Shadow King did not like the Kanarian gods.

Even though the god of shadows had no vendetta against Frost, he remained cautious and limited portal use. Frost was still technically a Kanarian, no matter how shiny his FBI badge was.

After parking at a gas station, Frost read Daniels' rush of texts on his cellphone. Ignoring the woman, who almost made him feel an ounce of emotion, he walked into the gas station and headed straight for the cashier. He was losing patience with his disguise.

"ID?" the cashier asked after grabbing a carton of menthol cigarettes.

Frost flipped open his wallet, showing her his ID.

"You don't look thirty-five." The cashier tried to flirt after she noticed the FBI badge next to his ID.

The cashier was cute, around her late twenties. However, the anti-fae bag resting behind her curled his stomach.

Frost leaned over the counter, grabbed the carton, and smiled. "Thanks. I'm actually older." He placed his finger to his lips and winked. "Don't tell anyone that I'm passing for human."

The cashier's face turned a bright red, and she spun around to stock the tobacco.

When Frost stepped back outside, he heard a familiar voice, causing him to scowl. He returned to his car, placing both hands on the steering wheel. He tried to pacify his anger, slowing his breathing, and cold air drifted from his lips as a voice laughed inside his head.

It worked! I can finally enter your mind, the voice said.

"Get out of my head, Cain." Frost drove back to his hotel.

Ignoring Cain's chatter, he pulled into the hotel parking lot and parked his car. Rushing up the stairs, he tried to tune out the electric voice that kept trying to recruit him to the other side of the Kanarian war.

The Kanarians were the overlords of the light realm, and they had fallen under the rule of the greediest god, Nao...

Nao was a poor king, for he was designed to be the god of diplomacy and records. He was not meant to rule—he was meant to gatekeep the Kanarians' resources. But greed consumed his heart. After gaining a powerful following among the gods, and having a stone within his grasp, he was able to overthrow Ezra, the first of the Kanarians. After he overthrew Ezra, he instigated the dismemberment of Ezra's soul. This betrayal had created two cults in the light realm: the Cult of Ezra and the Cult of Nao.

As Nao tried to do what he could not, he created individual mistakes that did not belong. He called these creations "abominations."

And Frost was the strongest abomination Nao had ever created.

Don't forget that Nao had brainwashed me into thinking I was his son after I arrived in this realm. I know how much hold he can have on someone, Cain said inside Frost's head. *Nao is not meant to be the Kanarian ruler. The light realm is breaking without the proper god on the throne. We need to restore Ezra.*

Frost burrowed his brow, irritated by Cain's presence in his mind. "Ezra became vulnerable when he fell in love with that demon you journey with, proving he was not fit to rule. The realm will be just fine."

What do you know? Cain grew angry. *You know nothing but the lies of our false father.*

Frost slammed the door closed after he walked into his room, eyes glossing over with ice. "Go away, Cain. I have nothing to say to you."

He walked up to the bar refrigerator, grabbing all the mini shots. He tossed them in the ice bucket on the brown end table and collapsed on the leather couch, opening the first bottle. He grabbed the tiny remote and turned on the Holo-disc, and a hologram of a TV appeared above the round machine.

"Tell me, how is the team getting along on the shuttle?" A reporter was interviewing Tabitha, the very short scientist who spoke to the news on behalf of the fae community.

Tabitha smiled and nodded. "They all get along great, but great it is not." A woman of riddled words, the world both hated and loved her.

Frost grabbed another shot and switched the channel. They were covering a segment on how Jesus was a nymph, if such a figure ever lived, causing him to pause. "Humans can't turn water into wine, but you know who can? Nymphs," the fae researcher said with his hands held up wide, thrilled. "The nymphs *love* their wine and can manipulate water."

Frost leaned back, closing his eyes, and listened to the man's soothing voice explain his theory. Mortals were funny with their religion and science debate. The two were one, and no man-made religion could ever capture the beauty of Kanaria.

Breaking Frost from his trance, a commercial came on. A woman was holding a green bottle of liquid with a spray nozzle. "With Empure, you can find out if you have any fae DNA." The woman smiled on the hologram's screen. "Ever thought maybe you were adopted? Maybe you want to find your roots? With Empure—"

Frost turned off the disc, gritting his teeth. A company profiting off naïve people—it pissed him off. If someone was fae, they would know it.

He sent a frigid chill throughout the room as he seethed. The base of the Holo-disc became caked with ice, splitting it. Leaning back on the couch, he slung another shot into his mouth. He was technically part of the Cult of Nao, but he did not want to be. Even though Nao had created him, he felt loyal to Ezra.

But that was not a surprise—he was a part of the first Kanarian...

Long ago, after Ezra's soul had been split into twelve fragments, Nao was able to capture one. And he had transformed this fragment of Ezra into an abomination whom he named Frost.

When Frost materialized, he possessed some powers of Ezra, for he was not just an abomination—he was also a fragment of the first Kanarian.

Pleased that he had created a successful heir, but also upset that he had had to rely on one of Ezra's fragments, Nao continued his mission. And his mission was simple: He wanted to turn Earth into his new kingdom. Among the trillions of planets in the light realm, Nao wanted Earth because Eden had been Ezra's favorite. Nao wanted to rule the very heart of Eden in mockery of the fallen god.

A pitiful man, Nao was.

Originally, Nao had tried to use his first son, Cain, for his cause during the times of Pangaea. But Cain was never truly Nao's son. Coming from another realm entirely, Cain had been brainwashed into believing that the Kanarian god was his father. After Nao forced Cain to be incarnated as the son of a zyula and katani—Adam and Eve—so he could gain the trust of Earthlings, Cain started to wake. And when he woke up to the truth of who he was, the world burned, and the one land of Pangaea cracked.

The moment Cain had abandoned his alliance with Nao, Nao used Ezra's spinal fragment to make Frost. Frost had been designed in Cain's image, as Nao wanted to create an abomination that could do what Cain could—fire and energy manipulation.

To Nao's disappointment, Frost came to life with the face of Cain and the frozen powers of Ezra.

XVII

Old Friends

MINUTES FROM THE DOWNTOWN hotel, Wren was waking up from her paralysis. Esme was trying hard to extract the ice from her system, and Ray was rubbing her arms, trying to warm her.

"Oh, sorry," Esme said when Wren flinched.

Esme pulled the water droplets from Wren's skin slowly, unfreezing her limbs. She raised her hands as she dragged out most of the water that infected her, then motioned her hands and sent the water toward the back doors, pushing the French doors open with the liquid and discarding it on the grass.

Among the bushes of thorn, not far from where the water had landed, drifted an extremely tall man dressed in all black. This man walked from the bushes and toward a gathering of trees to the side of the house, as he watched the runaway inmate with pitch-black eyes. He was not as cold as Frost, nor as impulsive as Kieran. No, he was wiser. The man's black hair drifted in the flowing wind while he surveyed Wren's property.

"Aren't you going to go get her?" a voice asked from behind him. "My fragment died early. She needs to return with the data."

"Soon, Cain." The man crept through Wren's gardens, analyzing the air waves.

"We need Syn back now," Cain said, irritated. He huffed impatiently. "Frost has found her reincarnation, and I don't want him interfering with my test. I can't leave my lab, so I need you to take care of this."

"We would not be in this mess if you had coded the tracking script correctly. Because of your negligence, we lost track of both Syn's reincarnation and your fragment—"

"Spare me your lectures, Lucifer." Cain interrupted him. "We should have conducted a spirit match—oh, we did! That was *your* responsibility when all those people were brought to your island for an evaluation. Maybe, then, we could have supervised Syn, and my test wouldn't be botched."

Lucifer looked back at a dark portal that led to Cain's lab and said, "The orb is not designed to detect spirits—it is a tool for reconstructing the planet. I have helped you to the best of my ability. Please, do not push your failure onto me." He squatted down, admiring the roses. "Syn still has a few more months. We have time to find her if Wren Sparrow is not her."

"She *is* Syn." Cain stuck his head out from his portal, goggles resting above his brow. "Frost isn't here for the kid. I'm sure you've noticed the psychic imprint on the kid's forehead—that's Syn's mark. Frost tracked him to her," he said bitterly. "I thought Frost was back in Kanaria. I bet you the fool is going off-script."

"A fool indeed..." Lucifer kept staring around the bushes. "Sorry, but I need solid proof before I drag a human to Limbo. Even if Isis thinks she is her and you see something mimicking Syn's mark on the boy."

"Damn it, Lucifer. I know you see her mark, too. She looks like her and is telepathic. It *is* her," Cain argued. "How can you be so dim?"

Lucifer ignored Cain, who was hanging halfway out from his portal in midair. His brown hair was messy, and a thin layer of mechanical dust covered his goggles. His dark brown eyes were glazed with a darkness that did not fit in with the light realm.

"You need to snag the kid, too." Cain rushed his words. "I need his energy. That's the main reason Syn is even here."

Lucifer thought for a moment, then said, "I thought Syn came to this planet to observe Earthlings' soul waves?" He paused. "By energy—do you mean soul? Please, do not tell me Syn is here to collect a soul."

Cain sighed. He was not a fan of Lucifer's attention to detail. "I have to go. The fires are starting up again," he said. "Try to keep Frost away and that half-breed close."

Cain muttered, and the portal closed.

"'Half-breed?'" Lucifer whispered. He walked toward the front yard of the house. After scanning the energy waves around Kieran, he noticed the half he was mixed with was not katani or zyula.

Lucifer's eyes widened with curiosity. "That should not have happened."

Through the muddled trees, he watched Kieran across the street. If Cain wanted the boy close, then he was going to make sure Kieran was close.

He stepped into The Shade and walked through the shadows that created the path that tied the three realms together—a scowl on his face.

"Hello," Lucifer said behind Kieran as he stepped from The Shade.

Kieran jumped from fright, turned around, and looked up to see a tall, pale man staring down at him. "Man, I thought that FBI agent was tall. What do you want?"

Lucifer noticed the blurry symbol on his forehead, but it was not clear enough to tell who had made it—a trickster mage or Syn? Even though the mages were not allowed to mess with one's mind, a few still did, but they would be kicked from the guild. As a being who knew most things about the universe, the cloudiness of Kieran's forehead troubled him.

"Let's go meet Wren." Lucifer tried to smile, only to sneer.

He snatched Kieran by the arm and pulled him toward Wren's house. He was not in the mood for pleasantries. Cain had annoyed him with his secret motive of collecting a soul. Cain knew of Lucifer's code of ethics. And if Cain had told him the truth, Lucifer would not have helped him send Syn to Earth to begin with.

Lucifer was not one to tamper with one's actual soul.

"Let me go. Who the fuck do you think you are?" Kieran shouted.

Lucifer waved his hand, and the lock on Wren's gate broke. He pushed a force field to shatter Wren's front door and threw Kieran into her foyer. Climbing to his elbows, Kieran tried to see the man who had thrown him, but the man was gone.

Damaging the body that drove the soul? Well, that was something Lucifer did not mind.

"Really?" Cain asked from a manifesting portal as soon as Lucifer stepped from The Shade and onto the streets of New York City. "You just *had* to toss around such a valuable resource? If the kid dies without me tying his soul to the Fires of Rebirth first, he will just become a regular spirit. His excess energy will be released into the universe, and then I'll have to wait for the next half-angelic to be born. News flash, Lucifer: Your species doesn't mix well with any other!"

Cain looked around the wide alley Lucifer stood in. "Why are you surrounded by trash?"

"Do you not have data to read? How did you know what I was doing?" Lucifer asked as he walked from the alley and onto a sidewalk. "Do not tell me you have satellites following me."

A woman turned around, thinking Lucifer was talking to her, and she almost had a heart attack. After locking eyes with Cain, who was leaning out of his portal, the woman screamed and dashed away. A seven-foot man talking to a face hovering in the air warranted a stir in the city. The others who walked on the sidewalk followed suit, save for a few who did not have the energy nor the passion to care that two extraterrestrial beings were there.

"Go away. You are scaring the humans," Lucifer said.

Cain returned to his lab, and Lucifer watched the dark portal close.

Signs shone brightly above Lucifer while noises from all around did not cease. The loudness of New York City, the horrid smell—he both detested and loved it. The few passersby who did not run eyed him, feeling a mysterious power he emitted. He smiled at the few strangers walking near him, and he started to whistle softly. An eerie tune filled everyone's ears, making the strangers finally rush away from him. His black trench coat wrapped around his pale frame, and his whistling grew louder.

Lucifer stopped walking right in front of an old shop. His piercing black eyes bored through the glass at the sight of a noticeably short man behind a counter ringing up a customer.

A dwarf ran the shop, but everyone thought the man was human. Like the other dwarves on Earth, the clerk kept their species a secret. The human world was finally adapted to the fae, but if they confused the humans even more with tales of how some Edenians still existed, it might have threatened the human governments in control. And it was well-known to the Edenians how humans enjoyed their false status of power.

The dwarf knew Lucifer was standing outside and hurried the sale along, then jogged to the front door and opened it. "My friend, come in," the clerk said with a smile.

"Good afternoon, Andvari," Lucifer said and walked inside the shop.

Andvari locked up his shop after making sure his store had no more customers. The short man flipped the sign to **Closed** and then rushed to a door in the back, unlocking it.

"Drink?" Andvari asked.

"We can drink," Lucifer replied and stepped through the doorway as Andvari rushed to his kitchen.

"So, any news?" Andvari asked his old friend. "Did you find her?"

A sheen of anticipation formed above Andvari's brow and sweat trickled down his light brown skin. He rushed back with a pint of beer and a glass of rum.

"We have located her." Lucifer took the rum from Andvari.

"Tell me about her," Andvari said and placed down his mug.

"She looks like her and sounds like her, but she does not act like her."

Lucifer said. "Cain is convinced she is Syn's reincarnation, but I am not as certain as him. The woman seems... ethical. Syn is not."

"True. Syn's a monster, like Cain." Andvari nodded.

"I would not call them monsters. Syn and Cain are both lore. And lores are a war-driven species," Lucifer explained to Andvari.

Andvari nodded in agreement, and then he leaned his bearded chin of gray on the back of intertwined fingers. His bright blue eyes twinkled as he fought the urge to gulp down his beer. Lucifer stopped speaking as he noticed the situation. "My friend, drink as much as you want," he then said.

"Ah, thank you." Andvari brought the mug to his lips and drank with sheer enjoyment.

The room the two old friends sat in was Andvari's small abode. A short bed, big enough for Andvari's dwarfish frame, and a wooden lamp were placed on the left side of the entrance facing in. Directly across from the entrance was a simple bathroom equipped with a shower, toilet, and sink. On the right side of the entrance was the kitchen and dining area, where the two sat at a round table made from willow. A hard wooden counter was covered in spoons, bowls, and mugs, and empty beer barrels were shoved in the back corner. In between the full barrel of beer and the empty barrels stood a cauldron on top of an electric stove and a cabinet stock full of bottles of various alcohols.

Andvari walked up to a barrel placed on a crate to refill his drink. "You want some? I know you prefer rum, but this batch turned out fantastic."

"Why not?" Lucifer replied and leaned back on the wicker chair, weaving his hands behind his head. "Let us enjoy your creations, Andvari."

In a pit of delight, Andvari grabbed another mug from the counter and filled both up from the tap at the bottom of the barrel. The sweet aromas of barley and hops filled the room.

Handing Lucifer one, Andvari could not help but grin widely.

"What is it?" Lucifer asked, staring into the dwarf's eyes inquisitively. "Say what is on your mind."

"It's nothing," Andvari said anxiously. "Well, ok. It's just that I have been waiting for a long time for a royal to drink my brew."

"We have tasted your alcohol before, back on Eden," Lucifer said.

"Yes, but not *my* brew," Andvari said. "I was never allowed to make the brew. I was always the toolmaker, the miner."

He narrowed his eyes and stared at his mug.

"I see," the royal angelic said and tasted the beer.

Andvari waited in anticipation while Lucifer drank half of his own mug. "So?" he asked. "How is it? Close to my brewmaster's?"

"Mm." Lucifer finished his cup. "Better."

"Blasphemy!" Andvari hissed. "Brewmaster Lastier made the best throughout Eden."

A bit mad and a tad pleased, he went to get a refill for them both.

"Seriously, Andvari—it is the best beer I have tasted," Lucifer assured him and brought out a small box from the inner pocket of his coat. "However, we must get down to business. We can reminisce another day."

After placing the mugs on the table, Andvari walked briskly to get something from under his bed. "Here it is." He rushed back to the table, waving a sharp knife capable of piercing angelic flesh in the air.

Lucifer opened the box he had brought out. Andvari looked into the box, and his eyes reflected the light of a gem within a black cloth.

"Is that what I think it is? A Gem of Reveal from Eden? I would love to add that to my collection. Wait..." The light in Andvari's eyes dimmed. "Is that what you want me to seal into your throat? Do I have to?"

"Yes. It must saturate in living angelic blood." Lucifer studied Andvari. "I designed it that way to prevent non-angelics from using our gems."

"Okay, okay, but once you use the gem, it shatters," Andvari protested.

Lucifer removed the golden gem from the cloth. "It is the only way I can know for certain this woman is Syn. Cain needs her back early, since his fragment died prematurely, or the data may be lost."

"Data... who cares?" Andvari asked.

"This data is important for improving the Fires of Rebirth," Lucifer said. "With this data, souls trapped in this cosmos can be reborn."

"I don't want to be reborn," Andvari spat.

"Easy for you to say." Lucifer raised an eyebrow. "Dwarves cannot die."

"We can die, just not of old age," Andvari said. "And you're one to speak. You royals are immortal, like the Kanarians. You guys are practically gods. That's probably why Nao despises you."

"We are not gods. We cannot do what the Kanarians can—even our skin changes on different planets, like mortals. The gods look the same no matter where they travel."

Andvari raised his brow to Lucifer. "True. I think I preferred it when you looked like a Citrine gem. Your eyes used to look like honey back on Eden, and now they're like soulless coins!"

The dwarf broke out into a light laugh. He had always adored Lucifer's yellow skin—it reminded him of the gems he used to mine back in the caves. Andvari wiped his eyes from laughing, then halted his giggles once he noticed Lucifer was becoming upset.

"My flesh came from the golden sands of Eden. Only on the hottest days would my skin look like a *'Citrine gem.'*" Lucifer twitched his eye. "My skin was normally a pale yellow."

"Sorry—sorry. I forgot how much pride you have for being from the Lucael Desert," Andvari said, not wanting to anger his friend. "But just because your skin changes in different galaxies doesn't take away from you being the same as a god."

"We are immortal because Eden bore us from its holy objects," Lucifer said. "And for the many souls who have brief lives and fall victim to an eternal confusion among the stars, rebirth would be a gift," Lucifer explained.

"Isn't that why Cain built Limbo, though? All the dead go to his planet anyway," Andvari said.

"Many do, but most do not," Lucifer said. "Aaeon takes most of the souls to his realm to play, and then he sends them back to their world."

Andvari shuddered. "That guy gives me the creeps. Promise me that when I die, Cain will grab me before that creep gets me. I don't want to spend eternity being tortured." He grimaced. "Better yet, leave me be. I don't mind flying around space. Maybe I'll become a star."

"That is until you get destroyed by a black hole or mangled in a wormhole," Lucifer said to the dwarf.

"I'd rather cease to exist than be tortured by the Shadow King for eternity." Andvari shrugged.

"It is not for eternity. Aaeon keeps souls in his world until he gets bored with them," Lucifer said, defending the lone god of the shadows. "It is not his fault. He thinks he is playing with them."

"You've always been keen on that god, and here I thought you hated the gods." Andvari eyed him.

"I detest *our* gods, but Aaeon is not from our realm," Lucifer said, and his stare became darker.

Andvari brushed off the dark glare. "Well, I don't care where that guy is from. I don't like him or his chains."

"Aaeon is honorable," Lucifer said.

Andvari stared up at the angelic in disbelief. "'Honorable?' *How?!*"

"Aaeon only drags corrupted souls to his realm—souls that do not learn from their mistakes. He is simply doing what Chaos designed him to do." Lucifer nodded at his own words. "While he thinks he is playing with them, he is actually teaching them."

"Must be nice to know the first god will never torture you." Andvari pointed at him.

"I would not say 'never.'" Lucifer folded his arms across his chest. "Aaeon has his tantrums, and I have broken many promises."

Andvari studied Lucifer's chuckling face. "You're severely messed-up," he muttered. He collapsed in defeat in the chair, placing his head on the table. Twirling the knife he had grabbed, he sighed. "You guys are planning on restoring Ezra, too, right?"

"Yes. If this test proves a success, we can use the fires to reconnect Ezra's spirit fragments. We need to restore Ezra, or our entire realm will collapse due to Nao's idiocy," Lucifer replied. "When Ezra rises, he will more than likely want to restore Eden back to its original form. The Restoration Society has already captured eight fragments."

"Good for them." Andvari mocked the society, which was run by the seven fallen angelics and the Cult of Ezra. "Restoring Eden... that means Earth will be destroyed."

"Most likely," Lucifer replied.

"I will probably never find a wife and start a family while the planet is still Earth," Andvari mumbled.

"Probably not," Lucifer said.

"I loved this planet. You're such a killjoy," Andvari grumbled. "Anyone tell you that?"

Lucifer smirked. "I have been told that a time or two."

Andvari stood up and sliced open his friend's throat with the blade. Silver blood trickled down as Lucifer looked unmoved, remaining still. Andvari shoved the gem in between the flaps of flesh and pressed the skin together as fast as he could. The wound sealed, and Lucifer moved the gem beneath his Adam's apple, eyeing the knife Andvari had placed on the table.

Andvari shuddered and went to go wash his hands in the bathroom sink. "You guys always freak me out with your pain tolerance," he said over the running faucet. He snorted, wiping his hands on a towel. "Oh, and—"

Andvari stopped talking when he looked at the table, where no one sat. A note with the words **Thank You, My Friend** had been placed under a mug. The dwarf took a seat in temporary loneliness, but his mood changed when he heard a few knocks on the front door.

As if he had won the lottery, he rushed from his room to unlock the store door, ushering in an elderly couple.

XVIII

ALIEN GODS

KIERAN WAS RUBBING BOTH of his arms as Wren, Esme, and Ray were staring down at him. The three had dragged him from the foyer and to the couch to interrogate him.

"So, this is Kieran?" Ray asked, trying not to be disgusted. "The man who ate his father's corpse?"

Wren nodded, then asked Kieran, "Couldn't you have just knocked? Why'd you break down my door?"

"I didn't. Some guy threw me into your house." Kieran glared up at her.

Wren ventured into his brain, causing him to look insulted when he felt her mind enter his. While his story was true, she could not see who the man was. The mysterious man's face was covered in a twisted web of shadows.

"He looks so innocent." Esme was eyeing Kieran up and down, prying Wren away from her investigation. "How can someone who looks like this be a cannibal?"

"The same could be said for anyone, really." Ray shrugged. "Never judge a book by its cover. The book may eat you."

"Ok, guys. Let him breathe," Wren told her two friends. "He literally ran all the way here."

"You guys are weird," Kieran stated, taking in Esme's obsession with him.

"No weirder than a cannibal who ate his father," Ray remarked.

"He's not a cannibal. I think he's half-Edenian," Wren said.

"The Edenians are extinct. How many times must we go over that?" Ray pried his eyes from Kieran to glance over at Wren. "They have fossils."

Wren felt argumentative. "And how many times must I tell you the fae's clay idol theory is real and surviving Edenians could still be living on Earth? Also, fossils doesn't mean they are extinct."

Ray did not want to participate in one of their ongoing debates.

"I don't care what he is. He's *fascinating*." Esme was sitting next to Kieran, poking his cheek.

"Quit it," Kieran said and grabbed her hand. He looked deep into her eyes. "I've never seen a nymph in person before."

Esme looked surprised. "How did you know that I'm a nymph? Most people think I'm human."

"Nymphs have a certain glow in their eyes," Kieran told her. "You don't look like a human at all."

Ray swatted Kieran's hand away from Esme's and said, "I thought she was human when I first met her."

"And I should care why?" Kieran asked Ray, then shifted his attention to Wren. "I have questions."

Kieran hesitated, eyeing both Ray and Esme.

"Guys, can you give us a minute?" Wren asked. "Why don't you go on ahead to the dinner? I'll be there later."

Ray glanced down at his watch. "It's only a little after four."

"I don't know. Figure it out. I want to be alone with Kieran," Wren told them.

Ray and Esme knew Wren and Kieran had things to discuss—things that did not concern either of them. Ray moved his head for Esme to follow him toward the foyer. "Let's go help Bernie and Bettie with the kids," he said to Esme while they walked under the archway and away from the living room. He then looked down at her formal white dress. "Aren't you changing into something more casual? Wasn't that outfit like fifty grand?"

"I want to wear it to dinner. And it was only thirty thousand dollars," Esme said and looked down at her gown, smiling at the glitter scattered over the fabric while Ray mouthed "*Only*."

Esme weaved her arm through Ray's, and they walked over the scattered pieces of wood that were once the front door.

"Let's walk," Ray said. "I don't want your dress to get ruined on my bike. Or we could take one of Wren's cars—"

"I don't want to walk. I did that this morning, and my feet regret it." Esme walked up to the bike and hiked up her dress. "Let's not disturb Wren and Kieran for car keys." She sat down sideways on the back of the motorcycle. She waited for Ray to get on the bike and said, "I've worn dresses on your bike before, Ray."

"Yeah, but not thirty-thousand-dollar ones!" Ray exclaimed.

"Yes, I have." Esme blinked. "And they're all fine."

"Seriously?" Ray shook his head, then slid in front of her.

Ray and Esme drove off toward the church. When they parked on the side of the road, Esme jumped off and looked back down the slanted road that led to Wren's house a couple of blocks away. "Do you think she'll be okay?" she asked.

"Of course." Ray slid off the bike and stared down the road with Esme. "She can set people on fire."

Inside the walls of the creepy mansion, Wren's black dress circled around her in its lacy way. She clutched a blue-skinned doll with bare hands—she had removed her gloves so she could work on the doll with ease. Strands of doll-making hair and paint were resting on the coffee table. Glancing up from the troll figurine, she eyed Kieran. But he seemed to have forgotten how to talk after Esme and Ray left them alone.

"My door," Wren said, taking the lead in their conversation. "How will you be paying me? Or would you rather replace it yourself?"

"I didn't break your door. Someone threw me into your house," Kieran said in objection.

"You're still responsible," Wren replied.

"Are you just going to make dolls?" Kieran asked. "That's a weird hobby."

"I'm waiting for you to ask me your questions. It's been a rather long wait." Wren batted her eyes up at him. "It's not a *hobby*. I'm a dollmaker. But you *already* know that. I know you recognized my voice in that jail."

"Ok—yeah—I did. You're the telepathic activist that's always in the news about fae rights," he said. "Your voice is unique. There's sometimes this metal-grinding sound when you talk. Almost broke my Holo-disc—"

"'Metal-grinding?'" Wren interrupted him.

"You know," Kieran said and held up his hands, acting like he was rotating two objects together, "yeek-yeek-yeek."

Wren narrowed her eyes at him. "And then you broke your chain and followed your nose to me like a faithful dog to his owner."

He did not like that analogy.

Wren smirked and returned to working on the doll. Something about her delicate movements while she worked on the doll's hair irked Kieran. Her existence bothered him.

He left his spot on the couch and tried to hit her, planning on catching her off-guard. But his punch was blocked by a shield, causing him to look surprised. He then threw more punches the dollmaker's way, but they were all reflected. "You're not human, are you?" he asked. "What are you? Fae?"

Wren picked up the comb to brush the hair she had just placed into the head of the doll. "I see the questions have begun."

"*What* are you?" Kieran repeated the question. "And why were you spying on me in jail?"

"I didn't mean for you to hear me," Wren said sternly and placed the comb down. "Sorry about that."

Kieran was hunched over her like a deranged animal.

"Oh, my," Wren whispered and glanced up at him, sarcasm radiating off her. "Are you going to kill me? From what I've seen, you have a knack for killing."

Kieran brushed off her remark.

Wren picked up a thin black brush and painted around the remaining bare eye of the doll with a swift movement, then placed the ceramic doll on the marble table in front of her to dry. "You *really* think I have the answers you seek?"

"You know *something*," Kieran hissed. He sat down next to her on the rug and threw the pamphlet of the city next to the doll that stood on her coffee table. "You can read minds and live with the fae. You *must* know something."

"Don't get me wrong—I'm happy to finally meet you, but I don't have the answers you're looking for. In fact, I was hoping you would have the answers *I* need. But from the sounds of it, you're clueless." Wren ignored his insulted reaction. "I can only guess what you are. I don't have your mother's memories."

"What do you mean by that?" Kieran asked. "Why would you even have my mom's memories?"

Wren looked at him for a moment and then asked, "You're a bit slow, aren't you? You said it yourself: I can read minds."

He frowned. "Yeah, but you never met my mom… So, how would you know to enter her mind?"

"I never met you before and can read your mind—ever since you were six, when you became addicted to my mother's book. But your mother was one I could never read," Wren said, noticing his shocked face.

"You've been reading my mind since I was six?" Kieran looked alarmed and a bit intrigued. "Do you see images or hear words? How do you translate my thoughts?"

"I hear them as you think them," Wren said.

"So, what do you know about me?" Kieran asked, fearing what she knew. He was not the most ethical person around.

"A lot." Wren twisted her mouth into a half-grin at his reddening face. "Don't worry. You can't help it—you aren't even fully human."

Kieran widened his eyes. "I'm not '*fully human*?' What the hell does that mean?" Before Wren could reply, he released a frustrated growl and rubbed his hair with both of his hands. He picked up the pamphlet and opened it. He turned it around to show her the middle section and pointed at a picture of her house under the headline: **Sparrow Manor Massacre: The Tragic Beginning Of The Fae Movement**. "You are a survivor of *this* and can read minds." He widened his eyes. "I *know* you can figure out what I am. Will you? I don't want to turn into a monster."

"Too late for that," Wren replied dryly as she stared at the picture of Sparrow Manor on the pamphlet. "That's an old picture. The willows were not even planted yet."

Kieran stared at her, wildness in his eyes. She was annoying him again. The side of Wren's lips turned up a tad, and she manifested her shield, sending it his way and knocking him back a few inches. He shook his head, regaining his sense of reality, and then side-eyed her.

"You do *not* intimidate me," Wren hissed, red flames exiting her pores.

"Well, aren't you just a goddamn freak," Kieran muttered, examining the small flames on her skin.

Wren pulled the fire back to her core and looked unapologetic about her attack as she straightened out her dress.

Kieran was at a loss for words and remained glued to the rug. "What the hell is going on?" He hissed out the words, frustrated, and slammed his forehead to her coffee table, exhausted. "*What* am I? And *what* are you?"

"I don't know what I am. As for you, my guess is that you're half-human and half-Edenian—possibly giant. You have inhuman strength, and you crave the meat of human beings. The giants were carnivorous, cannibalistic, and insanely strong. You have a magical aura, like the fae, but your aura differs from theirs," Wren said. "Eden was full of magic. A magic I think you possess. Plus, you don't *smell* human."

"What do humans smell like?" Kieran asked with raised eyebrows, his irritation with her subsiding.

"It's a weird mix of bakery and rot," Wren replied, sniffing her arm.

"Well, my dad wasn't my real dad," Kieran said with a shrug, humoring the idea he was not completely human. "But the Edenians are all extinct, so I can't be half-Edenian. They have a museum full of Edenian fossils in Birdsong."

"You know that having fossils and being extinct are not the same thing, right?" Wren asked him slowly. "I swear, you and Ray..."

As Kieran complained that the public were not allowed to visit the island, Wren became tired of his verbiage. "Birdsong Island is where the fae's government resides. It's natural for people to be prohibited," she told him, prying him from his dialogue with himself. "You must be part of the Mage's Guild or a fae scholar to come and go from the island."

"I know that." Kieran huffed. "Everyone knows that. It's just not fair."

"Life's not fair." Wren grinned at his wounded ego. To rub salt in his wound, she leaned toward him and said, "I've been."

"I thought not just anyone could go?" Kieran asked.

Wren laughed as his face filled with envy. "Don't feel too bummed. If I am right and you are half-Edenian, you will be allowed to go to the island," she said. "Shit, they may ask you to live there."

"Why were you allowed to go?" Kieran asked. "You're a mage, aren't you? That would explain your powers."

"I'm not a mage." Wren hesitated, then said, "My aunt and Rose took me to Birdsong when I was five to be evaluated by the mages."

It was not enough to satisfy Kieran's need to know more.

"My aunt wanted the mages to analyze my energy because things started to vibrate around me when I was in kindergarten. Tallahassee didn't have a guild yet." Wren leaned over the coffee table and placed her chin in her hand. "Since my parents tried to negotiate the first peace treaty with the fae, the Council liked them. And since my aunt is my mom's sister, they've grown to like her. So, the Council agreed to let us visit for a week."

She ended her explanation as if that were all.

"Yeah, that brochure has all your family information in it, like you're the goddamn main attraction." Kieran eyed the city brochure he had tossed on the coffee table. "So, what did they diagnose you as?" he asked. "Freak?"

"They couldn't figure me out." Wren sighed, ignoring his joke. "And my family is in there because the mayor wants us to be featured." She manifested fire in her eyes, spooking Kieran. "Zara thinks that if they mention my family in the city's brochure, along with the Mage's Guild, then it will prevent the rebels from coming here."

"Does it work?" Kieran asked.

"No, but it reduces the numbers," Wren said. "Mostly because of Vaan."

"Who's Vaan?" Kieran asked.

"He's with the Mage's Guild," Wren replied. "He followed us back from Birdsong. You can say he became obsessed with my aunt, but he doesn't ever talk about the island."

"So, is he fae?" Kieran asked.

"Something like that," she grumbled.

Enduring a melancholic youth, Wren had found comfort in the oddest of places: Kieran's mind. And within the walls of Sparrow Manor, Kieran was beginning to feel like he had found a place he belonged.

Wren turned the turntable near the elevator on, and a dark melody danced through the living room. She walked away from the spinning disc and sat down on the loveseat. She moved her eyes up to the antique clock on the wall—five. As much as she liked speaking to the monster she had wanted to befriend in her youth, she had to get ready for dinner.

Kieran stared at the silver-framed paintings hanging on the walls, and after he approached one behind the couch, he said, "This is... interesting."

The painting that had his head tilted in confusion was a painting of a man with huge white wings. His eyes were bright copper, and his hair was white as snow. He was holding a decapitated head in one hand and a gemstone in the other.

"What's this supposed to be?" he asked, unable to pry his eyes from the severed head.

Wren glanced over at him and looked at the painting he was fixated on. "Lucien. He's the first of the demonics." She stared at the painting. "He saved me and Esme when we were kids, or at least we think it was him," she said, shrugging.

"Saved you? Why?" Kieran looked back at her.

"I don't know. I really don't want to talk about that. It's why I'm in therapy. It was during the shooting..." Wren smiled forcefully, staring at the painting of the man with white hair.

Kieran nodded, noticing her discomfort. "Well, what are demonics? I've never heard of them."

"The demonics are the one hundred replicas of a Kanarian god, born from the fury of a god who was split apart," she replied.

"Gods aren't real." He placed his hands on his hips.

A man so against all man-made religions, Kieran would automatically shut down at the mention of any god.

"What do you think Isis is?" Wren asked him, snickering.

"Yeah, but..." Kieran looked baffled.

Wren stared at him, entertained by the look on his face. Confusion left his eyes, and horror seeped in. Then, she sympathized with him, after taking in his onslaught of despair. He did not like the idea of any form of a god being real.

She pointed at a thick silver tome on one of her bookshelves. "That book was written by a mage, and they wrote about the gods. But the mage never mentioned their name, so we don't know the writer's true identity."

Kieran followed Wren's finger and stared at the book bound in silver.

Everyone knew the mages were strict about recording the truth as they discovered it, for the mages were the most advanced physicists on Earth. There was no room for fiction in their world.

Even though the human science community had made magic part of the physical sciences, and it was being taught in public universities, the mages were still popularized as being magical in the sense of old-school fantasy characters. Late night shows and movies produced by humans who aligned themselves with the anti-fae would often have a mage from the guild be depicted as a wizard or a witch, or a demon's spawn, rather than someone grounded in science.

"The author is known as the First Mage—I'm sure you've heard of them. They created the Mage's Guild. It's mentioned in the book that Earth was nothing like Eden, which is why I believe the First Mage had lived on Eden. I think the mage is the same Edenian who created the clay idols."

"The Edenians died in the explosion. Evolution created the katani, just like the zyula," Kieran said, correcting her.

Wren ignored his argument. "The First Mage explained how there are advanced lifeforms in the Kanaria Galaxy and that the Angelic Empire would always visit a planet named Kanar." She paused. "You know who the angelics were, *right*?"

Kieran grimaced; her tone was belittling. "Everyone does. They were the dominant species on Eden and Isis' favorite type of fossil. But what's the Kanaria Galaxy, and why haven't I heard of it?" Kieran asked. "Why do you even have a mage's book, and how do you know if the author was a mage? Plus, Isis has said many times that the clay idols are just a fae myth."

"Isis loves to fib to calm her critics—she doesn't like drama. She talks about the idols at Science Now conventions all the time, but they are a fae network," Wren explained.

"I *like* Science Now," Kieran whispered to himself and then eyed Wren. "But the clay idols are a bit of a stretch, don't you think?"

Wren stared at him and said, "Kieran, we live in a *very stretchy* era."

She turned to look at the bookshelf where the silver book rested, clouded by magic. "To fix your doubt about the book being written by a mage, all you have to do is stare at it for a bit—you can feel the magnetic pull." She watched Kieran stare at the book on the shelf. He became alarmed at the vibrations he felt. "I found it upstairs when I moved back in. I think a scholar from Moonlight Hills brought it during the gala—only a scholar would have this book. There were many tabs on pages that talked about Kanar. So, I think they were researching the Kanarians."

Wren sunk back into the loveseat and glanced at the book the mage had written. Kieran knew what gala she was referring to. That night was all over the sky when he was five.

"I'm pretty sure it belongs to Birdsong's Primordial Library. I haven't contacted them because I want to finish reading it," Wren said. "The First Mage described Kanaria as a galaxy of bigger planets and brighter stars."

"Again, why haven't I heard of Kanaria?" Kieran asked.

Kieran was a man who prided himself on being an amateur ufologist. He used to spend hours watching the sky to observe the stars, and Johnny had often watched him geek out over a new alien conspiracy theory.

"Isis doesn't think humans are ready to know about the gods," Wren said. "When the fae came out, humans freaked out, and the anti-fae have been trying to start a civil war for decades. Humans are creatures of habit, and they don't do well with change."

Kieran liked Isis and the fae, so he did not want to mock them. "Ok... *if* these Kanarians are real, maybe they're just aliens playing god?"

"Savion Croix said it best: 'All gods are aliens, but not all aliens are gods.'" Wren recited the quote from a scholar of Birdsong, who was famous among the fae for his Kanarian research, to Kieran. "The Kanarians would be both alien and god."

"I don't know who that is, but if we're doing quotes..." Kieran straightened his posture. "'The very nature of reality is a confusing wad of crap,'" he said in a bad English accent, and he raised his hand to his chin and started stroking an invisible beard. "'All of this is merely an illusion. The gods are not real. We are not real.'" He bowed. "Said by *me*."

Wren sent a force field to shake Kieran out of his comical state. "Was that real enough for you?" she asked as he sidestepped to regain his balance.

"Say I'm coming to terms with the Kanarians... Did a Kanarian bring Isis back from the dead?" he asked.

"No—the Kanaria Galaxy is part of our realm. A god from another realm resurrected her. At least, that's what the fae claim, but the only fae that know who really resurrected her are the ones that live in Birdsong. And they like to keep their secrets. Isis won't tell me either. She thinks my 'human brain' can't handle it." Wren moved her eyes from Kieran. "Sometimes, it's hard to believe she's no longer human. You should see her love for strawberry frappés."

Kieran watched Wren laugh. "Oh, there's something I've always been curious about."

"Yeah?" Wren asked.

"Why did Isis single you out?" he asked. "I mean—why did she lead the fae to your house back then?"

"Something to do with an old wives' tale," Wren replied.

Kieran waited for her to continue talking.

"What?" Wren asked.

"Go on," Kieran said. "Don't leave me hanging."

"Oh, it's boring." Wren waved her hand, trying to change the topic.

"Tell me," Kieran insisted. What could be worse than gods being real?

"According to the mages, the Spirit has been reborn." Wren drifted her eyes to look up at the ceiling.

"And who is the Spirit?" Kieran asked her.

"Some ghost that lived in Pangaea," Wren answered. "The Spirit is infamous among the fae because she killed everyone who was a threat to the katani." She looked around the living room and nodded at another painting of a full moon with beasts and people dancing around a fire. "She also protected the zyula. It is said that the Spirit even raced with them during their full moon rituals in the woods."

"'Full moon rituals?'" Kieran asked.

"You've heard the fae's notorious children's rhyme, right? I mean, it's everywhere. The human world stole it. 'Blood and bones. Beast and drool. The Tyrant Lord is dead. The Tyrant Lord is dead,'" Wren said in a rush. "It's about how the zyula and katani teamed up to overthrow Lucien, who was committing genocide on the katani. The katani could drain all the blood of someone in under five seconds, and the zyula could morph into giant dire wolves. They would perform rituals under a full moon because the zyula's strength was stronger when the moon was full."

Kieran glanced over at the new painting Wren was staring at. "Huh. Didn't think the meaning was literal... Thought it was just a kid's rhyme about rioting against the system." He became fascinated by the painting of what looked to be tall beasts and humanoids under the moon. "Sounds like vampires and werewolves. Thought the zyula were more like dinosaurs... Wait, did humans evolve from werewolves? And the fae from vampires?"

Wren stared at Kieran in amusement and said, "Please don't walk up to a katani and call them a vampire. They don't even have fangs."

"Aren't they both extinct?" Kieran asked.

"The zyula are, but there are still a few katani alive—they live in Birdsong," Wren said. "Trust me. You don't want to be one of their victims."

"*Annnnd* you sound like you know a katani." Kieran's eyes widened in astonishment.

"Maybe," Wren said with dilated pupils, smoke escaping her nostrils.

"You're not going to say who it is, are you?" Kieran asked.

"Nope." Wren shook her head.

"If you're the Spirit, then that means you're an old hag," Kieran told her. He was upset that she would not tell him who the katani was. "Like *oooold*. As in Pangaea-old."

"Stop drawing out *old*." Wren scrunched her brow.

"So, are you her? And do you—"

Kieran was going to ask her if she remembered anything from Pangaea, but he noticed her embarrassment, so he stopped speaking mid-question. He turned around and folded his arms, moving his attention back to the painting of Lucien.

"I'm not the Spirit." Wren rubbed her forehead. "I'm just strange."

Kieran peered back at her slowly. "I know how you feel."

For a moment, silence befell the room, and the two shared a likeness of being abnormal.

"Does your family know?" Kieran asked. "About the mages thinking you're the Spirit?"

"Yes," Wren said in a depressed tone.

"You're not going to elaborate, are you?" he asked.

"No," she replied.

Kieran pointed at her with a spark in his eye. "Well, I think it's cool as fuck that you may have run with the katani and zyula. How badass is that for a past life? I mean, I was probably just a blob somewhere."

Wren looked up at him. She was digging her back into the loveseat, trying to vanish. His goofy grin seemed to be the cure she needed for her anxiety to go away. She nodded at him and said, "I never saw it that way."

"Well, you need to." Kieran placed his hands on his hips. "What's the worst that will happen if you're her? You become the Spirit? You were fine before, and you'll be fine again."

Wren spread her lips into a smile. "Yeah, who cares if I blew up a planet?"

"That's the spirit—" Kieran halted his cheerfulness. "Wait, what?"

XIX

IDENTITY CRISIS

KIERAN'S WIDE STARE MADE every inch of Wren's skin itch, as she tried to keep her fire inside. Her anxiety was returning, but he flashed an understanding smile and asked, "'Blew up a planet?'"

"I don't know much," Wren said, awkwardly. "According to the scholars of Birdsong, the Spirit caused the explosion that blew up Eden."

"Does that mean the Spirit was an Edenian?" Kieran asked.

"No one knows," Wren said. "She could have been."

"Just how old are you?" Kieran asked her.

"Stop saying I'm her," Wren snapped. She exhaled slowly, calming down. "She may have blown up Eden, but she wasn't all bad." She nodded toward the painting of Lucien. "When our ancestors lived in Pangaea, the Spirit stood united with the katani and zyula, and they overthrew Lucien, the demonic king known for his tyranny."

"Did she replace him?" Kieran asked her. "As king or whatever?"

"No." Wren shook her head.

"Then who did?" Kieran raised his eyebrows.

"A man named Cain," Wren replied. "Cain lived on the land outside of Lucien's castle and had joined their revolt. He killed Lucien, and the crown went to Cain. Or so the research into the Tyrant Lord claims."

"Where can I learn about this Tyrant Lord?" Kieran asked.

"The First Mage wrote about him in the book," Wren said.

"I'm not a fan of reading..."

"Well, the mages supposedly have a room that can replicate timestamps of the past. I'm sure you can watch memories of him there." Wren shrugged. "But I don't know how accurate that room is."

"How do I get to the room?" he asked.

"You can't. It's in Birdsong." After noticing Kieran's dampened mood, she added, "Maybe one day, the island will be open to the public."

Kieran stared at Lucien's coppery eyes and drifted his eyes down to the head the demonic was holding. He did not even want to ask whose head it was. He glanced at the gem Lucien held, and he decided it was best not to ask about the stone either, but Wren heard his confusion.

"I don't know what either is." She shifted her position on the loveseat. "I dreamed it when I was young, and Esme painted it."

Kieran stared at the painting in awe. "Your sister *painted* this?"

"Yep." Wren looked around the room at the paintings on the wall. "She painted all of them. I would tell her my dreams, and she would paint."

Wren chuckled at a small painting of a tree hanging on the wall that connected to the foyer. "Well, I painted that one." She pointed at the painting, proud of her tiny tree.

Kieran twisted his lips up into a goofy grin and said, "I can tell."

Wren shot her eyes at him. "Do you always have to make jokes?"

Kieran shrugged—a conflicted man.

Wren scooted on the loveseat, moving closer to where Kieran stood. She rolled on to her knees and placed her hands on the armrest. "I'll hide you from the FBI if you help me research into the Kanarians. I could use the help from an Edenian."

"I'm not an Edenian," Kieran said. "*You* are."

Wren fumed at his comeback. "My bad. *Half*-Edenian," she said, and batted her eyes at him.

Kieran glared down at her.

The two had each met their match.

"You know Isis. She would be more helpful than me. She has shuttles on several planets," Kieran said, crossing his arms.

"She says she's too busy, but I think she's scared," Wren said.

"Why?" Kieran asked. "She's a '*god*,' so I would imagine she'd want to."

Wren shrugged. "Think she's afraid of what she may find."

"So, Isis led the fae to your house because the mages think you're the reincarnation of the Spirit... Well, what does Isis think about you being the Spirit?" Kieran asked.

"She's my biggest supporter. The Council, not so much." Wren shrugged. "But the mages go back-and-forth on it. Talk about a mess—the Mage's Guild is all over the place."

Kieran grinned. "If Isis thinks that, then bitch, you're the Spirit."

"Isis thinks a lot of things. It doesn't mean she's right," Wren said. "Remember, I've been evaluated by the island. I'm just an anomaly. My energy is irregular—that's all."

"You just said the guild is a mess." Kieran raised an eyebrow.

"*Touché*," she muttered.

Wren became irritated with Kieran's smug smile and eyed the clock on the wall—five-thirty. "I need to get ready for dinner," she said. "But I want to show you the book first." She stood up and walked toward the bookshelf that held the book the mage had written. She picked up the silver tome, which looked like an ancient textbook. **Angelic Diaries** was carved into its cover. "This is long, but you will want to read the passage on Edenians to figure out what you are."

"I already told you—I'm *not* an Edenian." Kieran eyed the book and followed her into the hall behind the couch. "There's only one Edenian in this house, and it's not me."

Wren ignored his attitude.

They headed down the hallway and toward the front of the house, while

Kieran gazed all around him at the odd décor. Wren stopped at the tall oak kitchen door near the front of the house. She peered off to her right and stared down the continuous hall that led back into the foyer for a moment. The shattered front door aggravated her. Thankfully, it was winter, which meant mosquitos would not be flying in.

"I dig your wraparound hallway," Kieran said with a nod of confirmation as he looked around the wide hall. He then stared at a statue with dark gray eyes. "This guy looks like it ate many souls."

Wren pried her eyes from the foyer and looked back at Kieran, who was poking the eyes of the lion-like gargoyle. He walked around the statue and started poking the eyes of each of the four heads that emerged from the same body. "I wouldn't do that if I were you. They remember faces," she said as she opened the kitchen door.

Kieran stopped looking at the statue with a head facing each nautical direction and stood up straight, startled. "What's that supposed to mean?" he asked, walking away from the gargoyle and toward Wren, who held the kitchen door open for him. "You're joking, right? It's not alive, is it?"

She answered, "Maybe they are. Maybe they aren't."

"I take that as a yes," Kieran mumbled and walked into the kitchen.

He stopped walking as soon as he crossed the doorway's threshold and looked around the room. Straight across from where he stood was the kitchen bar, and to his left was the kitchen. To his right was the dining area, which Wren was walking toward. He watched her walk between the two pillars that formed an entryway in the middle of the white Victorian half-wall, separating the dining room from the kitchen. After she placed the book on the antique stone dining table, she walked into the kitchen to grab a glass and a bottle of red wine.

Kieran resumed walking into the dining room once he spotted a small statue of three women with wings. "Do those fairies come alive?" He pointed at the tiny statue of three fairies dancing upon the flat surface of the half-wall. "Or is it just a statue?"

"Poke one and see," Wren said.

Kieran walked up to the table and stared down at the *Angelic Diaries*. He pulled out one of the eight chairs nearest the book and sat down on the stone seat, which had a velvety blue cushion, modernized to comfort the person sitting on it.

Wren walked back to the table and placed the glass in front of him. She stayed standing and poured him a glass of wine. "Well, thank you," Kieran said in a more upbeat tone.

"I can't stay but help yourself to as much wine as you want. I know you need it." She brought the bottle to her lips to take a swig of wine and then released a sigh of relief.

Kieran took a sip of his own wine. "I'm still not reading the book—not even a page."

"After a few glasses, I'm sure you will. You're curious by nature." Wren grinned down at him. "The part about Edenians isn't long. It's about twenty-five pages. You can skim it."

"That's too long. I dropped out of high school for a reason. I don't like reading," Kieran said. He chugged his glass and reached for the wine bottle Wren was holding.

Wren played hostess and poured more wine in his glass. As his glass was being filled, Kieran eyed a picture hanging on the wall. It was a selfie of Wren, Ray, and Esme on a magnoyacht—a nature-friendly yacht without propellers or gas emissions that used magic-infused magnets to move, called magnetic weaving. With scuba gear on, Wren was the only one soaked and was smiling widely. Ray looked concerned, and Esme looked like she was about to freak out.

Wren noticed the picture Kieran was staring at and said, "We were sailing my magnoyacht to Puerto Rico. I saw a shark and jumped into the water. I wanted to take a picture to mark the occasion after. Ray and Esme were *not* pleased." She began laughing at the memory of Ray yelling at her for being reckless after she swam with a school of great white sharks.

"Of course you own a magnoyacht... Wait, sharks?" Kieran had a fear of sea creatures—mainly sharks. "You swam with goddamn sharks?"

"Yes," Wren replied as if it were a common thing to do, then placed the wine bottle next to Kieran's glass. "I guess you can call it a hobby."

"Have any attacked you?" he asked, completely disregarding the book Wren wanted to show him.

"No," Wren replied.

"Ah, because you do your telepathy on them," Kieran remarked. "They probably know you're like an old hag from Eden."

"No," Wren said firmly, narrowing her eyes. "Sharks understand body language. If you know their language, you're normally fine."

"Tell that to the victims in the movie *Jaws*." Kieran leaned back in his chair, folded his fingers behind his head, and said casually, "You're probably going to die by being eaten by a shark. Then, you'll be the Spirit again."

"One, that's a *very* old movie, and two, no, I will not," Wren replied, peeved at him messing with her.

"Right, your shield thing," Kieran said, looking around the dining room, grinning from her growing irritation toward him. "*Jaws* isn't old. It came out a few years ago."

"That. Was. A. Remake." Wren's anger was rising.

"No. It. Wasn't." Kieran argued, using her own diction.

"Kieran, *Jaws* came out in 1975. That's why the newest one is called *Jaws: 1975*!" Wren yelled at him. "It was to celebrate the *Jaws* franchise—"

Wren grew silent when she noticed Kieran was laughing at her. She realized the mutt was messing with her and leaned over the table, glaring down at the book. Tiny flames surfaced on both of her temples, and her eyes turned a lighter blue.

Kieran straightened his back in the chair and leaned forward, staring at the text to his left. "Put your damn fire away." He looked up at her and waved his hands over her black dress. "Johnny would have loved your dress," he said, trying to pacify her. "Not my thing, but he loved lace."

"Thank you," Wren said slowly in case his brain had short-circuited. She noticed a spark from her fire had made its way to Kieran's hair and burned the tip of a strand. She pinched off the burned end and said, "Sorry, I can get hot-tempered."

Kieran suppressed a laugh at the unintended pun she had made.

"Look, the fact you aren't trying to kill me makes me happy. But I really need to go—"

"Why would I kill you?" Kieran interrupted her.

Wren froze, afraid she had given him an idea.

"You're scared of me, aren't you?" Kieran picked up his glass of wine and took a sip.

Wren scoffed. "Kieran, a fly isn't even scared of you."

"You act like I didn't just burn down a town," he said.

Wren tilted her head down at him and released a wide and creepy grin with fire radiating from her eyes. "You forget I may have blown up Eden."

Kieran placed his wineglass down on the table and said in a very poor accent, "You win. You are the scariest of the land." He was not born to be a voice actor, despite how hard he tried.

"What are you trying to sound like?" Wren asked him.

"English..." Kieran looked confused. "Johnny loved my accent."

"No, Johnny loved *you*. Your accent is horrible." Wren walked away from the table and toward the door that led into the hallway. "I need to get changed. Bernie will have a hissy fit if I show up in black."

Kieran stood up and followed her from the kitchen. "I'm not staying. I want to go with you. Hey, I'm talking to you!"

Wren barely made it to the archway that led into the foyer before Kieran yanked on her arm. "Sorry, mutt, but you can't leave." She spun around to face him. "Frost is stalking around."

"That FBI agent? Doubt he's going to arrest me. He actually seemed happy that I burned Perk down," Kieran told her and then squinted. "Don't call me mutt."

"He may not, but Daniels will." Wren ignored his opposition to being called mutt and tapped a finger on her temple. "I heard it from Frost's partner. She's pretty easy to read."

The two stared at each other, at an impasse. Wren turned away from Kieran and ran off toward her bedroom on the other side of the foyer.

"Well, I guess I'll just stay here in *your* house. Me, a stranger who eats people!" he called out, trying to get a rise out of her, wanting her to skip dinner and talk to him more about Eden and Kanaria.

"Please don't eat people while I'm gone!" Wren yelled from her bedroom, changing into a light-yellow sundress.

Kieran walked through the foyer and looked over the stone statues and tall candelabras that decorated the large entrance. He then walked under the archway and toward Wren's bedroom. Before he reached her bedroom door along the left wall, she rushed out and almost crashed into him.

"You trust me to stay in your house alone?" he asked as she sped past him.

"You're not alone. I have house guardians." Wren paused and looked back at him. "So don't try anything. You'll regret it." She resumed walking into the foyer. "Be back in a couple of hours."

"It's the gargoyle, isn't it?" Kieran yelled after her as she walked away from the house and toward the wide-open gate.

Wren stopped walking to examine the broken lock on the open gate, then ran off down the street, not having time to look at it further.

"I guess I can at least fix the lock." Kieran walked out of the house and up to the gateway. He ripped a long rose from a bush and then wrapped the stem around the iron bars of both the broken and immobile gates. "There." He nodded. "At least it's closed."

Kieran walked back into the house, proud of himself for helping a stranger. The gate slowly creaked open, and the flower fell to the sidewalk.

"Way to go, asshat," a voice cursed from somewhere inside the house after Kieran walked into the foyer. "You ruined their roses for no reason."

"What the fuck?" Kieran asked and walked toward the voice. He walked under the right archway and down the hall. He stopped at the kitchen door and looked down the hall to his left. His eyes met the gargoyle's gray ones.

"It's you, isn't it?" He pointed at the stone gargoyle. "You're the one that spoke."

Silence.

"Well, fuck you." Kieran turned from the gargoyle and opened the kitchen door.

He wanted more of the wine and less of the confusion.

"No, fuck you," the voice said.

Kieran stared at the gargoyle. He abandoned his mission of drinking more wine and walked down the hall. He walked around the tall stone statue, observing the faces with different expressions on each side. "Well, aren't you just four shades of ugly..." He poked one eye.

Each of the eight eyes blazed red, making Kieran fall back on his rear. "Who ye callin' ugly, ugly?"

"I knew it!" Kieran widened his eyes at the statue.

"I know what ye are," the gargoyle stated. "I smell ye."

"You can smell?" Kieran asked and stood up. "I knew she was a mage. Mages can turn gargoyles into guardians."

"She's not." The gargoyle's eyes flashed red. "Me lord made me, and I was brought to life. A proper craftsman, me lord was."

"So, you know what I am?" Kieran asked. "Then, what am I?"

The gargoyle grew quiet.

"Well?" Kieran asked.

"A fucktwat," the gargoyle said. "You're a fucking filthy fucktwat. Get out of me house!"

The gargoyle went dormant, and Kieran was left puzzled at the foul-mouthed statue.

"Don't mind Red," another voice said near Kieran's ear. "Ever since the house was attacked, they've been a grouch."

Kieran jumped when one of the tiny fairies sat down on his shoulder. Instinctively, he swatted the fairy from him, sending her to the wall. "What the fuck?!" he exclaimed. "Talking bugs. Great."

"I'm not a bug." The three-inch tall fairy defended herself, rubbing the back of her head from the impact. "I'm a fairy. In fact, you were admiring me and my sisters not too long ago."

"The statue in the kitchen?" Kieran rushed back into the kitchen to see the statue on the half-wall. It was still there.

The fairy flew into the kitchen after him.

"I understand the gargoyle, but the last time I checked, none of the fae turn to stone." Kieran walked toward the cabinet to grab another bottle of wine, for the bottle on the table was empty. "Or can you?"

"We don't turn to stone." The fairy laughed.

She flew to the statue of her dancing with her two sisters. "This statue is a portal to our house in Moonlight Hills," she said and sat on top of her ceramic image. "My name's Twila."

Kieran did not have the time to understand fairy logic. He grabbed a fresh bottle of wine. After he placed it on the counter, he went to go rummage in the refrigerator. In a moment of weakness, he took out the platter of raw meat and drank the blood from it. But there was very little, disappointing him.

"Gross." Twila scrunched her nose. "I told Esme she shouldn't prepare food for people like you." She flew over to Kieran, who ate the steak with his hands.

"What do you mean by people like me?" he asked, glancing up at her.

Twila looked sickened as she watched him chew on the meat. "People who eat a poor animal's corpse," she told him.

"Ah, that's where you're mistaken." Kieran shoved the last piece into his mouth. "I eat live animals, too."

"Vile." Twila turned away from him and flew through the closed door and into the hall.

"Teach me that." Kieran placed the plate down on the counter and walked toward the kitchen door. "I want to walk through walls. It would be helpful the next time I get thrown in jail."

He stopped walking as soon as he opened the door. The fairy was gone, but Red's eyes were glowing once more. "Damn fairies. Always flyin' like it's their house," they grumbled, not moving any of their mouths.

"Wren said she has house guardians. I'm guessing that means you and the fairies," Kieran said. "So, yeah, it's their house, too."

"I don't like you." Red's eyes flickered like an all-red police siren.

"The feeling's mutual," Kieran said while he walked away from the kitchen and down the hall, passing the gargoyle.

Kieran made his way into the backyard through the large French doors that were placed in the center of the back hall, leaving them propped open. He needed a breather before reading through the long headache of a book, even if it was just one chapter.

"Wait," Twila said. She was carrying a yellow three-prong folder through the open French doors, following Kieran outside. "I'm sorry, but I eavesdropped on you and Wren's conversation earlier about the *Angelic Diaries*." Her face was red from carrying something much larger than her. "This may be easier to read than that book. It's one of Wren's journals about the species of Eden and Earth."

Kieran looked up at the fairy as she dropped the yellow folder with its pages clasped together into his hands.

"Stop helping him, Twila!" a woman yelled from a garden of flowers. "It's nearing night. The moon is about to rise high, and there's a lot of pollen in here. We can make *a lot* of nectar jam. Come help!"

Kieran snapped his eyes to two other fairies, who each poked their heads out of separate white tulips.

"That's Mari and Gold. They're my sisters," Twila said.

"I would have never noticed." Kieran waved at the two fairies, who quickly hid back inside of their flowers.

"Well, good luck with finding out what kind of monster you are," Twila said cheerily, then flew toward the circle of flowers to enrich the pollen for the hummingbirds, bees, and wasps with her laughter.

Kieran walked toward a stone bench near a water fountain and sat down. Opening the journal, he noticed tabs on most of the pages. He flipped to a tab that had **Edenians** scribbled on it, hoping a species would make sense to him, and scanned his eyes over the pages. Angelics, giants, dwarves, and outlanders were the four humanoid species of Eden.

"Nope, doesn't resonate," he muttered.

He quickly flipped to the **Ancient Earthlings** tab. The zyula and katani were the only two humanoids of Pangaea, and Kieran was not liking the idea of being half-zyula, who he viewed as puny werewolves, or half-katani, who he could swear were fangless vampires. Feeling irritated that nothing resonated, he was about to give up on reading the journal.

Then, his eyes glimpsed a small drawing taped to the bottom of the page. A man was covered in blood, clutching two long swords. In the corner of the small painting was a tiny signature that read **Wren**. "Something tells me she's proud of this painting, too," Kieran said as he studied the man's image. "The dude actually looks kind of scary."

He moved his eyes to read the name under Wren's signature: **Cain**.

"Ah, this is the guy she talked about. The guy who helped her former self kill that demonic guy holding the severed head!" he exclaimed as he jabbed his finger down at the painting of Cain.

Kieran scanned his eyes over the written scribbles explaining that Cain was half-katani and half-zyula. He traced a sentence with his finger and widened his wild eyes. The katani and zyula strains were not compatible. To top it off, Cain's mother was rumored to have giant's blood.

Kieran rolled his eyes. The giants were extinct. They had *fossils*.

"Hey, half-breed," a voice with a thick French accent said from his feet. "Quick, fetch me the *Angelic Diaries*. It's a large five-thousand-page book in a silver binding. You *can't* miss it. She's not here, right?"

Kieran looked down, but whoever had spoken to him was gone.

"Fine, I'll get the book myself," the voice hissed, and the French doors rattled as something ran inside the house.

"Hey, guardians," Kieran called out to the three fairies. "Something just broke into your house."

The sisters ignored him and continued singing and giggling with the flowers. Despite Kieran thinking the fairies were guardians of the house, they were only there to dance in the gardens.

Kieran rushed inside the house and ran down the hall. "Some guardians you are," he muttered as he ran past Red.

He threw open the kitchen door and ran up to the dining table. The book was still where Wren had left it.

"You were saying?" Red asked.

Kieran walked back into the hall and collapsed on the hallway rug near the kitchen door. "This is too much." He nodded to himself, contemplating leaving the strange house. "I should leave." He stood up, clutching the folder in his hands. "I'm taking this with me."

You can't. Wren's voice entered his mind.

Kieran looked up at the ceiling, as if Wren were up there, and said, "As soon as I meet you, you leave me alone with your fucked-up house. Thanks!"

Oh, my god. I'll be back in an hour or two. Stop being melodramatic. Wren groaned. *Two of my friends at dinner work for the police department and have been talking about you possibly being in the city. The entire city is on the lookout for you. It wouldn't be wise to go outside.*

"You make it sound like I'm a terrorist," Kieran mumbled.

You are! Wren shouted at him. *Blowing up a city falls under that category.*

"Then... what does that make you, oh, Great Spirit?" Kieran asked her.

Different planet, different rules. Wren shot back. *But I'm not her, Ezekiel.*

Kieran froze. The FBI duo had accused him of being Ezekiel during their interrogation with him. "I have no idea how you know that name, but I'm not him," he shouted.

They are saying your alias is Ezekiel in the news. How does it feel to be called someone you're not? Wren was being petty. *He's probably just a family friend, or something, because I also heard your mom say Ezekiel before she died.* The mention of his mom's death made her grow quiet. She had chosen her words poorly.

Wren suddenly cut the connection to his mind. She was not one to like emotions.

Knowing Wren's house was his best form of asylum from not only the law, but the vengeful citizens of Perk, Kieran ended up staying. He gripped the folder and was planning to head back into the backyard to read.

"Office," Red said when Kieran was about to walk past them. "To your right. More folders."

Kieran stopped walking and looked at the closed door to his right. "You're one odd statue." He looked at Red, whose eyes returned to gray.

Through the door on the right, Kieran walked into the office. A dark red oak desk, large to match the space, was in the center of the room, facing the door he had just entered. Underneath the desk was a large burgundy area rug, which covered most of the marble floor. He drifted away from the door and walked over to the brown chesterfield couch along the left wall.

"We had one of these growing up," Kieran said, bouncing up and down on the mahogany brown cushion, trying to communicate with Wren. He did not like how they had left their last conversation. He had taken a liking to the dollmaker. "Ours was tan."

Silence.

"Is that why you have one?" Kieran asked the air with a grin, waving his finger at the ceiling. "Reminded you of me?"

No, Wren said, irritation in her voice. *This room was my father's office. I left everything as he had it before he was killed. Now, shut up. I'm trying to converse with people. I can't have you calling out to me.*

"Then, stop reading my mind," Kieran said to her.

Wren laughed. *You are inside my house. I will not. Just shut up for a while.*

Kieran mumbled and laid back on the couch, spotting a globe on a shelf. After a quick moment's rest, he sprang up, ready to investigate the folders that Red had said were in the office. Rummaging through the desk, he found nothing. He swung open the closet door and noticed mounds of yellow folders stacked on the floor under hanging jackets. After he sat down, he pulled a tower of folders to him. He opened the top one and noticed it was in Spanish, so he went through more journals, but they were also in Spanish.

Feeling defeated, he shoved the folders back into the closet, messing up Wren's organization.

"Damn it!" he exclaimed.

A laugh echoed from the hall, and Red asked loudly, "Can't read them?"

Kieran ignored Red and tried to find the journal Twila had given him, but it was mixed in with the others. Trying to be patient, he opened each of the folders.

But his patience was running out fast.

"Come here, kid," Red yelled. "I got something to tell ya."

"I'll pass." Kieran finally found the folder Twila had handed him.

He flipped through the pages that described the humanoid species of Pangaea while he remained seated on the floor. Being thrown out of his frantic hunt, he stopped turning the thin pages. His eyes scanned a series of scribbles, causing his head to pulse the most wretched of throbs.

The page spoke about a disease that had plagued both the zyula and katani.

What disease?

In Kieran's recollection, no one had ever spoken about a disease—not even Isis. But here Wren was, scribbling away about plagues.

Kieran narrowed his eyes on the summary Wren had written.

He could not roll his eyes hard enough.

But just because Kieran did not know the truth of what had befallen the zyula and katani did not mean her words were false...

Vetus lupo primatus & Edax ossium

There are many names for the first land of Earth, but the zyula and katani called it the Gardens of Eden.

Since the beginning of Earth, Lucien was the ruler of all. But during the time the dinosaurs roamed, Lucien became angry. He threw the world into darkness for millions of years, and his demonics inflicted fear across the globe.

A man named Cain was born in the Early Jurassic period, and he openly opposed Lucien from an early age. As he aged, he and the Spirit were able to best Lucien and steal his throne. After all the horror Lucien inflicted, Cain offered the zyula and katani something they could not refuse: Hope.

The author of the Angelic Diaries (the First Mage) claims that Cain was the avatar of a Kanarian god. The validity of this claim is shaky at best.

With Cain's lenient rule, the people were free to form separate nations. But the meteors came to Earth and killed many civilizations, and the land broke apart. Not long after the continent broke, the zyula and katani became plagued with disease, and as time went on, some digressed. The two species contracted the same illness, and some lines evolved into what we modernly call primates and fae.

During the early formation of the continents, primates and fae were looked down upon by the zyula and katani. They were viewed as inferior.

The Angelic Diaries insinuates that the First Mage was trying to find a cure for the diseased katani and zyula. But what is this disease, and why were the katani and zyula the only ones affected?

Must research more...

"The fuck?" Kieran exclaimed after reading the page. "How the hell could primates and fae live *with* the zyula and katani? We come from them."

Wren mumbled, *Your thoughts are so damn loud. Let me go to the bathroom. Hold on.*

"Ew. I don't want to hear you go to the bathroom." Kieran scrunched his nose.

Idiot, I'm not actually going to the bathroom. I'm just excusing myself from dinner so I can focus on you. She sounded bitter.

"Oh, thanks," he said in surprise.

After a minute, Wren said, *Speciation. The theory common among humans is that populations of the zyula evolved into primates and the rest went extinct. They use this same theory to explain the katani and fae. But the fae believe in the First Mage's claims that a disease had altered the zyula and katani. Despite how agreeable humans and fae are with who our ancestors are, the details of how we all came to be are still argued—like the clay idol debate. Now, I know some katani survived, so the human theory is not entirely correct.*

"How do you know some of the katani survived?" Kieran asked. "Oh, that katani you just *happen* to know, but won't say who?"

Even though Wren knew Kieran was taunting her into admitting who the katani was, she still fell for his trap. *It's my aunt's friend. His name's Vaan. You'll meet him soon enough. Make sure to call him a vampire.*

Kieran did not respond.

Wren teased him. *Cat got your tongue?*

"What'll happen if I call him a vampire?" he asked.

He'll rip out your tongue, she said.

As wonderful as Wren's words were, Kieran lost interest. And he became immersed in his own thoughts.

"I've always wondered why the fae can talk to each other when they're different species." Wren was going to answer him, but Kieran continued his rant. "Why are humans the only primate that can speak?" he asked. "Hey! Do you know? And do the other primates know about the zyula?"

I don't know. Why don't you ask them? Wren asked. *We have communicated with gorillas using sign language, but they strayed too far from the zyula, so verbal communication is distorted. Many humans view themselves as superior to the other primates, so they don't care to communicate. Humans are a lot like the Upper Courts.*

"I mean, goblins are like tailless, hairless, talking monkeys with pointed ears. Why can they speak, and monkeys can't?" Kieran asked.

Don't let Rolf and Kyle hear you say that, Wren warned him. *The diseased katani evolved close to each other, practically staying one species. That's why goblins and elves can communicate and look more alike than, say, humans and gorillas. All primates come from the zyula, but we have more variation. Does that make sense?*

Wren paused. *I have to get back. We can talk more later.* She had to return to dinner. *I have journals that summarize the diaries back in the office. Read the one about the disease. It should be easy to find. It's labeled* Disease.

"They're all in Spanish," Kieran complained. "Well, except for—"

No, they aren't, Wren interrupted him. *I wrote them in English.*

After Wren watched Kieran's recent memories, she started screaming Red's name, causing Kieran to hold his hands over his ears.

✳ ✳ ✳ ✳ ✳

While Kieran battled Red in Sparrow Manor, the mages and officers continuously patrolled the area for rebels, and people throughout the city tried to continue to live their lives. Even Rolf and Kyle, who sat in front of a small window in the bookstore snacking on seaweed chips, wanted to see the nightlife. Their stones were up, and the magic was in full effect at the shop. They were protected from everyone and everything, but the two goblins wanted to be outside. Music was booming downtown, and the bars were packed with people who only wanted to focus on good moments.

Kyle noticed a billboard was flashing a new advertisement for an art show. "Can we go to the art district?" he asked Rolf. "Reme is having a show tonight at eight."

"No," Rolf told his younger brother. "You know Bernie's rules: 'No going out alone without an adult, and no going out at night.'"

Kyle turned from the window and pouted. "Reme's one of us, and she goes out at night."

"Reme's an adult," Rolf said. "If you want to go out, you can always go to the dinner at the church for the dead guy. We were invited. Think they are doing something in the courtyard."

"His name was *Simon*, Rolf," Kyle said, frowning. "That's like a family dinner—it doesn't feel right to go to that. And the courtyard isn't the same as an art show."

Kyle grabbed the remote and turned on the Holo-disc. Rolf looked down at his only family. "Reme is performing again in the morning. We can go to that one," he said. "Esme may want to go. Maybe she can take us."

"But they just buried Simon today," Kyle said. "Do you think she'll be in the mood?"

"An art show is good for mourning," Rolf told him. "Art heals everything. I think she will."

Reme was one of the earlier orphans Bernie had taken in, and when she had reached adulthood, she was allowed to move out of the church. Because of their metabolisms, goblins aged slightly faster than humans. But the difference was not large enough for the United States to form separate laws on age restriction, so the Lower Courts abided by human law, and the young artist had found it excruciating to wait a whole extra year to move out. She had riots to stir and things to create.

As the two goblins chatted about the local artist of goblin blood, Kieran continued to battle the voice in Sparrow Manor...

XX

UNDER A VIOLENT MOON

KIERAN WALKED OUT OF the office and watched Red laugh, their eyes blazing red. He did not want to deal with the shit-talking gargoyle. When the statue went dormant, he looked toward the back of the house.

The back of the continuous hall only contained décor and a set of French doors that led to the gardens. He had already explored the gardens, and he planned to sleep in the large, white-draped gazebo later. The stone hut had a very soft hammock.

He walked through the right archway and into the living room, taking a shortcut to the other side of the house. He stepped back into the hall on the opposite side of where Red was and looked both ways. The right led to the back hall, and the left led to Wren's bedroom, which was along the front hall. In the middle of the wall in front of him stood a closed silver door.

He had found his next voyage.

Kieran twisted the silver handle and pushed the heavy wooden door open. He felt a cool breeze and was taken aback by what he saw—a long narrow pool of crystal-clear saltwater, rose petals, and light foam. In the center of the pool stood a delicate-looking emerald statue of a goddess pouring water from her folded hands.

He stepped toward the pool.

A woman's voice interrupted his thoughts. "Let me know if you want the petals out. They tend to get stuck in your hair."

Kieran looked around and saw Esme pouring water above several plants. She looked up at him and smiled warmly. "When did you get back?" he asked.

"Not too long ago. I felt sick at dinner, so I'm recharging." Esme scrunched her brow. "They were serving Eudora's and Rose's new fried chicken special—made the salad stink."

Kieran looked around the chilly room. "That's inconsiderate of them."

"Simon loved Chicks 'N More. It was one of his favorites. We all used to hang out at Mom's restaurant after school, so Chicks 'N More is a fond memory. Even if I can't stand the smell... the dinner wasn't about me. Plus, they had veggies." As she defended the selection of food, Esme continued to pour water over the tall potted plants, which were under a series of wide windows on the opposite wall from where Kieran stood. "Dinner was almost over, anyway. Wren and Ray will be back soon."

Esme placed the metal watering can on a round table in the middle of two windows. Kieran did not want to continue their conversation about her dead friend's favorite meal and scanned his eyes over the wall of windows. Plants of all colors and species lined the wall from left to right.

He walked around the pool and said, "I really am no threat to you."

Esme stared at him. The blue-and-green strands of her long wavy hair sparkled in the sunlight as she walked toward him. Her mint green eyes hypnotized him. "That's comforting to know, since you killed hundreds of people this morning," she said gravely.

Kieran raised his eyebrows. "How'd you know about that?"

"Wren tells me everything," Esme said.

"You're adopted sisters, right?" he asked.

Esme looked surprised. "Did you run a background check on us?"

"No," Kieran said. "Your family has an entire page in the city's brochure."

"Ah," Esme replied and nodded her head. "Right."

"If you don't mind me asking... why'd you come to Tallahassee?" Kieran asked. "I feel like it would be neat to live in Moonlight Hills."

After Esme stared at him in silence for a moment, she turned from him and picked up her watering can again.

"I didn't mean to offend you." Kieran rushed his words. "Moonlight Hills is in Satan's Web, right? It's like thirty miles from Perk. Johnny and I used to ride out to the border of the woods and imagine what it was like living inside."

"Oh," Esme said and turned back to face him, flashing a sympathetic smile. "Johnny was kind."

Kieran fell mute, startled by her words.

"My family was one of the first volunteer families. We came here because my parents had believed the fae and humans could live in harmony." She stared at the flowers blooming near her. "It didn't go well."

Footsteps echoed off the floor behind Kieran, prying his attention away from Esme. He turned around and saw the illusion that haunted him. Next to Johnny stood a blurred image of an unknown man. "I'm so tired of these hallucinations. Go away," he hissed at the image of Johnny and the hazy man.

Kieran turned back to face Esme, who slowly faded into the air with a frightened look on her face. She knocked her watering can to the floor, and water leaked from its nozzle.

"Hallucination?" the distorted-looking man asked, then appeared in front of Kieran. "I'm not imaginary."

Kieran tried to walk away, but he froze when he felt a fiery hand clasp his neck. He tried to fight against the hand that clutched his throat, but the man threw him into the pool. He heaved from the saltwater that had entered his nose.

He stood up, the water reaching his chest. The hazy man hovered over him, his eyes darkening from a deep brown and into blackness. A rage fueled the unknown man, causing Kieran to crouch slightly below the water, hoping the water would save him.

"Don't kill him, Cain," Johnny yelled at the man.

"I'm not," Cain said. "I need him alive." He brushed a finger over his lip, staring at Kieran like he was a specimen. "So, you're the missing piece."

Kieran could hear Red shouting from the other side of the house, trying to banish the intruder. He finally realized that what was happening was not because of his mind playing tricks, but was, in fact, reality. And he widened his eyes at a newfound fear.

"This would be a good time to be reading my mind, Wren!" Kieran yelled out, only for her not to hear him. "Get away from me. Both of you!"

He did not want to find out who the man was, or why Johnny was back. Giving up and ready to meet whatever fate would befall him, he leaned back into the water and floated on his back, waiting to be killed—*wanting* to be killed.

But death did not come.

He stared up at the ceiling, tears flowing into the water, as he heard Johnny call out to him. He sank to the bottom of the pool, his body shutting down.

Heartbreak could ruin a man.

After hearing the clink of chains coming from The Shade, Cain walked toward his portal with Johnny following. "Yeah, yeah. Spare me your moans and groans, Aaeon," Cain said to the shadow god who hid in the unseen path. "I'm going. I'm going..."

Esme instantly reappeared. In a frenzy, she pulled Kieran from the pool. Before Cain and Johnny left, she locked eyes with Cain. Within his eyes, she saw a familiar spark.

After the two had left, Esme looked down at Kieran in her arms. No matter how much water she summoned to splash down on his face, he would not wake up from his nightmare—the night Johnny was stolen from him...

✵✵✵✵✵

It was beautiful, in a haunting way.

The silence of the night, the coldness of the wind—Johnny loved the cemetery. He enjoyed the quiet that always surrounded him near the tombstones.

But it was different on Halloween night. In Perk, it was a religious tradition to visit the cemetery and Christianize the spirits, and Johnny always hated the noise the others brought—the music, the loud prayers. The Hollow's Eve Memorial, they called it.

Johnny and Kieran made a mistake by going to the graves one Halloween night.

It was a mistake indeed.

Kieran and Johnny stood at the gates of the cemetery. It was too noisy, with too many people. A place for the dead was supposed to be calm.

"Are you okay?" Kieran asked. "We don't have to be here. You hate this festival."

"Look." Johnny pointed up at the night sky. "The moon has a ring."

"So..." Kieran said and walked with Johnny through the gates. "I know I asked you to live with me before I moved back into my parents' house, but I understand if you don't want to." They walked to a dark area where they could not be seen and laid a blanket on a patch of grass. "My parents died in that house. Like, I killed my dad."

"Of course, I still want to," Johnny said, and they sat down on the blanket. "It wasn't your fault."

While sobbing on the floor of his childhood home, Kieran had called both Johnny and the town's sheriff and told them the truth of what happened the very day he had killed the man that raised him. Johnny had arrived shortly after the sheriff. Being a family friend of the Crosses, the sheriff allowed the two to speak for a bit before dragging Kieran away.

The sheriff had cleaned Kieran up before bringing him to the jail, as his fingernails had crusted blood and between his teeth were strings of his father's skin. Blood was smeared across his lips. The sheriff, a naturally decent man, kept the aftermath of his defense a secret. He was afraid a disturbing event would send him into a system of mental institutions, particularly the town's own asylum.

At the jail, Kieran told the officers who were questioning him as little as possible, but enough to have them close the case as a homicide-suicide. There was clear video evidence from the neighbor's outside security cameras that Kieran's father had been strangling his mother. And Kieran had pried him off to save her. Self-defense was obvious for the defense, and Kieran was never charged.

Luckily, the security cameras did not capture everything.

But the coroner leaked the details of the corpse to the town in the local paper, claiming human bite marks. The coroner even released a photo of the corpse for all to see.

At city hall, the sheriff announced to Perk that the coroner did not pick up the body like he was supposed to, so he had personally brought the body to the medical examiner's office. He swore that the body had been intact, and no chunks were missing. The coroner argued that he was never notified and claimed the sheriff was covering up Kieran's disgraceful cannibalistic ways.

Cousins and rivals, the coroner and sheriff stood at odds. The more the sheriff had felt the need to protect the son of his high school sweetheart, the more the coroner felt the need to demonize him.

In the end, the other officers sided with the coroner, but they did not charge Kieran for desecrating a human corpse. It would have ruined the sheriff, and the nightmare that the sheriff was living made the office call it quits and close the case.

And Kieran became the town's dark secret...

"My mom killed herself there," Kieran said, pressing on, making sure

Johnny was certain that he wanted to live with him—the very man the town swore was possessed by the Devil.

"You said she was in shock," Johnny replied. "I don't care where you live. I want my last days to be with you."

Kieran's heart twisted as he listened to the words Johnny spoke. He did not want to think about the day that his boyfriend's heart would stop beating.

The local doctor had told Johnny that he would not live naturally past the age of thirty, and he was lucky that he had made it as far as he had. The Williams family had managed to place Johnny on a transplant list. But when time arrived for him to undergo surgery, he was no longer a minor. And he made the decision not to have the surgery. He feared a new heart.

The Williamses and Crosses were devastated, though over time, they grew to respect Johnny's decision.

"So, you wish to live with me in my lair," Kieran said in a horrible English accent, then pecked Johnny's neck, tickling him. "Your parents will not be pleased."

The Williamses had doted on Kieran and Johnny's love for years, and they once viewed Kieran as their son-in-law. But after Kieran had killed his father, the town began viewing him as a deranged cannibal, and the Williams family tried to keep Johnny from him.

Kieran quit joking. "I'll never hurt you," he said.

"Where is this coming from?" Johnny laughed.

"I'm serious."

Johnny nodded. "I know."

"You didn't go near town square today, did you?" Kieran asked.

"I had to. Was buying groceries for my parents." Johnny laid down on his side, placing a hand under his chin. "Are you worried that I saw you spray paint the church?"

"Yeah... Wait, you saw?" Kieran exclaimed.

"Everyone saw," Johnny said. "I'm surprised no one pressed charges."

"It's the only good thing of being feared." Kieran laid back on the blanket and placed his arms behind his head. "The Devil's son, they call me now."

He glanced over at his old childhood friend, who had become his boyfriend when they both turned seventeen.

"He's scared of you. I like that he's scared because I feel safe," Johnny said. "If a man like him is a man of god, then I want to be with the Devil's son." He rolled back on his back as well. "And to be fair, we don't actually know who your father is."

"Look here, you little punk." Kieran was about to roll onto his side and tickle Johnny, but he grimaced at the sound of old-school fireworks being set off. "Should we go back to my house? They're getting louder." He sat up, staring toward where most of Perk was gathered, and cupped his hand around his mouth. "They are prioritizing holographics for a reason! You guys are going to get the town fined!"

Johnny laughed and pulled Kieran down to lay beside him. "You know no one cares what we do. I mean, we're the town that the Pope condemns," he said. "They kicked Preacher out of the church years ago for showing public support with the anti-fae. But everyone still treats him like a priest." He avoided his dark memories and smiled at Kieran. "We always sleep out here under the full moon. Let's stay."

The moon shone brightly over them, and the two kissed. The dark area they had plotted themselves on was visible for a moment, so when David and Brian saw them, it was a complete surprise.

"There," Brian told his friend and pointed at the two. "Weren't you looking for Johnny?"

David stared angrily in Kieran's and Johnny's direction.

"What do you want him for?" Brian asked David, trying to keep up with his pace. "I thought you hated the Williamses."

David ignored his subordinate and had his hands gripped around Johnny's neck before Kieran could see who they were. Brian freaked out and tried to pry his friend off Johnny.

"Hold him, Brian," David shouted. "We need to test him for fae DNA."

"I thought you were just kidding," Brian shouted back. "He's Sarah's brother—"

"Stop talking about that damn bitch and do it!" David yelled. "Only a fae would be with a cannibal. It makes sense. They eat humans, too. The town should lock you both up!"

Brian, not having an ounce of backbone, restrained Johnny. David had once bullied him in their younger years, and he felt it was better to be his underling than to be bullied ever again—to the point Brian had broken up with Sarah when he was in ninth grade to avoid David's wrath.

"You can't be serious?!" Kieran yelled and swung at the two, who were part of Johnny's high school graduating class. "The fae are all vegans, dumbasses! Johnny hunts!"

"No, Kieran," Johnny yelled when Kieran shoved David into the grass. "They're just drunk!"

With the power Johnny's words had on him, Kieran froze like a deer in headlights. And right when he had stopped shoving David into the dirt, David pulled out his hunting knife and drove it into the weak heart of Johnny Williams.

The whites of David's eyes reflected the moonlight as his face chilled in horror. "I—I didn't me—mean to..." he stuttered. The plan had been to cut off a piece of his hair and run it through an Empure test kit. But during the scuffle, the knife had gone elsewhere.

While Kieran could not move, David and Brian ran away as the night cried for the death of an innocent. It was an act of cruelty, an act that Kieran would never forget—a test to see if Johnny Williams were fae gone wrong from the prejudice of idiots.

Kieran collapsed and held onto Johnny, crying while he died in his arms. He picked up his limp body and walked through the cemetery, people thinking it was their costumes. He walked all the way to the town's hospital, a small brick building with a few doctors.

The sight of Kieran covered in dirt and carrying the corpse of Johnny in his arms startled the staff, who were hosting a Halloween party.

XXI

GHOSTLY GHOULS

WREN HELPED RAY CLEAR the dishes from the table as Father Bernie led everyone outside to the inner courtyard. It was only a small group of people: Ms. Beckman, Bettie, Jackson, and Connell. Rose could not attend, as the mages were hosting an initiation dinner for her at the local guild. Eudora and Vaan were out of town on a business trip. And while the goblins and trolls were invited to dinner, they stayed in their individual places of comfort—whether that was inside closets, under the pews, or among the bookshelves.

"Do you feel sick, too?" Ray asked Wren as they walked from the kitchen.

"I'm fine," Wren lied. "I'm just worried about Esme."

"She'll be fine once she's around her plants." Ray shrugged. "It's her fault for not taking the ginger pills. The kids take them, and the smell of meat doesn't make them sick."

Wren scoffed. "She doesn't like ginger. She'd rather get sick."

The two walked out into the inner courtyard.

"You never worry about Esme's nausea. What's really bothering you?" Ray looked down at her. "Kieran?"

"No, we actually seem to get along, but he made me talk about the Spirit," Wren said. "What if I *am* the Spirit? I mean, I blew up my yard and supposedly the Spirit could create force fields and was a pyromancer. I don't want to be some ghost story."

"Don't forget that the Spirit could read minds, too," Ray joked. He stopped walking and took hold of her arm, preventing her from taking another step, and said, "But you're not her. Even the Council thinks Isis made a mistake. Stop worrying. You're just similar. Even the mages are similar to the Spirit in other ways."

"The mages are trained. I was born this way." Wren shrugged roughly, feeling the crawl of irritation behind her neck. She then smirked, thinking about Isis. "Imagine Isis' reaction if I am proven not to be the Spirit. She would run away and stay on Mars for a century!"

"Remember, Isis was once human," Ray said, making her feel better. "No matter how badass she is, she was still one of us mere mortals."

Wren nodded, and they resumed walking toward Father Bernie, who was holding a medium-sized golden chest. Before dinner, everybody had placed something of Simon's into the container. They were planning to bury it under his favorite tree, a small Eastern Redbud.

"Let us begin," Father Bernie said. He lowered the chest to the ground under the Eastern Redbud and groaned at the pain shooting through his knees.

Wren and Ray rushed to help hold the chest, and the three lowered the container into the hole. Ray helped steady Father Bernie as Wren took his arm, and the two led him to a steel bench near the tree.

"Thank you, kids," Father Bernie said and wiped his brow, sitting down. "Eighty-three is no joke."

"Let us bury the chest," Ray said. "You rest."

Father Bernie watched the two bury the chest Simon had cherished. The priest was quiet that evening, lost in his own memories. They were burying Father Bernie's most valuable possession, for it was not just a chest—it used to be his own son's. And the priest once wanted to be buried with it. However, Simon was obsessed with it, admiring the golden color.

The kind priest had wanted to adopt Simon during the Coys' custody battle, as his own son was taken from him in his early years, and Simon had always reminded him of him. But Father Bernie knew Simon was better off living with his grandparents, so he chose to bury his son's chest with Simon's things inside on the day they put him to rest.

Before Bernie became a priest, he had been a mechanic with a wife and son. As if Tallahassee tended to attract catastrophe, he was robbed of both during a riot before the fae came out of hiding. The old priest was twenty-four, and it was the winter of 2165. North Korea was becoming free, and the world was promoting an era of peace.

But as with all civil progress, cruelty hid in plain sight. Bernie used to be opposed to getting mixed with civil rights, and he had only wanted to focus on raising a family. But his wife was not. She was mixed, with Nigerian and Irish blood, and she had wanted to raise their son aware of worldly issues.

When Bernie's wife had taken their young son to a peaceful celebration at the Capitol, which was organized by Korean Americans, they were attacked by the same group that evolved into the anti-fae.

At first, Bernie was angry at his wife for going to the event. But that anger turned into compassion, and a priest he had become. And when the fae had appeared, he heard his wife whisper into his ears, "Help them."

As Bernie thought fondly of his late wife and son, everyone helped fill the hole. Ms. Beckman could not stop crying, and she rubbed her eyes until they became red. Wren backed up from the hole, clutching her stomach from an oncoming vision. Before the darkness filled Wren's sight, she saw Ray rush toward her.

❋❋❋❋❋

Simon felt it was safe to walk about the city. Tallahassee had increased their mages and police officers on patrol, and he had a restraining order against his parents. While Wren and Ray were working at their store, and Esme was at the bookstore, he planned to make everyone dinner. He had just finished an interview and wanted to celebrate getting the job.

Walking back to Wren's house from the grocery store a few blocks away, he saw his father's old worn-down truck pull up behind him. His eyes grew wide, his face pale.

At that moment, Simon regretted not taking his car.

"Goddamn it, Simon," his mother yelled from the passenger seat. "I know why you moved back to this sinful city. You and that fae girl eloped!"

"Go away," Simon said in a choked voice as he dropped the grocery bags and walked backwards from the truck. "How'd you even find me?"

"Susan spotted you at that fae church. She's been following you all week," Simon's mother shouted from her rolled-down window, arm hanging out. "I told you not to go to Novus. It's a house of evil! And evil spreads!"

Susan was Simon's aunt and part of the local cohort of rebels. Unlike Simon's grandparents, who had sided with peace, their daughters had not.

"And you know what must be done about evil, Simon?" his mother asked.

Simon's monstrous parents kept following him as he ran to the grocery store where he had seen a police officer patrolling. He kept shouting out for help while his father drove his old truck close behind him. It was daylight, and no one really cared or bothered to help him until his father crashed into him and the side of a burger joint in the shopping plaza. The cop, who had been in the grocery store, ran across the parking lot and yanked out the un-wounded maniacs.

※※※※※

Wren regained control of herself, batting her eyelids from the memory of Simon's murder. She had never wanted to see how Simon died, and she refused to pull it from any witness' mind. But she had somehow dragged the memory from his insane mother, who was being held at the jail.

After Wren reassured everyone that she was fine after her brief vision, everyone resumed the burial. Ray would not leave her side. He knew she had seen something—her veins were a little dark.

When the last pile of dirt had been scattered over the hole, Wren rushed away from the inner courtyard. She slung open the doors and ran back inside the interior of the church. She heaved again, her throat closing.

Scattered footsteps ran around as the children spied on her. "Go back to bed," Wren told them. The kids ran from the church's lobby and rushed back down the hall toward the living quarters.

Wren needed to distract herself, so she tried to check on Kieran and Esme. Unable to connect to Esme's mind, she attempted to link with Kieran. Neither would connect, and she panicked. She raced to the door that led to the street the bookstore shared and opened it.

"How darling. You *loved* him," a woman with a deep French accent said the moment Wren walked down the steps.

Wren had first heard the woman, who sounded like an evil French villain, one month ago. And the woman would speak to her when she was alone. She kept demanding jewels and gold, claiming Wren had to show her respect. And recently, the woman had demanded for Wren to give her the *Angelic Diaries*.

"What do you want?" Wren asked, walking toward the bookstore. "Let me guess, the book?"

"Yes, the book," the woman said snobbishly. "It belongs in the library."

Wren could not read her mind, so she was clueless as to who the woman was. All she knew was that the woman was obsessed with stealing the *Angelic Diaries*.

Despite Red being incredibly troublesome, for they loved shit-talking and pranks, they were an excellent house guardian. They were always able to banish the thief, but they could not figure out who the bandit was. The French-sounding rogue was too fast for them to see. Red was an expert at eliminating aggressors from a perimeter, but they were not great at sight.

"Wren Sparrow?" Frost called out to her from the sidewalk.

Wren cringed at the sight of the FBI agent and his slicked-back blond hair. He had just returned from a brief nap in his hotel room and was once again following her around. "Stop stalking me," she shouted at both the unseen French woman and the agent.

"Wren Spar—"

"Stop!" Wren screamed in the agent's face, interrupting him.

She rushed across the street to the opposite sidewalk and resumed heading to the bookstore.

"I don't know why you're ignoring me when your life may be in danger," Frost yelled after her, smoking his cigarette casually.

"Leave me alone," Wren yelled back at the agent, who had followed her across the road. She threw her hands up, muttering Spanish insults to calm herself down, then pounded on the front door of the bookstore.

"Runes are up. Can't open the door until morning," Rolf shouted from the inside.

"Is Esme here?" Wren asked.

"No," Rolf replied. "She came by about an hour ago, though. How could you serve meat to a nymph?"

"She didn't eat meat. She ate greens and salad," Wren replied.

"Reme!" Kyle shouted, disrupting their banter. "I was going to ask Esme earlier, but she was sick. Can you or Esme take us to go see Reme tomorrow morning at ten?" he asked, almost pleading. "Or both of you! We can all go to Reme's art show! It'll make you feel better about your dead friend."

Wren stood on the other side of the closed door. If a human had said the words Kyle just had, it would have been viewed as insensitive. But he was not human, and goblins often gave off an uncaring attitude, even though they meant well and spoke from the heart.

"Yes, Kyle," Wren said. "We can go see Reme."

"Yay!" Kyle cheered, then turned to Rolf, who was still seething about meat being served. "Esme said chicken was Simon's favorite."

"So?" Rolf asked. "If someone's favorite thing to eat is human, then is it okay to watch them eat it?"

Wren thought for a moment, listening to the brothers bicker back and forth. She shrugged, thinking about Kieran, and asked, "Why not?"

Rolf and Kyle grew quiet for a moment.

Wren was about to turn, but then stopped when she heard Rolf ask Kyle, "'Why not?' *'Why not?'* Did she really just say that?"

Wren slowly turned around from the bookstore, facing Frost, who was smoking his cigarette near his car along the road. She hesitated before walking away, eyeing the agent. "What do you want from me?" she asked. "I already told you I don't want you around me."

"Is that because you are harboring a fugitive?" Frost inhaled his smoke.

"You tell me." Wren entered a staring contest with him.

Wren leaned toward him and inhaled the smell of alcohol and cigarettes he was emitting. "You need a shower, *Frost*." She glared up at the agent.

Frost grinned darkly and walked to the driver's side of his car, flicking his cigarette butt into the street. "I'll be seeing you later, *Sparrow*."

Wren could not sense the French woman nearby, but she noticed Ray was standing near his parked motorcycle in the bookstore's small parking lot. He was watching Frost drive away from them.

"Ok, the government guy... Is this something we should worry about?" Ray asked Wren when she walked up to meet him.

"No, he's just following Kieran," she said.

"Oh, is that all?" he asked.

Wren tilted her face sideways at a loud buzzing sound, and Ray's voice became muddled. He rushed from his bike and held her face between his hands. "You almost had another panic attack," he complained.

"I'm fine. Quit it." Wren slapped his hand away. "Let's go. We have a friend's ashes to spread at midnight."

While Simon's grandparents had his ashes, they had given some to the remaining members of the Sad Guy's Club. They knew how much Simon had treasured the three and how he had wanted to be free. So, everyone planned to toss his ashes into the wind. While the three friends were set on spreading Simon's ashes in the gardens of Sparrow Manor, his grandparents were going to take a cruise and sprinkle them into his favorite sea.

Ray nodded, saying, "You better be okay, or Simon will haunt me."

Ray drove them away from the bookstore, under the risen moon. He sped down the hill and through the broken gates of the manor. In an anxious frenzy, he parked in front of a goddess statue to the right of the front door—his usual spot. He retrieved the small box of ashes from the compartment of his bike while Wren walked through the broken doorway.

Kieran cleared his throat from where he sat on a black wingback chair near the archway that led to the left hall. "About time," he mumbled. "You will *not* believe what fucking happened. I'm surprised you didn't reach out to me with your mind crap. It was *horrendous*."

Esme was seated in the other wingback chair next to the opposing archway that led to the right hall. "Johnny's ghost and some monster broke in," she said, full of unease. "But they left."

Kieran pouted, looking for sympathy.

"Are you okay?" Wren asked Esme as she ran up to her sister, ignoring Kieran. "I tried to call out to both of you, but no one was responding."

Esme nodded. "I kept transitioning—my atoms were going haywire. I was barely able to stay solid in order to drag Kieran out of the water. You know I can't hear you telepathically when I'm invisible... Sorry."

"What about me?" Kieran asked, wanting someone to inspect him for injuries too. "I was thrown into your pool. I woke up like five minutes ago."

"What about you?" Ray asked him after he walked into the foyer. "You broke in and now expect us to take care of you?" He forced a laugh, then walked up to where Esme sat and asked her, "Do you want some soup?"

Esme nodded happily, with brightened eyes.

"I was *thrown* in," Kieran said, correcting Ray. "Way to blame the victim. Why do people keep throwing me?!"

Wren turned to look at him. "You are far from a victim."

Kieran was about to feel out of place, thinking he had mistakenly assumed he had bonded with the creepy dollmaker. Then, she walked up to him and held out her hand, prying him away from his approaching doom. "Come, I'll check your wounds," she said.

"Esme is more delicate than you. Nymphs are physically frail out of water. It's natural to check on her first," Ray explained to Kieran, peering back at him. "Didn't mean to insult you."

Kieran was about to let down his guard until Ray's next words.

"Plus, why the hell would we prioritize an escaped convict who has burned and eaten people alive over family?" Ray raised his eyebrows and turned to walk with Esme from the foyer.

Esme nudged Ray as they entered the kitchen. "What?" he asked.

"I thought you always liked Kieran?" Esme asked.

Ray placed the box on the counter and opened the refrigerator. "I do."

"Then, why are you being mean to him?" Esme asked and sat down on a bar stool, twirling around to check on the fairy sisters, who were asleep in their cottage back in Moonlight Hills.

"How is checking on you before him being mean?" Ray asked, placing a bowl of left-over pumpkin soup in the microwave.

Esme looked up at the ceiling, twirling around on the stool, trying to think of an answer. Ray watched the timid woman continue to spin around and placed the warm bowl in front of her on the bar. He walked around and placed both of his hands on her shoulders to stop her from avoiding his question. "You can't find an answer because I was not mean," he told her.

"Your words were mean," Esme said.

"I was honest," Ray told her.

"You could have chosen better words." She squinted at him.

He nodded and sat down on the stool next to her. "Eat."

"Thank you for the soup." Esme took a bite of soup, glancing at Simon's small box on the counter. "You should go apologize to Kieran."

Ray smeared soup on her cheek. "Hey!" she exclaimed as he walked away and picked up the box of ashes.

"Simon approves," Ray said. "Hurry up so we can go spread his ashes. He probably hates being trapped in this thing."

"That's not how it works," Esme said, placing her spoon down on the counter. "The spirit is released from the body the moment death comes."

"That's what you believe. Maybe the spirit is trapped in the remains," Ray countered and patted the box.

When they realized they were debating where the spirit went with part of their dead friend in Ray's arms, the two became awkward.

"I'm going to go outside. Come join once you're done." Ray rushed out of the kitchen door as Esme pushed the soup away from her.

Walking past the gargoyle, Ray spotted Wren tending to Kieran's wounds in the hallway bathroom next to the office. He stopped at the doorway and folded his arms, watching the two. "You fit in nicely," he said to Kieran, apologizing in his own way. "Welcome to the house of freaks."

Kieran looked up at him. "Thanks?"

Ray nodded and walked away toward the backyard.

As Wren bandaged Kieran's arm, Ray released a scream.

"What was that?" Kieran asked. Wren shoved him to the floor and darted from the bathroom to see what was going on.

Outside, Ray was sprawled in the grass, lying on his back near the steppingstones that led to the gazebo. His arms were clutching Simon's urn like it was the Holy Grail.

Wren ran up to Ray and squatted next to him. "What happened?" she asked, propping him up in her arms.

Ray did not speak. He could only point at the odd shadows drifting inside the gazebo. Wren looked over at the hut, noticing a pair of red eyes staring through the white fabric of the gazebo's drapes. The drapes fluttered in the wind, and a man's face was revealed in a butchered sequence of broken images.

"Oh, that's what we saw earlier," Kieran said, walking from the back door of the house with Esme following him. "It threw me into your pool."

"What is it?" Wren asked as she helped Ray sit up.

Kieran continued speaking about what happened in the sunroom while Esme nodded at his tale. Neither Ray nor Wren paid him any attention, as they kept staring at the blurry image under the steel tent.

Thick smoke circled the tall man and dark shadows danced around his face. Atop the blurred man's head were what looked like goggles, and appearing next to him was Johnny.

"You think it's a demon?" Kieran asked. "Well, that's my dead boyfriend standing next to him."

"Who are you?" Wren asked the intruder, standing up.

Kieran placed his hands over his face, sitting down next to Ray while Wren stood in between the group and the invaders. Exhausted, Kieran tugged on Wren's light-yellow dress and said, "Ask Johnny why he's back."

"Why are you—" Wren was about to ask the ghost of Johnny why he was on Earth, but she then looked back at Kieran. "Why don't you just ask him?"

Kieran simply grinned in response. Ray looked up at Esme, who reached out her hand for him to take. He stumbled to his feet at the same time Kieran collapsed back onto the grass, closing his eyes.

"Kieran, this is not the time for a nap," Wren hissed down at him.

"You can protect us with your mind crap," he told her.

A roar came from the intruder, who soon walked toward them.

"Get back," Wren exclaimed.

Kieran did not move, so the group circled around him with Wren standing in front. He opened his eyes and saw Ray and Esme standing on both sides of him while Wren stood at his feet. "I have guards. Nice," he said.

Wren's eyes twitched at Kieran's words, glowing a light blue. She held up her hand and summoned a force field, manifesting a dome, which radiated lights that mimicked arctic glaciers. "Go away!" she screamed loudly.

"Well, that won't do," an arrogant voice said from a shrub.

XXII

Thorns & Wine

A LONG-HAIRED WHITE CAT who looked much like a Norwegian Forest Cat walked out from behind a bush of lilies and ran inside the dome. The cat sat down next to Wren's feet. She briefly groomed her paw and glared up at Wren. The cat shook off her coat and twitched her whiskers at what she observed. She groaned and stood back up after she had finished grooming herself, releasing a long yawn, full of suffering boredom.

"You?" Wren asked the cat. "The book thief?"

"It's better to be a book thief than a peasant," the cat said, looking over at the intruders. "Why are you so scared? Is that not your beloved?"

"My beloved?" Wren asked and glanced at the twisted-looking man.

"The one whom you mourn," the cat said. "Simon, was it?"

"No," the man with the distorted face said, "I am not Simon, though Simon is me."

The man, shrouded in smoke, stood right in front of their energetic dome. He placed a hand on the shield, and his image became stabilized. His red eyes pierced into Wren's, and long, medium brown bangs fell into his face. He stood tall and glared desperately down at her.

"Come home," the man said to her.

Flames poured from the man's eyes, revealing dark brown irises. Fire had been brewing at the base of his eyes, making them seem red from afar. A symbol with fire along its edge was carved into his neck.

In the *Angelic Diaries*, a being had carved such a symbol into his own neck with a sacred blade, forever marking his soul. The symbol represented the Fires of Rebirth, a machine that could give souls skin.

And there was only one person who was obsessed with creating a machine that could grant life to those who had died: Cain.

Red flames began to dance around Cain's lightly tanned body while he sent his fire to pierce through the dome. His fiery cords wrapped around Wren, holding her still. Cain's eyes narrowed, focused on Wren's. She tried to summon her own flames, but Cain's fire had suppressed her powers.

"Our test is done," Cain said to her. "I need you and the half-breed to come with me."

Before Cain could continue, a silver chain emerged from the grass and circled around him. A hooded man with ghostly flesh broke through the soil. Amid the smell of death, the hooded man tossed more chains Cain's way. The shadowy chains surrounded him, causing him to look back at the hooded man.

"You're seriously tossing your chains at *me?*" Cain sneered at the man who smelled of decay. "I don't care if you're a god. *Release me!*"

The hooded man released cracked and raspy words. "He said... no."

Before Cain could speak further, he was completely wrapped from head to toe in cold chains and yanked under the soil.

The four humanoids and cat waited a few minutes to make sure the threat was gone, and then they all moved from their frozen state. Wren dropped her force field, and Kieran finally stood up. "Tell me I'm having a fucking nightmare." He cursed and walked inside the gazebo, inspecting the interior.

Wren left her spot on the grass and walked into the hut, taking a seat on a wide stone bench. After Kieran realized Johnny and Cain were gone, he sat down next to her. She tilted her head to the side, flashing a disturbing smile at him. Ray and Esme entered the gazebo after them and sat down on a bench opposite of the two. Soon, the cat trotted in and sat at Wren's feet, staring up at her.

"Something tells me this is normal for you," Kieran said to Wren.

"Pretty much. But it's normally the rebels breaking in," Wren replied and leaned back on her hands. "What?" she asked the cat after she noticed she was being watched by the furball.

The cat did not speak, but she released a *humph* and trotted away from the gazebo and back out into the gardens.

"We'll figure out the talking cat later." Wren raised her eyes to the cat as she ran into a shrub. "I need a drink."

"I need a lobotomy," Ray muttered.

Esme jumped up, saying, "I'll grab the drinks. I'll grab some snacks, too. We'll need the energy to figure out why those men were here." She tapped her fingertips together like a mastermind. "Y'all want to play a board game while we brainstorm?"

"No, Esme," Wren told her sister. "This isn't the time to play games."

"Playing a game will calm everyone down," Esme protested. "Simon loved games. It will be a nice homage before we spread his ashes."

Wren was not big on games, but she knew Esme needed to calm her nerves. "Fine, I'll play whatever game you pick," she said.

Ray eyed Esme. "I'll play if it's chess and *not* a board game." Like Wren, he did not favor board games. Simon and Esme had somehow always persuaded them to play, though.

"I like board games." Kieran rivaled Ray.

"I'll bring both." Esme clasped her hands together, smiling.

"Who do you think they were?" Ray asked Wren, drifting his eyes away from Esme and Kieran, who were discussing what board game to play.

"The man with the mark on his neck was Cain," Wren said. "And the ghost was Johnny, Kieran's boyfriend."

"*Ex*-boyfriend," Kieran tried to say humorously after he and Esme had settled on the board game. "I don't see us working out. It's like we live in different worlds or something."

Wren registered the emotional undertones in his voice, and she watched him look away, holding in his tears.

"Cain, from the book you're obsessed with?" Ray asked Wren while Esme patted Kieran on the back caringly.

Wren nodded. "I'm not the only one who's obsessed with it," she whispered, staring out toward the bush the cat had vanished into.

Silence befell the group, and Esme took that as her sign to run into the house to play hostess. Wren and Ray locked eyes briefly, and she turned to Kieran for suggestions, but he only shrugged. No one knew what was going on.

Words were not necessary, and for a few minutes, only the night birds made any noise. The moment Wren stood up to find the talking cat, Esme ran out of the house smiling.

"She's too carefree," Ray said as he watched Esme run toward them with a large basket of goodies. "Wren's right—this really isn't the time to play games."

"Being carefree isn't a bad thing," Kieran snapped. "And there's always time to play games."

Ray studied Kieran. "Are you forming a crush on Esme or something?"

Kieran moved his eyes to Ray, growing pale.

Ray looked defensive. "Not a good idea. Plus, your boyfriend's back, and something tells me we'll see him again."

"You're speaking nonsense." Kieran shook his head as he watched Esme stop walking on the stone path to speak to Wren.

"Then, why are you arguing with me every time I talk about Esme?" Ray asked.

"I don't. I just argue with you every time you talk." Kieran shrugged. "It's not my fault you're always talking about Esme." He looked like he had an epiphany. "*You* like Esme," he whispered and leaned forward, pointing at Ray.

Ray became annoyed by Kieran's accusation and eyed Esme standing on the steppingstones. Wren was pointing around the yard while Esme was nodding.

"Obviously, she's one of my best friends." Ray brushed off Kieran's words. "I think you're projecting your growing feelings for Esme onto me. Don't."

He stood up, prepared to help Esme carry the large basket, then paused and looked down at Kieran. "You just got here, but I talk about Wren just as much." His scalding glare burned Kieran's eyes. "Does that mean I like Wren? Why do you even care? I talk about them because I worry about them."

Ray walked down the gazebo steps and toward his two best friends. Kieran leaned forward—his forearms onto his knees—baffled by Ray's words. "He started it," he hissed, looking down at the gazebo floor.

Kieran ruffled his hair, frustrated. His boyfriend was a ghost, and he had a growing fascination toward a nymph. His life was far from sensible.

"Where are you going?" Ray asked Wren when he approached both women, overhearing part of their conversation.

"I need to find that cat." Wren placed her hands on both Ray's and Esme's shoulders. "Set up the picnic. I won't be long."

Esme nodded and walked into the gazebo, handing Kieran a wine glass. "Forget the glass. Hand me a damn bottle," he said as he stared into the large wicker basket at the wine bottles, giving the wine glass back to her.

Kieran grabbed a bottle and ripped out the cork with a corkscrew. Instantly, he started chugging the red liquid. He noticed Ray, who was standing at Esme's side, staring at him. He felt like being nice and held out the bottle for Ray to take.

"I don't drink that," Ray responded while he investigated the basket.

"You're telling me you don't drink?" Kieran asked.

Ray reached into the basket and found his poison. "I said, 'I don't drink that.'"

Esme was holding out a glass for Ray to take, but he followed Kieran's example and chugged from the already-opened whiskey bottle, then sat down on the stone bench across from Kieran.

"A whiskey man." Kieran nodded, approving, and then drank more from his own bottle.

"*Barbarians*," Esme said, shaking her head while placing the basket on an empty bench.

Out in the bushes and away from the chatter of three misfits, Wren was in a crouched position while she searched through the twigs of thorn. Cuts ran deep as she frantically pushed roses away from each other to look for the cat.

"As much as I love watching you in your natural habitat, I'm right here," the cat said from the steppingstones that wove through the gardens like a maze.

Wren looked back in annoyance at the cat, who was grooming her ears with her paw. "*You*," she hissed and left the bushes of roses and tulips.

"Yes, it is *I*." The cat nodded with closed eyes. "*The* Madam Marie of France is sitting before you, so I advise—"

The cat was going to continue her egotistical introduction until she noticed Wren's piercing glare toward her and ran away.

"Get back here and tell me what the hell is going on!" Wren yelled after the cat. She chased Marie around the backyard, getting lost in her own maze of flowers and shrubs.

"That is no way to speak to me," the cat yelled from the other side of a tall shrub. "I was *the* madam—"

"I don't care who the fuck you are!" Wren shouted and shoved through the tall shrub, stepping out onto another path that led to a small pond. "Get back here!"

"Well, I'll be..." The cat was shocked. "You're not at all like the stories of my ancestors. They spoke of you as a hero, but here you are, acting hopeless. Like a peasant."

"Cool," Wren hissed and ran toward the pond. After a moment, she stopped running and leaned forward with her hands on her knees, catching her breath. "Fuck!" she shouted down at the grass below her feet.

Silence.

The cat was gone.

Moments later, laughter filled Wren's ears, and she walked back to the gazebo near the back door of her house. She walked up the steps and entered the stone hut, walking through the sheer drapes.

"Damn it!" Kieran exclaimed. "I thought you were another ghost."

Wren noticed the blanket Esme had set up in the center, which the three were sitting on. Ray and Esme were playing chess, while Kieran, who sat next to Esme, seemed to feel his role was to drink everything in sight.

"I lost the cat." Wren scowled.

Kieran pointed at the cat curled up on a blue hammock that was hanging opposite the entrance and between two benches. "She's right there."

The cat stared over at Wren with a smirk on her face, like she had won.

"Of course," Wren muttered and sat down on the blanket next to Ray.

"What happened to you?" Ray asked, stopping the match with Esme when he noticed the scratches on Wren's arms. "We need to disinfect those."

When he was about to stand up, Wren pulled him back down. "I'm fine. You should see the rose bushes, though."

Ray settled back into his spot and resumed his game with Esme.

"So, cat..." Wren grabbed a wine bottle and poured herself a glass. "Why did Cain attack us? Start explaining."

The cat sat up in the soft hammock, yawning. "My name is Marie, *not* 'cat.' I was born in the year 1309 and served as the main mage in France for King Jaquez in the year 1354. You may address me as *Madam* Marie."

Marie glared at the four, annoyed, waiting for them to be amazed at her accomplishments as a fae king's mage. Realizing she was not going to receive recognition for being a mage of noble rank, she continued, "I am a nakori mage from Birdsong, and I am here to retrieve the *Angelic Diaries*. A gentleman checked out the book over twenty years ago, and it's long overdue. As for why Cain was here, I don't know. Lucifer—"

"Wait." Ray interrupted the cat. "The only person to mention Cain was the First Mage in Wren's book. Does that mean the First Mage is real? I thought the First Mage was like a mascot for the Mage's Guild."

"'Mascot?'" Marie asked, alarmed. "The First Mage created the Mage's Guild. And the *Angelic Diaries* is not Wren's book."

"I see..." Ray grew quiet and looked down at the chessboard.

Esme fumed, shocked by Ray's words.

"'I see?'" Esme asked. "We've been telling you that the First Mage is real for years." She jumped up to her feet. "Moonlight Hills even has a statue of the First Mage!"

Esme abandoned the game and went to go sit on the bench farthest from Ray. She folded her arms and looked away from everyone, pouting. Ray stared from her to Wren and then at Kieran, who was absorbed in his own world of drunkenness. "To be fair, the *talking* cat convinced me."

He stood up and walked over to Esme. "And, you know, Cain and the man with chains." He sat down, causing Esme to lean away from him, in a mood. "Oh, come on! You know we can't leave a match unfinished."

"*You* can't. *I* can." Esme bit her tongue.

Wren looked away from her best friends and realized her glass was empty. She took the bottle from Kieran's hands and poured another glass of wine.

"Why?" Kieran whined and nodded at the basket full of bottles of wine and whiskey. "There's more."

"Yours tastes better." Wren smiled at Kieran, handing him the bottle. She scanned her eyes over the empty wine bottles surrounding him. "How many bottles have you drank?"

Kieran looked around him, swaying, and said, "No idea." He burped, and the horrid smell of gassy wine filled the gazebo. Marie scrunched her nose in disdain. Wren and Ray looked impressed by the loud burp, and Esme looked offended.

"Cat, why was Cain here?" Wren asked Marie, focusing back on the issue at hand. "I thought he died in the river. That's what the First Mage implied in the book."

Marie tried to ignore being called "Cat" and jumped down onto a bench to be closer to Wren. She stared at her in silence, quietly judging the woman who sat on the blanket. "I don't know, but he looked very alive to me. It might have something to do with the fact that you are the reincarnation of Syn."

Everyone stopped what they were doing and looked over at the cat.

"My ancestor Loki journeyed with Syn on Eden." Marie was excited and then returned to her cynical demeanor. "I volunteered to retrieve the *Angelic Diaries* after I found out Syn's reincarnation had it. But imagine my surprise when I found out how plain you are." She released a sinister laugh.

"First the Spirit, and now I'm someone named Syn?" Wren asked the cat, humored by the accusation. "The island really needs to get their reincarnation myths straight."

"They are the same—" Marie was about to lecture Wren, but she was cut off by Esme screeching.

"The hooded man!" Esme yelled and locked eyes with Wren. "The man who dragged Cain from us—he's the same guy who saved us from the white-haired man when we were kids." She waited for Wren to react, and then asked, "Remember?"

"Of course I remember. It's why I'm fucked up," Wren told Esme.

A brief silence fell over the group.

"I'm probably mistaken." Esme shook her head with a nervous laugh.

"Yeah..." Wren looked down at her hands, which were twisting together anxiously.

Kieran broke out in a laugh. "What?" He looked around at everyone, who were now glaring at him. "That wasn't a joke? I don't know exactly what happened, but if you both saw a dude that looked like that grim reaper we just saw, it's probably the same guy."

"Cat, who was the guy with chains?" Wren asked.

"My name is not '*Cat!*'" Marie finally snapped at Wren. "I don't know who the hooded man was. I'm not an encyclopedia." The cat slammed her tail down on the bench with full force. "I need to return the book."

Wren thought of her next question for Marie and said, "Fine. At least tell me who Syn is?"

Marie was growing contempt toward Wren. "No one knows her origin, but she lived on Eden. She was called the Spirit after Eden fell." She looked far from impressed. "The zyula named her that. They always liked their nicknames." She squinted. She was not fond of the zyula and the primates.

Marie jumped down from the bench and walked up to Wren. "You came to the island as a child, right?"

Wren nodded down at the cat, surprised.

"I *knew* it. I was part of the evaluating team." Marie dropped her head and stared down at her paws. "I knew the orb was glowing back then. No one agreed with me because he said the orb was faulty." She tilted her head. "I mean, yes, the orb sometimes glows accidentally, but we fixed it," she said, arguing with herself. "But the orb does break often... maybe he's right?" Her eyes widened as if she had just snorted an enormous bag of catnip. "Then, you are *not* Syn, and I've wasted my time."

"What do you mean?" Wren interrupted Marie's monologue. "Who's '*he?*' What are you even talking about?!"

Wren grabbed a full bottle of wine and tore the cork out with her teeth. Kieran clapped, impressed by her display of barbarianism. He reached for one of the bottles and tried to do the same, but he winced at the pain in his gums.

"The leader of the Mage's Guild," Marie said, and watched Wren swap wine bottles with Kieran. "He just returned from his stay on another planet, and he is currently going through invoices and records. That's why I'm here—he realized his book was still checked out. Are you listening?"

"What book?" Wren asked Marie. She had become distracted with watching Kieran hug his new bottle of wine. Everyone was becoming intoxicated.

"The *Angelic Diaries*," Marie said and became annoyed at the four, who were laughing in a drunken stupor. "The royal magician from the Angelic Empire is back." She stood up and swayed her tail swiftly. "He's known as the First Mage." She glared at the four, who did not hear her. "He's from Eden!"

Marie fell silent when she noticed no one was listening to her. She jumped onto Wren's lap and pawed up at her, then pulled her ears back and started hissing.

"Is this her war face?" Kieran asked and picked up Marie, cuddling her. "Show me your war face!"

XXIII

Ashes

Later that evening, Marie ran around the house, looking for the book. Esme followed the cat tranquilly, intervening when Marie got near the *Angelic Diaries*. Esme would always giggle after she moved the book to another hiding spot, thinking she and the cat were playing a game. Kieran laid on the couch, entertained by Esme and the talking cat playing chase, until he fell asleep.

After Ray and Wren pried Esme away from her game with Marie, the three made their way into the backyard, each carrying a tiny bowl of ash. The cat followed the three into the backyard, for Esme was clutching the book tightly in her arms.

"Are you sure you should be doing that while intoxicated?" Marie asked Wren, nodding at her bowl. "Is this not a memorable event?"

"I feel fine," Wren said, stumbling.

Marie turned to Esme with a mischievous stare. "You should place the book down. You don't want to spill the ashes."

Esme was about to place it down on a stone bench along the path, but Ray stopped her, saying, "She's trying to get the book."

"Curse you," Marie hissed, then trotted off back into the house where it was warm.

The three walked around the gardens, and Esme walked away to sprinkle some ash on a bush of lavender. When Wren was about to follow her, Esme stopped her with the shake of her head, saying, "I want to be alone."

"Simon still exists," Wren told her. "Don't cry, Esme."

Esme clutched the bowl of ash to her stomach, forcing it to merge with her essence, and both she and the bowl disappeared into the air. Ray walked up to Wren's side and surveyed the bushes for any sign of her.

"I think that man named Cain knows where Simon is," Ray called out to Esme. "Maybe Simon will return, like Johnny did?"

Wren was about to agree, but she decided not to when she remembered what Cain had told them earlier. She turned to him and yanked on his elbow. "Cain said Simon is him, but he isn't Simon. What do you think he meant by that?" she asked.

Ray looked down at her. "I don't know. He was probably trying to sound intimidating."

"Maybe..." Wren took a pinch of ash, rubbing her fingers over the grinds, and watched the particles fall over the wildflowers.

Ray walked away from her and sprinkled some ash from his own bowl over a separate bush of wildflowers. He watched Wren while she tossed ashes over the flora. She then turned from the flowers, causing Ray to walk around the edge of an apple tree, stopping a few feet from her, a worried look upon his face.

"It's been a long day, hasn't it?" Wren asked when her bowl was almost empty, glancing at the time on her watch—midnight.

"Are you okay?" Ray asked.

"Yes, Simon still exists somewhere," Wren replied.

"No, not that. What if you are the Spirit, after all?" Ray asked.

Wren's hair lifted behind her, and the remaining ash spilled from the bowl that fell from her hands. Tiny flames covered her flesh. She stared at him, taking in the possibility, and said, "We don't have to talk about this. I know you don't like the legend of the Spirit."

"It's not that I don't like the legend. I just don't like how it consumes you," Ray said. "There's more to life than trying to find out why you are the way you are."

Wren looked back at him. "Like what?"

"I don't know. *Living?*" Ray suggested.

"How can I live if all I think about is death?" Wren countered.

The wind flew between the two, dividing them.

"It's getting cold," Ray said and poured the last of his ash under the apple tree. "We should go inside."

The flowers, which were decorated with ash, hypnotized her. She walked into the middle of the flower patch. "You can go in," she said. "I want to stay outside for a while."

The dark sky became crowded with clouds and the air grew colder. Wren snapped her eyes up the moment Ray pulled her to him. "It's okay to cry," he whispered into her ear.

She tightened her lips and cried into his chest.

Esme reappeared, sitting on a bench near the apple tree, staring at her best friends. She was mumbling at them in incoherent words. Wren stopped crying abruptly, and she and Ray both stared at Esme—neither had ever seen her cry. Wren sat down next to her and resumed crying, and Ray looked away from them, fighting his own tears.

"You said it was okay to cry!" Esme yelled at Ray. "So, cry with us, Ray."

Ray turned back to face them, placed his hand over his eyes, and joined in with their mourning. After the three released a million tears, they walked back into the manor.

Emerging from The Shade, Lucifer walked into the yard with his black coat whipping behind him. He walked up the stone path that led to the backdoor of Wren's house. He clenched his jaw after the gem shook slightly, and he walked closer to the house.

Cain was right.

It *was* her.

"How?" Lucifer asked. "They hold no similarities, save for the flesh and magic. Syn is more... sinister."

The angelic rubbed the gem in his throat.

"It is *her*," the voices said rapidly from The Shade, the path only one angelic could walk.

"Indeed. It appears I have been proven wrong," Lucifer said, looking back at the pitch-black darkness where the voices came from. "Now, we need her alone."

"We are sure you will come up with something," the many voices said, almost jeeringly. "You are Lucifer, the wisest angelic to ever live."

Lucifer ignored the mockery and stepped back into The Shade, which consisted of dewy ash and shadowed death. The angelic stayed within the path, waiting for the moment Wren would be alone. The voices from the shadow realm started talking over each other, pulling him toward their plane of existence.

"Play with us," the multitude of voices said. "We are alone. Play with us."

"Not now, Aaeon," Lucifer said, his eyes focusing on the hazy image of Wren's house. "I'm busy."

The voices became one, and a loud scream came from the shadow realm, echoing within the path. Lucifer glanced over at the frame of a ghostly man in a black hood. Aaeon's chains lurked behind him, and the smell of rot filled Lucifer's nose.

"My apologies," Lucifer said and bowed his head. "Thank you for helping me with Cain. My associate is rather reckless. However, I do not have the time to play."

Aaeon looked up and screeched out a lonely cry, black blood falling from his eyes.

Back in the house, and away from The Shade, everyone did their own thing. Esme had entered a deep coma in the sunroom, and Wren was lying on the floor of the living room, passing out. Ray was about to pick Wren up to carry her to bed, but Kieran had other plans.

Kieran had woken up and pinned himself to Wren, his mouth clinging to her arm. Sharp points pierced her flesh.

"Filthy peasants," Marie said, standing behind a bewildered Ray.

Wren opened her eyes from the pain, sobering up completely. Kieran's canines were longer than before, with delicate points. "What in the actual fuck, Kieran?" Wren asked, pushing him off her.

"He's feeding; it's what half-breeds do," Marie said with an expression on her face like she just ate shit.

Ray placed a hand over Wren's wound.

"Don't tell me you didn't know?" Marie asked, pacing before them while Kieran scooted away from Wren. "I smelled his stench before he came into this god-awful city."

"I knew he was half something," Wren said, looking down at the wound on her forearm, which was being inspected by Ray. "Do you know what he's mixed with?"

"Half-breeds are half human or nymph and half zyula or katani," the feline said. "Every half-breed develops their parent's genes in their own time." The cat pounced onto Kieran's lap and pawed up at his fangs. "But never have I seen their teeth change."

Kieran felt his teeth, which did not retract. "Will they go away?" he asked Marie, panic rising.

"Maybe. I don't know. Lengthening of the canines has never happened before," Marie said tenaciously. "Your father was a katani, right? And your mother a nymph?"

"What?" Kieran asked in defense. "No. My mom was human."

"Your father must have been a katani. Humans are the only primate and nymphs are the only fae that can mate with the archaic lines because they inherited certain traits during their evolution. It's almost as if the nymphs and humans are trying to become the katani and zyula again. So, if your mother was human, then your father would *have* to be zyula, since humans share their likeness. But they are all extinct," Marie said, staring at Kieran with a twitch in her eye.

She was intrigued with uncovering Kieran's DNA, and she looked down at the floor to think. She became troubled, realizing she had no idea what Kieran could be mixed with. After a moment of thought, the cat then looked back up at him. "Well, *what* are you?" she asked.

"What are *you*?" Kieran asked the cat, not fond of how she stared at him like a bug being examined. "You said you're a nakori mage? Is that a level of mage or something?"

Marie was about to answer Kieran's question until the half-breed burst out laughing at her.

"What about Edenian?" Wren asked Marie, interrupting a growing feud between cat and half-breed.

"The only Edenians who survived that *may* be compatible with humans are the angelics and dwarves." Marie paused.

"Some Edenians actually survived the explosion?" Ray asked. Realizing he had lost his ongoing argument with Wren and Esme, he fell silent.

"What about the giants?" Wren asked, excited about uncovering Kieran's genetics. "They are humanlike. Plus, Kieran is carnivorous. He also has cannibalistic tendencies."

"The giants became extinct before the explosion of Eden." Marie twitched her whiskers. "'Cannibalistic... tendencies?'"

Wren turned to Kieran and asked, "Then, what the hell are you?"

Kieran shrugged. "You tell me."

"The angelics on Eden were herbivorous, but the seven left behind on Earth became carnivorous because of the darkness." The cat muttered to herself with knowledge she had about the Angelic Empire. "If—and only *if*—one of the fallen angelics on Earth is the boy's father, then the offspring would resemble a half-breed. But that is highly doubtful, considering the fallen angelics detest humans," she said coldly. "Hypothetically speaking, of course, if one of the angelics had mated with a human, then... I guess the offspring would be half-angelic. They *don't* exist, nymph nor human."

"Maybe that's why you have fangs? You weren't supposed to exist," Wren told Kieran. "Isn't this great? You're not a cannibal since you're not completely human. You're just fucked-up, DNA wise."

Marie stared up at Kieran. "Congratulations... you're *special*."

Wren glanced for a moment at Ray, who was lost in his thoughts. She shrugged, mistaking his discomfort for drunkenness, and turned to Marie, asking, "Hey, what did you mean about the darkness changing the angelics?"

"Hm?" Marie groomed her paw, eyeing Wren with a glare smothered in superiority. "Energy from the dark realm invaded our world when Eden was intact, and it altered the few angelics left behind. Bloodlust, carnivorousness, savagery... the fallen angelics are no longer part of the peaceful nation who once ruled Eden." She smirked. "The darkness is also what cracked Eden. It's why the solar system is so, well, *dark*. I thought everyone knew that. What are they even teaching in your schools?"

"The scholars in Birdsong claim the Spirit blew up Eden," Wren said.

Marie stayed still and then broke into a mean giggle. "What scholar said *that*? Syn did many things, but she didn't blow up Eden. She could barely blow up the Angelic Empire's castle." She snickered. "There's an old story in my clan that Syn had stood against the angelics, and she led all the giants to attack the empire. And that's why we don't have any more giants."

Kieran patted Wren on the shoulder. "So, you didn't blow up a planet, but you did lead the giants to extinction."

"It's just a story," Marie told them. "It's most likely not true, but I like to think it is."

The cat preached how there were only nine half-breeds throughout history, and that all of them were half-nymph and half-katani. She chattered about how the few surviving katani lived in the woods of Birdsong Island, which Wren already knew. Marie shifted her banter to talk about spirit fragments as she snorted with maniacal laughter. The cat enjoyed the fact that some primates and fae were not complete, soul-wise. While she detested the primates, the cat was not fond of the fae either. She suddenly stopped talking, embarrassed by her friendly attitude toward *peasants*.

"Listen, I really just want the book. As much as I had a wonderful time meeting Syn's reincarnation, I don't want to become your friend," Marie said. "The quicker I get the book, the faster I can return to the library."

"You keep mentioning this library... You probably live there," Kieran said, pointing at Marie. "Nerd."

Ray stood up from the living room chair, leaving his mental prison, exhaling a long breath from all the noise. He stretched and said, "I would love to stay and be yelled at by a cat, but I'm tired. I'll be back later."

Marie stood her ground to Kieran's mockery and scolded him about possibly being an angelic half-breed, as if he had any control of his genetic makeup. He kept calling her a nerd, and the two continued their squabbling.

"Good idea. I'm going to bed." Wren jumped up and walked with Ray under the archway behind the Holo-disc.

Wren and Ray turned left and walked down the hall toward her bedroom. He looked down at her, a solemn look on his face. He rubbed his eyes—a throbbing was spreading.

"Do you have a headache?" Wren asked him after she opened her bedroom door. "You keep messing with your eyes."

"Meh." Ray shrugged.

Wren's bedroom was the same size as the kitchen and dining area, but it harbored fewer materialistic possessions. The room was decorated with a king-sized bed on a wooden platform, a set of nightstands, a rocking chair, a few standing candelabras, a wooden armoire, and a door that led to a boudoir—which was also connected to Esme's sunroom.

"Don't worry about me. I'll take some medicine," Ray said, standing at the door. "Get some sleep. I'll be by in the morning."

"It is morning," Wren grumbled as she walked toward her bed. She laid down and grabbed one of her silver decorative pillows, hiding behind it.

"You know what I mean," he said.

"Oh! Rolf and Kyle want to see Reme later today. I'm going to go with them. Want to go?" Wren asked. "Think they want to cheer us up."

"What time?" Ray asked.

"Ten," Wren replied. "I'll make coffee."

"Sure." Ray nodded. "Might be fun. We should bring the cat and set up a puppeteer act."

He walked from the bedroom, leaving Wren stumped at his joke. He narrowed his eyes down the wide hall and paused before walking back into the living room. He rubbed his eyes, trying to get rid of the pain behind his eyelids.

"Why haven't you guys got together yet?" Kieran asked Ray when he walked back into the living room. "I'm curious about that."

Kieran kept shoving Marie away, only for her to keep getting in his face about the dangers of half-breeds.

"What?" Ray asked as he picked up his keys and bike helmet from under the coffee table. "First Esme, and now Wren? You're speaking nonsense again."

"Well, I'm just saying—"

"I need to go home," Ray said, interrupting Kieran, trying to ignore the pain in his eyes.

"You shouldn't leave the house," Marie said. "Who knows what the rebels are planning?"

"We'll be fine. Vaan always takes care of them..." Ray scratched his cheek.

Vaan's job was to clean up the city if the criminal mischief became too much for the police and mages. This was applauded by the city. However, the city was not always keen on how the quiet man from Birdsong Island went about it. He had a bloodlust that could make Vikings cower. But when he saved the city from the nineteen-year-old shooter, the city had started to see his value differently. Tallahassee realized that someone like him was needed, and the former mayor gave him a custom-made city job as Damage Control Alpha. And when the city got a new mayor, she kept the job active.

The world was safer with people like Vaan in it.

The opposite could be said for Vaan's victims.

"They can't do much damage with Vaan working for the mayor." Ray looked down at Marie. "Plus, Zara's giving a speech at the courthouse during the arraignment on Friday. Every time she gives a speech, the city calms down for a bit. Talk about charisma—the Adams family is full of it."

"That's Friday. Today is barely Sunday. Rebels could be everywhere. You don't have special abilities like your friends do. It's not safe for you to leave," Marie said. "Plus, *no one* is leaving until I get the book."

"Ah, the real reason." Ray rushed into the foyer.

Marie ran past him, her body growing into the size of a horse. "I said no," she hissed, whipping her large tail behind her.

Ray held up his hands and backed up, not caring to know how the cat grew. "Okay, okay."

"Wren *is* Syn. As for you, you have a weird aura all around you." Marie looked frustrated. "You all must abandon your current lifestyles. We have things to do."

"What do you mean, we have to abandon our lifestyles?" Ray asked the mage, who shrank back down to the size of a house cat.

"Your family, your job—"

"No." Ray narrowed his brow down at the cat. "I am not abandoning my parents, and the store is Wren's life. She lives, eats, and breathes our store."

"I'm aware," Marie stated. "I don't mean to sound harsh, but you all have more important things to do from now on."

"Whatever... I'll at least hire a stand-in manager and ask Eudora to monitor the store," Ray said as he thought out loud, quick on resolving problems. "*Fine*—I'll tell my parents I'm going on vacation."

"You speak as if I'm talking about temporary. You need to get rid of all obligations to your human life so you can focus," Marie snapped. "The sooner that happens, the quicker we can save Earth from blowing up."

"Earth is going to blow up?" Ray asked. He stared blankly down at the cat, light flickering in his eyes. The silver light lit up like lightning, causing Marie to step back.

"What spirit are you communicating with?" Marie looked captivated by the light in his eyes. "That light reeks of spirit possession."

Quickly, Ray's demeanor changed, and his eyes became overwhelmed with light. "You are nakori, correct?" he asked in a deep voice.

Marie nodded, unable to speak. Her tail swayed right to left rapidly as excitement fueled her. She recognized the king of the Angelic Empire's voice. She sat down at Ray's feet, puzzled that she was speaking to the very being who had sacrificed himself to save Eden's cosmos. The library she worked at only had recorded audio footage and documents of Eden.

"Even on this shattered planet, you still protect us." Ray's eyes were completely silver. "Nakori were always the most trusted steeds." He kneeled and scratched Marie behind her ears. "Guide Wren, so when Syn wakes, this broken cosmos will not break further from the darkness."

Ray's eyes turned back to normal, and he stared down at the cat in confusion. "What are you doing?" he asked Marie as he picked up his hand from her ears.

Marie stopped purring and looked disappointed that Ray was back and the angelic trapped inside the sun was gone. She ran off, excited about her brief conversation with Azazel, the angelic who kept the solar system from breaking further.

Ray shook his head, lost about what had just happened. Confused at the cat's sudden departure, he stood up and walked into the living room with plans to sleep on the couch. When he was about to lay down on the loveseat, Kieran, who had already claimed the couch, shooed him out of the living room. "Turn off the lights." Kieran waved his hand.

Ray flicked the switch on the wall that connected to the foyer and then walked toward the entryway. He took a seat on the black wingback chair near the archway that led to Wren's bedroom and sunroom. He looked to his right and stared at the doorless front door.

Ray leaned his head back, exhausted, as Wren walked out of her bedroom wearing a long burgundy robe. She was planning to take a shower before bed, but she wanted to make a temporary door for the night. Her hair was loosely waving behind her as she hurried toward the front door to create an energetic barrier. "What the fuck, Ray?" she asked in surprise, jumping back when she saw him dozing off in the foyer.

"That cat won't let me leave," Ray explained.

"She's a tiny cat—what can she do?" Wren asked and walked up to the doorframe.

"She grew," Ray replied, watching Wren create an energetic door. "Will that hold? Doesn't energy manipulation drain you?"

"Worth a try," Wren said. She stepped back and observed the foggy door of energy. "I feel fine."

She turned to face Ray, and the energetic door collapsed, returning to her the moment she let her guard down.

"I got it!" Red shouted from the hall. "Go to sleep already!" The gargoyle summoned thick branches to the doorway, which sealed out the wind and debris, shouting, "This won't hold forever, so you should get a new door!"

"Thank you, Red," Wren called out. "No idea why I didn't think of asking them to create a door." She paused. "We might as well stay up until Reme's show." She then yanked Ray out of the chair. "Who needs sleep anyway?" she asked excitedly, annoying him. "Esme, Kieran, want to have a slumber party of mourning?!"

From the couch, Kieran shouted, *"Fuck no!"*

At the same time, from her lounge on the pool's steps, Esme yelled, *"Be quiet!"*

"This is why they created coffee, guys!!" Wren yelled out to Esme and

Kieran, who kept shouting for her to be quiet. She turned to Ray. "You're in charge of making the coffee. I want to shower."

"You don't need coffee. How are you so energetic after all we drank?" Ray asked her, groaning. "Why can't you be normal? Just take your damn shower and go to sleep."

As Wren suggested all the things they could talk about, Ray tried to look away from her. He caught his reflection in the hallway mirror and noticed the light emitting from his eyes. Not knowing what the light meant, he ruffled his bangs to try to hide his eyes. He was one to talk about normality.

XXIV

HOUSE OF FREAKS

WHILE WREN WAS IN the oversized shower, everything hit her at once. Leaning against the wall, she covered her face with her hands and slid to the floor. She had a hard enough time grasping the reality of Simon's departure. Now, she thought she might actually be the Spirit because of a talking cat, and something odd was going on with Ray—his headaches were becoming daily.

As she cried in her hands, dark energy swirled together in front of her. Lucifer emerged from The Shade, squinting from the hot water, and as he peered down at Wren, he said, "Stop that insufferable sound." He squatted down in front of her as she pressed her back further into the wall. He appeared amused by her reaction and flicked her on the forehead. "Come on out, *Syn*," he ordered, while the gem in his throat moved. "We have no time for games, and we all know how much you love your games."

"What do you want?" Wren asked, stunned. "Who are you? How'd you get in here?"

Wren tried to shove Lucifer away and summon a force field, but she failed. Then, she tried to pull the curtain back to yell for help, but he took her wrist in his hand. "Yelling is of no use. So, please, do not bleed my ears," he said politely.

He tossed Wren over his shoulder, walking out of the shower. After leaving the boudoir, he flopped her onto the bed next to Ray, who was asleep. She tried to raise her force field again, only for Lucifer to wave his hand, temporarily disabling her powers with his magic.

"What did you do?" Wren asked and scooted back.

"Go to sleep," Lucifer told her in a familiar voice.

Wren rubbed her temples and looked up at the extremely tall man. She tried to summon her flames, but her fire would not start, and sleep overcame her. "Do we know each other?" she asked, her eyelids closing while she yawned from Lucifer's spell.

Lucifer watched her fall asleep and turned to Aaeon, who emerged from The Shade, his chains dragging behind him on the floor.

"Cain wants... you," Aaeon said, about to toss his chains at Lucifer.

"Uh-uh. How many times must I remind you?" Lucifer held up his hand. "No chaining me."

Aaeon looked sad and held back his chains. Chaining was the Shadow King's way of being friendly. It hurt him that no one liked his chains. Lucifer was his only friend, so he listened and decided not to fling his links of shadow at him.

"Tell Cain I am busy," Lucifer told Aaeon.

Aaeon drifted back into The Shade and burst into numerous particles of darkness. Voices came from the path, chattering over each other, trying to lure Lucifer into the shadow realm.

"Aaeon, I am busy," Lucifer said, as if scolding a child.

Once the path closed, he sliced his throat with the knife he had taken from Andvari. His silver blood splattered onto the floor. After retrieving the gem, he tossed it above her unconscious body, and fire engulfed the stone, which stayed motionless in midair.

"Is this woman Syn?" Lucifer asked the gem.

The stone burst, and its specks spread over Wren, clinging to her form. For no, the dust would turn black, and for yes, the dust would turn gold.

Wren was soon shimmering in a million sparkling specks of golden broken rock.

Lucifer walked outside while the others slept inside the house. Aaeon opened a door to The Shade and, once again, tried to call Lucifer into his world.

"I am still busy, Aaeon." Lucifer wanted nothing but silence.

Aaeon left as his many voices criticized Lucifer. The Shadow King had taken a liking to Lucifer after Lucifer found entrance into the shadow realm one day, back on Eden. From the moment the Shadow King met the angelic, Aaeon had attached himself to Lucifer.

The shadow realm was created long before the other two realms, and it was made from both light and dark. The shadow realm's only inhabitant was a god named Aaeon, the lost and forgotten king. The god drifted The Shade as he watched the light and dark realms, often wondering why he was created in a world of his own. And with a realm all to his own, he never knew how to treat others, so he often dragged spirits from the other two realms to play—or torture, depending on one's perception of fun. Consequently, when he returned the spirit to their proper realm, the spirit would often be a broken shell.

Lucifer sat on a bench and stared at a sleeping bird nestled in a tree. His lips slowly spread into a smile. He remained still, waiting for dawn to come.

※※※※※

When dawn came, so did the alarm that Wren had forgotten to turn off. She hid from the sun, which filled the room in protest, and she tried to fall back asleep, but she could hear people talking in her living room. She then remembered the man who had invaded her shower.

"She is the reincarnation of my pupil," Lucifer told Ray as the two talked in the living room. Ray was questioning him. "Her name is Syn."

"Told you," Marie told Ray in a pompous tone and then ran around the couch, trying to get Lucifer's attention. She wanted to inform him about Ray communicating with Azazel, but the cat side of her kicked in, and she started to stalk a small spider on the wall fifteen feet from the backside of the couch.

Wren sat up, tuning out the discussion in the living room, spotting gold dust clinging to her body. She tried to brush off the gold specks and noticed she was wearing a red silk nightgown she had never seen before. It reeked of magic. She tried to extract information from Esme or Kieran about who the intruder was—and what had happened—but it was knowledge she could not obtain from their minds. Esme was not receptive to Wren's thoughts, as she was deeply concentrating on preparing her breakfast while chatting with Twila, and Kieran was busy laying on the couch, blaring music in his ears from a vintage headset he had found in the study. The runaway hated knowing his mind was being read.

So, Wren tried to pry into the stranger's mind, only for Lucifer to push her out with ease. "Damn it," she muttered to herself.

Wren was too tired to scream her way into Esme's mind, and she picked off a golden fleck from her wrist. She grimaced at the rustic wall clock, which was releasing another alarm—seven-fifteen. She stood up and walked down the platform steps. She pushed the small button on the bottom of the clock, turning off the alarm. She walked up to the solid wooden door that led to the boudoir, which was on the right wall of her bedroom if one looked in from the hall. The boudoir connected her bedroom to the sunroom, and it was constructed to make it easier to walk around the rooms of the house, though she had to get used to maneuvering inside the boudoir after it was renovated, as the room often made it an adventure or chore, depending on how awake she was.

Walking into the boudoir, Wren groaned from the bright lights that shone in from the sunroom's glass door. Esme had always kept her living quarters bright. The room Wren walked into was almost half the size of her bedroom. To the right of the entrance, from her bedroom, was a tall glass door that led into the sunroom, which Esme claimed as her bedroom. All the walls in the boudoir were made of light, green-colored marble, and they were decorated with many long mirrors that lit up the room from the light of the sunroom. The white marble floor had a hint of crystal in it so that it sparkled lightly. Mirrored walls reflected the floor, making the room have a quasi-mystical glow.

The brightness of the boudoir was Esme's idea. She was obsessed with a sunlight-and-water theme, but Wren loved steampunk and gothic décor, so the interiors of Sparrow Manor were far from Wren's parents' humble country cottage. The mixture of Wren and Esme's fashion preferences had developed into a gothic-hippy aesthetic.

A huge painting hung on the wall opposite the door that led into Wren's bedroom. It was a lost and untitled piece by Leonardo da Vinci. Eudora had purchased it in France from a private underground auction on a trip with her daughters after they decided to renovate the house. If Wren and Esme wanted to live in a mansion that the city considered haunted, then Eudora would make sure it was the most sophisticated haunted mansion.

Under the painting was a grand piano from Italy. To the left of the piano was a wall that extended eight feet, separating the entryway from the enclosed bathroom. To the left of Wren's door was an L-shaped light green couch that rested in the corner. Between the deep-cushioned couch and enclosed bathroom was an oak vanity table with a soft yellow stool facing the left wall. There was no need for a standard vanity mirror; all the walls acted as mirrors. And in the middle of the boudoir were two rectangular island dressers, with a vase full of flowers placed in the center of both wide surfaces.

Wren walked over to the sliding door that led to the bathroom in front of the couch. She stared at her reflection and saw the gold sparkling all over her body. Sliding the door open, she entered the bathroom. She thought the bathroom was going to be a war zone from the previous night, but it was clean. The tiled wall had its normal soft blue hue, and the white rug was spotless, resting on top of the clean marble floor. The toilet on her left was closed and tidy. She peeked around the protruding wall that separated the toilet from the shower.

The room harbored no strangers.

Wren slid the door closed behind her and walked toward the shower, which was the size of a hot tub. Drawing the curtain open, she scanned over the shower-bath for any signs of tampering. Content with the state of the room, she drew her bath. She climbed into the scorching hot water and dipped her head under, holding her breath.

"Good, you're up! We all woke up, like, ages ago," Kieran yelled out and barged into Wren's bedroom once he noticed her bedroom light was on. He, Ray, and Esme had only woken up thirty minutes before Wren. "This guy says you're Syn, too!" he yelled over the music blaring in his ears. "Where the fuck are you?"

Wren did not reply. She was focused on how Kieran was rummaging around her bedroom. She was expecting him to break something, as he was not the most graceful. He then managed to enter the boudoir.

Kieran circled the boudoir and placed the headphones around his neck. "I like your piano room. Um, where the hell are you? I just heard you banging around in here."

"It's a boudoir. I'm in the bathroom," Wren said loudly.

"Fancy." Kieran rummaged through all the drawers on both sides of the black island dresser, smirking at Wren's lingerie. "32G," he said as he read the tag on a black bra. "Your back must hurt." He then smelled the snapdragons in a light pink vase that smelled like lavender.

"My back is fine, thank you! Stop going through my clothes," Wren yelled out to him. "And don't you dare go through Esme's!"

Kieran placed the headphones back over his ears and turned up the volume. He smirked at a sweater with **Moonlight Hills** sewed into it. The sweater was hanging above a white island dresser that was a few feet away from Wren's. Something told him that it belonged to Esme. He was not planning to go through her drawers, but he saw a pink laced bra hanging near the sweater. He felt it was harmless to read the tag, since he was curious by nature. **34C**. He grinned. A light blue vase with yellow sunflowers rested in the middle, but they smelled like roses. He turned, spotting Esme lying down on a chaise lounge through the glass door that led to her room.

"Well, you're boring. Later!" Kieran yelled out to Wren. He left the double island dressers and flowers that smelled like other flowers and walked into the sunroom. He stared at Esme lounging under the wide windows in a floral sundress. She was reading a nymph lifestyle magazine. A bowl of porridge was on the end table. He removed the headphones from his ears and said, "Morning."

Esme looked up, startled, and she almost fell off her pearl-colored chaise. "Don't just barge into people's bedrooms, Kieran!"

"I thought this was the poolroom," Kieran said, placing the headset on a wooden bench next to the pool. "This doesn't look like a bedroom. There's no bed. Where do you sleep?"

"I can say the same about a human bedroom," Esme argued. "I sleep in water, not cloth."

She turned to Kieran, who was studying the statue of the goddess in the center of the pool.

"Wait—you're telling me you sleep in this thing?" Kieran looked down at the bubbles and rose petals. "Why?"

"You know why." Esme grew annoyed that he was asking idiotic questions. "Stop acting stupid. Wren told us all about you. I know you know all about my culture."

Kieran looked surprised by her tone. "Where did you go when I was attacked last night?" he asked.

"Nowhere," Esme replied, and she glanced down at the page she was reading. "When I turn invisible, I'm still here. You just can't see me. I was scared. Sorry I left you alone."

Kieran cleared his throat. "You're forgiven. What the hell even happened last night? That guy attacked us twice. And Johnny just stood there."

He waited for a reaction from her. Esme simply nodded—her eyes glued to the words on the page. She did not want to deal with anyone until she was completely awake. As he stared at her calmly reading, he entered a temporary fit of panic. "Why is no one overreacting to the invasion from last night? What about the ghost of my dead boyfriend? How about this guy who's in the living room? Ray is just like 'Oh, okay, nice to meet you,' and he's talking to him like they're old friends," he ranted. "What about your sister being the reincarnation of some old hag? What about me? I eat people, and you all just let me roam around your house while you had dinner last night! Why are y'all so fucking calm?!"

Kieran huffed as Esme continued to read. "Stop reading!!!"

In the living room, the angelic who had temporarily disabled Red and broken into the manor listened to Kieran's tantrum. His eyes narrowed at the half-breed's diction. Lucifer knew *exactly* who Kieran's father was. There was only one of the seven angelics on Earth who had exploding episodes.

Then, Lucifer started to fret. Being near the offspring of the very angelic he found to be the most annoying in existence was a cruel joke—a joke he did not have time for.

"Should I check on them?" Ray asked as he stared at the closed door that led to Esme's room. His hands were resting on his hips. "Why is he yelling?"

"That is your choice to make," Lucifer said. "The half-breed is having a crisis, that is all. He will be fine. Like father, like son."

Ray looked back at the tall angelic. "You know who his dad is?"

Lucifer did not respond.

Feeling all-black was appropriate, Wren emerged from the boudoir dressed in jeans and a tank top. Her destination was Esme's room to see what the loud commotion was.

To Wren's bewilderment, Esme had Kieran in a chokehold. They both had fallen into the pool after Kieran had stolen Esme's magazine. "What's going on?" she asked, raising an eyebrow at the two, who were laughing.

"He took my magazine," Esme told Wren.

"So, you put him in a chokehold?" Wren asked.

Esme quickly released Kieran. "I thought nymphs weren't strong?" he asked as he rubbed his neck.

"On land, our strength is drained," Esme said, and her eyes spiraled with a million waves. "But in water, we can make hurricanes."

Wren watched Esme laugh at Kieran's reaction when she manipulated the water to move around him on its own. He splashed her with water, which she easily sent back to him with her golden tail.

"Well, this is weird," Wren said, and left them alone to their game. After she stepped out into the hall, she noticed Ray was staring in her direction. "I think Esme and Kieran have a crush on each other. Out of all the crazy stuff that's been happening, I think *this* is the most shocking."

Wren walked up to Ray. "I knew it," he said with a slight grin.

"I thought he preferred men," Wren said. "Johnny died two months ago. Isn't this too fast? I really don't want Esme dating some cannibalistic half-breed. Can you imagine? A pacifist and a cannibal? Talk about odd couples. Would he even be a cannibal if he's only half-human? My brain hurts..."

"Well, liking each other doesn't mean romantic. Look at us," Ray said. "They could just be forming a platonic bond."

Growing irritated with their mortal behavior, Lucifer walked up to Wren and glowered down at her, saying, "We need to talk."

Back in Esme's room, Kieran was scrubbing his face with petals that looked like roses in the water. He liked how they felt. It was almost as if they were exfoliating his skin. He did not know roses even had a species of flower with rough petals. Then, he examined a petal and thought maybe it was not a rose. "What are these?" he asked Esme.

"Rose petals." Esme looked at the petals floating around them.

"But they're rough," Kieran said and scrubbed his cheek with one.

"Roses in Moonlight Hills grow that way," Esme said. "The florists design them with regenerative properties. That's why they're not like other roses."

"I thought florists only assembled bouquets?" Kieran asked.

"Not in Moonlight Hills," Esme said. "Our florists are more like plant geneticists who *also* assemble bouquets. The pool is medicinal. Check your wounds. They should be almost healed by now."

Esme watched Kieran examine his arms. He patted the back of his head, feeling no scabs from when he had often banged his head on the wall back in Perk's jail. His wide eyes informed her that his wounds were vanishing. His brain was becoming more focused.

After Esme and Wren moved into the house, Esme had claimed the sunroom because of the pool. It was well known that nymphs preferred to sleep in water. Feeling bad about turning the sunroom into her bedroom, she had amplified the pool the Sparrows had designed with roses and herbs from Moonlight Hills. She left the room open during the day, so Wren and guests could swim in the pool, but she assigned a timeframe for pool use, considering it was inside her bedroom. The pool was open from sunrise to sunset unless it was an emergency. Then, the sunroom turned into an infirmary.

And they had a good share of emergencies.

"Are you sure that it's okay I'm in here? Isn't it your bed?" Kieran asked.

"The water cleanses itself every second. You're fine. Just enjoy the water," Esme said and walked out of the pool, her sundress clinging to her body.

"The water is clean, even with my filth?" Kieran looked away from her and played with more petals.

"That's why you can't see any of the blood from your wounds in the water." Esme pointed at the water surrounding him. She grabbed a towel from the wooden rack. "I infused the water with herbs that mend and cleanse. The water stitches cuts closed, and the petals absorb dirt. You only have to spend three-to-five minutes soaking to become clean. Ten minutes to seal superficial wounds. Thirty minutes for severe wounds. And an hour to fully heal the body of internal injuries. You should be clean by now."

"Why didn't the water clean me last night?" he asked.

"Because you were only in the pool briefly before I saw you drowning," Esme said. "I mean, you did become a little clean... Didn't you notice your stench was gone after I woke you?"

"No..." Kieran was slightly offended, but he shrugged it off. "Thank you for not letting me drown. Johnny was just watching."

"That *was* odd," Esme said, nodding. "But I'm sure there was a reason. Johnny's always been kind-hearted."

"You said the pool heals injuries?" he asked and fell back into the water, floating on his back. "What about heartbreak?"

"Oh, I don't know. But it should. Heartbreak is associated with real bodily issues," Esme told him. "Feel free to use the pool during the day. But please, don't get nude. Always wear at least trunks." She suddenly widened her eyes. "You can dry your clothes out under the sun or in the dryer. I prefer the sun." She rushed her words and rambled on anxiously. "I'll see if Ray has any clothes you can borrow. He usually keeps clothes here in case he stays over. Clean towels are on the rack. Help yourself."

Before Kieran could speak, Esme quickly walked into the boudoir. She closed the door and screamed into her hands. How could she say the word "nude" in front of a man? No, in front of anyone, for that matter?

As if Esme had forgotten that the door was made of glass, she grabbed the sides of her head with both hands and shook her head back and forth. A smile crept up the side of Kieran's mouth. He leaned over the edge of the pool, watching her scream silently into the void.

Lucifer was still glaring down at Wren in the living room, waiting for her to speak to him. But she was still talking to Ray about Kieran and Esme.

"Stop ignoring me. We need to talk," Lucifer said to her.

"Why?" Wren asked the angelic, looking him up and down. "Who are you?" She leaned in and stared into his pitch-black eyes. "*What* are you?"

"He's looking for Syn... he thinks you're her," Ray said.

Kieran walked out of the sunroom, drying off his bare torso with a towel, and another towel was wrapped around his waist. He had decided to leave Esme alone with her breakdown. "He's obviously an alien," he said, eyeing Lucifer.

"His name's Lucifer," Marie said loudly from the hall as she crouched down chasing a spider. "Show your respect. He's the First Mage."

Kieran waved his hands in the air, scrunching his face, mocking both mages. Lucifer moved his eyes from Wren and looked down at Kieran, narrowing his eyes at the half-breed.

"Wait, what?" Wren asked, staring at the angelic who was glaring down at Kieran's foolishness. "The First Mage?"

Kieran tilted his head at Wren. "Your telepathy is failing you."

Lucifer grimaced and said to Marie, who was jumping down the hall, "I told you not to tell them my name, Marie."

Kieran looked over at Wren and Ray, absorbing the information, and then he looked up at Lucifer. "Seriously?" he asked. "You're the fuck who wrote that huge fucking book?"

Lucifer did not speak.

"So, I can just ask you all my questions and not read?" Kieran looked relieved. "But why keep your identity hidden?" he asked. "You're the First Mage. Like, the first of the mages—"

"That is why," Lucifer said, interrupting Kieran's praise, and he pointed at Wren, who was leaking fire from her eyes.

Ray and Kieran stared at Wren, who was entering a rampage. The corners of her mouth had turned upwards while she glared a deadly stare at Lucifer. Marie, who had been running around the house chasing a spider, began following a fly and circled around Kieran, trying to capture the bug.

"Why's she frozen?" Kieran asked as he walked up to Wren.

"She is in a trance," Lucifer told him. "It is what she does."

"I've never seen her do this," Ray said. He walked up to Wren, who would not move, to look her in the eyes.

"I would not get too close if I were you," Lucifer warned Ray. "That is not your friend at the moment."

"Not my friend?" Ray asked. "Then, who is she?"

"Syn," Lucifer said. "Even though she is in a different body, her soul is still aware of what is going on. Before Syn came to live as Wren, we had an argument."

"Ok," Ray said quietly and stepped back from Wren. "Say that I believe you about Wren being Syn... What was your argument?"

"Cain wanted to send her here, but she disagreed," Lucifer said.

"So, you forced her to reincarnate?" Ray asked.

"Sort of—"

Fire flickered around Wren, causing Lucifer to stop talking.

"Dude, is she going to blow up?" Kieran asked jokingly. "Esme! Come hose her down!"

As if Kieran's stupidity had snapped Wren out of her trance, she calmed down. She shook the fire away from her, confused about why the knowledge of the man being Lucifer angered her. As fascinated as she was with the *Angelic Diaries*, she should feel ecstatic to meet its author.

"You shouldn't have attacked me in the shower," Wren told Lucifer, trying to justify her rage. Something about the angelic made her feel odd. "Are you the reason I look like this?"

"I did not attack you," Lucifer replied. He examined her light golden arms. "Yes, I am afraid that was my doing. I had to verify."

"Verify what?" Wren asked.

"That you are Syn," Lucifer replied.

"About that..." Ray chimed in, looking at Wren. "I think Isis is right about you being the Spirit."

"I am not." Wren looked offended.

Marie abandoned the fly when she found a small jumping spider near Kieran's foot. She pounced on his bare foot, causing him to wince. Her claws were sharp. He looked down at her staring at the jumping spider, which kept jumping away from her, and asked, "Can't you just use your magic to catch it? Aren't you a mage?"

"That's no fun," Marie mused and moved her whiskers, about to pounce. She was forced to abandon the fast spider, who escaped from the living room by jumping into a vent.

"Who exactly is Syn?" Kieran asked, after moving his eyes from Marie. "The cat only said she lived on Eden."

"Yes, Syn lived on Eden, but she is from the dark realm." Lucifer held his hands behind his back, walking around the living room, looking over every painting. "The artist is quite talented."

"'The dark realm?'" Kieran asked, stepping away from where Wren stood, pointing at her. "Is Wren a demon? She's a demon, isn't she?" He quickly walked between Lucifer and a painting the angelic was walking up to and gazed up at him, trying to hypnotize him into admitting Wren was, in fact, the reincarnation of a demon.

"No. Syn is not a demon. She is lore, a species known for war," Lucifer said, trying not to sound bitter. "Excuse me, but my mood is foul. Wren presents herself in a noble manner, and I find that annoying."

"I'm not annoying," Wren blurted out.

Lucifer looked back at her. "I never said that. I said how you present yourself is annoying."

"Isn't that the same thing?" Kieran asked.

Lucifer looked concerned that Wren was starting to overthink his words. She turned to Ray and asked him, "Am I annoying?"

"No, the guy's kind of an asshole." Ray shook his head and waved his hand Lucifer's way. "Don't listen to him." He eyed the angelic. "Look. I don't care if you have a hard on for Syn. But that is no reason to be mean to Wren."

Lucifer was taken aback. "'Hard on?'"

When Lucifer realized what "hard on" meant, the angelic straightened his back and looked disturbed. Everyone in the Angelic Empire knew he was a scholar of the universe. The wise angelic did not have time for anything other than research, nor did he get *hard ons*.

"You seem all uppity and high-class, too. That's the pot calling the kettle black," Ray said to Lucifer.

"If you knew Syn, you would be just as surprised as I am that Wren is her reincarnation. Think of Syn as the ghost of a graceful hunter who loves to eat all kinds of animals, especially humans. The reason she did not want to reincarnate to help Cain was because she has a habit of venturing to Earth to possess people, kill others, and eat them." Lucifer paused. "Well, I suppose Syn is actually similar to your demon myths..."

"That sounds troubling," Ray said, locking eyes with Wren. "Is she going to turn back into her?"

"Stop staring at me," Wren said to him. "And I'm right here."

"Yes. On her twenty-fifth birthday, after her human development is complete," Lucifer said in response to Ray's question. "Cain's fragment died early, so he is trying to bring Syn back earlier to continue building his machine. However, I think Syn should live her life as Wren for as long as possible. Maybe she will pick up on some new ethics."

Wren was about to get mad again for being spoken about and not to, but then she exclaimed at Lucifer, "Hey! I have no idea what you just said, but that sounded like a diss."

Lucifer smiled. "See, you are Syn."

"No, I'm not."

"Why else would you get mad if you are not Syn? I insulted her and complimented you." Lucifer studied Wren's eyes as she processed what he had said. "I am proud of the life you have been living, Wren. Helping those being hunted, donating to those in need..." He walked up to her and placed a hand on the side of her face. "You have done well."

Lucifer's touch soothed Wren's pain, and she took a step back. She did not like the way it felt.

"You'll probably start craving human meat, like Syn," Kieran chimed in. "We can go on food runs. *Sweet*."

Wren glared over at him.

XXV

SPACE & TIME

ESME FINALLY WALKED INTO the living room with a pair of clothes for Kieran. After she cleared her throat, she said, "Sorry it took me so long. I was thinking."

"More like freaking," Kieran joked.

"What?" Esme asked.

"What?" He asked back and took the clothes from her. "Did you even hear me call out to you? Wren was dying."

"Seriously?" Esme glanced at Wren. "You were dying?!"

Wren shook her head at Esme, who was known for her gullibility.

"Are those my clothes?" Ray asked, noticing the dark blue jeans and blue shirt celebrating North Korea's freedom in Kieran's hands.

"Thanks," Kieran said. He walked into the hall to put the clothes on.

"You can keep them!" Ray yelled out, giving Esme a disapproving look. "I *loved* that shirt."

"I assumed you wouldn't mind lending him one. You have so many freedom shirts. But I can choose another one," Esme said, about to walk back to the boudoir.

Ray grumbled. "It's fine."

His words caused Esme to burst. "Of course it's fine! If I can share my bed with him, you can share your clothes," she argued. "Besides, it's what Simon would have done!"

The air in the living room grew tense for a moment, and the remaining members of the Sad Guy's Club exchanged looks.

"That may very well have been the case, but Simon is dead. And Cain would certainly *not* share his clothes with anyone," Lucifer said

"What does that even mean?" Esme asked.

"Your friend is Cain," Lucifer said bluntly, after realizing the mortals were not fully comprehending the situation. "To clarify, Simon was a fragment of Cain. When Cain sent Syn to be born on Earth, he also sent a part of himself to watch over her and to record information. After Simon's death, he retrieved his fragment and collected the data. His fragment's murder was not planned. Simon was supposed to live a few more months."

"'Data?'" Ray asked. "Are you saying Wren and Simon are part of some kind of an experiment?"

"Hold up," Kieran said as he walked back in, wearing Ray's clothes. "Shut up. You're speaking too alien for me." He had a towel draped over his head. "It sounded like you just said their dead friend is that fire guy who attacked us last night."

Lucifer nodded and said, "His name is Cain. He is the ruler of a planet named Limbo."

"According to your book, he's the son of Adam and Eve," Wren said. "And he's also the son of a god. So, who exactly is Cain to be the son of so many?"

"Like Syn, Cain is from the dark realm. When they crossed into the light realm, they had both lost their memories and became separated from each other. While Nao had found Cain in the lands of Kanaria, Lucien had found Syn asleep near an asteroid belt. That is why Cain thought he was the son of a Kanarian god for so long," Lucifer explained, and then noticed everyone's cloudy stares. "Questions?"

"*That* Lucien?" Wren asked, glancing at the painting of Lucien holding a decapitated head and stone. "The demonic who ruled Pangaea?"

"We call that land the Gardens of Eden." Lucifer walked up to the painting. "Lucien has higher cheekbones." He lowered his eyes to the head and the stone Lucien was holding. "Dramatic... Exodus and some guy's head." He released a *humph*. "Lucien beheaded many people when he ruled the planet, but he never held Exodus. Still, well done."

"Exodus? Why does that sound familiar?" Wren asked herself.

Lucifer turned around from the painting of Lucien, and after he landed his eyes on Wren, he said, "Because it came from the dark realm. You should know all about Exodus, *Syn*." He walked up to Wren and bared his teeth in an unpleasant grin.

"Why should I?" Wren asked, ignoring the fact he had called her Syn.

Lucifer leaned in close to Wren and whispered only for her to hear, "Because you are from the dark realm. Please, try to follow along." He smiled at Wren's face, which was becoming red with anger. Leaning away from her, he continued his explanation. "Exodus is why the gods of our realm are at war with each other. Nao, once a lesser god, was able to overthrow the First King of Kanaria merely by holding Exodus in his hands. If a stone from the dark realm has that much power, imagine how powerful their gods are."

Lucifer stared down at his hands, imagining holding Exodus.

"Have you ever met a dark god?" Kieran asked him.

"No. No one from our realm has," Lucifer replied.

"Then, how do you know they're real?" Kieran asked with confidence, like he had just asked something brilliant.

"Cain and Syn are from the dark realm, and Aaeon is the god of the shadow realm, which is the oldest of the three realms." Lucifer stared down at Kieran with a growing darkness in his eyes. "Aaeon has spent eons watching both the light and dark, and he watched our own gods and worlds be born."

Lucifer wanted to scare the son of the angelic he loathed. "Aaeon is also the one who invaded your dream when you were in that cage. All those chains and burns—that must have hurt." He snarled. "If it was not for me, you would be in his world, hanging upside down from his ceiling of skulls. And the fangs you grew last night? That has never happened before. Be careful, *half-breed*. The Shadow King likes rare things. And *you* are a rarity." He took a step closer to Kieran. "It is a good thing Aaeon does what I say."

A cold sensation creeped up Kieran's spine, and he took a step back from Lucifer. He turned from the angelic with a face full of fear. He laughed nervously and locked eyes with Wren. "I bet he's just a rogue magician. He and the cat are probably not even part of the guild. I bet he's helping the cat swindle you for the book. He's just playing games."

Esme had missed Lucifer's introduction from earlier and was about to ask him who he was, but the cat jumped in.

Marie looked up at Kieran and said, "Peasants should know when to be silent."

Before Kieran could respond to Marie's scathing words, Lucifer raised his hands into the air above him and said, "If I am playing games, then allow me to begin."

In an instant, the living room transformed into an image of outer space. Marie looked around as the planets rotated around the sun, which took the place of the Holo-disc. Lucifer snapped his fingers, and all the planets raced toward the sun, merging. Time reversed, and the rocks of the solar system became a giant golden planet, and the neighboring clusters of stars became brighter. The darkness of space turned into a pale amber.

Lucifer snapped his fingers again when he found the scene that he wanted to show them. "This is Kanaria." He pinched a star, zooming into another galaxy. "And this—this is Ezra."

While it seemed like everyone was racing toward the kingdom of the gods, they still stood in the living room. But that did not stop Kieran from getting motion sickness. He leaned over a tall man's foot and vomited. "Sorry about that," he told the man. "Whoa." He looked up at the man who had the most intense copper eyes, and his long, white hair was adorned with a radiant crown. "Who's that?"

"Ezra. He just said his name." Marie glared up at Kieran. "Next time you feel the need to throw up your insides, don't pick a god's foot."

"Why? He's not real," Kieran argued with Marie.

A loud roar interrupted the half-breed and cat, stopping them from arguing with each other. More images appeared around Ezra. Then, a group of Kanarians restrained Ezra and pushed him to kneel before a shorter Kanarian who was clutching a small stone...

"How mighty kings fall," the shorter Kanarian said as he walked up to Ezra. "You are weak. You keep us weak." The short Kanarian summoned a scythe and slammed it over Ezra's neck, then picked up Ezra's head, whose eyes were still open. Turning around, he held up the head for the other Kanarians to see. "We are not weak!" the short Kanarian screamed, and soon, thousands of Kanarians appeared around them. "We are the gods!"

"Long live Nao!" one Kanarian shouted as he walked up to the head of Ezra and took the crown from the fallen king. He placed the silver crown on Nao's head and bowed. While Ezra's dismemberment scared a few of the gods, most of the Kanarians bowed to the new king.

Nao, the short Kanarian, dropped the former king's head next to his mutilated body. Before Ezra could reassemble himself, Nao hacked up Ezra's body with the scythe he had stolen, then reached down, grabbed Ezra's golden heart, and said, "You will be the first Kanarian to die."

Nao squeezed the heart, but he could not shatter it. The Kanarians fell silent. All eyes were on the new king. He looked around at the Kanarians as embarrassment spread over his face.

The images became blurred, and Lucifer brought everyone to a new scene...

Nao tried to shatter the heart again while sitting on his throne, but he could not. A goddess walked up next to him as he was growing frustrated from not being able to crush Ezra's heart.

"Dear Nao," the goddess told him, "you cannot kill him. Though you can split him."

"Nyria, explain." Nao stared into the purple eyes of his wife.

"Fragments," Nyria said. "The god in the dungeons explained it to me."

"He is not a god," Nao told Nyria. "He is just a mistake."

"Oh, dear husband. If he is not a god, then we are certainly not." Nyria's eyes gleamed. "He is the first and only being of the shadows. Why does his existence frighten you?"

"I am not scared," Nao lied.

"Good, because we came to an agreement," Nyria said.

"What do you mean?" Nao asked.

"He will split Ezra apart for us," Nyria answered.

"Why would he do that?" Nao asked.

"I released him," Nyria replied. "And I promised to give back his scythe."

Nao stood up from his chair, dropping the heart. He shouted at Nyria as the heart rolled away from them. Both of them stopped talking and looked at the person who picked up the heart. The Shadow King looked down at the golden organ of Ezra and seared his stitched-shut eyes into the heart's soul. His executioner's hood was not covering his face, and black blood seeped from under his purplish eyelids as he cried.

"I... will not," Aaeon said and placed the heart inside a shadowy pocket near his waist.

"You cannot lie," Nyria said and walked up to Aaeon. "Everyone now knows that you are not just a visitor to our kingdom. You come from The Shade. You cannot lie, for the path reflects Chaos' purity." She choked up. "We made a promise!"

Aaeon moved his face toward the goddess. "I... did not... lie," he said. "I... changed... my mind."

After Chaos, the creator of the universe, awoke to their inexplainable existence, they roamed an abyss of nothingness. The nothingness was denser than matter and lighter than gas. As they pushed through the void, blood leaked from their wounds. Walking against such contradictory forces, they suffered immense agony. The pain they bled came from their center, where only innocent intent lurked. And the first formation from their blood grew into a path that would spread across the three realms.

Only one being was born from The Shade.

The Shadow King summoned his scythe from Nao's hands and tossed his chains at Nyria and Nao. Both Kanarians were bound together. Even the stone from the dark realm was no match for the king of shadows when he had his scythe. Being captured was not what he had planned, but he had been lured into the dungeon when the Kanarians who supported Nao saw him roaming their planet.

After tricking the honest god into giving them his scythe, the Kanarians had caged him. For two days, they had kept the god from the shadow realm in their dungeons, trying to figure out what he was. As Ezra opposed what had been done and ordered the immediate release of who he announced as the first god, Nao called him a liar and overthrew him, taking his throne.

But when the Shadow King looked into the heart of Ezra, he realized Ezra had been mutilated for wanting to free him.

Aaeon looked down at Ezra's body, which was trying to move. He kneeled and grabbed the decapitated head that was resting on Ezra's chest. He placed the head above the god's neck, then took out the heart from his pocket and tried to place the heart back into Ezra's chest.

But with the power of the Shadow King, the energy was too much, and Ezra's body blew up into ten more pieces.

Aaeon looked up at the twelve fragments hovering above him, and before he could grab them, each flew off in different directions. "I'm... sorry," he said to the sky.

Feelings of guilt washed over the shadow god. He had not meant to shatter Ezra. And with every chain, he summoned all of his links. He sent them across the planet, and he obliterated the surface of Kanar. Every structure and tower fell, and the light of the stars of Ia began to go out.

Then, the Shadow King returned to his world.

"Enough," Lucifer said. He changed the surrounding back into the living room when he noticed that Kieran was about to throw up again.

"Okay, you win. First Mage or whatever. I don't care." Kieran exhaled slowly, trying to stop his mind from spinning.

"What was that?" Ray asked.

"Ezra's fall," Lucifer replied. "Aaeon accidentally split Ezra apart when he was trying to put him back together. This is why he is trying to help us resurrect him."

"The hell, Kieran?!" Wren exclaimed when she noticed where Kieran had thrown up.

Wren stormed up to the coffee table and glared at the vomit covering the doll she had made.

"I can fix that." Esme summoned her water, but Wren placed her hand up to stop her.

"No. It will still smell." Wren shot Kieran a dirty look, like he had purposely thrown up on the doll when the living room was gone.

Lucifer walked up to stand at Wren's side and flicked his finger the doll's way. The vomit and smell were gone. She squinted at the cleaned doll. "I still *know* it was vomited on." She looked up at the angelic. "Thanks, though."

Lucifer nodded and remained standing at Wren's side.

"By the way, who are you?" Esme finally asked Lucifer. "Are you with the Mages Guild?"

Lucifer gazed into Esme's eyes and said happily, "You are the artist."

Wren walked up next to Esme's side, whispering, "The First Mage."

Esme became anxious. "Seriously?"

"Maybe," Wren whispered to her. "I don't know... The cat said he is."

"He's right there. Ask him," Esme whispered back and nodded over at Lucifer.

"You ask him," Wren told Esme.

"Why?" Esme asked her sister.

"Because you and Moonlight Hills are obsessed with the First Mage." Wren shrugged.

Lucifer brought the side of his lips up as he listened to their private discussion. Whispers were not typically so loud.

"Give me a break." Esme was baffled at Wren's words. "We may idolize him, but you're so obsessed with the First Mage that you haven't returned the *Angelic Diaries* to Birdsong. You even keep romanticizing—"

Wren and Esme stopped talking when they realized everyone was staring at them.

"Yes, I am the First Mage," Lucifer said.

"Did you really create the katani from clay idols?" Esme asked, thrilled.

"Yes." Lucifer nodded. "When the zyula became overpopulated, I molded the katani to balance them. That did not sit well with Azazel. And his light became hotter for a thousand years."

"Azazel?" Ray asked.

"I know this one! The Sun King!" Esme raised her hand like they were in class and turned to Ray. "Azazel's the king of the Angelic Empire. According to one of our creation myths, Azazel sacrificed himself and became the sun after Eden blew up. If you had ever taken an interest in the fae's folklore, you would have known that."

"Not a myth," Lucifer told the intelligent nymph. "History. Azazel created the barrier that protects your planet from the dark, and the vegetation that gives you breath. He is the main reason why you all exist. He is also the reason Eden is not completely gone." He narrowed his eyes at Wren. "Well, not you. You came along long before Eden fell."

"How many Edenians survived the explosion?" Wren asked Lucifer.

"A few species survived, but most died. My people found sanctuary in the Kanaria Galaxy before the gods sealed their borders, so the empire's current whereabouts are unknown. Our gods do not want their home to be infected with the dark leaking out from our cosmos." Lucifer paused. "If we do not neutralize the dark energy, the entire Milky Way will be consumed by darkness, and the other galaxies will then be invaded."

"Do you guys breathe, or can you just hop galaxies?" Kieran asked.

Lucifer hesitated and then said, "The commoners have masks that allow them to breathe Eden's air in different atmospheres."

"So, that's how you can walk on Earth?" Kieran asked, pointing at him.

"No. I am a royal. Even though we can technically breathe, we do not need to," Lucifer replied. "Though I enjoy it from time to time. It makes me feel like I was born from the maelstrom. I do not recommend Saturn—it's very gassy."

"Damn it, that ruins my vacay to Saturn." Wren snapped her fingers, breaking Lucifer from his explanation of masks and angelics' anatomy.

"You really want to go there?" Lucifer asked Wren.

Wren raised an eyebrow. "Jokes go right over your head, don't they?" Her words made Lucifer sigh—he did not have time for jokes.

"What if someone loses the mask? Do they die?" Ray asked, curious.

"What's a royal?" Kieran asked in unison with Ray.

"Yes." Lucifer nodded. "Though, losing one's mask is very hard. The masks are buried inside the commoners' bodies. When their body needs air or sustenance, the mask automatically gives them what they need."

"I take it you don't have a mask?" Ray asked.

"None of the royals have need of one." Lucifer said, thinking back on Eden. "At the end of the night, angelics who were granted a child would go to the shrine at the shore and dozens of cradles would be shipped to them from the swirling sea. Once the babies reached land, they merged with the masks that acted as their cradles."

"Ok... that is a weird way to be born. What about the other Edenians?" Wren asked.

"Every species of Eden came from the Maelstrom of Origin." Lucifer looked at her. "You always loved the maelstrom. You said it was beautiful."

Wren folded her arms and said, "I'm not saying I'm Syn, but I *doubt* that."

"What's a royal?" Kieran asked again, not liking that he was ignored.

"The royals are the first eight angelics—born from Eden's holy objects. We come from the land itself. Azazel is the sun, and I am one of the seven royals on Earth." He turned his attention to Kieran. "One of whom is your father."

"Who's that?" Kieran asked, intrigued.

"Ezekiel," Lucifer replied. "I'm sure you know that name. Your government has been calling you that. Your father is part of the Restoration Society, and he is known for hacking the planet's human governments."

"Really? Why?" Kieran asked.

"The society's purpose is to correct everything that is broken in our world. We must re-create Eden, neutralize the dark energy, and restore Ezra. Aaeon has already fixed the cracks between the realms. Meaning, new energy cannot drift where it does not belong." Lucifer paused, making sure everyone was comprehending what he was saying. "Eden was Ezra's most valued planet, and Nao wants all of Eden's cosmos to be his new kingdom, so he has been placing followers around the world since the time of Lucien's reign in the Gardens of Eden." He crossed his arms, his voice became bitter, and his mood: petty. "Lucien may have been able to create the animals, but he cannot do much else—he is too weak."

Lucifer paused, waiting for questions. None came, so he continued. "Ezekiel is trying to stay one step ahead of Nao to prevent him from conquering the heart of Eden. Without the heart, Eden cannot be rebuilt," he told them. "We are not gods, so we do not have their abilities to create worlds, but we can mend broken planets if we have the core fragment. That fragment is Earth."

"What'd you mean, 'Lucien created the animals?'" Wren asked, addressing what Lucifer had said about the demonic king.

Lucifer looked down at her and said, "After Eden fell, Lucien competed against Azazel—we call this the Creation Wars—and through that petty competition, Lucien created the first organisms in the oceans, trying to recreate the ecosystem of the Maelstrom of Origin. Even though Earth has some of Eden's waters, the creations Lucien made are not the same."

"Why did Lucien compete with you guys?" Wren asked. "What's his interest in all this? Is he really a god, like your book claims?"

"Yes. He is the heart fragment of Ezra. Since the soul of a god dwells within the heart, he is practically a weakened version of Ezra. That is why he fought so hard to rule Earth back then," Lucifer explained. "He feels Earth is his, but he is not Ezra, who ruled with a benevolent fist."

"The other demonics... are they also heart fragments?" Kieran asked before Wren could continue questioning Lucifer.

"How many hearts do you think a god has?" Lucifer asked, amused.

Kieran glared at the angelic, not liking his response.

The angelic took notice of the half-breed's temper and granted him a better response. "When Ezra's heart was slung from Aaeon's power, it was flung into deep space. The heart tried to recreate Ezra, but it could not without the other fragments." As Lucifer spoke, he reread the universe's imprint of the moment Lucien came into existence in his mind. "But the heart ended up creating Lucien, a poor version of Ezra who was fueled by rage. And Lucien manifested his fury as a hundred versions of himself. These, we call demonics." He twisted his mouth up into a sneer. "Does that better answer you, half-breed?"

Kieran stepped back from Lucifer.

Looking troubled, Wren asked the angelic, "You said Nao found Cain on Kanaria and Lucien found Syn... Can you explain?"

"After crossing realms, Cain was thrown onto Kanar soil. Nao noticed his power and took him in as his son," Lucifer said. "While Nao brainwashed Cain, Syn slept in deep space near where Ezra's heart was flung to. Once the heart grew into Lucien, he saw Syn growing a galaxy from her limbs while she slept. From the moment Lucien broke Syn from the branches that grew from her essence, they became close in a shared pain."

Lucifer stopped talking, and his mind left his private memory of Lucien holding Syn, surrounded by his demonics.

"And then what?" Wren asked.

"I fear I do not wish to continue Syn and Lucien's story," Lucifer told her.

"Why not? It was getting good!" Kieran said to the Edenian.

"I do not wish to talk about it." Lucifer turned away from everyone and stared at the painting of Lucien. "When Syn wakes, Wren will remember."

A few minutes went by as everyone stood in awkward silence.

Ring. Ring

Esme answered the phone near the foyer—it was Rolf and Kyle. It was nearing nine o'clock, and they were dead set on seeing Reme. After Esme explained to the goblins that they could not go, as they were held up with something, Lucifer took the phone from her hands. "We will meet you there," he told the goblins.

"Don't go alone!" Esme yelled into the receiver. "Ask Bettie or Bernie to take you."

Before Rolf could ask Lucifer who he was, the angelic hung up the phone. "Never break promises," he told Esme and walked back toward Wren, who was sitting on the couch.

Esme nodded slowly and ran to her room to get ready.

"How'd you know all of this?" Wren asked Lucifer after the angelic leaned back on the arm of the couch. "I get that you're the First Mage and an Edenian, but how do you know so much about, well, everything?"

"I may have become a mage, but I was created as the Angelic of Wisdom." Lucifer looked a bit smug. "I can read the energies of an area and absorb its history."

"Get ready!" Esme yelled from her room. "You can hound the Edenian at the art show."

"We're still going to that?" Wren asked Esme, who stood in the hall, glaring at her.

"Yes, we promised Rolf and Kyle," Esme said sternly.

"I figured with, you know, the First Mage in our living room, *that* could be rescheduled." Wren shrugged. "Just a thought."

Lucifer slid over the armrest, sat next to Wren, and whispered in her ear, "You can hound me at the art show."

Wren's face flushed, looking up at him.

"Why is your face red?" Lucifer asked, alarmed. "Are you feeling ill?"

Wren pushed him away from her. He was taking a liking to Syn's reincarnation, who was acting completely differently than Syn, who was not one to get easily flushed.

"What's wrong, Syn?" Lucifer asked. "Does your reincarnation find me attractive?"

"Can you at least tell me why Lucien saved me and Esme back then?" Wren asked him, wanting to distract herself from Lucifer teasing her.

"Maybe," he said.

Wren glared up at him. "You and Lucien are so close that he broke out of his imprisonment to save you," he said, after registering her annoyance.

"Why?" Wren asked Lucifer, who quickly looked away from her.

He stared at the painting of Lucien. "Even a broken god can love."

XXVI

THE CROWN

KIERAN WAS WATCHING ESME, who was sitting on a floor pillow behind a row of tall potted lemon trees. As she brushed her long hair, she eyed him in confusion.

"Are you just going to stare at me?" she asked.

"Yes," Kieran replied. "Until we go to the art show."

"You're not going to that," Esme said and placed her brush down.

"Why not?" Kieran asked.

"You're on the wanted list," she reminded him.

"We have the First Mage. I'm good," he said. "If anything happens, he can do mage stuff."

"I don't think he likes you." Esme stood up.

"Well, I'm half-angelic... I bet I can learn that magic trick from before." Kieran stood up with her.

"Do you even know what the angelics were capable of?" Esme asked him.

"No," Kieran said. "But Lucifer can do magic."

"Everyone was different in the Angelic Empire. Most didn't have powers and lived short lives. The scholars don't know much about the angelics, but they claim a few had special talents." Esme looked engrossed in what she was saying. "I bet those are the royals... Lucifer said your father is one."

"Cool... What was Ezekiel's?" Kieran asked. "Do I have a special talent? Wait—do I have one of those masks in my body?"

"I don't know. I'm not from Eden." Esme walked past him and headed to the door. "Lucifer would know."

Kieran followed Esme from her bedroom and toward the back hall. He stopped walking when she turned invisible, and he looked around the hall, near the open French doors. He then walked into the backyard. "Yo, Esme. Where'd you go?"

"Away from you!" Esme cried out from the air. "Stop following me."

"Oh, you like it," Kieran whispered, grinning, and heard her footsteps rush from where he was.

He gave up on finding the invisible nymph and looked over at the tulips, expecting to see the three fairies, but they were not there. He heard the Edenian's voice around the side of the house and went to go see what Lucifer was up to.

"No, this is not the right design," Lucifer mumbled as he tried to find the right door to The Shade that was near Limbo's portal. Concentrating on the wide tree that radiated energy from the Shadow King's path, he said, "Here. This one will do."

Kieran walked through the trees and found Lucifer and Wren staring at a wide tree. "What are y'all doing?"

At the exact moment Kieran asked them what they were doing, a spiral formed in the middle of the wide tree, creating a door.

Lucifer looked back at Kieran and said, "We are going to Limbo."

"What about that art show?" Kieran asked.

"Change of plans," Lucifer said, not liking how Wren made him feel. "I want Syn back. Her human reincarnation bothers me."

Wren stepped back and said, "That is not what you said we were doing. I thought you wanted to show me The Shade, or whatever it's called."

Lucifer grabbed Wren's wrist. "I am. But after we enter The Shade, we are returning to Limbo."

"I don't want to," Wren shouted over the swirling wind. "Even if I'm your friend, I don't care. I'm going to the art show."

When she turned to walk back to the house to return to its interiors, Lucifer pushed her through the door.

"What the fuck? Where'd she go?" Kieran asked him.

"Home," Lucifer said and walked into The Shade after her.

Before Kieran could chase them through the rift in the air, the door shrunk and vanished. He searched behind the trees, thinking they had been eaten.

Outside of Wren's gated property, Rose was examining the broken lock. She mended it back to its proper form. At Rose's feet sat Marie, who asked, "Why are *you* fixing the lock? You're not a locksmith." She had been taking a nap on top of Sparrow Manor, but when she opened her eyes to yawn, she had spotted Rose inspecting the broken gate.

Rose had become her mentee while she was in town. Marie was only in Tallahassee to retrieve the *Angelic Diaries* for the Primordial Library in Birdsong, but she was pulled into mentorship. The nakori hated the fact she could not tell the guild no.

"Because Wren and Esme are my nieces, and I don't like their gate to be wide open." Rose glanced down at Marie. "I don't care how weak this gate is in comparison to their abilities. It's comforting."

She looked down at the fixed lock. She was pleased at what she could fix with her novice magic.

"Look. I know you said that you can't attend the meeting tomorrow, but we need all the guild members there," Marie told her.

"I told the guild when I joined that I can't work weekdays from eight to five. Those are the hours I am on call for the restaurant," Rose said. "The weekends are when I'm most free."

"Have that woman fill in for you. What's her name? Eudora?" Marie spat. "You're business partners, right? I don't see the big deal."

"Has anyone ever told you that you're extremely rude?" Rose asked her mentor. "Eudora is out of town at a business meeting—she'll be back tomorrow afternoon. She is on call every single night and every weekend. So, I'd rather not ask her."

"I'm so tired of you primates. Even in the forest, your cousins irritated me." Marie groaned. "I can't wait for Eden to be restored."

"What do you mean?" Rose asked.

Marie stared up at the humble woman. "You just joined the guild, but our primary mission is to raise Ezra and restore Eden."

Rose looked surprised.

"You didn't read the mission statement, did you?" Marie narrowed her eyes. "No one ever reads the mission statement... You even interned with us for two decades." She twitched her nose. "You at least read about the gods' war, right?"

Rose kept her eyes wide and asked, "'The gods' war?'"

"I take that as a no." Marie looked away, annoyed. She looked back at Rose and said, "Tonight, you must memorize the entire mission statement and read the *About Us* section of the welcome pamphlet."

"I will." Rose was wondering what she had gotten herself into by joining the guild. She had interned with them off and on for almost twenty years, but that was not the same as being a member. "Are Wren and Esme inside?" she asked. "I have important news to tell them."

"How would I know? I'm not their guardian." Marie hissed.

Prying both mages from their conversation, a door opened in Wren's front yard, and Wren was shoved onto her lawn from the other side. Lucifer walked out after her and wiped ash from his shoulders.

Wren had fallen and was sitting on the grass. Her eyes were dull, her black tank top was ripped, and ash was smeared across her face.

"Well, that went horribly wrong." Lucifer looked down at Wren. "Sorry about that. Aaeon was not happy to see you."

"Ah, found her." Marie looked at Wren and twitched her whiskers.

Rose widened her eyes. She did not know why Wren had jumped out of something that looked like a portal, but she brushed it off. She looked down at her niece and said, "Wren, dear, Simon's parents' arraignment has been moved to start an hour later on Friday."

"*That* was the important news?" Marie asked Rose. "You forgot to read the mission statement, but *this* you remembered?"

Marie was not used to a Mage's Guild having so many humans. The location in Birdsong was her home guild, but she had temporarily transferred to the guild in Tallahassee while in pursuit of Lucifer's book. Human views on importance failed to impress the noble cat.

Wren stood up, not seeing Marie or Rose, and walked into her house. Lucifer noticed the mages and waved at them.

"How is the guild treating you, Rose?" Lucifer asked.

Rose knew what the guild master looked like, for the guildhall had a picture of him on their wall. She was surprised that he was at her niece's house and stuttered, "G-good."

"My little protégé there is the best mentor in the guild. You're in good hands," Lucifer said.

Marie wagged her tail, thrilled she had been called the best by the very being who saved her from a life in the woods...

Nakori were felines capable of speech who were normally larger than lions and faster than cheetahs. They were also one of the few species who had survived Eden's explosion. They were once highly respected as the mounts of the royal angelics during the Angelic Empire and could live thousands of years.

So, when Marie was born tiny, like a house cat, she was ridiculed. She was often laughed at for her frame, and her clan used her as an example of what not to be. The only ally Marie had was her mother. And when Marie was a cub, her mother would tell her stories of their great ancestor Loki from Eden. Loki was once small like her, but he grew during his older years. "Some of the greats take time," Marie's mother would often tell her.

Marie never viewed herself as great, no matter her temperament, but her mother and one other being did.

Nine hundred years ago, during a festival of the Spring Equinox, the leader of Marie's clan had invited Lucifer to their home in the woods in East France. The Mage's Guild was the most prestigious organization for anyone to join, and the clan had five they felt were worthy of joining such a guild.

Pleased at Lucifer visiting their land, the clan leader showed the angelic the sights. As the angelic was being introduced to their five smartest nakori, he kept noticing the small cat staring at him from her spot under a huge leaf.

Lucifer returned from the nakori village in France with a recruit, but not with who they wanted to join the guild. He brought back the tiny cat who flinched at everything, and Marie soon called Birdsong her home. From then on, she was taught magic by Lucifer himself. And a great mage she had become.

"I'm sorry for asking, but why are you here?" Rose asked Lucifer.

Marie looked up at Rose and said, "You know why. The Spirit."

Rose looked from Marie to Lucifer and back to Marie. "That's a fairytale."

As Rose laughed, the seriousness of Lucifer's face scared her. "Isn't it?" she asked him. "Eudora said the Spirit is just an old wife's tale."

"It's not an old wife's tale," Lucifer said.

Lucifer studied Rose's quiet face, not wanting to explain further.

"Are you certain Wren is the Spirit?" Rose asked.

"I am certain." Lucifer nodded.

"Then, why did the mages turn Wren away..." Rose trailed off, thinking about when they had visited Birdsong.

When Eudora had taken Wren to the island nineteen years ago, Rose accompanied the family of three to help with the girls. Having long come to terms with their new reality of fae and magic, Eudora and Rose were open to the possibility that Wren was who Isis claimed. But from what the mages saw after pulling energy from Wren's soul to test, she was just an anomaly. And when they returned from the island, Rose was clutching a pamphlet for interning with the Mage's Guild. While the guild had no interest in Wren, believing she was not the Spirit, they had taken an interest in Rose, who possessed a powerful aura.

"I knew I sensed Eden's energy on Wren," Marie snapped. "I tried to tell them to redo the evaluation, but they wouldn't listen."

Lucifer looked down at her. "It seems you would be a better fit to run the orb."

"Me?" Marie asked Lucifer, alarmed.

The orb was a basketball-sized glass marble full of pure Edenian energy. Lucifer had placed some of Eden's amber light into a ball of glass before the golden planet had exploded. While it was meant to be used for reconstructing Eden, the mages often used it for other means.

Though, the orb often malfunctioned.

"I'm so sorry." Rose stared at Lucifer blankly. "I'm afraid I'm lost."

"Marie, you are responsible for filling Rose in on who exactly Wren is." Lucifer looked down at the cat, who did not look enthused. "Your historical dissertation was on Syn and your ancestor, Loki, was it not?"

"I would love to read your dissertation, Marie. But—"

"This is why you need to pay attention, *human*," Marie said and glared up at Rose, interrupting her.

"—who is Syn?" Rose asked, nervous from Marie's blazing gaze.

"The answer varies. It depends on who you ask," Wren said in a vibrating voice.

Lucifer looked back at her. She was standing in the doorless doorway. Fire was radiating from her eyes. "Syn?" he asked.

Wren did not reply as she walked from her porch and down the steps. Tracing her hand over Lucifer's chest, she leaned in close to him. "My, you've always been beautiful, but you look even more so when I'm in this body," she whispered with an echo in her voice.

"Syn…" Lucifer said and took a step back from her.

The fire left Wren's eyes when she saw Rose standing there. "Rose?" she asked in her own voice. "What are you doing here?"

As Rose spoke about the arraignmnet and Wren told Rose how Simon's remembrance dinner went, Lucifer walked around Wren to inspect her. Syn had just taken control of her body, puzzling him. "Odd," he whispered, staring at the back of her head. "Why are you waking up on your own?"

In the original sequence Cain had coded for Syn's reincarnation, Wren was supposed to die once her frontal lobe reached development. Rather than having her complete a life cycle, he had estimated twenty-five years was sufficient for his test. Despite having told Lucifer that he was only observing her interaction with light souls, so he could create a code for calibration, Cain's goal was always to capture the soul he had detected when running his pre-test calculations: Kieran Cross. With the half-breed's excess energy feeding the machine, the Fires of Rebirth would be completed much faster.

Limbo was a planet of the dead, and there were plenty of souls for Cain to reincarnate for his test. So why did it have to be Syn who had to interact with the living? If Cain could, he would have sent one of his loyal lab technicians instead of his untrustworthy Echo, a lore's partnered half. But he had to reincarnate someone like him—a being of darkness. His machine ran off both dark and light energy, and he needed more light in order to rectify the machine. In order to do so, a dark soul would have to interact with living beings of light. Besides, Syn was telepathic, and he often exploited her skill for his gain. So, he had sent one part of himself to Earth, and with Lucifer's help, he had tricked Syn into entering the machine to reincarnate as a human.

While Wren was coded to intertwine with Kieran's mind and collect his soul, Simon was ordered to observe Syn's reincarnation. And after Simon returned to Cain, he planned to alter his existing code for the machine he had been endlessly building.

But Cain was not a god, even though he often acted like he was. And the only codes he had written for Simon were to be born near Syn's reincarnation and to observe her. There were two critical elements he forgot to clarify in his coding of Simon's essence: when and how he would die. Because of Cain's carelessness, Simon was murdered—ending Cain's test early.

"Why is everyone outside?" Ray asked and walked out of the house. "Why do you look like you just rolled in dirt, Wren?" She looked up at him. "We're about to go to Reme's. Esme will flip if you go like that." He looked over her ripped tank top and dirty skin.

Wren looked down at her shirt, noticing the scratch on her stomach, and said sarcastically, "It's artistic expression."

Esme walked through the broken doorway when she realized everyone was outside already. She had a clutch purse in her hands and was smiling—until she saw what Wren was wearing. "Why, Wren?" she asked. "Why can't you just dress nice for once?"

"This *is* nice," Wren argued. "This is Gucci. You love Gucci."

Esme and Ray stared at Wren, who was tugging on her top.

Kieran finished inspecting the trees, to no avail, and he walked back into the house. After realizing everyone was in the front, he walked toward where everyone had congregated. "Yo, Esme!" he yelled from the foyer. "Wren and Lucifer went into this swirling thing. I tried to stop them. I looked around the trees for a bit, but I think your sister's gone. Sorry."

He stepped out of the house and saw Lucifer and Wren in the front yard. "Wait. You guys were walking into a tree, like just now." He stared at Wren's ripped shirt. "Why do you look like a homeless person?" He noticed the ash in her hair. "What's with the dirt?"

"Long story," Wren said and eyed Lucifer. "Ask the alien."

"It is ash, not dirt." Lucifer shook the ash from his hair. "Aaeon gives souls new bodies—sometimes, he gives them several bodies. He loves to burn souls alive as an ultimate lesson. The ash tends to drift into his path."

"Ew." Wren brushed the ash off her immediately.

Lucifer felt her anger toward him, so he went to go fix the front door. He walked up to the front entrance and waved his hand over the space within the frame, building a door from thin air.

"Alert. Alert. Alert," Red yelled loudly from all over the house, as the gargoyle disappeared and reappeared in every hall.

"Shut up!" Kieran shouted and covered his ears.

Lucifer walked up to the gargoyle, who had settled back in their preferred spot after the door was finished, and he sent a small orb into their stone. "Stabilize yourself, gargoyle," he said. He was standing near the study while he inspected the gargoyle. After confirming Red was stable, he walked back outside to the front yard.

"I'm getting tired of their shit," Wren said after Red went dormant. "Next time you do that, Red, I'm selling you!"

"Someone's in a mood." Rose gasped at Wren's words. "Red deserves more respect than that. They have been loyal to you and your family from day one."

"I don't want to hear it, Rose," Wren said. "Why don't *you* be stuck in darkness for, like, half a year?"

"It was not for half of a year. We were only gone for a few minutes," Lucifer said from the porch.

"Oh, is that all?" Wren yelled from the yard.

"What are you even talking about?" Ray asked them both. "What darkness?"

"I brought Wren into The Shade, but Aaeon did not like that. He blocked the gateway to Limbo and kept us in his darkness until I bargained our way out." Lucifer looked over at Ray, who stood a few feet away from him. "He can be quite childish. I really should ask Cain for another portal key. It would be useful in times like these."

Wren shivered from Lucifer's short retelling of their trip into The Shade. Esme was standing near Ray, and she turned to Lucifer and said, "I wanted to say earlier that it is an honor to meet you. Should I call you First Mage, or I don't know... *Creator?*"

"Please, do not call me First Mage. My name is Lucifer," he said with a scowl on his face. "And calling me 'Creator' is a little much. All I did was manipulate the energies that were already in existence to design the katani."

"Isn't that the same thing?" Wren asked the angelic.

"No," Lucifer replied.

"Then, technically, no one created anyone, and we're just blobs of gas playing dress-up," Wren exclaimed at the angelic, who widened his eyes at her outburst.

Esme nodded slowly at Wren's explosive words, and she said to Lucifer, "Moonlight Hills has many structures built in your honor, but you never visit."

"I purposely avoid major fae metropolises," Lucifer told her.

"Why?" Esme asked.

"The fae's classism turns my stomach," Lucifer said. "That is why I told the Council they could build a guildhall in this city. Tallahassee gave the goblins and trolls asylum." He saw Esme's disappointment and added, "My apologies. I do not mean to insult you."

"Oh." Esme waved her hands in front of her. "The classism turns my stomach, too."

"Then, why do you idolize Moonlight Hills?" Wren asked Esme, still in a foul mood. "You keep ordering everything from their air malls and insist I go with you whenever you visit."

"Because I was born there," Esme said with sad eyes. "I love my culture, but I'm not happy about our current politics. Nymphs weren't always this way. Our former queen was pro-equality of the courts."

"That is true." Lucifer nodded at Esme. "With your queen's death, and the new queen's reign, your people soured. The former queens would be greatly disappointed in the new crown."

"Since our queen lives in Birdsong with the kings and queens of the other courts, can't you persuade them to all... to get along again?" Esme asked. "You created our ancestors. If anyone can convince the fae to coexist again, it's you."

"I cannot," Lucifer told her. "I have more important things to do."

Esme looked down at the rug under her feet. She was known for her unrealistic optimism in others.

"But *you* can," Lucifer said, staring at her. "The island is holding the election for council positions in the middle of the coming year. You can run for the Sapphire Court's position on the Council."

"No, I can't!" Esme exclaimed and clasped her hands over her mouth. "Our queens have always come from the same royal family."

"Are you not a McKnight?" Lucifer asked her.

"Yes, but we are only diplomats," Esme politely argued.

"You can run for council since you are of royal blood," Lucifer told her. "Just because your queens have come from the same family does not mean it should continue. Sometimes, tradition is best broken."

Esme laughed lightly. "That does not mean I have the right to fight for the crown."

"You would have a significant chance of winning if you ran. You harbor a lot of Queen Avasavia's grace," Lucifer said.

Esme placed her hands over her ears. "The current queen comes directly from Queen Avasavia. Not me. I'm more of a great—times one thousand and more—niece."

"Wait, are you and your queen cousins?" Kieran asked Esme.

She glanced at him and said, "Yes, on my mother's side. The women decide the crown."

While the Council lived in Birdsong, the birthplace of the Mage's Guild, each court had a capital city. In each major city, the extended family of the kings and queens of the courts acted as diplomats. Regarding the Sapphire Court, Moonlight Hills was the capital city for the nymphs.

Wren stretched and said, "You should see Moonlight Hills greet Esme whenever we go. Talk about celebrity treatment."

Esme looked down at her watch, feeling embarrassed. "We don't have time to talk about my family tree. Rolf and Kyle are waiting for us at the art show."

She walked speedily to the gate.

XXVII

A Festive Morning

"WHERE ARE YOU GOING?" Wren asked Esme, who was approaching the gate with shaky footsteps. "It's too far to walk. Let's take the Jeep."

Esme turned around with flushed cheeks. Without looking at anyone, she walked toward the side of the house where the garage door was. Wren trailed behind her, and the others soon followed.

"Did I hear correctly? Are you going to Reme's art show?" Rose asked enthusiastically. "Do you mind if I tag along? I love Reme. Maybe I can find something for Addison's graduation. You don't mind if your aunt comes along, do you, girls?"

Wren turned around abruptly and faced Rose near the garage door. "Oh. My. God. You and Esme are the politest people I've ever known," she snapped and spun back around, following Esme down the steps to the underground garage. "It's sickening."

"You *are* in a mood," Rose said and entered the stairwell.

"Of course she's in a mood," Ray said from behind Rose. "Wouldn't you be if your entire reality changed in a few hours?"

With perfect timing, his eyes flickered. "What was that?" Rose asked, looking behind her. "I thought I saw a lightning bug."

Ray shrugged.

Everyone walked away from the staircase and toward the wide parking lot, where ten cars were parked. A heavy podium was stationed between the stairs and the lot with a console of buttons. Wren walked up to the podium and placed her fingerprint on one button to unlock the black Jeep from its secured hold to the ground.

"I want to drive!" Kieran ran over to the old Jeep. "Is it a stick shift? Please, let it be old school." He pinned his face to the driver's side window to look inside the Jeep. "I see a stick!" he exclaimed.

"Of course, it's a stick. That's all my dad drove," Wren said, pushing him away from the driver's door. "Ray likes to drive the Jeep."

She walked around to the other side of the Jeep and waited for Ray to unlock the doors. He took the keys from the podium and walked by Kieran with a smug grin, unlocking the Jeep. Kieran opened the rear door and scooted over to sit next to Esme, who was sitting behind the passenger seat, where Wren was buckling her seat belt.

"Are you sure this thing is even safe to drive?" Kieran asked, sulking because he could not drive. "How old is it?"

"Yes," Wren said from the front. "It's a 2184 Obsidian edition."

Kieran leaned forward to keep talking to her. "That's old, but I guess old people like old things, huh?"

"Shut up, mutt." Wren rolled her eyes and glanced at Ray, who started the Jeep.

Lucifer somehow found himself squished in between Rose and Kieran, while Esme sat on the other side of the half-breed. Marie had decided to stay at the house and continue her nap on the roof.

As if the lightbulb in his brain was broken and a new one had just lit up, Kieran looked to his left at Lucifer. "You're the jerk who threw me through the door!" he exclaimed at the angelic, who was sitting uncomfortably.

"You just made that connection?" Lucifer asked, lips tilted up in a sneer. "*Bravo.*"

Feeling a bit out of place from being around so many Earthlings, Lucifer fell backwards into The Shade. Normally, he liked to pinpoint where he would end up in The Shade, as the path existed everywhere. But he was impatient to leave.

"Where'd he go?" Kieran asked after the angelic vanished into a cloud of dark fog.

Wren looked back at where Lucifer had been sitting. "Who cares?"

As Ray drove everyone to the festival that was hosting Reme's art show, Kieran playfully ignored Esme, who was gently shoving him closer to the middle to give her more room, while Wren lectured Rose and Esme about being too nice. After a few minutes, Ray pulled into the crowded public parking lot in the art district.

Shouting at Wren to be quiet, Rose leaned close to the window to her left and stared at a few people fighting in the street. "Maybe I should get back to work." She looked over at a police officer trying to break up the fight.

"I thought you worked from eleven to three today?" Esme asked as Wren applauded her aunt's attempt to silence her. "It's only a little after ten."

"Really?" Kieran asked, following Rose out of the Jeep. "That's a short shift. *Jealous.*"

"Kieran, you don't work. What are you jealous about?" Wren asked before he closed the door on her. "Plus, Rose and Eudora work long hours at the restaurant. Their hours aren't anything to be jealous of."

Kieran ignored Wren and went to go stand on the sidewalk to watch the police officers tackle a group of rebels to the ground. "Nice," he exclaimed when an officer had a burly biker in a chokehold.

"Fuck, his *face*." Wren locked eyes with Ray, and both left the Jeep in a hurry. "We should have left him at home." She cursed as the two yanked Kieran away from the officers. "Your face is on wanted posters," she whispered to Kieran, who looked disappointed that he was being dragged away from the brawl. "We need to find you a mask."

They pulled Kieran toward a booth that marked the entrance to the festival. Esme rushed behind them while Rose stayed back, watching the fight, worried the rebels would overpower the officers.

"Nuh-uh, I'm not wearing that," Kieran said when Wren pointed at a pink tiger mask.

"Well, pick one," Wren said.

Kieran looked over at the masks. "Are they all kid masks?"

"We're out of stock on adult masks," the vendor said. "But many adults like the zebra ones."

"He acts like a kid anyway," Wren said. "How about the zebra one, then?"

"No, I don't," Kieran argued. He eyed the plain-looking zebra mask and then saw a blue puppy mask. "I'll get the dog."

Wren paid for the mask and then placed it over Kieran's face. "Good, it fits you. You finally have a face that matches your name."

"Thanks," Kieran said. "Hey!"

Esme walked up to Wren's side. "What's wrong, Esme?" Wren asked after she noticed the worry on her sister's face.

"Just what Lucifer said about me running for my court's seat," Esme replied and purchased the pink tiger mask from the vendor.

Kieran watched Esme put the mask over her face. "Are you wearing one so I don't have to be alone?" he asked.

"No, a lot of humans in one place make me nervous," Esme told him.

"If you run against your queen, I don't see that as a bad thing," Wren said to Esme. "You're a natural-born leader and love all the courts."

"It's just too much," Esme said. "Everything is too much. You're, what, someone named Syn? And me, run against the queen?" She looked back at Rose, who was talking to one of the officers who broke up the fight. "And Simon is some alien who rules a planet for the dead?"

"Zombie planet," Kieran said with a slow nod, repositioning his mask.

"I'm sorry to intrude, but did you just say, 'planet for the dead?'" a tan man in a zebra mask asked Esme from a few feet away.

Esme looked at the man wearing the zebra mask. Kieran studied them, and when he realized they were having a moment, he walked up next to Esme.

The man bowed and stared into Esme's eyes. "Greetings. My name is Davios Echols."

"Nice to meet you. My name is Esme McKnight," she responded.

Davios studied her features. "Are you a nymph?"

"She's wearing hair dye and contacts," Wren said to the man in the zebra mask, not liking his friendliness.

As Wren and Kieran both stood on guard, Ray looked over Davios suspiciously and said, "We're talking about a video game."

"I see," Davios said.

"Okay, nice chatting," Kieran muttered, then yanked on Esme's arm. "Let's go."

Davios flashed an unpleasant smile at Kieran and told Esme, "Your boyfriend is in a hurry."

"He's not my boyfriend," Esme said, trying to take her arm from Kieran's hold.

After Davios bowed to Esme, she ran off with Kieran chasing her. "Can I help you?" Davios asked Wren, who was staring him down.

"I don't like you," Wren told him. He smelled too much like Frost's smoke. "Stay away from my sister."

"You don't even know me," Davios said, still smiling awkwardly.

Wren stepped closer to him. "People who are overly friendly to strangers tend to have hidden motives." She sniffed the air between them. "Plus, you smell too much like someone I don't like."

Wren's eyes turned a light blue, and the masks from the booth started to vibrate. In a flash, she turned and ran after Esme and Kieran. Ray eyed Davios and followed Wren away from the entrance.

Wren and Ray were always suspicious of nice people, whereas Esme loved good-hearted people because she was authentically a nice person.

"Davios," a woman wearing a tiara said as she walked up to his side, wrapping his arm with her own. "Who were you talking to?"

Davios turned to the woman and said, "Someone interesting."

However, the man the three best friends and the escaped inmate had met was not a good-hearted person. Covered in a mysterious allure, Davios Echols walked away from the entrance of the festival with the woman, who clung to him. "Come," he told the woman. "Let's go meet Frost."

"Whatever you say." The woman looked up at Davios.

Wren stopped walking away and looked back at the booth, preparing to attempt to read Davios' mind. But he was gone.

"Are you coming?" Ray asked Wren. "Something tells me that balloon down there is Kyle's."

Ray pointed at a very large heart-shaped yellow balloon that had **Reme** printed on it.

"You go ahead. I need to check on something," Wren said. She trotted off back toward the entrance.

Down the road from the vendor of masks, Rolf and Kyle sat at a picnic table with balloons and a cake. Bettie had volunteered to escort the brothers to the art festival for Reme's show, and while she sat reading a brochure, Rolf and Kyle were playing poker at the table, with cake smeared on both of their faces.

"There they are," Kyle said when he spotted Ray walking toward them. "Finally! Where's Esme and Wren?"

Esme and Kieran walked up to the table, and it took Rolf and Kyle a moment to realize Esme was wearing a pink tiger mask.

"Wren will be here in a second," Ray said.

Kyle pointed at each of them, while saying, "Ray, Esme... Who are you?"

"Who are you?" Kieran asked the short goblin, who was holding a handful of cards.

"This is Rolf and Kyle." Esme volunteered to introduce everyone. "And this is Kieran. He's staying with me and Wren for a while."

"Why?" Kyle asked and placed a card down to rival Rolf's own card.

"He's a friend," Esme said.

"Why?" Rolf asked and then placed a card on top of Kyle's.

"Oh, god, not the *whys*." Bettie groaned as she stood up and greeted Esme and Ray with a hug. "They've been on a kick all morning."

Kieran sat down next to Rolf and leaned over the table, staring at Kyle. "I'm not really their friend. I did some bad things, and they're hiding me." He bared his teeth and extended his canines. "Pretty neat, huh? I can retract them, too." His canines slid back into his gums. "According to some mage, I'm a half-breed."

Rolf and Kyle stopped playing their card game and stared up at him in admiration. They did not know if they should say "Why?" or "Cool." In the end, both resumed their game after asking Kieran, "Why?"

"What did I just hear?" Bettie asked Esme.

"It's complicated," Esme said.

"He said he was a half-breed. What does that mean?" Bettie raised her brow.

Esme whispered, "He's half-human and half-angelic."

"'Angelic?'" Bettie stared Esme in the eyes. "But they died when the planet exploded."

"That's what our government wants the humans to believe," Esme said.

Bettie looked around and whispered, "Don't tell anyone. If the government knows, they'll dissect him."

"Most of the courts' people don't even know the truth—I didn't until recently. I think the Council keeps it secret because they fear that we may tell the humans since we live together now," Esme said. "I don't blame them for keeping it hidden… A few sectors in America wanted to dissect us before the federal laws were written. Just imagine what they would do to an offspring of a human and an angelic."

Bettie looked over at Kieran, who looked depressed at what he had heard. He looked back at Bettie and Esme. "Child, I don't care what you are," Bettie said and went to sit next to Kieran. "You're safe with us."

With Ray standing at her side, Esme watched Bettie pat Kieran on the back. The two looked entertained as she soothed him.

"Should we tell her that he burned down his hometown?" Ray asked Esme.

"Definitely not," Esme said, staring at the older woman say kind words to the runaway inmate.

Shoving through the crowds, Wren was searching for the man in the zebra mask. She stopped walking and looked around at the random faces.

"Sorry!" a young boy exclaimed after he dropped his ice cream cone on her shoe, looking mortified.

Wren looked down at the frozen dessert covering her black tennis shoe. She looked up slowly at the child. The boy's mother came up and started wiping a napkin on her son's face, ignoring Wren's shoe. "Oh, I'm so sorry. Kids will be kids—"

The mother of the boy trailed off her cheery words when she noticed that Wren was puffing smoke out of her nostrils. The woman dragged her son away from Wren, who was entering a fit of rage. "Fucking brat!" she hissed and kicked the ice cream off her shoe.

The woman turned around and stared at Wren, horrified by her tone. "What did you call my son?" she asked.

"Not him. *You.*" Wren glared at her. "He's young, so he gets a pass, but you didn't even attempt to clean his mess from my shoe."

The woman looked around at the passersby, who ignored them.

Wren walked up to the woman, who was hiding her son behind her. "You just wiped your son's face even though he had nothing on him. And then you trotted away like a whore."

The woman stepped back from Wren when she walked closer. Before she could continue cursing the woman, she spotted the man in the zebra mask staring at her from behind the mother and child. Next to the man in the mask stood a woman wearing a tiara, and next to the glittery woman stood Frost.

"I don't have the time to deal with you," Wren said and rushed past her. Before leaving the woman and her son, she whispered to her, "Some people are not meant to be mothers, and you are one of them."

Leaving the horrified woman and her crying son, Wren ran off to where Frost stood.

"Making children cry..." Frost said with a slow clap when Wren approached them. "Harboring a fugitive is not enough for you?"

"Oh, shut up," Wren said. "Who the fuck are you, anyway, Frost? You're not *just* FBI."

"She is such a delight," the glittery woman said.

Frost walked up to Wren, looked down at her, and said, "If I tell you who I am, then you must answer my question honestly."

"I'm not playing that game," Wren said.

"Then, you won't ever know until you die, and by then, it will be too late."

Frost turned around and was about to walk back toward his two friends when Wren spoke. "Wait—fine. Who are you?"

Frost turned back to face her. "My name's Frost."

"That's not what I mean." Wren folded her arms. "Your identity. I want to know what you are and where you come from."

"I'm what the Kanarians call an abomination," Frost said.

"Abominations are?" Wren asked.

"That's not the question," Frost said in objection.

"It's part of your identity, and your identity is the question. So, elaborate," Wren ordered.

"Abominations are the creations of Nao," Frost said.

"He is what you humans call a demigod," the shiny woman said while clinging to Davios. "Abominations are the lesser gods of Nao."

"Or mistakes," Davios said, not liking his girlfriend's idolization of Frost. "Nao prefers to call them 'mistakes.'"

"The others are mistakes, indeed. But Frost is not like the others..." The woman turned her eyes to Frost, mesmerized. "He is the first functional god *created* by a god that is not Ezra."

"What about Isis?" Davios asked the woman, wanting to ruin her feelings for Frost. "She is a demigoddess and practically on our level."

The woman laughed. "Isis is not a demigoddess. She is an imposter. They claim the *Shadow King* brought—"

Wren did not like the bubbly woman who spoke ill of Isis. She interrupted her, saying, "Who the fuck do you think you are?"

"My name is Siar, and this is Davios," the woman said, fixing her tiara.

"Kanarians..." a raspy voice said from the surrounding air, and people broke out into dramatic screams.

Clink. Clink. Clink.

Wren turned and saw Aaeon dragging his chains behind him as he emerged from The Shade.

Boom. Boom. Boom.

Trees collapsed around the festival, and booths crashed to the ground. Wren had her eyes locked on the man who wore the blackest of hoods. Dark drool dripped down his chin, and blood was smeared across his bare white chest of the ghastliest skin. No being was comparable to the fury of the oldest god, who was disrespected. As he walked upon the bright green grass, the pebbles shook, and the earth rumbled.

"No. No. No." Lucifer rushed out of The Shade. "You cannot be roaming Earth. I told you I am sorry for bringing someone into your path."

"You are... forgiven," Aaeon said, gripping his chains. "They caged... *me*."

Walking toward Siar and Davios, he wrapped his chains around his arm. He was about to throw them at the two Kanarians.

"What is that?!" a man screamed from behind his broken booth, and then he ran from the festival.

After Aaeon's chains sank into the two Kanarians, he looked around at the people running toward the exit. The Shadow King pulled the chains to him as Davios and Siar cried out in pain. "Friends..." He peered down at the two gods crying at his feet.

Lucifer was standing at Aaeon's side and said, "I am glad you made new friends, but you cannot be roaming Earth. They do not know about the gods yet."

"They know... Isis." Aaeon sounded sad. "Why not... me?"

"There is an enormous difference between you and Isis," Lucifer said. "For starters, Isis does not drag her friends by a chain."

Understanding Lucifer's words, Aaeon was about to release the two Kanarians.

"No. You already have your fishing rod hooked, so you might as well go back to your home and fillet them," Lucifer said.

"I will... go back." Aaeon looked around the realm he had traveled to. "I have... new friends."

"Have fun. Go on." Lucifer shoved Aaeon toward the foggy door that led into The Shade like he was a child.

After the Shadow King disappeared into The Shade with Siar and Davios, Wren looked around to find Frost. But he had taken the opportunity of Aaeon's arrival to leave.

"What the hell just happened?" Wren asked Lucifer.

"The Kanarians rarely visit the other galaxies because Aaeon can sense them outside of their locked cosmos. You just saw what Aaeon does to the Kanarians. He may not split them or kill them, because of his creed, but he does other things." Lucifer looked around at the ruined festival. "Back in Kanaria, they have built totems to hide from Aaeon. They do not want him back on their planet."

Wren walked over debris and muttered, "I take it Frost is a demigod?"

"Yes, like Isis," Lucifer said. "He is Nao's right-hand."

Lucifer looked around as the blaring of police sirens and the trumpets of the mages' alarms sounded throughout the city. "This is a nightmare," he complained. "I cannot have Earthlings knowing about the Shadow King."

"Can't you erase their minds?" Wren asked as she spotted Ray and Esme walking from the picnic area.

"No," Lucifer said. "I do not mess with one's mind."

"That's stupid," Wren said. She waved her friends down until they saw her.

Behind Ray and Esme walked Kieran. And on each of his arms, Rolf and Kyle swung.

"They won't get off!" Kieran yelled out.

"Can't touch the floor!" Kyle shouted. "It's an earthquake."

"Earthquake!" Rolf exclaimed.

"Tallahassee doesn't have earthquakes, kids," Bettie said from behind them. "What in the world happened?"

"An... earthquake?" Wren asked and looked at Lucifer, who nodded.

*****

The rest of Sunday was chaotic as news exploded through Tallahassee with reports of a tremor. While most of the attendees believed the earthquake explanation, for the planet was already going through a drastic climate change, a few people came out to claim an executioner with chains broke the road using a scythe. But they were laughed at. "Calling all humans and fae! Be careful, we have the grim reaper on the run," one news reporter said, jeeringly.

The city concluded that anti-fae rebels were rioting using fear tactics at the same time the quake had happened. Even the police had many rebels from the art festival in custody from fighting.

And the rebels happily took credit for the hooded man with chains.

While the city chatted about the shattered festival, Sparrow Manor was quiet. After such a loud disturbance, the silence was welcomed by all. The fairies had returned from Moonlight Hills to dance with the birds who sang in the evening, which Kieran listened to while he slept in the hammock. Esme was alone in her room, contemplating whether she should run against the existing queen. And Wren was sleeping soundly in her bed after she reassured Rose, who was at the police station with Connell, that they were fine.

Ray had returned to his apartment when his eyes started flickering again before the cat could prevent him from leaving. He needed to get a good night's rest away from any drama, and Sparrow Manor was full of theatrical surprises. Despite their otherworldly interruptions, he still had a store to run in the morning.

Lucifer had escorted everyone safely back to the house in case more Kanarians were drifting about, and he was now standing on the front porch, surveying Wren's property. While Cain wanted Syn back early to end his test, and Lucifer had tried to bring her to Limbo before, he was now on the fence. The angelic was becoming more concerned about Syn's reincarnation's wellbeing.

Marie leaped down from the roof and sat down at Lucifer's feet. "It wasn't an earthquake, was it?" she asked. "The entire city is going on about it. I could hear people scream about the festival from the street over. It woke me up."

"No. It was Aaeon." Lucifer looked down at the nakori. "Kanarians were at the festival, and he came to Earth to take them prisoner."

"That's foolish of them." Marie groomed her paw. "But I'm glad the creep has new toys. Maybe he won't appear anytime soon."

"Aaeon is misunderstood," Lucifer said. "He is a gentle giant."

Marie snapped her head up to stare at the man she idolized. "He's evil. Everyone sees that but you."

Lucifer squatted down to pet Marie on the head and told the cat, "You would not think so if you had journeyed with him for as long as I have. One cannot be evil if they lack intent. Aaeon does not share our opinions of morality. It is how he was designed."

Marie grunted and purred at the same time. "I still don't like him."

"Many do not." Lucifer stood back up. "Though Aaeon takes an interest in everyone."

"Yeah, to the point he kidnaps them and tortures them!" Marie exclaimed.

"We all have our own view on what is righteous." Lucifer walked toward a dark fog manifesting a few feet away from him. The First Mage looked back at the young mage. "Aaeon is trying to teach their souls."

After Lucifer stepped into The Shade, Marie hissed, "If people knew that their devil myths are based on Aaeon, they would be better people."

"Ah, that is where you are wrong. Avoiding evil deeds knowing you will be punished does not make you a good person," Lucifer said from within The Shade. "Aaeon's purpose is to teach us all to become better, so the universe is a better place for everyone."

Before Marie could object to the angelic, the portal to The Shade closed.

XXVIII

CHICKS 'N MORE

THE NEXT MORNING, AND not far from Wren's house, the quiet mall was scarce. It was the beginning days of January, and Wren sat on the steel stool behind the coffee counter, eyeing the two gossiping store clerks. She was trying to decide whether she should buy Kieran a bed and necessities. However, she already had three furnished rooms on the second floor. She tapped her fingers on her chin, debating opening the second floor of the manor.

Something told her more *guests* were coming.

She did not need to have a vision to know that.

Wren stopped obsessing over what to do and watched Ray from across the store. He was helping a customer find the right book, but it was not a book the customer really wanted. She could not help but laugh along with two nearby employees when Ray got flushed after the customer asked for his number. He walked away and placed the new dolls Wren had made near the checkout lanes.

"He's *so* clueless," Ashley, one of the two employees, said.

As the three of them watched Ray fix a sign that read **Protection Dolls**, another customer rolled her eyes and made a snide remark about how a toy could not protect one from earthquakes and rebels.

"If you don't like our store, then why are you here?" Ray asked the snooty customer.

The customer looked offended and rushed out of the department store.

Tallahassee was not fond of the trendy company that used to occupy the store, and when the mall freed up the spot, Eudora, who was a businesswoman already, helped Wren and Ray set up their own business. Being a tremendous supporter of fae's theory of how Earth came to be, Wren had named their company *Eden*. Having been accused of being the reincarnation of someone who had lived on Eden, it came to no surprise that Wren was obsessed with the golden planet. Ray, who was laid back about everything, agreed to the name.

In the windows of Eden, the clothes of a local goblin who was making waves in the local fashion scene were always displayed. Magic-infused dolls Wren had crafted, which mages would then sanctify, lined the front. Rare books on how to tap into one's magic, antiques, unique art, and other miscellaneous items were sold.

Wren's goal was simple: She wanted to support the local fae community and educate the public on their history and culture.

Originally, she had wanted Esme to co-own the store with her, but the public made Esme skittish, and she preferred to help Father Bernie with the orphans and work at the bookstore. After she rejected becoming a partner, Wren asked Ray. She did not want to run a business alone, and she certainly did not want her aunt to become her partner. She saw how Eudora ran her chicken business. Relaxed, Eudora was not.

"Asian hottie, hello," a teenager with a group of friends said, giggling as they stared at Ray from where they stood at the entrance. "Told you an earthquake wouldn't stop him from working. He works *all* the time."

The girls ran spastically out of the store, giggling louder.

"I swear those girls come by just to spy on Ray," Ashley said, amused.

"Right?" Lisa, the other employee, laughed. "It's almost daily."

Wren smirked. A couple of medium-sized bags were hanging from her fingers as her chin leaned on her palm. Ray turned around and walked back toward Wren at the coffee center.

"Oh, Wren," Ashley said, eyeing Wren. "Where are you and Ray going?"

"Yeah, about that... Are you selling the store?" Lisa asked, her tone becoming more serious. "I really don't want y'all to sell."

"We aren't selling the store," Wren reassured her two store clerks. "We're just needing some time off."

"For how long?" Lisa asked.

"About a month, I think." Wren took a sip of her coffee, full of anxiety.

"Six months," Ray corrected Wren after he approached the counter. "Shouldn't you two be stocking the new supply?"

Ashley and Lisa quickly left the coffee center.

"Why six months?" Wren asked.

"You're seriously not understanding the situation." Ray leaned over the counter and stole the coffee from her hand. He took a long gulp and handed it back. "Neither of us are ever probably returning here." He plopped a manila folder in front of Wren. He had been aggressively recruiting people for management positions all morning. "We really should be looking to sell the store, not hiring a stand-in."

Wren looked down at the folder. "Why sell?" she asked as she flipped open the folder, staring at a stack of applicants.

Ray leaned closer to her and whispered, "You're underestimating the shit that we've been dragged into." He was inches from Wren's face. "And we've been dragged into some *shit*."

A few aisles down, Ashley tugged on Lisa's sleeve and nodded at Ray, leaning over the counter to talk to Wren. From where the two girls stood, it looked like Ray had kissed her.

"I bet they're eloping," Ashley whispered to Lisa. "That's why neither of them ever dates anyone."

"Because they're dating!" Lisa quietly shouted to her work best friend.

As the two employees continued their gossip, Ray poured himself a cup of coffee. He looked down at Wren's empty cup and poured her some coffee to replace what he had stolen. "I found the perfect applicant. Found him on the mall's billboard. He was looking for a mall job, even though he has an economics degree," he said. "I mean, he does have an arrest record, but he has lots of experience running a store. Plus, he sounded pleasant on the phone interview. Think everyone will like him."

"Arrest record? What'd he do?" Wren asked, not happy that Ray wanted to sell the store.

Ray took the application from the top of the stack of papers and handed it to her. "Looks good to me," Wren said, reading about the drug possession charge. She laughed. "That's a light crime compared to what many people secretly do."

She handed the paper back to Ray, who nodded in agreement. "Maybe we can convince him to buy the store," he said.

"I'm *not* selling," Wren scolded Ray. "I don't care if we are in some *shit*."

Ray stood up. "Let me go call Bill back and tell him he has the job."

As Ray walked away toward the office that was on the second floor, Wren slumped her shoulders.

She knew they were going to sell.

When noon came, Wren and Ray walked from their store. The sunlight hit them as they walked out toward where their vehicles were parked. Wren locked her shopping bags in her black two-door Vicar, which looked like an old Lamborghini. The model was currently the fourth-fastest sports car in the world. It was also the only car she had bought for herself, as she had inherited the others from her father.

"Let's just take your bike. It'll be easier," Wren said after she closed her door.

The two had plans—plans they did not tell Esme about.

She would have talked them out of it.

"Your car is faster," Ray said. "We may have to outrun them."

"Yeah, but the bike can get into places my car can't," Wren said.

Ray felt the light return to his eyes, making him rush ahead of her. Worried, Wren chased him. "Ray, what's wrong?" she asked as she stood next to his bike.

Ray shook the light from his eyes and looked at her, placing the spare helmet on her head. "You worry too much. I'm fine. Let's go."

He placed the helmet he never wore on his head, trying to hide his eyes, raising Wren's suspicion. She took the sides of his helmet and forced him to look at her. His eyes were chaotic, with silver light bouncing over his pupils and the whites.

Wren's jaw dropped. She convinced Ray to drive them to Rose, who was working at Chicks 'N More near the mall, to check his health before carrying out their plan. Since Rose was a mage, she had to know what was going on with Ray. And Wren was not in the mood to talk to the *cat*...

Rose looked over the counter of the fast-food restaurant and stared at Wren and Ray walking in. Her freckled, fair skin looked red from being overworked. Her brown hair was pulled back into a messy bun, and her brown eyes looked tired.

"Why are you running the register?" Wren asked Rose.

"Call outs," Rose said.

"You are way too nice. Sometimes I think Esme is your real daughter." Wren walked behind the counter and helped stock cups for Rose. "Can you close the store for five minutes and check out Ray? Something weird is going on with him—like, magical weird."

"Isn't Marie at your house?" Rose asked. "She knows more than me."

"Are you two friends or something?" Wren asked. "I can't believe that cat is a mage. Did you know she stalked me for, like, a month? Always bitching to me at the church. Fuck that cat."

Rose looked at the people in line, alarmed at Wren's foul mouth. "Sorry for my niece. We just buried her friend. She's not taking it well."

"Oh, I'm fine," Wren said. "Didn't you know that Simon is still here in the form of Cain? You're a mage, so you should have known."

She closed her hands around the paper cup stack, crumbling them.

A man in the back of the line looked appalled, but he did not leave. He wanted chicken despite not liking the mages.

"So, Ray's eyes. Can you check?" Wren asked as she placed the ruined cups over the existing cups.

Rose walked up behind Wren and tossed the cups in a bin quickly before she rang up the next customer. "I can't at the moment, but I will after this line clears." She looked up at the eight people in line.

Wren finished stocking the cups and condiments, which Rose re-did.

"Hey, Wren." A young woman came out from the grill area with a plate of boxed chicken meals. "Wanna help?"

The young woman placed the tray of boxed chicken next to Rose and turned to look at Wren. Her dark brown hair was pulled up into a similar messy bun to Rose's, and her flushed face hid the dark freckles that normally complimented her light brown skin.

"Sure, Addison," Wren told her.

She walked with Addison to the grill and helped box up the chicken, which she was better at. Ray helped by ringing up customers, and the customers often stared at the light flashing in his eyes.

"I see what Wren's talking about." Rose gasped and stared into Ray's eyes. "This is spirit communication."

The customer at the back finally left, accusing Ray of being fae. Rose just stared after the hostile man. It was common knowledge that Chicks 'N More was owned by two supporters of fae integration—one of whom had recently announced her status in the Mage's Guild. It was also an establishment that advertised they hired fae, but the local trolls and goblins had yet to apply. There was too much risk working in such a busy place.

"Why are you working fast food?" Wren asked Addison, back in the kitchen. "I thought this sort of work was *beneath* you?"

"William is sick." Addison plopped the chicken in the frying pan. "Cindy is at a baby shower. Tara is out of town, yada yada. You know how it goes. I couldn't let my mom do all of this on her own. I can't *wait* for Eudora to return. My mom can be such a pushover." She looked mad at the thought that her mom was always being taken advantage of.

"Excuse me." A woman named Samantha waved from the drive-thru area, wearing a headset. "I'm here, aren't I?"

Addison grinned at the employee. "That's because you're scared of Eudora."

"Who isn't?" Samantha turned back to her screen to ring up a customer at the drive-thru.

"Well, the employees who called out aren't," Wren said and carried a box to Rose. "Can't wait to see the shitshow that unfolds when she comes back." She broke out into a calm and delirious laugh, eyes glossing over with sadistic joy as she locked eyes with the customer she handed the food to, sending a shiver up his neck.

"You are turning into your aunt." Rose slowly took a box of chicken from Wren and handed it to the last customer.

"According to Lucifer and the cat, I'm going to turn into Syn," Wren said bitterly.

Rose walked to the front door and taped up a scribbled note, saying they were having a ten-minute break. She turned around, facing Wren. "That's *not* something to joke about. That day is going to ruin Eudora and *me*. Not to mention Esme, and everyone else that loves you."

Following Lucifer's order, Marie had educated Rose on who Syn was back at the guild the previous night. The small mage would not stop bragging about how Loki had been Syn's travel companion.

"Why don't you just close for the day?" Wren asked, ignoring her sentiment. "You're lacking staff."

"Loss of revenue," Rose explained.

"Closing for the day will not dent your revenue," Wren said, raising an eyebrow. "Everyone loves your chicken. They'd all come rushing for it once you re-open tomorrow."

"We'll be fine. Eudora will be back soon. She always returns before one," Rose said and glanced down at her watch—quarter past noon. "And Connell is on his way to help."

"Did I just hear *Connell*?" Addison shouted from the back.

She walked out from the kitchen with a huge grin on her face while Wren became sidetracked by trying to communicate with Vaan—to inform Eudora about the callouts.

"Not a date, Addy." Rose shook her head at her daughter.

"And who's Syn?" Addison asked.

"No one," Rose told her daughter and then looked over at Wren, shaking her head.

Addison shrugged off her mom's peculiar behavior, thinking it was mage talk. She took advantage of the break to play on her phone, while the only employee present took a mini-nap in a chair. Rose went to go sit with Wren and Ray at a table to observe him. Wren leaned back in the booth as she watched Rose hold Ray's face in her hands.

"Sooo... *Eudora* just got off the exit. She should be here soon. She's furious," Wren said.

"Why is she furious?" Rose asked and stopped examining Ray. "Don't tell me you just read her mind."

"I may have." Wren looked out of the window to search the parking lot.

Rose squinted her eyes at her non-biological niece. "I don't care if you can read minds. Forcing your mind into others' is rude."

"I didn't read her mind. You know I can't read that woman's mind," Wren said.

"Then, how do you know she's back in town without calling her?" Rose asked skeptically.

"I read Vaan." Wren shuddered at Vaan's thoughts and looked at Rose. "Only for a little. Think I angered him. I told him to chill the fuck out—

think that angered him more. Seriously, I only wanted to know their location. I mean, Vaan is not someone I enjoy glimpsing into. You know? His mind is like a horror show. I just didn't want to call Eudora and be the victim of her temper."

Rose grinned. "That's what you get for prying," she said, and she flitted her eyes away from Wren and resumed inspecting Ray.

"They started this when they went out of town instead of attending Simon's funeral." Wren folded her arms. "I mean, I get it. I really do. But Eudora had the *audacity* to order me to go. Like, how is *that* fair?"

Rose looked away from Ray's eyes and stared at Wren with concern. "I am so sorry for missing the funeral, Wren." She apologized for the umpteenth time. "Father Bernie gave me a recording of the eulogy at the lunch." She turned to look at Ray and told him, "You did so well." He nodded.

"All mages were ordered to work this past weekend, and it was your first day. Can't fuck up your first day." Wren narrowed her brow. "Eudora went out of town to check on the new Chicks 'N More. Not the same. She could have postponed the trip. I bet Vaan's going to do his red-eye glare at me when they get back. If they didn't go out of town, I wouldn't have had to read his mind to begin with."

"You still shouldn't have read Vaan," Rose said, glancing at her.

"Rose, telepathy is the same as a cellphone," Wren said. "Plus, it's easier on my eardrums when dealing with Eudora."

"No, it isn't," Rose said, astonished. "You literally enter people's minds and can hear every thought. It sometimes gives us migraines. It's like a cellphone... Yeah, right!" She paused when she saw the light in Ray's eyes flicker brightly for a moment. "Did you know Wren called me before the service and tried to weasel her way out of attending the funeral?"

"At least I *called* you," Wren said, trying to joke, and then realized what Rose had told Ray. She did not want Ray to know that. As he snapped his eyes from Rose to Wren, she froze in his scalding glare. Rose moved his head back her way to continue her examination.

"I would have killed you if you didn't go," Ray muttered to Wren. "Then, I would have two dead friends."

No one said anything further.

After Rose examined Ray's eyes and concluded he was in fact being possessed by a spirit, he and Wren walked out of the restaurant to attend to other matters. Taking down the sign on the door, Rose stared worryingly at Ray climbing onto his motorcycle.

When Ray drove out of the parking lot, Detective Connell was turning into the establishment. Wren pointed at the detective and said something while laughing, which was muffled by Ray's bike. Connell just stared at the crazy woman on the motorcycle.

"You can't stop us." That was what Wren had yelled at the detective.

"Did Wren and Ray help y'all?" Connell asked after he walked in and approached Rose, who was behind the register again.

"Hardly!" Addison yelled from the kitchen.

"Ray's being possessed by a ghost, I think," Rose said, concerned. "They swung by for me to check him."

Connell poured himself a drink and went to go stand next to Rose. "I always found Ray to be odd," he said and then took a long sip of Diet Coke.

Rose hit him, and the detective released a chuckle.

"*Not* a date?" Addison asked and walked out of the kitchen, eyeing her mom and the detective.

"Addison, quit joking." Rose kissed the gold cross necklace that her deceased husband Louie had given her when Addison was born. "I would never do that to your father."

The detective looked away and refilled his drink. "Quit joking about your mother and me, Addison. Your father was my best friend," Connell said.

Addison grumbled, walking back to the kitchen. Her father had died when she was ten, eleven years ago. While she missed her dad greatly, she only wanted her mother to be happy. Rose *deserved* to be happy.

Addison peeked out from behind the wall and eyed Connell and Rose reminiscing about her father, Louie King. She could not be the only one who saw it. "Marry her!" she yelled out, then ran back near the fryer, trying to avoid the wrath of the loyal detective. She sighed and tuned out her mother and Connell, who were speaking to a new customer.

"Um..." Samantha, the employee, stared through the drive-thru window at a short black limo pulling into the parking lot. "Eudora is back."

Addison abandoned her duty in the kitchen and told the employee to cover for her. If anyone could get through to her mom, it would be Eudora. She fumed at the number of callouts they had received simply because Eudora was on a business trip.

"Hello, dear." Eudora looked over at Addison walking up to her as she exited the backseat of the car. "I see Wren was telling the truth." She looked around at the empty spaces where her employees usually parked. "Normally, invading Vaan's mind is unwarranted, but I can see the situation is dire."

Addison looked mad. "They all called out, except for Samantha." She huffed. "Connell and I are covering for them because my mom couldn't tell them *no*."

"Vaan..." Eudora looked over at her closest friend, who was closing the driver's door. "Remind me to fire the callouts and hire a new staff."

Vaan nodded. He was irritated that Wren had yelled at him on their way back into the city. He may have been seen as vicious in how he handled criminals, but loud he was not.

"Oh, I don't think you have to go *that* far." Addison looked surprised. "Maybe just write them up and reduce their hours?"

"Nonsense," Eudora said and waved her hand. "If they don't value their job, then someone else will."

Eudora and Rose were like fire and ice—the two had nothing in common except their love for business. Where Rose was apologetic, emotional, and humble, Eudora was cold, controlled, and outspoken.

"How was the trip?" Rose asked Eudora after she and Vaan followed Addison into the chicken joint. "The new manager doing okay at the Atlanta location?"

Eudora and Rose were the same age, forty-eight, and they had met at the local university in their twenties. Both coming from well-off families and sharing the same major, they bonded. Over the course of their college life, they collaborated on a plan for a fast-food business. Both women earned degrees in marketing, and they started their fast-food chain as soon as they graduated. Over the years, their restaurant became popular in the South, and the local business magazines often portrayed Eudora and Rose as powerful and distinguished women.

"Everyone, get your food and leave my restaurant," Eudora said, ignoring Rose and staring at the scattered customers eating in booths. "*Now!*"

Rose rushed out from behind the counter and handed the customers coupons for a free meal, making Eudora roll her eyes. Vaan locked the store and turned on the neon **Closed** sign. He folded his arms and followed Eudora's pace around the store with his dark brown eyes, where red was seeping in. There were only a few dozen katani left on Earth, living in secrecy on Birdsong, and Vaan was the most feared. While he viewed everyone as a threat, there was only one who he treasured.

"Call everyone to a mandatory meeting, Samantha," Eudora told the employee who stood at the drive-thru area. "And congratulations, you just became the store manager."

No one could match Eudora's personality—it was calculating and distant. She had a way of making the proudest person crumble. Something told Rose the meeting that Eudora was going to hold would make it on the local news channels. Every time she felt wronged, the entire city fell victim. That was what had happened when Louie died, and the upper class gossiped about how "poor Rose" would be lost without a man.

With a calm and threatening tone directed at the higher-class society chattering about Rose after Louie died, Eudora had recited a quote.

"'Strong minds discuss ideas, average minds discuss events, weak minds discuss people.'" The famous quote from Socrates had escaped Eudora's tightened lips as she bored her gaze into everyone's soul, making the city freeze in their tracks. She had gone on local TV for her business' advertisement, but she targeted those who slandered her dear friend and honorary sister. She had stood there, staring into the camera, holding a basket of fried chicken. As if she were an abyss of truth, she had sent the coldest chill into the viewers' stomachs. Something about how she had held the basket made the spectators rush to buy her chicken. Silent intimidation and a fabulous chicken recipe were a deadly but perfect combination for a business in the South.

Locals loved Eudora and Rose because while they both came from the upper class, they often preferred to mingle with the lower and middle classes. Eudora did so because that was who their customers were, while Rose was just a loveable woman who adored everyone.

As Samantha texted everyone in the store's group chat about what was taking place, Vaan walked up to Eudora, who would not stop pacing. He placed his hands on her shoulders and hummed a melody from Birdsong Island. As the tune filled the stoic woman's ears, Eudora relaxed.

Turning to Vaan, Eudora looked up at the man who had followed her from the island when Wren and Esme were both children.

※※※※※

Rose and Eudora were walking down the hiking trails, following their guide around the island. It was 2205—the year they went to Birdsong. Wren and Esme were playing in the pool with the local children. As the mages watched the children, Rose and Eudora attended a sightseeing tour, which both Wren and Esme found to be a boring thing to do.

"What's that sound?" Rose asked, looking down the mountain to an area in the woods where a bonfire was lit.

"No need to know about them," the elven guide said and waved his hand, not wanting to tell the two humans about their lineage. "It's just a tribe."

Later that evening, Eudora snuck out when Rose fell asleep with a Mage's Guild pamphlet clutched in her hands. Surprised that a strong empath was human, a mage recruiter quickly wanted to bring the first human into the Mage's Guild. Reluctant to join such a foreign organization, Rose humored the idea of interning with them. And her dreams reflected that interest.

Eudora left the hostel where her family slept and ran toward the trail that they had walked earlier that day. The Council had told both women to not go out at night—that it was dangerous for humans. But Eudora disregarded their warnings. She climbed to the top of the mountain with her flashlight and looked down at the bonfire, which was still lit, then walked toward the flame.

As Eudora edged closer toward the fire and walked further through the woods, opposite the city they were guests at, she started to hear chanting. She crouched behind a bush and watched people dance around a bonfire. They were taller than the humans and fae. Like the fae, their skin was of different colors, but the shades were more vibrant. One woman of dark orange skin wore a mask over her eyes, and she bared her teeth as she raised her arms toward the sky.

Without making a sound, Eudora watched in horror as two men dragged a fair-skinned man toward the bonfire. The woman in the mask sliced her hands through the air to silence everyone from chanting. Strapping the man to a wooden cross, the two men were about to place the cross above the fire.

"Stop!" Eudora ran from her spot before reason could tell her not to.

The people of varied shades turned to stare at the human. The woman in the mask widened her eyes, looking overjoyed to see a human in their woods. She pointed at Eudora, and the men laid the cross down and walked toward her.

The woods became Eudora's shelter, as she huddled behind a fallen tree branch while the tribe of unknown inhabitants searched for her.

A low growl emitted from the small village, and screams spread through the woods. Eudora dared not look over the trunk, and she remained clinging to the grass as the growling that radiated from the village suddenly stopped.

And when it resumed, the growl was inches from Eudora's ear. Wanting to see the one who would end her life, Eudora raised her head and peered into the eyes of the reddest wildness she had ever seen.

The man before her did not look like the others, as he was pale, and there was a difference in his nature. The others of the village stood tall and straight with a frightening grace, while this man crouched like a beast.

"You were strapped to the cross," Eudora whispered.

The barbaric man knocked Eudora over the head with a rock and tossed her over his shoulder. He ran to the nearby city and threw her on the doorstep of the hostel where she stayed.

When Eudora woke, their guide and a few members of the Mage's Guild were hovering over her.

"I told you not to go to the village," the guide told Eudora. "A guard saw one of them bring you back."

"Almost back to normal," a mage said, healing Eudora's head wound.

A group of guards marched out from the woods holding flashlights. "Everyone is dead." One guard looked to be in shock. "The katani are dead."

"Impossible," the mage healing Eudora said. "What about their healer?"

"Dead," the guard replied.

Three guards walked up from behind the head guard and pushed the man who had knocked Eudora on the head in front of them. "We think this demon is responsible," the guard said.

"I am not a demon," the man who was shoved in front of the guards said in broken English. "I am katani."

The guards laughed and pushed the man to walk in front of them. He was tied to a rope. "Katani do not eat each other," a guard said. "And all of them are orangish."

"Actually, they do." A woman walked up to them. "Not all are burned with amber."

The queen of the Sapphire Court emerged from under the lamppost, and the mages and guards bowed to her.

"This man is one of the one thousand katani who started this island with the First Mage ten thousand years ago." The queen of nymph blood walked up to the frozen guards and freed the man from his binds. "He is far older than the island itself. Show him more respect."

The guards backed up from the katani they mistook for a demon and bowed in apology. The katani hissed at them.

Meanwhile, Rose had awoken from the commotion outside and made her way to stand next to Eudora.

"I'm sorry for killing the Anu Tribe," the katani said to the queen. "They were sacrificing the other tribes. It had to be stopped. Please, tell Lucifer."

The only ones who knew the truth about the First Mage and how the katani still lived were the residents of Birdsong: renowned scholars, the Council, and the Mage's Guild. It was an island secret of the highest decree. Most common fae thought the First Mage and katani were long-deceased.

"Is this why you had yourself abducted by the guards?" the queen asked the katani. "You wanted to inform the First Mage of the katani's politics?"

The katani nodded and then growled at Eudora. "But that woman interfered."

The queen looked over at Eudora, who was standing behind the healer. She then walked up to meet her and Rose at the hostel door. "You are the humans here for an evaluation?" the queen asked. "Isis believes that one of your daughters is the Spirit. We shall see about that. What is her name?"

Rose did not speak. Something about the elegant queen made her feel meek. And Eudora refused to answer.

"Answer me." The queen's voice thundered.

"I do not answer commands," Eudora replied, making Rose look at her in disbelief.

"This is not the time to have a power struggle," Rose whispered.

The queen brought out her magnifying glass and started staring through the glass at Eudora, then narrowed her eyes at the stubborn woman.

Eudora glared at the queen. Tired of her playing with her glass, she asked, "What do you think you are doing?"

Everyone gasped at the human's behavior in front of one of the court's queens.

"We are here because I want an answer as to why the fae think my niece is the Spirit. And here you are playing with your magnifying glass," Eudora said furiously.

After becoming fascinated by Eudora, the katani followed her back to the United States. It was an interesting encounter when she found the man from the island standing outside of her house in the rain.

He had been waiting patiently for hours.

XXIX

ONE SLY ALLY

MILES AWAY FROM THE Chick's 'N More, Wren and Ray drove to the jail that had Simon's parents in custody. While the two were on board with the fact that Simon was a fragment of Cain, they still had a need for revenge.

It did not matter that Simon was part of some alien that ruled a planet for dead beings.

Simon was once their best friend.

"Can you hear anything?" Ray asked Wren after he braked.

"Are you sure that you're alright?" she asked. "Your eyes—"

"I feel fine," he replied. "What can you hear?"

Wren let go of Ray's sides and slid off the bike. She scanned the jail, trying to find Simon's parents. To no surprise, the Coys were too insane to think structured thoughts. Luckily, she could read the minds of most of the inmates who were housed near them.

"Simon's parents are bragging about how they will avoid prison because of their defense," Wren told him.

"'Defense?'" Ray asked. "Didn't Connell say they're going to be assigned Jack from the Public Defender's Office? He always gets the cases Vaan wants to take care of. The only thing awaiting them is Vaan's teeth."

"True... Oh, my god, this is too good." Wren could not help but laugh. "Their club hired them a private attorney." She tried to concentrate on the scattered inmates' thoughts. "Their defense is ridiculous as fuck."

Ray turned to her and asked, "What's their defense?"

"They're going to say Simon was a terrorist because he was in love with a fae. And they were carrying out their American duty," Wren said as she listened to Simon's mother's voice inside an inmate's memories. She looked at Ray. "I thought they were going to claim that they were being mind-controlled by a fae?"

"They're insane—nothing they say makes sense." Ray raised his eyebrows. "Was Simon even seeing anyone?"

"No," Wren replied, then stopped snickering at what she heard. She looked surprised at the new information. "They think I'm fae."

"Well, you are Simon's first love." Ray folded his arms, staring at the brick building in thought. "But it's entirely evil to kill your own son because of that. People shouldn't kill their children. People shouldn't kill each other, period."

He turned to face his bike and punched the metal frame of his motorcycle, bruising his hand. "Fuck!" he exclaimed and kicked his bike. "Fuck them!"

"'First love?'" Wren asked and took Ray's hand into her own to check. "I didn't know that."

"Really?" Ray flinched at the stinging in his hand. "How did you not know? He dragged you everywhere in kindergarten, *forcing* me to be your friend."

"You sound resentful," Wren grumbled.

Ray took his hand from her and shook it from the throbbing. "That's not what I meant. My hand just freaking hurts."

"We should get your hand looked at." Wren stared at his hand. "You may have fractured it."

"My hand's fine. Did you get it?" Ray asked.

"Yep." Wren tapped her head with her finger and slid back on the bike.

"Good." Ray drove them away from the jail, ignoring the pain in his hand.

The address Wren had retrieved from one of the inmates was the location belonging to the first anti-fae club twenty miles from Tallahassee. They did not want to look up the location online, afraid to leave a paper trail. Luckily, many of the people housed in the jail were members of the Human Coalition.

Ray and Wren had a message to send to the rebels. And the only way for them to be heard was to visit their headquarters.

What's taking you so long to come home? Kieran asked, forcing his voice into Wren's mind. *I thought you were returning at noon.*

"Holy fuck," Wren shouted, making Ray swerve while they turned onto a narrow road that led into anti-fae country. "How the hell did you just communicate with me?!"

Think my mind is used to yours, Kieran told her.

"Damn it, Wren!" Ray shouted, driving.

"Sorry!" Wren shouted back. "Kieran is talking to me!"

"I don't care! Do your mind crap quietly!" Ray drove down the twisting dirt road, not wanting to wreck his new bike.

Why are you and Ray driving to the anti-fae club? Is this what it's like to be telepathic? Cool! Whoa... you have some dark thoughts. I thought I was morbid. Well, when you get there, throw a Molotov for me. Kieran snorted. *Oh, I want pizza. Pick me up some pepperoni.*

Aren't Lucifer and that cat there with you? Wren asked, deciding it was best to speak with him internally and not spook Ray with random outbursts. *Ask them to get you some.*

The cat is, Kieran said, *but Lucifer just left. I'm starving.*

Esme works down the street. I'm sure she'd be happy to get you some. Wren rolled her eyes at her sister and Kieran's growing bond.

Kieran objected. *I'd rather not. It feels wrong asking her to order meat.*

There's food in the kitchen, Wren told him.

I don't want that crap. It's all healthy. He sounded bitter.

Did you check the freezer? Last time I checked you like blood, Wren said.

You have blood pouches in the freezer? Kieran sounded amazed.

No, you idiot. Wren sighed out loud. *I have steaks. Eat that because we may not return until tomorrow. We're going out of town to attend to something.*

I already ate the steak in the fridge, but I didn't see any in the freezer—

Lucifer appeared next to the motorcycle, running to match their pace, breaking Wren and Kieran's link.

"What the hell!?" Ray exclaimed as, again, he almost wrecked his bike.

Lucifer walked up to them after Ray parked on the edge of the narrow road. "Whatever you two are planning, do not do it." He stared down at Wren.

"How'd you know what we're planning?" Wren asked.

"Kieran was talking loudly to you from your living room." Lucifer walked up to Ray and reached out to take the motorcycle keys from the ignition. "Just the two of you going up against the primary group that leads the anti-fae? You may have powers, Wren, but you are still human. Are you two trying to end up dead like Simon?"

As if Lucifer's words manifested an onslaught of bullets, an old car drove past the three of them while a crazed lunatic hung outside of the backseat, shooting at them.

"Fae scum," the madman shouted as he shot at Lucifer, thinking he was fae because of how he looked. "Die, mutants!"

Lucifer looked unphased when the bullets tried to pierce his stone-like skin. He turned to the car and watched it roll to a stop. The rebel, who looked to be on uppers, left the car holding a machete. Swinging the blade, the madman walked toward them, and the driver stood out of the car, pointing a shotgun Lucifer's way.

"Fuck. If bullets don't work, this sure as hell will." The crazed man approached Lucifer and stabbed his chest with the machete.

Lucifer looked down at the blade, which broke through his clothes: two inches of faux leather and cloth. "You ruined my jacket—I loved this jacket." He caught the machete before it could fall and waved the blade to his side. "I'm keeping this as compensation."

He stared down at the weapon, liking the look of it.

"What the hell are you?" the once-proud maniac asked, taking a step back from the angelic. "S-some kind of mutant fae?"

"'Mutant fae?'" Lucifer asked. "You are human, therefore a primate. Primates and fae are the mutated lines from the zyula and katani. To call someone a mutant when you are one is pretty hypocritical."

The man looked back at his friend, who had jumped back into the car and driven off, leaving the guy behind.

"No." Lucifer leaned over the scared man. The rebel's high was wearing off. "I am not one of the fae." He extended his white wings from his shoulder blades, and blood trickled down his back. The whites surrounding his black eyes turned pitch-black, and the sound of his bones crunching together made the drugged man's stomach clench.

Glaring down at the man, Lucifer said, "If you have a problem with the katani and their descendants, then you have a problem with the empire. If you do not like us, then *leave* our world."

The man soiled himself and tried to run from Lucifer. The darkness that had befallen the seven angelics took over, and Lucifer rammed his fist through the stomach of the man, pulling out his intestines. Roping the intestines around the man's neck, he wrapped the organs tightly, then shoved a piece of intestine into his mouth to chew. Spitting out the meat, he wiped his mouth from the blood as the man fell over, entering a slow and painful death.

"Even your insides are disgusting." Lucifer turned from the dying man.

Ray was kneeling beside Wren, who was lying still on the grass. Blood was leaking out of her chest.

"How did this happen?" Lucifer walked up to the two.

"A bullet hit her," Ray said, panicking as he held his cotton jacket down on her wound. "Can you heal her? The pool is out of the question—Esme is having it cleaned today."

"I can, but I do not have the time for this," Lucifer said. "This wound will take one hour to mend, at the very least."

"Damn it." Ray exhaled. "What about the Mage's Guild? You run it. Can't they skip a few people and heal her?"

"Are you asking me to ask the mages to heal her before kids—before the children of Child's Heart?" Lucifer asked him. "The same charity you and Wren donate a portion of Eden's profits to?"

While the mages could not cure cancer, they could slow it down to give someone a much longer life. The guild worked with Child's Heart Charity, an organization that aided both fae and human children with terminal cancer. Since they had to regulate their magic, the mages focused on the most severe conditions: cancer, disease, severely injured limbs, and organ punctures. Even if Wren had been a child, the mages would have sent her to the hospital because the bullet did not pierce a vital organ.

"Well, the hospital it is," Ray said, feeling rattled that he had even suggested such a thing.

Wren was out like a blown socket. Lucifer and Ray spoke while she drifted into a paralyzed darkness where the dead waited. Images of the deceased flashed through her mind. Trapped in a dark pit of anguish, she landed her eyes on Simon. He stared at her lifelessly, then turned from her, pointing at a man who was covered in flames: Cain.

As Wren was stuck in what seemed like an endless nightmare, Ray started his motorcycle, despite the bullets grazing it. And Lucifer took it upon himself to fly Wren to the nearest hospital—luckily, they were only three miles outside of the city limits. Seeing a man flying in the sky was yet another reality for the human world to freak out about.

Lucifer dropped from the sky, causing the ground to shake lightly. A paramedic froze while escorting a patient strapped to a gurney inside.

"Can you take her?" he asked the paramedic. "I do not want to walk in there looking like this."

The paramedic pushed the gurney with the patient on it to the approaching nurse and staff, then nodded. Lucifer walked up to the paramedic and placed Wren in his arms.

"Take care of her. She deserves to live for a few more months." Lucifer looked down at her unconscious face.

"O-oh." The paramedic stumbled over his words. "Name?"

"Her name is Wren," Lucifer said.

"What is your name?" he asked. "They will need to know."

"Lucifer," he said.

The paramedic turned around, about to rush Wren inside, then glanced back and asked, "Lucifer?"

But the angelic was already gone.

Even though the human and most of the fae world were blind to who Lucifer was, the paramedic was aware of the First Mage. His crush was a local elven mage, and even though she was not allowed to speak of the guild, she had told the cheerful human everything.

Feeling giddy about meeting the one who ran the Mage's Guild, and worried about the status of the patient in his arms, the paramedic ran inside to check Wren in.

✵✵✵✵✵

Days later, Wren tasted stale cigarette in her mouth when she woke up to the intolerable singing of morning birds. She loved birds. Really, she did. But that morning, she wanted to kill a few birds.

"Fucking birds," she muttered without opening her eyes.

"Tell me about it," a voice said above her.

Wren opened one eye to sneak a peek at the person who sounded just as annoying as the birds.

Frost.

Before she could overreact to seeing the son of Nao sitting casually in a chair near her bed, Frost muted her by placing his hand over her mouth. "Look. I'm just doing my job," he told her. "Please don't overreact and attack me. I quite like my job."

She shook her mouth free from his hand and whispered, "Yeah, which one? As an errand boy for a fucked-up god, or an errand boy for the FBI?"

Frost stared at her in disdain and whispered, "I'm not an errand boy."

"I wouldn't be here for too long if I were you, Frost. That shadow thing doesn't like you guys," Wren spat. "Do you want him to drag you into his world, like your friends?"

"It's a good thing I'm not a full Kanarian," Frost said. "Just a part of one."

"What does that mean?" Wren asked.

"Aaeon won't attack me," Frost replied. "He has no grudge against me. I wasn't there when they caged him. Well, in a way, I was." He paused, confused by his very existence. "Did you notice how he didn't drag me into his world? Did you even question why he didn't include me when he took Siar and Davios?" He leaned toward Wren.

"*Dramatic,*" Wren muttered and sat up on the hospital bed.

The two glared at each other, neither backing down.

"Can you put your evil god vibe on hold for a second?" Wren asked.

"I'm not evil," Frost claimed. "When you remember everything, you'll remember your alliances." He stood up.

"Remember what?" Wren asked, not liking that it sounded like they were allies. "There's no fucking way we were friends."

Frost looked down at her and whispered, "In the Gardens of Eden, a blind bird would sing. Grand kings tend to fall, and spoiled princes always rise. But the bird... the bird always sings."

Before Wren could ask Frost the meaning of his words, Ray opened the door. She looked away from Frost and watched her best friend walk in with two cups of coffee. Following Ray, a nurse walked in to check on her health.

"Where's the agent?" Ray asked, placing the drinks down on the table. "I have his change."

Wren looked back at where Frost once stood, but she only saw the rapid closing of a portal. "Guess he left."

Neither Ray nor the nurse saw the portal, and Ray took a seat next to her bed. The nurse walked up to check the IV bag. After scribbling on her pad, the nurse asked Wren some questions and inspected her vitals. Wren looked down at the nurse's clipboard and read the date.

It was Friday—the day of the arraignment.

"Mr. Frost was concerned about you," the nurse said grimly as she started tapping a screen to read Wren's vitals. "Two handsome men caring for you. Not even my husband's like that. He doesn't care about me."

Wren looked up at the nurse, who was releasing a depressed laugh. "Well, you can always leave him," she told the nurse. "I will not pity you for being with someone that does not care about you. Grow a backbone."

The nurse looked down at Wren in shock.

"Wren," Ray hissed at her.

"Oh..." The nurse stared at Wren with startled eyes. "It's okay, Mr. Kim. Ms. Sparrow has a point. I've been wanting to leave him, but my backbone is too weak." She forced another laugh. "I should take notes from you, Ms. Sparrow," she said.

Wren did not feel bad for the nurse as she stared at the door, wanting to leave.

"We recommend staying at least one more night to observe you—"

"No." Wren interrupted her and nodded at the door. "I'm walking out of *that* door today."

"That's what Mr. Kim said you would say." The nurse glanced over at Ray and exchanged a concerned grin with him. "Your health is good, and you recovered surprisingly fast. You're free to leave, but please contact us at the first sign of irritation or infection. You had surgery on Monday."

"Understood," Ray told the nurse. "She's going straight home."

"Ah... That's why I have stitches in my boob..." Wren told the nurse sarcastically and looked up at her. "I would have never guessed."

Ray said farewell to the nurse, who left the room with an upset smile and teary eyes. "Why did you have to be so mean to Sandy?" He picked up his coffee and gulped the remaining liquid. "She has been watching over you all week."

"That's her name?" Wren looked up at the ceiling. "Maybe if I didn't have an aching pain in my chest, I would have been nicer to her."

"I shouldn't have driven us there." Ray tossed his empty coffee cup into a small trash bin. "This is my fault. This was my idea to begin with."

"No, it isn't." Wren looked at him. "You aren't the one who pulled the trigger."

Ray fell silent.

"Think this was life's way of telling us not to kill people?" Wren joked.

"'Kill?' I thought we were just going to vandalize their cars and set fire to their club?" Ray stared at Wren, waiting for her to respond, and narrowed his eyes, saying, "Were you planning on killing the people inside of the club?"

"No?" Wren asked, hoping it was the answer he wanted. Ray sighed. "I mean, you agreed when I suggested I set their building on fire."

"Yeah, not with them in it!" Ray exclaimed, looking rattled that Wren's choice of vengeance was murder.

"How was I to know?" she asked.

Ray eyed her cautiously, pulled out a change of clothes from a bag, and handed the set to her. "Murder is not the answer."

"Yes, it is." Wren snatched the clothes and rushed inside the bathroom to change out of the gown and into a clean navy-blue T-shirt. "Murder is always the answer when it comes to those pricks!" She fumbled with the gray sweatpants. "They all deserve worse than death." Opening the door, she looked up at him. "Sorry. I forgot you're a softie under all that sarcasm."

"The fuck you did," Ray exclaimed. "You've known me since—"

"Yeah, yeah. I get it. Murder is *wrong*." Wren shrugged.

Ray looked disturbed. "You're seriously freaking me out. Ever since that Edenian appeared, you haven't been acting like yourself."

Wren had always clowned around and loved to intimidate others, especially bullies. But there was now something sinister in how she delivered her words, whereas before, her intent was more on the side of comedy and defense.

"I'm the same as always." She scowled.

"*That.* That is what I'm talking about." Ray pointed at her. "You've always been loud and weird, but you are getting angrier by the day. And meaner. What did the nurse do to you?"

"I just had surgery!" she yelled.

"You've had surgery before." Ray stepped back from her to grab her bag. "For your leg. And all you did when you woke up was brag about how high the roof was."

Wren smirked at the memory of her jumping off Eudora's roof to see if she could fly. Having just watched a superhero movie when she was nine, she had thought it was possible that she could fly, since the main character in the movie could also read minds. Back then, the local Mage's Guild only healed the fae, and she had to go to the hospital for a torn ligament and fracture the old fashion way.

"Well, I can't fly." Wren laughed. "But I can start fires. And you know who can burn easily? The rebels."

Ray was speechless.

Wren gathered her hair in her hands, tied it into a high ponytail, and put on her sneakers.

After some hesitation, Ray said, "Don't forget me and Esme when you turn back into Syn. And if you go around possessing and eating people like Lucifer said you love to do, can you... not kill us?"

Wren twisted her mouth in thought. "Maybe. I don't know how I will be if I turn into her."

Ray lightly scoffed and said, "Brat."

"Of course I won't hurt you guys," Wren said as she placed the hospital gown on the bed. "And sheesh... Sorry, I'm acting *'mean.'*"

Ray pulled her to him and hugged her carefully, trying not to disturb her stitches. "I forgive you."

"Good." Wren looked up at him. "I still think we should kill all the rebels."

Ray pushed her away, becoming serious, and turned toward the door. "Don't even joke about that."

"Prick." Wren grinned.

XXX

Syn

WREN STOPPED THREATENING TO kill the rebels when she saw that it was upsetting Ray. He was one for a good revenge story, but he drew the line at murder.

Pausing at the administrator's area, Wren asked to see who had checked her in. After the receptionist looked through the thin computer, he said, "Someone named Lucifer."

After she had been discharged, they walked into the lobby.

"Why didn't you just ask me?" Ray asked.

"I didn't want to," Wren said. "My words bothered you." She batted her eyes up at Ray, who was calming down. While he thought an apology was about to escape her mouth, she said, "You seem to have a weak stomach. And I don't have time for sensitive bitches."

She rushed out of the door in the lobby. Ray shook his head at the woman, who looked like his friend but acted like a crude jerk, as he followed her outside. He spotted a black limo with Eudora and Vaan waiting for them. Noticing her adopted mother, Wren speedily walked in the opposite direction, not wanting to speak to her.

"Wren!" Ray called out after her and chased her down. "Where are you going? You're doped-up right now. You can't walk home!"

"Yes, I can! I don't want to speak to her," Wren yelled back sharply. "She chose business over Simon's funeral."

"You were trying to get out of going, too!" Ray yelled behind her and caught up to her, taking a hold of her arm. "Stop being a hypocrite. Just talk to her."

He fixed Wren's messy hair when she pouted. "I'm glad you're acting more like the Wren I know."

Across the parking lot, Eudora and Vaan watched the two from within their limo.

"I always thought those two would have made a wonderful couple. They balance each other so well," Eudora said as she stared at Wren and Ray. "But Wren was always so fixated on Simon."

Vaan stared at Eudora in silence.

"Oh, it doesn't matter. She's almost twenty-five." Eudora was not ready for Wren to leave her. "Are you certain Wren is the Spirit?"

"Yes," he replied.

"And the Spirit is named Syn?" she asked.

"Yes," Vaan answered again. "I have never met her, nor have I seen the recordings of the Angelic Empire back on Birdsong, but Lucifer is convinced Wren is Syn. So, I am convinced as well."

"Your loyalty to that mage…" Eudora fell quiet.

"He created my kind," Vaan said. "Do you have any idea what it's like existing without form? It's cold. Lucifer gave my spirit warmth."

"Wait, Vaan," Eudora said. "Do you have memories from before life?"

Vaan sealed up his emotions. As much as the katani adored the woman of snake's blood with a venomous tongue, he kept his memories to himself.

He drove the limo up to where Ray and Wren stood, which was in the middle of the road that wrapped around the hospital.

"Oh, enough of these dramatics, dear child," Eudora said after she had rolled down her window. "Get in the car."

Wren let Eudora's words roll off her shoulders, and she and Ray walked up to the car door. "Get in the limo, both of you," Eudora said, her sternness turning into irritation.

"I'll take a taxi." Wren turned to face Ray. "Wait, did you drive here?"

"No. Eudora dropped me off." Ray scratched his head. "My bike's in the shop. It got grazed by some bullets."

"I'll drop you both off at the house before the arraignment begins. Neither of you are going to *that*." Eudora stared at Wren and Ray like a hawk.

"I'm going—"

"Yes, Eudora," Ray said, cutting Wren off.

"I'll meet you and Esme at the Diamond Club at seven." Eudora tried to sound motherly, but she failed. "Please be there on time."

Wren was used to Eudora's strict demeanor and cold speech. "Warm" was not the word to describe Wren and Esme's adopted mother. When kids received barbie dolls and roller blades for Christmas, Eudora would gift survival kits, defense weapons, and socks to the girls. Despite her focus on practicality, Wren and Esme still received sparkly things. Rose had always spoiled the two like they were her own daughters. And she would give the girls sparkly doll dresses, which they grew to adore.

When the limo came to a halt at Wren's gates, Wren and Ray climbed out of the car. Wren looked back at Eudora, who always hid behind her oversized sunglasses. While Vaan drove away, Eudora stared in the side mirror and watched her niece's house grow smaller.

Vaan pulled up to the courthouse downtown, and Eudora moved her strict eyes over the crowds of rebels shouting to free the Coys.

Wren was being bombarded by Kieran's questions back at Sparrow Manor. Esme took hold of Wren's arm and tried to force her to heal in the newly filled pool. But Wren ignored her and headed into the living room with Ray. All the loud chatter woke Marie up with a startled snort. The tiny mage had been enjoying a deep nap under the coffee table.

"Is Lucifer here?" Wren asked, looking around her living room for the angelic who intercepted most of the bullets.

Marie walked out from under the coffee table and up to where Wren stood. "No. He found the book for me and took the *Angelic Diaries* to the library," the cat said. "He'll be back."

"Why'd he do that?" Wren asked.

"He wrote it. So, it's his to do with as he pleases." Marie felt superior, giddy that the First Mage had aided her in retrieving the book.

"Good for you. You won," Wren said curtly.

Wren sprawled out on the couch, as Esme persistently tried to convince her to heal in the pool. Marie jumped up on the back of the couch and glared down at Wren in annoyance at her false praise, preventing her from resting.

"If you got what you wanted, then why the hell are you still here?" Wren asked Marie, irritated that her favorite book had been stolen—even though technically Wren was the wrongful owner of the book in the first place.

Marie twitched her nose in contempt. "Loki was my ancestor, and—"

"Good for you." Wren closed her eyes, not caring to hear the cat's story about her ancestor.

"Marie wants to stay here and help you transition back into a demon." Kieran walked up behind Wren, leaned on the back of the couch, and scratched Marie on the top of her head. The runaway inmate and cat had bonded while Wren was in the hospital.

"The pool—"

"When the drugs wear off, I'll go into the damn pool," Wren interrupted Esme. Looking hurt by Wren's tone, she sat down quietly in the armchair.

"Syn's not a demon." Marie purred while Kieran continued to scratch the top of her head. "But Wren is."

"What proof do you have that I'm Syn?" Wren asked Marie, feeling aggressive toward everyone.

"Oh, I don't know." Marie scrunched her nose at Wren's idiotic question.

"It may be because you fit her description, and you set things on fire. There's also the fact that Cain tried to drag you to Limbo last weekend." The cat whipped her tail back and forth. "Or the fact that Lucifer performed a test of reveal on you, confirming that you are her..."

Marie kept her stern look on Wren. "I don't know why we think you're Syn. *My gosh*, what a mystery." She widened her eyes in fake shock, then noticed Ray was staring into a mirror on the wall to check his eyes and said, "Also, Ray's been communicating with a spirit."

"We know that. Rose already—"

"Azazel." Marie interrupted Wren, clarifying her words. "Ray's been communing with Azazel."

Marie groomed her paw as Esme jumped up from the chair, freaking out. She ran around the living room, splashing random areas with water. "Do you mean the Sun King?" she asked in a panic. "Oh, dear. Oh, dear. First Lucifer, and now *him*."

Wren stood up instantly as her sister continued to flip out, wincing at the shooting pain in her chest from the surgery, and said, "Fuck, Esme. Calm down."

"The end is near." Esme placed her hands on her cheeks in panic. "If the Sun King has been speaking to someone, that means the end is near."

Ray pried himself away from the mirror and looked back at Esme. "I'm not communicating with some angelic locked inside the sun."

Esme stopped running around and tried to calm down. "Isn't the person Azazel is said to communicate with katani?" she asked, thinking about the fae legend of the Sun King. "Since the idols were made by an angelic?"

"Yes. So, stop freaking out." Wren looked at Ray, who resumed checking his eyes in the mirror. "I highly doubt Ray is katani. You know... because he's human."

"Your prophecy is false, and Rose is an amateur," Marie said and jumped off the couch. "Ray is Azazel's Crown."

"What do you mean by 'Crown?'" Wren asked.

"The Crown is Azazel's avatar," Marie told them, nodding with closed eyes. "In simple words, Ray is Azazel's incarnation."

"Then, how are we all still alive?" Esme asked, with fright in her voice. "Azazel is our sun. He cannot be in two places at once, can he? He's an angelic, not a god."

"I don't know." Wren tried to ignore Esme's hysteria. "Ask him."

"I'm not Azazel," Ray snapped. "The cat is not always right about everything. Stop believing every little thing she says."

As everyone argued, Lucifer emerged from where he was hiding. "Enough. Stop screaming." He looked down at the pompous cat. "I am afraid you are wrong, my little protégé. Ray is not Azazel." Everyone stared at him as he walked up to Ray. The angelic smiled sinisterly and bent down to look into Ray's eyes. "He is being possessed by Azazel."

Marie ran up to Lucifer's feet, trying to ignore the fact she was just wrong. "I knew it."

"You don't know shit, cat," Wren barked. "You just said he's Azazel."

"I wrote the tale of Azazel's Crown as a fairytale back in the Gardens of Eden. Most of the fae's prophecies are just fictitious writings," Lucifer said as he watched the light flicker in Ray's eyes. He looked away from Ray when he noticed Esme's hurt expression, turning to face her.

"Really?" Esme asked. "Are any of the prophecies real?"

"Are you talking about the ones featured at the university in Moonlight Hills?" Lucifer asked. "Near that *horrendous* statue of me?"

Esme nodded and said, "Yes."

"No," Lucifer replied. "They are fairytales. I had written them for the commoners to have hope during Lucien's rule. Now that you know this, please stop idolizing me. I am not a god. All I did was reform some of the existing energies the gods had already created to manifest the katani, and then I founded a guild for their diseased kin to find solace."

Esme thought for a moment. *"That's* why we worship you!" She clasped her hands together, full of appreciation. "Your humbleness."

Lucifer turned back to Ray, grumbling. After realizing Azazel was not going to speak to him, he turned to Wren. "I hate to be a bearer of bad news, but we actually do need you to return to your original form before your twenty-fifth birthday."

"Why?" Wren asked, a cold liquid shifting inside her head.

"I have just learned that the rebels have been joining Nao's cause, and Nao has been feeding them his power—two wars are merging. We need you and Cain back as one *now*. Syn's ego has already controlled you before, so it should not be difficult. However, this was not part of the code, so we must help you transition, or the planet may shatter by your darkness."

"Ok? If Earth shatters, can't you just remake it?" Wren asked, surprising Ray and Esme. Kieran looked amused by the dark undertones in Wren's voice, but Marie sat next to Lucifer's feet, staring up at her with contempt. As more of Syn's persona crept through, Wren's demeanor became more ominous. "Just rebuild. You're good at that. This life is boring anyway."

Wren turned away and walked toward the front door. "Syn?" Lucifer asked and followed Wren into the foyer, with Marie trotting behind him.

But when he entered the foyer of the house, Wren was gone.

"Why is Wren being so scary?" Esme asked Ray. "Did you see her eyes? They looked so empty."

"I like it!" Kieran exclaimed.

Lucifer stood under the archway near the foyer, staring into the living room. "Marie, watch them. Do not let them leave the house."

"Why?" Ray asked. "What's going on?"

"Syn is rising, and she is not in the mood I thought she would be. Her being bored is never a good thing," Lucifer said. "I fear she may worsen the war rather than help stop it."

Before anyone could ask the angelic what was about to happen, he stepped back into The Shade to gather the followers of Ezra.

As people started showing up at the door of Sparrow Manor, mostly by the means of Isis' portal, Esme kept following people around—she wanted to make sure the strangers did not break anything. And every time Isis brought someone who was far away through her portal, Kieran would cheer from his perch on the top of the staircase.

"Wren won't like the fact you opened up the second floor," Ray told Lucifer, who was ushering people inside. "And if this Syn person cares about Wren's life, then we're fucked."

"Well, let's hope Syn is understanding," Marie said from her spot next to Kieran's side. "She's one of Ezra's followers, after all."

Lucifer stopped talking to the people arriving in groups and told Marie, "Cain and Syn are not followers of Ezra. They could not care less about our gods' war."

"I thought they were," Marie said. "If they don't care, then why are you always on Limbo helping Cain with his machine?"

"We have different goals, but the methods of obtaining them are linked. So, we have a deal," Lucifer told her. "I help them with designing Cain's machine, and they will allow us to use it to piece Ezra back together."

"What's their goal?" Marie asked.

"What machine?" Kieran asked at the same time.

"I do not know," Lucifer said to Marie, then looked at Kieran. "Cain has been building a machine that can resurrect the dead, the Fires of Rebirth."

Marie stood on all fours. "Are you telling me Cain has been building a machine that can bring the dead back to life? A machine capable of rebuilding a god—but you don't know why?" Her fur stood on end, and she hissed. "Cain used to be part of Nao's cult, and he's from the dark realm!"

Lucifer was shocked that the small cat was hissing at him. He walked up the steps and sat down below Marie and Kieran, scratching the cat behind her ears. "Don't fret, little one. You forget we have the Shadow King's aid. If Cain thinks of doing anything that can pose a threat to our realm, Aaeon will drag him to his domain," Lucifer said.

"Is Aaeon a follower?" Kieran asked.

"Not of Ezra," Lucifer told him. "But he follows *me* everywhere."

As if the god from the shadow realm knew Lucifer was talking about him, Aaeon decided to watch him talk to the half-angelic and cat from within his shade. Sensing that Aaeon wanted to speak to him, Lucifer excused himself and entered the path.

The many voices of Aaeon spoke over themselves, asking Lucifer why he was worried about the woman from the dark realm.

"She is my apprentice," Lucifer told the Shadow King.

"Do you... love her?" Aaeon asked him, his many voices becoming one.

"No." Lucifer looked at the god, who had manifested next to him, standing at his height. "I have known her since Eden. Whenever Syn is bored, she becomes destructive—both to herself and others. I am worried about her and what she may do. That is all."

The Shadow King nodded. "Lies... You lie."

"Even so, there has only been one person worthy of Syn," Lucifer said. "Ah, my apologies. I am reminiscing. You probably have friends over."

"Tell me..." Aaeon said, always loving Lucifer's stories.

"Long ago, when Syn journeyed with Lucien, they sought sanctuary on Eden. At the time, Azazel was to be married to Shiva, the Lady of the Silver Lake. Shiva was created to be the queen of the Angelic Empire, and she adored Azazel. But after Syn arrived on Eden, Azazel slowly became obsessed with her, and it created conflict throughout the empire," Lucifer said. "That is why he possessed Ray. As selfless as Azazel is, he is still a king with a resentment toward Syn. Spoiled, kings are. No offense."

Aaeon released a low growl and nodded, understanding Lucifer's words—offense not taken.

"You see, Syn and Lucien were once deeply in love, and they were companions from the time of Ezra's fall. They had arrived on Eden seeking asylum." Lucifer motioned with his hands, explaining. "Azazel was known to have many consorts, and when he approached Syn asking her to be one of his wives, it stirred tension between Lucien and our king. For some reason,

Syn kept losing her memory while on Eden, and I helped her restore her mind a few times. She grew fond of the angelics, and Lucien acted out by frequenting the brothels of the empire. He grew to loathe the Angelic Empire, mostly because of Azazel. But he stayed to watch over Syn. A poor bastard, Lucien is—a broken god who is in love with a woman from Hell."

"You're wrong..." Aaeon said.

"How, pray tell, am I wrong?" Lucifer asked, turning to him.

"Syn loves... only Cain," Aaeon replied.

"Yes, but Cain is not worthy of her affection. I have watched Syn for a very long time. The person who cares about Syn is Lucien, but one from the light realm and a being from the dark realm are not meant to co-exist." Lucifer crossed his arms. "Cain's love for her is not pure, and he has treated her with so much cruelty in the past. Fated love is a tricky thing, and the lores are indeed cursed." He placed his hands behind his head and tried to grin at Aaeon. "It is a fool's game to fall in love."

"Then... you are... a fool." The Shadow King looked down at Lucifer as he slowly became taller, then turned from the window that led to Sparrow Manor and walked toward his realm. When he reached the height of thirty feet, he turned back to Lucifer and said, "You care... more."

❋❋❋❋❋

While Sparrow Manor was turning into a stronghold for the Cult of Ezra, Wren's mind was tangled with confusing images, and she roamed the streets of Tallahassee. Her mind was constantly bouncing between Wren and Syn. She gripped the sides of her head and screamed silently at the pain inside her mind—memories foreign to her, memories of chaos.

Without any control of her motor functions, Wren entered a hardware store. Ignoring the welcome, she walked down an aisle and grabbed a small jar of black paint. Opening the jar, she smeared the paint on her lips and eyebrows.

Flashes of people in black war paint danced around a fire inside of her mind, along with drool and the beat of drums. Her vision was lost, and her inner sight conquered her. She listened to the rhythm of the music and heard the chanting of the zyula and katani. Half of the ancient people transformed into wolves and howled up at the full moon, and the other half hissed into the fire with glowing red eyes. The two species were getting ready to go to war against Lucien together.

Before Wren could paint symbols upon her face, a clerk rushed up to her and said, "You can't be doing that. You gotta buy the paint first before... you wear it?" The clerk stared at her, stumped by what she was doing. "Are you *eating* it?" The clerk asked, noticing the paint dripping from her lips. "Don't tell me you're trying to get high?"

Wren tilted her head down at the paint. As if she mistook the clerk's words for a suggestion, she tasted the thick liquid.

"Well... that's what you get for eating it." The clerk widened his eyes at Wren gagging as she swallowed a small amount of paint.

Wren did not know why she was doing what she was doing. It felt like something was crawling out of her—something evil.

"Well, that will be two hundred and seventy bucks." The clerk placed his hands on his hips. "Come on, lady. I don't wanna call the authorities."

Wren walked up to the clerk, dumped the paint on top of the man's head, and said to him, "You speak too much."

"Damn it, lady!" the clerk yelled. "Who will it be?! The cops or the mages?!"

As the clerk tried to wipe the paint from himself with a nearby towel, Wren walked past him.

"Na-uh, you aren't going anywhere." The man reached out to take a hold of her arm.

"Don't touch me!" Wren exclaimed when he gripped her wrist. She pushed him toward the shelves with her force field, and he slipped on the painted floor.

She shook her head, trying to regain her sense of self. But which self? Syn was battling for control of her mind, and Wren was far from winning.

The clerk pushed himself up from the floor. He was about to call out for the other employees to stop her from leaving, but what he saw made him decide not to. With every step Wren took, fire sparked beneath her feet, leaving burned footprints.

"Are you okay?" another clerk asked the employee covered in paint. "Who did this?"

"It was an accident," the man in paint said, for he did not want to tattle on someone who left fire when she walked.

As Wren left the store, every employee and customer gathered around the man she had dumped the paint on. She turned the corner and walked down the street while loud explosions sounded throughout downtown.

"Did you see their faces!?" a woman who stood with a group of rebels hollered down the road from the store.

"That alien knew exactly what we needed." A man grinned at his magic-infused rifle. "I didn't like magic before. But I like it now!"

The man released a shot toward a car, and the car exploded.

As citizens quickly realized what was happening, everyone panicked.

"That was no alien. That was God," a woman in the militia said as she played with her wand. "We *met* God. We're his chosen!!"

As rebels lined the streets with weapons gifted from Nao, Wren stumbled upon a small army.

"Isn't that *that* Sparrow chick?" One rebel, who acted as the leader, aimed his machine gun at Wren.

"Dude, this stick's awesome," the rebel who swore Nao was God said, blowing up a mailbox with her wand. "We should blow up that fae church next." The woman then pointed her wand and blew up a trashcan. "You know, the one with that priest who loves the fae."

"We know who you're talkin' about," the leader told the woman. "Later. Let's finally kill this Sparrow chick. She's a thorn in our spine."

A few of the rebels whistled to get Wren's attention. "Hey," the leader yelled out to her. "We didn't see you at the arraignment—"

Wren looked confused by the rebels yelling at her, and she started walking toward them.

"—when we picked up the Coys," the leader snickered.

"You should see the courthouse," the woman with the wand shouted, releasing a cackle. "Or maybe you can't. Since it's gone!"

Wren stopped walking, unable to register who the people in front of her were. As she looked around her environment, nothing seemed familiar.

"Like your aunt," the woman taunted Wren again.

"She didn't die," a man whispered to the woman. "That *thing* saved her."

"I know that. I'm just trying to rile her up." The woman grinned foolishly and placed her wand on her shoulder like it was a rifle.

"Well, it ain't workin'," a rebel in the back said, noticing Wren's absent look. "Let's just shoot her."

An explosion stole Wren's attention as the woman from the small group in front of her blew up another car. Unable to remember who she was, she ran toward the woman who held the wand, viewing her as a threat. Fire spread through her veins, and as she leaped into the air, she summoned all her flames. She dropped down in front of the woman and pried open the woman's lips with both hands, then released a piercing shriek, sending fire into her mouth. And as the fire swept down the woman's throat, the rebel's insides began to burn.

"The fuck?! S-shoot it!!" a rebel barked at the others.

Bullets and magical flares penetrated through Wren's flesh.

"Is she dead?" one of them asked as they looked down at Wren's butchered body.

"What do you think?" the leader asked and turned his back on Wren's corpse. "We did it! All the Sparrows are dead. Can't wait to tell the club. Bet you we'll be given new jackets."

"Let's get the nymph next," a rebel spat. "The dead bitch's sister."

"No, the priest," another rebel said.

"Why are all the Sparrows dead?" someone asked near Wren's corpse.

The leader turned around, and his face went white when he saw what looked to be a see-through version of Wren. "W-what—"

"Did you kill the birds?" the woman who looked like Wren asked.

The spectral woman walked away from the rebels, who looked beyond frightened, while fire crept from her translucent form, and she remembered everything other than Wren's life. The flames engulfed the vile people as the trees turned to ash.

Then, the planet started to shake.

And Syn began to wake.

EPILOGUE

A Broken Wing

THE SKY WAS POURING rain the color of blood, and the ground shook with each step the woman who looked like Wren took. A thick fog spread across the city, as thousands of people hid.

"Blood and bones. Beast and drool. The Tyrant Lord is dead. The Tyrant Lord is dead." Syn whispered the ancient rhyme repeatedly as she stared through the store's window at people taking cover from the rain. "It's just a little blood."

Pinning her face to the window, she acted like the wall kept her from being able to enter. She pounded her fists, shaking the glass. "It's just a little blood!" she shouted.

Remember, a woman spoke into her ears at the exact moment she was about to walk through the glass.

Syn looked around at the voice and growled in every direction. Her next target was spared, and she walked away from the people who hid inside a clothing shop. Through the fire and debris, she walked on the burned road. She could not feel the heat since her flesh was no more.

Remember, the voice said again, speaking from a direction that led away from the clothing store.

As Syn followed the familiar voice, her fire drifted from where it burned and back toward her core, though the flames had already claimed many lives. Stopping at a music store, she looked through the windows, searching for where the voice was coming from.

She then collapsed on the sidewalk and gagged. As Wren's consciousness tried to battle for control, Syn tried to throw up part of herself in hopes of ridding herself of Wren.

Remember, the voice said again.

"Stop telling me to remember. I don't want to remember!" Syn yelled, placing her hands on the window to help herself stand back up.

Red rain showered down above Syn as she stared at her reflection. But it was not Syn staring back. It was a broken ego, a broken soul.

Syn was split in two.

"Remember!" Wren shouted and pounded on the other side of the glass. "Remember me!"

Covered in the blood of Azazel's tears, Syn stared into Wren's eyes. "Don't forget me," Wren pleaded.

"You were never meant to exist," Syn told her. "I'm sorry."

"Strip us from all our memories and see how we lived?" Wren asked Syn. "We were good. We were happy."

Syn tried to ignore her alter ego while she crawled down the sidewalk from the music store, but Wren took control of their spirit, and they entered the store.

"Things like 'good' and 'happy' are not real," Syn hissed. "Die already."

She was forced to crawl until she reached a wall of instruments. An image of Wren appeared on the surface of a shiny classical guitar. "Things like death are not real," Wren said.

"Oh, shut up." Syn grabbed a guitar and smashed it into the reflection of Wren. "Shut up!"

Syn made her way back up to her feet, then searched around the broken guitars in hopes of not finding Wren.

Silence.

THE RISE OF SYN

As soon as Syn believed she was finally gone, Wren began yanking at where Syn's heart would be if she had a body. Feeling pain that she should not be able to feel, Syn clutched her chest and looked down. Fire was seeping out from in-between her breasts. As the flames spread around her, more voices spoke.

Syn screamed and covered her ears. "Do you really want to forget them?" Wren asked quietly from the air.

Still able to use magic separate from Syn, Wren summoned a memory from a stranger who had witnessed her parents' first encounter. The room then changed into the interior of a train.

Syn lowered her hands from her ears and stared at a man playing a guitar. A woman with a high bun stood near the man, recording him with her camera. Unable to look away from the memory of the Sparrows, Syn entered a trance...

Mia always had her brown hair tightly pulled back in a high bun, and her brown eyes would always appear to be smiling brightly. Calvin was taller than Wren's mother and lacked her grace, but he displayed such honesty that it was second nature to any stranger to like him.

Calvin was playing a guitar on the train for money that would feed him, while Mia and Eudora were filming him. The sisters were completely mesmerized by his performance in New York City. The video camera was passed to Eudora so Mia could give him some cash. Wren's future father, who did not know anything about her future mother, kneeled before Mia and held her hand ever so delicately.

"So brown, your eyes. So brown, your hair. In this light of such dim rays, just a mere touch of this hand makes my life have meaning," Calvin said to Mia with a genuine smile.

Mia leaned down, brushing Calvin's long blond bangs from his pale blue eyes. As if the universe itself took control of her, she said, "So blue, your eyes. So gentle, your smile. Strike me down with your electric kiss."

Mia pressed her bright red lips to his, cold from the winter air.

Syn looked around at everyone who sat on the train, watching the two strangers kissing on the floor with only a guitar separating them.

"When you forget me, you forget them," Wren told Syn. "Don't you remember what you always wanted back on Hell?"

Syn's eyes would not blink.

"To belong," Wren whispered. "You belong here—so don't just throw us away."

Syn was about to make herself throw up again, but the sound of Wren's mother's voice stopped her. The surrounding room changed from the train, and she looked up at Mia in a ball gown, laughing while attending a party.

Wren had pulled a memory from her father's life—a memory dear to her...

Mia was standing at Calvin's side, and he looked nervous. She was a woman from high-class society, and her family reunion was being hosted by the Acostas in Puerto Rico. Calvin felt out of place, since he was an orphan who roamed the streets of New York City. He did not even have a name for years, as he was born in an alleyway and raised by those without a home. An old man who helped guide him had named him Calvin Sparrow because he was always reading a torn comic book named *Calvin* and always whistling to the birds.

Mia and Calvin were so different, but they were born from the same star. And the members of the influential Acosta family always had a way of reminding Calvin that he was not good enough for Mia.

During the reunion, Mia and Eudora's father, Joaquin Acosta, witnessed a cousin of his scold Calvin for not being worthy of being part of their family. "Nobility is in the blood, and a street rat will always be a street rat," Joaquin heard his dear cousin tell Calvin.

Being the direct heir to the money Joaquin shared with his extended family, the patriarch of the Acosta line interrupted his cousin and approached his soon-to-be son-in-law. "My great-great-great—all the greats—grandmother was like you, Calvin," he told him, handing him champagne in a crystal class. "She would play the guitar on her parents' farm, and the locals would give her food and money in return for her music. She didn't have much family—only her ailing parents."

Joaquin's cousin was about to greet him, but the Acosta's patriarch turned his back on her to speak to Calvin. "Come, let's go for a walk," he said, patting Calvin on his back, and the two walked away from the party at the seaside resort to take a stroll.

The celebratory holographic fireworks blazed across the night sky, and hardly any stars could be seen.

"Her name was Maria Marcella." Joaquin smiled and admired the fireworks. "She was the daughter of a farmer, and she lived in the village where the Acostas made their money."

Calvin watched Joaquin take a long sip of his drink.

"The one who started my family's legacy was a man named Juan Acosta. Before he met Maria, he was a womanizer." Joaquin chuckled. "Or so I'm told. He would hide on Maria's family farm to escape the women he played with. And he would sleep under the deck where Maria would play her guitar. Maria didn't like Juan at first. She was a strong-minded woman, a feminist. She didn't care about Juan Acosta, the man who started the most successful wine company in the area. She only cared about taking care of her parents in their old age."

Joaquin took another sip of his champagne. "Maria and Juan were both in their forties when they met. It was unusual for a woman to be unmarried and childless at that age back then. Especially in Spain..." He became sidetracked, looking for something in the sky. "Ah, there it is. Look."

He pointed at a diamond-shaped firework. The words **Welcome to the Acosta Family, Calvin!** were displayed for all who viewed the sky to see. "But Juan won Maria over, and they got married and moved to Puerto Rico."

While Calvin kept staring at the words in the sky, feeling an ache in his chest from never having a home, Joaquin continued speaking. "They only had one child, and then the Acostas just kept on multiplying." He laughed. "I probably have cousins out there back in Spain! Juan was a bastard in his younger years."

He turned to Calvin and noticed the young man was trying not to cry. "My boy," he said and extended his arms wide. "If you tell anyone I gave you a hug, I have a bullet with your name on it."

Joaquin released a rolling laugh, and the older man of Spanish blood gave Calvin a hug—a hug Calvin had never received as a child. "My cousin is wrong. Nobility is not in the blood, it's in the soul." He pushed Calvin away and held onto his shoulders. "You were born noble—I can see it in your eyes. Your soul is bright, like the North Star."

The images disappeared, and Syn was seething, while Wren was staring at her from a mirror with hopeful eyes.

"Did you really think that would work?" Syn asked.

"Then, why are you crying?" Wren asked her.

Sitting among the broken instruments, Syn was left with her own conscience as she stared into the mirror. Tears streamed down her face, and the fire she had reabsorbed drifted once more from her pores.

Before she could burn everything inside of the shop, the door of the music store creaked open. The smell of stale smoke made way to her nose, causing her to release a scowl—much like Wren's. Then, the lore looked back, and her fire turned to ice.

Memoirs of The 3 Realms

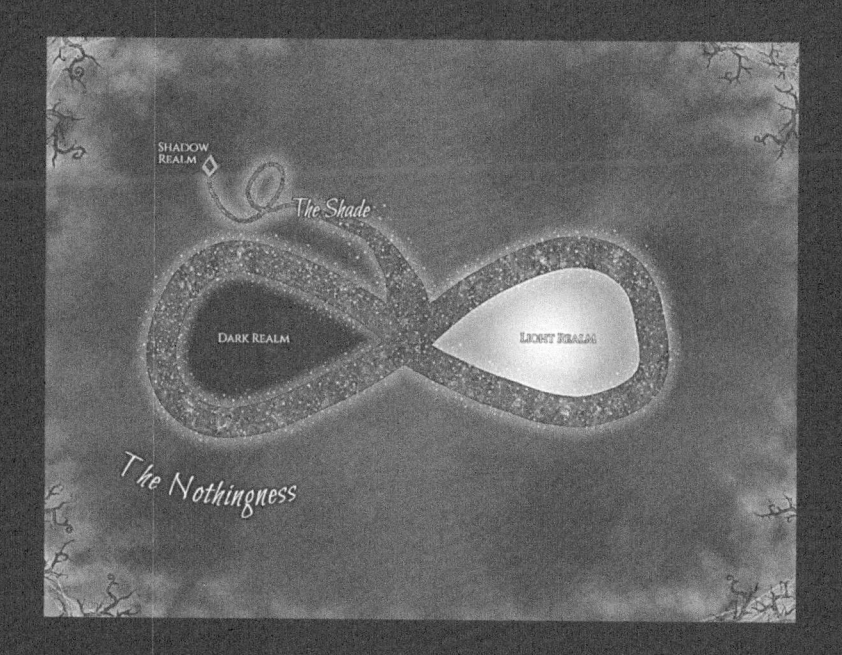

Chaos Theory

Chaos, the tortured and sad designer of the universe, began their endless walk searching for purpose. They roamed among the blankness of nothingness, forever longing to find meaning.

But the reason for their existence was not what they found.

As if Chaos felt the energies brewing behind them, they looked back, and what they saw, they did not like. They did not know they were bleeding, and their blood was creating rocks and stars. Soon, the rocks and stars made objects of their own.

Three worlds were created by their blood: a realm of light, a realm of dark, and a realm of shadow. Then, the gods came. The gods of these three realms, birthed by the sufferings of Chaos, were constructed to maintain balance. However, their egos caused the realms to become unstable, and the universe became a battleground. The pantheon of gods in the light and dark realms feared each other's energy, worried they were not the most powerful. All the while, the lone god of the shadows watched the light and dark fight a senseless war, which created rips in the three barriers.

The mesh of all the energies that drifted through the cracks of the realms caused Chaos to flee—a dire consequence of their endless walk.

Frightened by their creations, Chaos continued their path far away from their children… I do not blame them.

Lucifer

Lucael Temple
Scroll No. 666 of the *Three Moon*

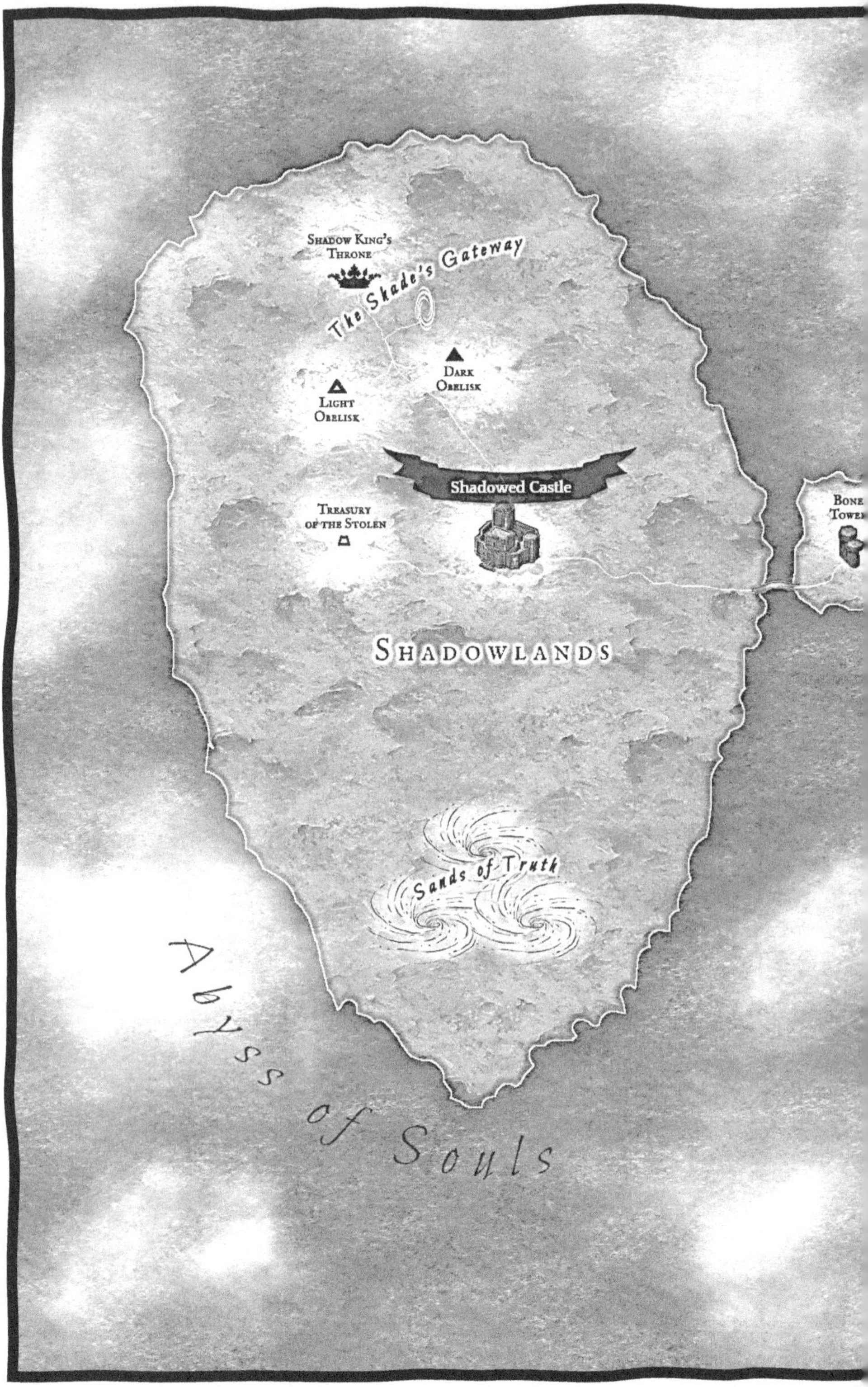

Shadow King's Throne
The Shade's Gateway
Dark Obelisk
Light Obelisk
Shadowed Castle
Treasury of the Stolen
Bone Tower
Shadowlands
Sands of Truth
Abyss of Souls

Shadowlands
Realm of One

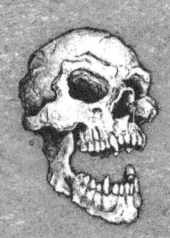

"The light... is too radiant.

The dark... is too sinister.

They both... are wicked.

For Chaos... I will be... their pedagogue."

Aaeon, The Shaodw King

Shadowlands

Memoir of a Lonely God

FROM A SHADE THAT was not of light or dark drifted the most tragic of all of Chaos' children. Stitches bound his eyes closed, though he still could see. A hood of death covered his face, for he did not like his own reflection.

This was Chaos' firstborn.

Watching from a distant cosmos where only he existed, he witnessed the other two realms thrive from both light and dark. Walking the path Chaos created from their blood, he cried out for companionship. Imprisoned in a grueling torment of a world he did not ask for, Aaeon, the Shadow King, knew not the reason for his existence.

Then, he saw...

"Again." A tall man of pale yellow lectured a woman with the palest pink skin and long blond waves. "Syn, you need to learn this."

"I do not care for Kanarian folklore." Syn stared up at the angelic with blue eyes. "Why are you teaching me about this galaxy, Lucifer?"

"To understand the world is to understand ourselves." Lucifer kneeled next to the slightly translucent woman, who sat under the shade of a tree. "The gods from Kanaria created Eden, and Eden created us."

"But are they real?" Syn asked her tutor.

"That is what we are going to find out," Lucifer told her.

Syn stared at Lucifer's face. She leaned up and tried to kiss his lips, but she fell through his face. Looking shocked, the angelic held her shoulders with his magic-laced gloves and pushed her away from him. Shaking his head, he gripped the magic-infused clothes bound to her arms.

"Do not do that again." Lucifer looked upset.

"When I learn how to touch solid objects in this world, I will kiss you." Syn smiled up at the angelic, who only looked down at her in annoyance.

"Why do you want to kiss me?" Lucifer unwrapped a scroll. "I am boring. I do not have emotions like the others."

"Because I want to," Syn said, honest as Lucifer was wise.

"And Lucien?" Lucifer asked, tired of her games. "Have you forgotten about your companion?"

"He frequents the brothels." She stared down at the scrolls. "He's consumed by the redheaded maiden and has forgotten me."

"Aren't they all?" Lucifer sighed, leaning on the tree's trunk. "No one wants to research the universe with me. It is irritating."

"I do." Syn looked up at him with a mischievous grin.

"You have ulterior motives." Lucifer laughed at her.

Syn fell silent.

"Every day I'm in your world, I remember a little more of where I come from. I feel my spirit being ripped to shreds, and I fear I will one day burn everything." Syn grabbed a different scroll from Lucifer's bag and unrolled it. "That is why I wish to kiss you. You make me calm."

Fire drifted from the top of her head, and Lucifer placed his hand above her hair, extinguishing the fire with his peaceful touch. "Do not do that," the angelic told her. "If the others ever find out what Azazel and I know, you will be exiled by the majority vote."

"Would you and Azazel really exile me if the other angelics vote to cast me out?" Syn asked.

Lucifer stared down at the woman from the dark realm. "It is best not to test that theory," he said, then turned his gaze back down to the scroll.

As if fate had rewritten the lore's story, Syn pressed her lips to Lucifer's cheek.

The Shadow King wanted to watch more of the scholar and his apprentice, but the realm that radiated such blinding light pushed Aaeon back into his shadows, burning his eyes.

He recognized the woman. She was the one who had invaded his world not that long ago with a companion from the world of darkness. The king then turned from the window of light and walked toward another.

Aaeon was forever searching, forever yearning. Like Chaos, he roamed. However, unlike Chaos, his path was confined.

He paused his venture within The Shade and turned his gaze to a scene of giants fighting two small creatures in an arena. The darkness swirled in the air as cheers echoed throughout the stadium, drawing him to the window of night...

"And there you have it!" the announcer screamed with enthusiasm. "The lores are outmatched."

Several giants stood on the field, snarling, with drool and blood dripping from their gaping mouths. The two small beings the giants surrounded were lores, scared of their very first battle.

The Shadow King drifted closer and almost passed into the unknown world of darkness. Unlike the world of light, which he found too bright, Aaeon had found that the darkness was far too dark for his liking. He backed up from the eeriness of the dark gods, who laughed at the death of the giants. Aaeon had his pleasures in pain, but something about the darkness sent the Shadow King running from The Shade and into a corner of his own kingdom.

Stranded, unable to understand the two worlds, Aaeon cried. Frustrated, feeling alone, the shadowed path that connected the three realms attracted an intruder into the shadow god's domain. Voices spoke over each other. Aaeon never had visitors to his kingdom, and no one had ever been allowed to use his path before.

"So, this is where the shadow realm hides. A loop of fog hides you well." Lucifer looked around the shadowed kingdom of stone, often glancing down at his scroll—his skin turning gray. "I am glad I wrote Syn's verbiage down over the years. I was questioning her tale of how she came to our realm."

Out of instinct, Aaeon summoned chains from all around and smashed them through the angelic's flesh. Wrapping the hard steel, he forced the chains to squeeze around the Edenian. Silver blood oozed from Lucifer's wounds.

"Ouch." Lucifer looked unmoved. "Is that any way to treat a guest?"

"What... do you... want?" the Shadow King asked, clutching his scythe, as he stood from his throne of skulls.

Lucifer looked around the world of gray. "You should think of adding in colors." He stared up at a hanging corpse above him. "It would really spruce up your décor."

Laughing for the first time, Aaeon retracted his chains and walked down the large stone steps toward the Edenian of graying yellow hues. Angelics were a colorful species and were indeed impressive. Still, they were not one to be compared to the oldest god, who lived deep within the shadows. The Kanarian and Hellion gods could not even compete with the lost king. Aaeon hovered over the angelic, standing about thirty feet tall.

Lucifer looked up at the ghastly god. "Well, aren't you quite tall?"

The Shadow King decreased his size to match the angelic's height. "How... did you... enter?" Aaeon asked. "No one... can use... my... path."

"My apologies. I was not aware of that," Lucifer said, causing the god to take an interest in him. "I simply found your path and walked in."

"Desecration..." Aaeon cried out, his voice rattling the chains above him. Lucifer shuddered at his voice. "Your voice matches your style."

The Shadow King looked both alarmed and intrigued.

"My apprentice spoke about you," Lucifer said as he looked up at another corpse hanging above them. "She and her companion had traveled through your world to enter ours."

"*Lores.*" Aaeon turned his hooded face to a distant blob of darkness that led toward The Shade. "They came... and... they left."

Sounding a bit disappointed, the Shadow King turned around to walk up the enormous steps to sit upon his throne, returning to his original size. Taking a seat on the stone chair, the king of the shadows eyed the angelic in silence.

"Syn told me about the pathway that repelled them, so she and Cain had to enter your realm through a crack so they could use your doorway to enter The Shade." Lucifer looked down at the small critters, which were fragments of Aaeon, following him while he walked closer to the first gigantic step.

Aaeon groaned. "Crack?" he asked, surprised by the news of a broken structure in his domain. "How did... that happen?"

"Exodus being misplaced cracked the realms. It's an interesting tale. Would you like to hear?" Lucifer asked, then jumped onto the first step to sit on the stone. "I only know what Syn has told me. She remembers more with each day. I assume her words are true. I mean, I did find your pathway."

The Shadow King nodded.

"While she lived on a planet named Hell, Syn was a devout follower of the oracle of her world and learned about our realms." Lucifer pointed at the Shadow King and then at himself. "Syn lied to her own gods, known as the Hellion, and claimed that their life force, called Exodus, was stolen by someone from my realm. She retrieved Exodus after coming to my world and hid the stone to protect it from the Kanarian gods. Everyone wanted the stone from Hell, you see. With Exodus, one could destroy or re-create an entire cosmos without sacrificing parts of themselves. You can see why my gods became interested in Exodus, particularly Nao."

"Why did... she lie?" Aaeon asked, enjoying the story.

Lucifer stood up and paced on top of the stone step. He finally had someone to tell his stories to. "Syn told me that she conspired against her own gods, but not for a noble cause. I am afraid my apprentice only wanted to explore the universe. I hope there will not be any ill consequence."

Aaeon released a muffled sigh, and he asked Lucifer, "What is... a lore?"

"The only thing I know about lores is that they are fighters for the dark gods," Lucifer said.

"Is that... their purpose?" Aaeon asked. "What is... yours?"

"What is anyone's purpose but to exist?" Lucifer asked. He held up his hands, trying to imagine what the dark realm looked like. "The universe is fascinating, is it not?"

"Indeed..." Aaeon leaned back into his throne, shadows creeping around him. "Tell me... about... your world."

Lucifer widened his eyes. "My world? What do you wish to know?"

"Everything..."

As Lucifer spoke, the Shadow King felt a sense of belonging. Feelings emerged—feelings the lost king had never experienced. The sadness that bound him, the tears that were always there, ceased.

Then, the Shadow King laughed.

DWARVES CITADEL
FROZEN FORTRESS
BARTER'S WALK
SAPPHIRE'S CRADLE
LAND OF GIANTS
TEMPLE OF ALL
COMMON LANDS
Nakori Hills
ROYAL GUARD'S WATCH
ROYAL GUARD'S WATCH
ROYAL GUARD'S WATCH
GABRIEL SHRINE
Gall Pond
ROYAL CAPITOL
URIEL SHRINE
ROSE THORN
AZAZEL SHRINE
Url Forest
ANGELIC EMPIRE
TWIN SANDS
TEMPLE OF LUX
LUCIFER SHRINE
MICHAEL SHRINE
ALTAR OF TIME
Lucael Desert
BRONZE VALE
Marskes of Azlel
EZEKIEL SHRINE
AZRAEL SHRINE
Lux Ocean

EDEN
The Golden Planet

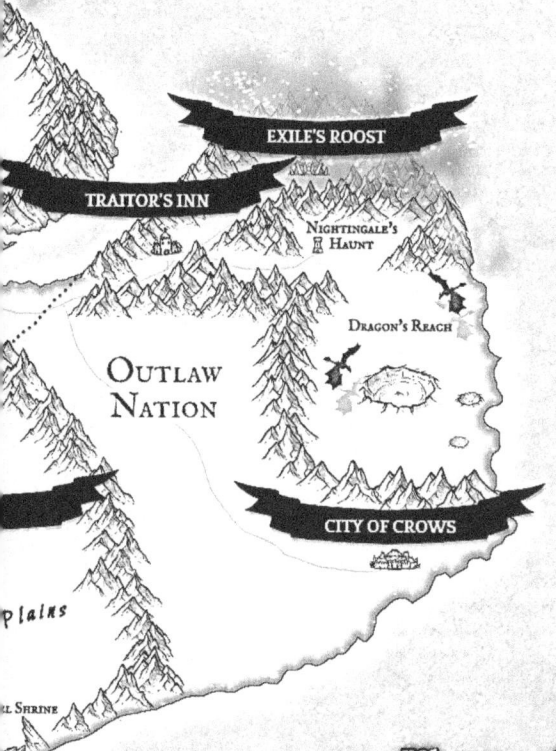

- EXILE'S ROOST
- TRAITOR'S INN
- NIGHTINGALE'S HAUNT
- DRAGON'S REACH
- OUTLAW NATION
- CITY OF CROWS
- Plains
- Shrine
- Maelstrom of Origin

"She was a land of light.

And she was scared of the night.

Thus, the darkness made her weep.

So, she fell into pieces."

—Lucifer, the Angelic of Wisdom

YELLOW SKY

MEMOIR OF EDEN

EDEN WAS ONCE A planet of nothing but light, and this golden planet was ruled by the Angelic Empire. A species of all colors with majestic wings, the angelics were. All the creatures of Eden were created, not born, for the planet itself was their mother and father.

The myths the angelics believed in said nothing about darkness, nor did it mention two other realms in the universe. News about a multiple-dimensional overlap was not a topic on Eden, save for the times the angelic Lucifer preached about the endless multiverse throughout the kingdom. But the angelics did not listen to the hermit who lived in solitude.

Lucifer was merely a magician.

Though, as he was the wisest angelic of them all, it was foolish to ignore his words.

Many angelics visited Kanaria when the mint-blue ocean of Lux released a silver fog. Once the largest ocean of Eden, Lux was a sight to see. The ocean would release a mist after Eden's cluster of three moons finished orbiting around the planet, and the sky would reflect lights of blues and greens across the golden globe. When the lights came, every being of the planet would temporarily live in harmony. Conflict would pause until the last moon finished its orbit, and everyone would be a spectator to the lights.

During the mist, the empire traveled to the Kanaria Galaxy to pray at the ruins of a planet named Kanar and its grand spiral of spectral stars called Ia.

It was Eden's tradition.

But, when the mist of the three-moon orbit vanished, conflict always returned to the nations of Eden.

Azazel never went to Kanar to see the stars of Ia, and he always remained behind. A loyalist to Eden, he knew nothing else. While the others would go to the lands of Kanar to pray to the gods of myth, no gods were ever spotted. The gods did not care about the angelics; they just could not see it.

And, as Azazel was the king of the angelics, Lucifer was his most trusted advisor. The wise magician had told him numerous times that Kanar was barren, but the king wanted to give his empire hope, so he encouraged the angelics to visit Kanar, to liven their souls under the bright stars of Ia, and Lucifer both proudly and begrudgingly led them there.

An angelic of both faith and skepticism, Lucifer was.

One day on Kanar, Lucifer was standing by himself as the empire walked through the ruins, praying and singing to the gods. Bored, he looked around the planet of stone and broken temples. One of the tiny minions he conjured to absorb new information about his surroundings stole his attention. As the minion danced near a crack, Lucifer noticed a pair of green dots staring at him.

On that day, he had stared into the eyes of the greediest pair of eyes: Nao's eyes.

Lucifer learned that Kanar was not at all barren, and the gods dwelled under the surface, and he shared his findings with Azazel, trying to persuade the king to forbid anyone to return to Kanar. But Azazel ignored his warning, and he continued the tradition. It gave the empire morale.

The more the empire traveled to Kanar, the more the gods became irritated. As the angelics pranced and danced upon the surface, Nao, the king of the Kanarians, grew furious. Eden was created by the very god that the new king had overthrown, after all.

Time and time again, Lucifer warned the empire of happenings in the universe. But when they finally listened to him, it was too late...

※※※※※

Eden had never been without the soft amber light that surrounded the planet. So, when the darkness that seeped from the dark realm's rip created a wormhole, panic arose in each of the creatures of Eden. Several brave angelics flew from Eden to face the rip that invaded their world, planning to fight everything that came through.

Those who faced the rip in the sky were sucked into the wormhole that had formed nearby. A few became scorched, and their skin was flayed from their bones before they were dragged into the unknown. The angelics left behind on Eden watched those who tried to fight the darkness vanish within the hole in the sky.

Soon, most of the angelics left behind flew from Eden and toward the home of the gods in the neighboring cosmos of Kanaria to find asylum. The darkness that seeped in from the rip had consumed the entire cosmos of Eden.

However, eight angelics stayed behind. They were the royals of the Angelic Empire, and they refused to leave Eden, for their love of their land was enormous. As the dark energy spread over Eden, the royals roamed the ominous planet, feeling darkness enter their souls.

And when all the light was gone, Eden shattered.

The shards of the planet went everywhere in the new blackness of space, and the eight became scattered upon the remnants of their once-golden home. Their skin was braised by the heat of the ruined planet's inner core, which leaked out into the Milky Way Galaxy. The gold hues of Eden's liquid center turned black.

The royals finally left, but when they reached the portal that held the light on the other side, they were rejected. They were trapped inside their fallen kingdom. The portal to the galaxy where the Kanarian gods dwelled was closing, and the eight tried to enter Kanaria again, but their newfound darkness kept them chained to Eden's broken rocks.

One, named Azazel, who had come to life from a silver fountain, managed to gather some energy from the Kanaria Galaxy before the portal fully closed. He held the light close to his hollow chest, silver as the fountain he had emerged from. His eye sockets used to be full of beautiful energy, but now, they were full of nothing but emptiness—empty craters of darkness.

The trapped angelics reunited on the main fragment of Eden, a small rock formation. Their wings were welted from the darkness' wrath. Standing tall in a circle, they surrounded Azazel as he raised his hands to his chest and prayed. He was their king, the first angelic to have been *born* on Eden, and no angelic loved Eden more than he.

The other seven angelics recited words of hope to Chaos.

But it was not Chaos who heard their pleas...

A bright light came from within Azazel, and the others stopped chanting. He was sacrificing himself to save Eden from the infliction of darkness.

The energy cupped inside Azazel's hands hummed, and soon, the energy rushed over his entire body. The silver angelic smiled genuinely at his comrades, and the king became a pure light of silver, yellow, and all the other shades of color. Then, the pure energy that he had become raced over two rocks and settled in the silent space.

Several broken shards of Eden raced over to the light of Azazel and mixed with the pure energy the angelic had transformed into. Soon, the combination of angelic and rock formed into a rock of light. Hot, bright flames swirled around the gigantic star.

The seven angelics who lingered on the main fragment of Eden stared at Azazel and his light as a faint glow befell them, giving them a sensation of peace. A new invisible shield spread around the broken planet, forcing the chaotic energies the dark realm had brought from their bodies. This drove the angelics into a hypnotic state. Lucifer, Michael, Gabriel, Uriel, Raphael, Azrael, and Ezekiel were the names of the seven who remained.

And as the common angelic was born from the Lux Ocean of Eden, the royals had emerged from holy objects across the land.

Lucifer and Michael were born from the whispering rocks of the Lucael Desert, south of the capital city of the Angelic Empire. They were both the second-born of the angelics, twins of hard yellow skin. Their skin, tough as metal, shone like the summer sun that chased the blue sky away, leaving only a pale-yellow sheen in its wake.

Gabriel, the third angelic of Eden, was born from the pure waters of the Gail Pond, which was north of the capital. His skin, hard like metal as well, was the soft blue found just outside the bright ring around the sun, where the blinding yellow bled into pale, pale blue.

Uriel was the fourth, born of the trees in the Url Forest, far west of the capital. He held a beautiful forest green shade for his stiff flesh, as if forest green came in pastel and bark could withstand the harshest punishments.

Raphael, the fifth, was born on the highest mountain on Eden in the Rahe Plains, southeast of the capital. He had white skin so smooth that one would think he was cotton, but the solidity of his stone skin countered that.

Azrael and Ezekiel, the sixth and seventh, came from the Marshes of Aziel, south of the Lucael Desert. Azrael was a little older than Ezekiel, but they both were shiny as new pennies and as tough as ancient ruins.

The seven royals stood about the same height, except for Lucifer, who reached half a foot taller. They were entranced by the new light in their cosmos, as it was so beautiful and soothing. But it was not the same as Eden's light, and soon, the color of the angelics' skin dulled into shades of brown and peach. The seven then understood that this new light, which was created by Azazel, was not at all like their old light, which was reflected off the Lux Ocean.

As the others bantered about what they should do next, Lucifer noticed a series of numbers within the sun. The light was not the only thing Azazel had stolen from the Kanaria Galaxy. The angelic king had taken some of Kanaria's data with it.

Lucifer fretted over what was to come. Taking a handful of energy from a cosmos was one thing, but to steal a copy of its blueprint was another. Especially when Kanaria was the home of Nao, the corrupted king of the Kanarian gods.

With mixed emotions, Lucifer glared at the sun. How could an angelic steal a god's blueprint, and then try to create an entire system of worlds? Angelics were not meant to create planets. They were to maintain Eden, but without Eden, the destiny of each angelic shifted. What was Azazel trying to become? A god?

As Lucifer stared into the light, he decided to keep his knowledge to himself. Azazel never did anything without good intentions.

Kanaria's light... it did not belong in the cosmos of Eden, shattered or not.

Lucifer turned away from the newly formed sun and the Kanarian codes. He stared at the mass, which looked much like a wormhole, and it continued to grow. His pitch-black eyes stared at the oddity, which was pulling everything into it, and he realized what it really was.

While the spiral mass, in fact, linked two points throughout space, it was far from the casual transport he had studied back in his cave.

"Black as night, bright as day, that is both worm hole and dark." Lucifer grimaced at the oddity. "That is a one-way trip to Hell's Tundra."

The other six turned from the sun of Azazel and stared at what Lucifer was glaring at. They had once raised their eyebrows at his words, but they realized that scoffing at the intelligent angelic was not the wisest.

Lucifer knew what he preached.

The seven noticed two creatures flying from the rip near Hell's Tundra and stared at the two new arrivals, which were covered in shadows. They were smaller than the angelics. They were strange, with their reddish flesh and fierce eyes that radiated darkness.

The seven were cautious and were prepared to face the newcomers. The two beings of darkness descended onto the heart fragment of Eden and stared at the seven of different fading shades.

They, the visitors, looked up at the new sun. The two's eyes turned dim in horror. They let out screeches of torment for reasons unknown.

"What do you want?" Lucifer asked the strangers in a language the others did not know.

"You speak our tongue?" one of the two hissed, her voice echoing off the stars. "This will be easier... We have come for Exodus since our predecessors failed. Speaking of which, do you know Syn and Cain? They traveled here long—"

The woman's partner elbowed her and hissed, "We didn't come here to find Syn and Cain. We're here for Exodus. Don't act friendly, Naya."

Naya stared into her partner's eyes with a solemn nod.

"Hand over Exodus, or become imprisoned inside our tundra," Naya shouted at Lucifer.

The seven stood still as the woman looked up at Hell's Tundra swirling in the sky.

"But I am feeling merciful. Return with us to our world, and we will spare you the coldness of our jails." Naya, the woman of darkness, spoke once more. "You can tell our gods where Exodus is. You will be rewarded graciously."

"Leave, demons!" Michael yelled at the two creatures, and then he turned to Lucifer. "Brother, you understand them. Who are they? What do they say?"

Lucifer knew all too well what the two creatures were. His apprentice was one of them.

While Lucifer was created already knowing the languages of the light realm and all its creatures, the dark realm was a mystery. Thankfully, his apprentice had taught him their language while they studied his scrolls on the grounds of Eden.

"They are called lore. They come from Hell, the home of the dark gods," Lucifer told Michael.

"Are they gods?" Azrael asked as he eyed the two creatures from the dark realm closely.

"No," Lucifer replied.

Azrael sighed with relief.

"They are the fighters for the dark gods," Lucifer warned. "Do not underestimate them. They can be just as powerful as a god when they are paired."

Naya's counterpart, Samelle, narrowed his eyes and released a battle cry, sending splits through the ground with the mere vibrations of his vocal cords. "Enough. Your gods are evil. Thievery is shunned. Come with us," he roared.

The couple snarled at the seven. Did the pair think they were convincing the angelics with their dark aura?

"I will agree that some of our gods are certainly on par with your energy, but to say that all of our gods are evil is untrue," Lucifer told the two.

He then turned to face his comrades and spoke to them in his native language. "I know someone who can help us. He lets me walk his path. But it may take some time before he trusts me enough to help. Until then, we shall rebuild and abide by Chaos' law. Our fate was decided by their stars. This is what I advise we do."

The six angelics nodded at Lucifer's vaguely confusing words.

Lucifer turned back to the two creatures and shouted, "We follow Chaos' law. We trust in the universe. Exodus is not here. Begone!"

The two creatures hissed and cackled. Their skin slowly became redder as fire exited their pores.

"Chaos?" Samelle asked in a softer voice. "Chaos cares not."

"How darling. They abide by Chaos' law," Naya said, mocking the fallen angelics. "Next, they will say they believe in the shadows. There are only *two* realms: ours and yours. Your gods are nothing more than weaker copies of ours. As for Chaos' rumored firstborn, he is nothing more than a child's rhyme."

Lucifer narrowed his eyes at the two small creatures flying above them with mechanical wings. "You speak as if Chaos and the Shadow King are not real. You speak as fools. I have traveled Aaeon's path, and I can assure you of how *real* he is." He stepped closer to the two who had entered their world through the dark rip. "I'm sorry Exodus was stolen from you, but we do not know of its location."

"But you do know of Exodus?" Naya shouted. "You have a liar's tongue. I think you know where it is."

"Then, you and your cosmos will continue to wither by our darkness," Samelle said, gripping hands with Naya. "You failed to give us Exodus; now, you must suffer the consequence. Consider our words a declaration of war from our gods. Our *darkness* will consume you all."

Content with having the last word, the two flew away from the heart of Eden and toward the rip that led to the dark realm. The two vanished through the rip, and the portal instantly closed after.

Hell's Tundra then fell apart and vanished from the light realm.

Lucifer's eyes drifted toward the sun, taking in Azazel's new form, and he whispered, "Azazel, my friend, we will restore Eden."

The six joined Lucifer, and they all sat on the ground. The seven sensed darkness within their spirits, and as they felt the wilting of their wings, they fell into a deep sleep.

After the rock began moving around the sun, life came to the heart of Eden, and once they smelled the freshness of vegetation, the royals woke up from their hibernation.

"Look." Gabriel pointed at a small and fast-growing plant.

All around them, plants were growing.

The smell of life, the raindrops that fell.

"It's beautiful," Ezekiel said, touching a green leaf of the small plant.

"Azazel is creating this," Uriel said brightly. "He is turning this broken shard into its own planet."

"Should we call this planet Eden?" Azrael asked.

"Why not?" Raphael looked at Azrael, thinking it was a great idea to name the new world after the old. "New Eden?"

Lucifer looked down at the ground, where more foliage grew as their wings healed from their charred state. "No," he said to his comrades. "This rock is the heart of Eden. Let us name this planet Earth."

Near the approaching greenery, the woman who had chosen the light over the dark was lying on the ground. Her pale eyes were open, frozen in time.

Lucifer crouched down next to the limp energy form of the woman no one else could see. She was wrapped in his magic, as he had wanted to protect her from her the conflict of energies. His eyes stayed on her entranced ones in complete torment.

He leaned closer to the woman, and he whispered a few words softly into her ear, but his apprentice could not hear.

Map

WASTELANDS

Charred Sea

VAKU CITY

ETERNITY VALE
HORACE

NIGHTINGALE

RED STEAM

CITY OF ECHOES

SANCTUM

ECHOES

The Wired Thicket
LYRIE'S DEN

HORACE'S TOMB

Lake of Fire

DUBH

CROM HAVEN

WILDLANDS

HELL
Planet on Fire

FORTRESS OF HELL

Hell's Tundra

HELLION RISE

GATE'S KEEP

Arena of Sorrow

Keep's Road

GIANT'S LANDING

"Most beloved by the gods.

Once fifty thousand strong.

But we fell in number.

So, the gods bound our skin with wire."

-Syn, Daughter of the Temple

Nightmare

Memoir of Hell

AMONG THE MANY PEOPLE dwelled two lores: Syn, a woman with blond hair, and Cain, a man with walnut-brown strands. The dark clouds above them reflected the redness of the Charred Sea, and the dim lights of the cloudy buildings bounced off of their reddish skin.

Syn was nervous but played calm so well that it fooled Cain, her mirrored self. She glanced up at him, walking behind his lengthy frame, feeling guilty that she was keeping secrets from him.

He stopped walking and stared at another pair of lores passing by, causing Syn to bump into him. The passing lores were full-grown, and fire radiated from their eyes. Their veins were enhanced with spiked mechanical wires to prolong their life—mimicking a god's immortality.

While every lore had wire hidden under their red skin of varying shades and intertwined in a few of their veins, only the strongest lores were given the blessing of a full-body wiring. This made Cain excited they would become adults the following day. Only grown lores could enter the arena to challenge those who were given the blessing. If the new team won, the wiring would be transferred to the winners, and the old lores would perish.

Syn did not care about their birthday. She was too wrapped up in her thoughts of the other worlds.

She wanted to know more.

"Hey, Syn!" A small boy of around five hundred years ran up to the two, who were only one day away from being three thousand years old. "The king wants you." The boy pointed at her.

Syn did not want to see the king and her eyes darkened, which was hard to do because they were such a light silver with bitter blue. Cain's eyes were a dark brown with crimson, and he was enraged by the news. "What does he want?" Cain asked the younger lore. "And where is your Echo, Samelle?"

"Oh." Samelle kicked a pebble on the ground. "Naya is petitioning for a new partner. She doesn't like me."

"She's questioning the shards' design? *Outrageous.*" Cain cursed under his breath. "Go back to her and convince her to stay with you. Echoes are only divided in death."

The young child ran away quickly at the power of Cain's words.

"I thought you agreed we should be able to pick our own Echo, Cain?" Syn asked him and walked up to his side, brushing her blond hair behind her ear. "You thought so when we were kids."

"People can change their minds. It's wrong to want a different partner. Echoes are supposed to be together," Cain said, then studied her face.

"What?" Syn asked.

"Why do you hold resentments?" Cain asked her.

The two fell into silence as they walked down Keep's Road, which led to Hellion Rise—the island of the gods.

"Wait—what's going on?" Syn asked, disregarding Cain's question as she looked over at a growing circle in front of the border of Gate's Keep, the city of giants along the road they traveled. "Are they preparing for battle?"

"No, I don't think so," Cain said, looking over at the arena in the distance. "If they were, the arena would be packed."

Cain spotted Samelle and his Echo, and he pulled Syn along toward a crowd of lores near the city. "Samelle," he said to the young lore from before, "do you know what's going on?"

Samelle held hands with his Echo, the annoyed Naya. "Lord Ecorah," he said in a low voice, frightened. "He's been imprisoned."

"What?" Syn asked. "Why?"

"He said something about other worlds," Samelle stated.

"'Worlds?'" Cain asked. "That's nonsense."

"What's so unreasonable about that?" Syn asked. "What if there is another world outside of Hell?"

"The gods would tell us," Cain simply said.

"Ecorah did tell us. Why does everyone ignore that he's a god?!" Syn exclaimed, exasperated by the politics of the planet.

With those last words, Syn let go of Cain's hand and ran toward the end of Keep's Road, which was guarded by giants of dark red skin who stood roughly fifteen feet tall.

"The king summoned me," Syn yelled and stared up at an aggressive giant. "My name's Syn."

The giant looked at three other giants, who nodded. "Okay, lore," his voice thundered. "Come on."

"Wait," Cain yelled. "I'm her Echo."

"Hurry through, lore," a different giant told Cain, then moved back into his guarding place after Cain reached Syn on the other side.

"I'm not letting you face him alone." Cain forced out the words.

Syn stared down at the stone bridge as she walked with Cain toward Hellion Rise.

When they were created from the Eye of Horace in one of the lore temples near Vaku City, Cain could not believe the connection he had felt with Syn. The two of them had emerged to be named, in a short form of four feet, from a burning shard in front of all the gods of Hell. They were created already knowing things, and Cain walked out knowing he was lore, a member of the fighting species for the Hellion gods. Lores were created to go to war on behalf of the Hellions. If anyone went against the gods of Hell, the lores would eliminate them.

However, the lores were also created for another reason. Knowing even the gods were capable of corruption, the first god of the Hellions, Horace, had turned himself into a crystal called the Eye of Horace, and from his crystal, a species was born—a species that could overpower any of the gods if needed. If a god became corrupt, the lores would become a hive and behead the god in question.

To prevent the lores from turning tainted themselves, Horace created them in his image—with justice and fairness. It was hard for a lore not to be honorable, but if one strayed from the flock, the other lores would judge, and they would stand trial.

This did not mean that the young lores did not go through fits of anger toward their Echo. A few wanted to be cut from such a strong connection to another soul, so some would end up volunteering to enter the arena, beyond training. Thinking death would free them from their bindings, the aggravated lores would show weakness on purpose so the opposition would kill them.

It would always be the wrong move. The lores left behind would enter a state of darkness unmatched to the dark gods, and eventually commit suicide. Feeling lost and alone, never truly having a real Echo, the newly created lore that would be paired to the lore left behind would often go insane. And the new lore would be exiled out to the wastelands by the majority vote.

Splitting up a lore team went against the fundamental design of Horace's shards. Horace did not create the lores to be re-paired.

Syn snapped out of her trance. She looked up at the arena's gates and turned to Cain. He looked down at her, bangs falling into his eyes. She was only a few inches shorter than him, but he was growing taller, and he did not like that. He liked looking his Echo straight in the eyes.

"Come on," he said and pushed open the gates, going in first in case of any danger.

Cain looked around the dark room and led Syn inside. The two lores were born with Horace's grace, and they had been given extra blessings from the high king, as the shard that bore them was the closest to Horace's third eye. Cain was given the gift of innovation, and Syn was given the gift of vision. Horace had spoken to Syn during her creation within the shard, for she had inherited his sight. The god had told her how his son, Ecorah, spoke the truth.

Horace had told Syn *everything*.

If Ecorah's preaching was truthful, then there was deceit among the gods. Which gods of the Hellions were honest, and which were not?

It almost pained Syn to think that Prometeo, the current king of the Hellion, could be a deceiving god. If she were to believe in Ecorah, the son of the former king of the gods, then she could not believe Prometeo at all.

"Syn," said a deep, electric voice. A tall man walked from a cracked door that emitted a low light from another room.

"Lord Ameethus." Syn smiled forcefully.

"King Prometeo sent me to get you, but he failed to inform me of Cain coming to the banquet," Ameethus said.

"'Banquet?'" Syn asked.

They followed the god known as Ameethus to the cracked door and entered the room that emitted the faint light. Lores were the gods' most prized creation, but they were not treated like it. Many lived on the streets, often begging for food or fighting for it. It was not uncommon to eat the deceased among their kind. That was how starved the average lore was.

"Ah, Cain." A god with dark red hair and even darker red eyes stood from his seat at the end of a long table with twenty-seven large chairs. His skin was scorched a light reddish brown. "I already prepared you a seat. I knew you would not let Syn come by herself."

The god smiled a smile that Cain did not like. "Thank you, my king," he said. He was then escorted to a seat farthest away from Prometeo, next to the two empty chairs once belonging to Ecorah and Horace.

Syn looked back at Cain, who sat in isolation at the other end of the table, head bent at the blank plate.

"Come," Prometeo said, and patted the seat to his left. "Sit down, Syn."

Syn sat to the king's left and stared across at Ameethus. "I thought you weren't feeling well, my lord?" she asked Ameethus. "The city was worried about you."

Ameethus, a fair-skinned god with light gray hair and dark gray eyes, smiled absent-mindedly. "I wanted to see Prometeo's favored lore," he said. "However, you are right. I feel ill. I should be excused."

Prometeo nodded and stared after Ameethus in silence. Syn was whispering words of enchantment, and she quickly closed her lips when Prometeo looked back at her.

"I had wanted to ask you some things with Ameethus present." Prometeo paused. "But you and I should do well alone."

Syn grew nervous.

"The lores and I need to be alone, my brethren," Prometeo said to the other gods and goddesses who were seated at the long table.

"I knew I should not have come," one god with tanned skin and dark green hair said under his breath. He stood up, smoke escaping his emerald eyes, and raised his voice to Prometeo. "It is no surprise that your banquets have fewer guests with each feast. You always cut them short." The god grabbed his forest-green cane, each finger layered with bright green rings, and scoffed at Prometeo. "Now Crom Dubh knew how to throw a banquet!"

"Understood," Prometeo told the god. "The next feast shall be in your territory, Pan. And if you fail to impress, I shall claim your treasured cane as mine."

Before Pan vanished into a cloud of smoke, he laughed loudly at Prometeo and said, "In your dreams, cousin. In your dreams."

The Hellions all exited the room in various ways. Some vanished into smoke like Pan, which Prometeo found to be quite rude, so most of the others walked out of the door to disappear into the haze of their smoke.

"The questions I wanted to ask you have changed." Prometeo took his hand and brushed a finger over his jaw in thought.

The air became still.

"Exodus," Prometeo said. "Our life force has been stolen. A few of the giants chased the thief through a crack. I believe this crack leads to a world that is not part of ours. Ecorah may have been telling some truths about our universe having multiple dimensions."

"Why imprison him, then?" Syn blurted. "If there are indeed other dimensions, then why—"

"Do you question me?" Prometeo interrupted in a loud voice, making both lores shudder.

"No, my king," Syn whispered.

"Good," Prometeo said. "On the first night, you will acquire your fire, as it is your birthright. On the second night, you will be sent through the crack and travel to a shadowy dimension. Be careful in these shadows. Make sure the demon that lives there does not take you."

Syn stared up at the king.

"On the third night, you will arrive inside the dimension where there is only light." Prometeo handed Syn a potion and held another bottle out for Cain. "Come get the vial, Cain, and take a seat next to Syn. This will lead you directly to Exodus. The potions may have certain side effects—memory loss and fury are the most prominent. Find Exodus fast to avoid these symptoms."

The lores did not speak. Syn stared down at the vial in her hand. Drinking a potion that potentially created memory loss was not part of the deal. Knowing she should not speak up, for she had stolen Exodus in the first place, she remained quiet.

Cain walked up to Prometeo and grabbed the other vial, then sat down next to Syn.

"Now, drink," Prometeo ordered, and Syn and Cain drank the bitter potions. "Tomorrow, your first night will begin. Follow the three nights, and in no time, you will find Exodus." He looked down at Syn. "The ear of night knows why you are doing this."

Syn snapped her eyes up at the knowing god. Prometeo's eyes lit up with energy, fire illuminating from his red eyes. Both Syn and Cain tried to stand from their chairs, but they were held in place by invisible chains.

"Until night one begins, you will remain seated," Prometeo said. "Rest. You will need your strength." He turned away from the lores, and then looked back. "Oh, I almost forgot the deadliest symptom of the potion: You will die when you arrive in the world of thieves. There is no reason. It is just a side effect of the potion."

Prometeo smiled sinisterly before he vanished from the hall.

For the remainder of the night, Cain and Syn sat bound in the chairs, staring at the meat before them. As if it was a punishment from a god who was aware of Syn's trickery, the lores' stomachs hungered. And their approaching death crept much faster than naturally intended.

Yanked by sudden jolts to their hearts from their concentration on the food they could not eat, the two looked around while the air swirled around them. The environment around the two drifted away and shadows came, surrounding them both in the chilly wind. They looked up at the dim sky swirling together with smoke.

The first night began with Cain and Syn huddling together as creatures approached them. Fire drifted from the lores' eyes, marking their three thousandth birthday.

After the lores were sent through the shadows and into the light, they were stripped of their bodies, and their minds went blank. And the two became separated...

❋❋❋❋❋

Amidst the Kanarian gods' war, the two were thrown into a mess in which they did not belong. Kanar, the home planet of the Kanarian gods, was in the middle of a crisis, for Nao had just overthrown Ezra, the first king.

After angering the shadow god, Nao had led the people of Kanar into the center of the planet in a fit of cowardice. And as Cain was thrown before Nao on the grounds of Kanar, Syn was slung near Cubi—a tight cluster of asteroids inside the Kanaria Galaxy, and the home of the Kanarians loyal to Ezra.

At the same time the lores had traveled to the light realm, Ezra's fragments were scattered, and his heart fragment was flung to where Syn was. As Syn's spirit fell into a deep sleep—a side effect of the potion—bark grew from her essence, and Ezra's heart tried to restore the god back to full form.

After the heart bore Lucien, his fury manifested itself into one hundred coppery versions of himself. However, he calmed his temper as he watched the woman from the dark realm grow a galaxy from her limbs. Growing curious, Lucien flew toward Syn, and his demonics followed. When he noticed her spirit was dim, he ripped her from the roots of the tree.

As Lucien flew Syn from the tree and the stars that stemmed from its branches, she regained consciousness. When she stared into the heart of Ezra, the lore accidentally exchanged essences with him.

And the two became tied by a string of fate that was never meant to be woven.

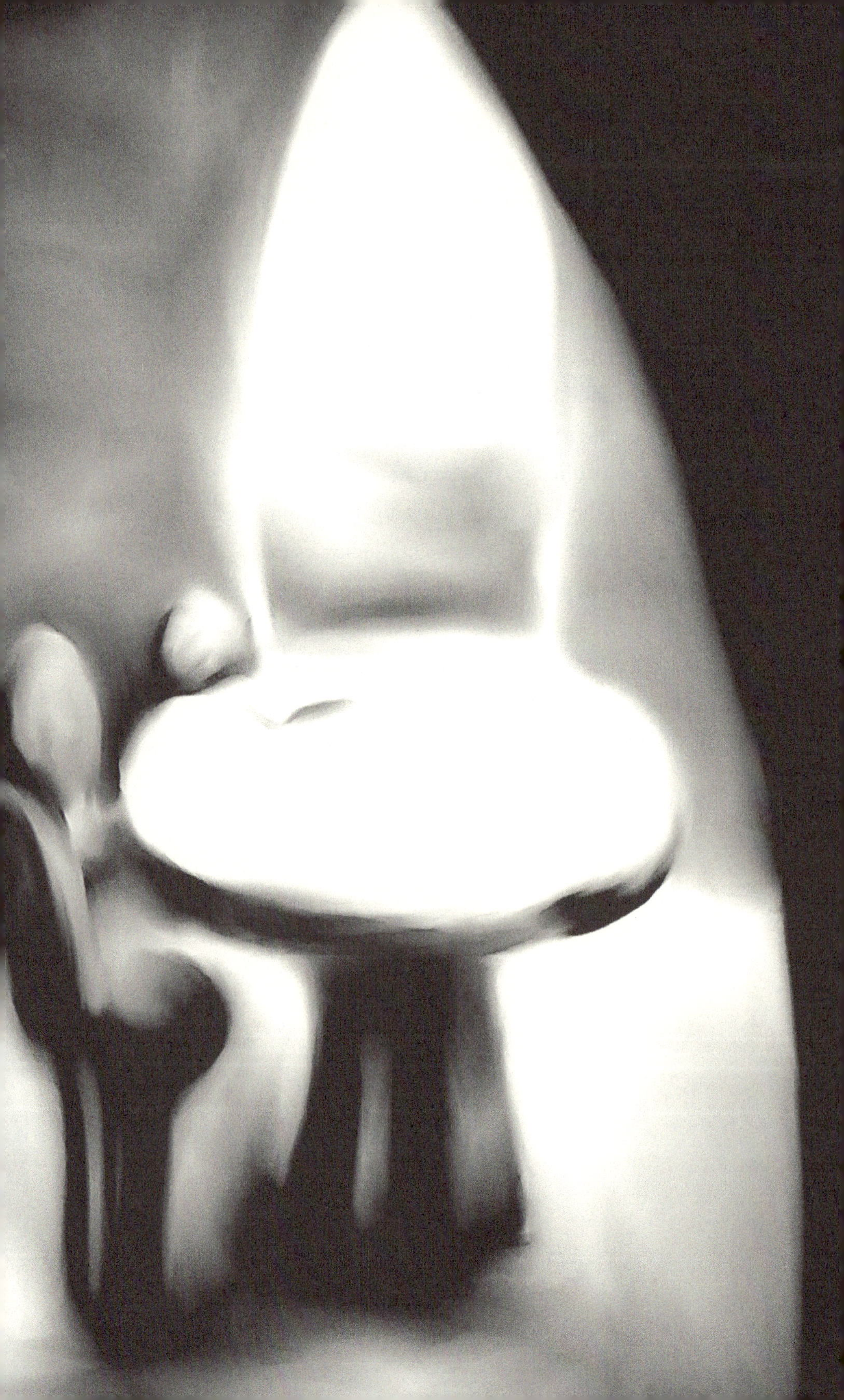

Fae Courts & Council

"I hereby condemn all forms of greed, hate, and cruelty. The courts have no place for division. On this day, we stand united. And through our common blood of katani born, we merge with the other courts of Willow, Dragon, Onyx, and Ruby. As it was, so it shall be. We are one people. For evermore."

—Queen Avasavia, the Sapphire Court,
Oath in the *Book of Creed*

Sapphire Court
Governors of the Seas | Element: Water

Nymphs once lived in the ocean, and they swam alongside sharks and orcas. They are the reason mermaid myths exist. They fed off primarily seaweed and all sea life respected them—for they protected the waters.

After noticing the sea was becoming contaminated by land animals, the queen of the nymphs had led her people to land to propose the other courts to become one government. Queen Avasavia wanted to fight human corruption and bring peace upon the land.

On land, they are fragile. In water, they are mightier than a trident. In both environments, they can summon and manipulate water. While most still follow the late queen's command and migrate to live on land, a few rogue nymph colonies still roam the sea.

WILLOW COURT
Governors of the Forests | Element: Air

Elves never left their original habitat of forests and jungles. In fact, the other courts joined them and built communities within the woods for the five courts to live. The elves are known for their tall height, long ears, and empty stares. Despite manmade stories of them working in the North Pole, the elves are not one to start fights with.

Masters of air, they can manifest tornados and wreak havoc across the globe. You will never feel alone in an area where an elven camp is. They are the ones who follow people when they are lost, after all. Feeling at home with grizzlies and wolves, the elves thrive off of the macabre.

They have an odd tradition of stealing humans' faces to carve into masks—which was sparked by humans leaving trash in their woods. Similar to the other courts, they do not eat meat. But they do not hesitate to kill, and hikers should not fear only bears. They are why some humans think the fae are carnivorous.

DRAGON COURT
Governors of the Animals | Element: Earth

Fairies used to live in the flowers, and many still do. They love to dance and laugh with the wild animals on the planet, especially the birds. They write songs and send music notes through the air so the birds can hear, and the birds then sing their lullabies. When they are not dancing to the bird's song, they are harvesting flower nectar to make jam for the other courts.

Do not let their joyous persona fool you. The birds are more than happy to do their bidding, and the fairies can anger easily.

Unlike the other courts, they are born in a small clear marble, and as they age, the marble expands and becomes a three-inch orb. It then creates a duplicate and becomes a portal between two areas in time. Without the orb, they must travel by flight. They keep the orb close, as they love their leisure. It is a common trend among the Dragon Court to have their birth orbs seared onto a stone base.

ONYX COURT
Governors of the Sands | Element: Fire

Trolls conquered the desert long ago. Experts at fire manipulation, they were once feared throughout Egypt. As they lived peacefully within their tribes, humans would try to find them—only to be killed by the harsh winds. The humans would blame the trolls, and humans had created stories about monsters haunting the sands.

While most may not live in the sands of Egypt any longer, nor walk the paths where most mortals perish, they still summon flames of heat and harbor strength that rivals the Nile. However, their sensitive and caring nature makes them targets of viciousness.

They often adopt a parental role among groups, especially over the goblins. Sharing a bond of not looking like the others, the trolls share a commonality with the Ruby Court, and the two journey with the other throughout time.

RUBY COURT
Governors of the Mountains | Element: Spirit

Goblins once surveyed the skies from the peaks of mountaintops and acted as guardians of Earth. Using symbols and runes, they could bring the rain. They would never be without vegetation, and even used this ability on other communities across the globe, including the human world. These acts were perceived as miracles.

Goblins were once a people who loved everyone and everything, but they grew to be defensive after realizing that many people did not like them. And the nymphs did not take kindly to the idea that they were messing with the rain.

There is an old fae tale that states goblins are the most powerful of the katani descendants. But their timid nature holds them back.

LOST GLOSSARY

CAUTION!

Make sure Aaeon does not see you.
He loves rare things...

GLOSSARY

Aliens—Lifeforms that live across the cosmoses. Some are wacky.

Angelics—Humanoid species that lived on a planet named Eden. The commoners were born from the Maelstrom of Origin. However, the royals were created by Eden's holy objects and did not succumb to the illness of mortality. Not everyone liked the angelics—especially the giants. (Part of the Ossa Antiquorum)

Angelic Empire—Kingdom that ruled Eden.

Anti-fae—Moronic people who are against human and fae integration.

Birdsong—City on Birdsong Island. The Mage's Guild main branch, the Council, and the Primordial Library and Museum are located within.

Birdsong Island—The island is in the middle of the Bermuda Triangle. Home of fae government.

Cubi Colony—Cluster of asteroids where the Kanarian gods loyal to Ezra dwell. They oppose Nao's throne.

Cult of Ezra—Followers of the first Kanarian god Ezra.

Cult of Nao—Followers of the greedy Kanarian god Nao.

Dwarves—Humanoid species that lived in the icy mountains of Eden, north of the Angelic Empire. They made the best brew. One still does... (Part of the Ossa Antiquorum)

Earth—Heart fragment of Eden.

Earthlings—Lifeforms that live on Earth.

Eden—Huge golden planet. Eden's animal kingdom was similar to Earth's, except that most of them lived for thousands of years. A few lived longer, and some had no end. After Eden blew up, its fragments became the solar system.

Edenians—Lifeforms that lived on a planet named Eden. Most were born from the waters of Eden and lived for thousands of years. Humans and fae had struggled with how to categorize Edenian fossils. So, Isis created a new tree of life for the Edenian fossils that kept appearing across the solar system: the Ossa Antiquorum.

Fae—Descended group from the katani. There are five species: nymphs, elves, fairies, goblins, and trolls. They all are herbivorous, but that does not mean they are weak. They all stayed close during evolution and can communicate with each other.

Fae Court—A body of government that rules each species of fae.

Giants—Humanoid species that lived on Eden. There is a funny story about how they became extinct. It makes a wee cat giggle. (Part of the Ossa Antiquorum)

Gods—Three species of aliens that are immortal. They think they are special just because they can create stuff. They are known as the Hellions, the Shadow King, and the Kanarians. Superiority complex. Well, the Shadow King is okay.

Hell—Planet in the dark realm. Parts of it are on fire.

Humans—Descendants of the zyula. They think they are better than the other primates because they know how to use tools and speak a different kind of language. (Scientific name: *Homo sapiens*)

Human Coalition—Club of anti-fae radicals. Their idiocy has no limit...

Katani—Ancient humanoid species. Ancestor to the fae group. They are known for their bloodlust and savagery. Rumored to still exist. (Scientific name: *Edax ossium*)

Kanaria—Far away galaxy. The gods of the light realm are believed to live on a planet named Kanar and the stars of Kanar are called Ia. Ancient folklore of the fae.

Limbo—Planet of ghosts and ghouls. The leader of Limbo really likes wires. Frighteningly so.

Lores—Species from a planet named Hell.

GLOSSARY

Mage's Guild—League of fae healers and fighters. The healers reassemble matter back to its proper form and the fighters, well, fight. The main guild is located in Birdsong. They allow humans into their guild if the humans have a powerful aura. The leader of the guild is abnormally tall.

Moonlight Hills—Fae city hidden in the North Georgia woods called Satan's Web. The Blue Capitol of the Sapphire Court is located within.

Nakori—Huge talking cats that lived on Eden. They acted as the angelics' steeds. A few clans survived Eden's explosion. One in particular loves to remind everyone about how special they are. (Part of the Ossa Antiquorum)

Ossa Antiquorum—Phylogenetic tree of life that classifies the species of Eden. Located in the library of the Primordial Library and Museum in Birdsong.

Pangaea—Super continent. Also called the Gardens of Eden. But it broke apart because some guy had a meltdown. Or so the legend goes...

Perk—Small town in North Georgia. Located near Satan's Web. A very religious community. Home of Saint's Prison and Saint's Asylum.

Primates—Descended group of the zyula. During evolution, the many species drifted apart, and most have limited vocalizations. Unlike the fae, the primates often live separately, and most are not involved in the civilization of human order.

Primordial Library and Museum—Found in the city of Birdsong. Safeguards ancient relics, fossils, and various recordings. It has a neat room that can reenact events that happened on Eden, but the accuracy of the footage is up for debate.

Satan's Web—Forest near Perk, Georgia. Moonlight Hills is hidden inside. The trees supposedly eat people—good for them.

Tallahassee—Capital city of Florida. Sanctuary for the fae. While it has a Mage's Guild, the anti-fae love to cause trouble in the city.

The Council—The fae's top government. It was created when the five fae courts came together to create one civilization. The leaders of each court form the Council.

The Three Realms—Three primal dimensions of the universe where star systems and clusters of planets overlap each other. Each realm is made up of shadow, light, or dark energies and matter.

Zyula—Ancient humanoid species. Ancestor to the primate group. They evolved alongside small shrew-like animals over two hundred million years ago. They are believed to be extinct. (Scientific name: *Vetus lupo primatus*)

About the Author

Sun Sign: Taurus | Moon Sign: Pisces | Ascendant: Sagittarius
Blood Type: A-
Favorite Animal: The Humble Rat

K.D. Thomas was raised in Tallahassee, Florida, and most of her stories are set in or around that area. Drawn to the mysteries of the universe, she seeks to unravel the meaning of existence. But being kept in darkness, the human mind can handle so much. Other than writing, she is obsessed with learning and rescuing animals. Two of her dreams: to obtain a Ph.D. in Physics and have ethics become an international trend.

Made in United States
Orlando, FL
06 November 2024